PENGUIN BOOKS

The Chosen Ones

Howard Linskey is the author of a series of crime novels set in
the North-East, featuring detective Ian Bradshaw and journalists Tom Carney and Helen Norton. Previously he has
written the David Blake series, the first of which, *The Drop*,
was selected as one of the 'Top Five Crime Thrillers of the
Year' by *The Times*. Originally from Ferryhill in County
Durham, Howard now lives in Hertfordshire with his wife
and daughter.

D0317688

The Chosen Ones

HOWARD LINSKEY

PENGUIN BOOKS

PENGUIN BOOKS

UK | USA | Canada | Ireland | Australia
India | New Zealand | South Africa

Penguin Books is part of the Penguin Random House group of companies
whose addresses can be found at global.penguinrandomhouse.com.

First published 2018
002

Copyright © Howard Linskey, 2018

The moral right of the author has been asserted

Set in 12.5/14.75 pt Garamond MT Std
Typeset by Jouve (UK), Milton Keynes

Printed and bound in Great Britain by Clays Ltd, Elcograf S.p.A.

A CIP catalogue record for this book is available from the British Library

PAPERBACK ISBN: 978–1–405–93314–8

www.greenpenguin.co.uk

This one is dedicated to Danielle & Cameron Pope
with much love. I'm so proud of you both.

On looking up, on looking down,
She saw a dead man on the ground;
And from his nose unto his chin,
The worms crawled out, the worms crawled in.

Then she unto the parson said,
'Shall I be so when I am dead?'
'O yes! O yes,' the parson said,
'You will be so when you are dead.'

– 'Gammer Gurton's Garland', 1784

Chapter One

1997

When Eva woke, imprisoned in a large metal box, the one thing that terrified her more than the prospect of her captor returning was the thought that he might not. Then she would be trapped here for good, or at least until she ran out of the things she needed most: food, water, air.

Oh my God, how long would that take? She didn't want to die like this. She didn't want to die at all. She had to stifle the overwhelming feeling of panic and face the reality of her situation. As her eyes became accustomed to the gloom she realized she was in a container of some sort, with thick corrugated-metal sides, floor and roof. She felt dizzy and tried to focus on her surroundings so she could clear her head and begin to understand what might have happened to her.

She was lying on a cheap camp bed with no memory of how she had got there. The only light came from a single battery-operated lamp set upon a packing case that acted as a makeshift bedside table. She felt incredibly weak and had a splitting headache which added to her conviction that she must have been drugged somehow. Had someone put something in her drink, or did something happen after she had left the pub? She couldn't remember.

How had she got here? Who had trapped her in this airless metal prison, no bigger than her bedroom at home?

Then there were the unfamiliar clothes. She hadn't been wearing them before. Her dress was gone. In its place there was a thick, dark-blue sweatshirt that was a little too big for her, its cuffs riding down over her hands, and a pair of loose tracksuit bottoms. Eva didn't remember removing her dress voluntarily, or putting these other items on. Someone had stripped her then dressed her, but she must have been unconscious while it happened. She was still wearing the same underwear, minus her bra. The thought made her feel physically sick.

In her fear, Eva's hand gripped the side of the bed. The mattress sagged in the middle where it had once been folded for storage. It smelt new, as if it had been bought with her in mind – that was another chilling realization.

The metal box was a rectangular shape and around twenty feet long and eight wide, with a door in the far wall. There was barely enough room to stand up. Eva tried to do just that but rose too quickly and her legs immediately buckled and she fell back on to the side of the bed, slipped off and landed heavily on the cold, hard floor. She managed to crawl towards the door, fighting the effects of the drug she was sure she must have been given. Once there, she struggled to pull herself to her feet. When she was finally upright, she tugged on the door then pushed at it. Even in her weakened state, she could tell it was stuck fast, locked from the outside.

She returned to the bed, feeling as if her legs were about to give way again at any moment, and allowed herself to fall back on to it. Then she tried hard to remember what had happened to her, and fragments of the previous evening slowly came back to her.

She had been in the pub with the girls. She didn't think she had been all that drunk. Eva had a flash of recollection: the girls laughing together about something someone had said, then, later, they were leaving, some on to a club, but Eva couldn't go with them because she was meant to be at work the next day. Would her colleagues at the gym have missed her and reported her missing, or would they just have assumed she had overslept or felt ill? Was anyone looking for her?

She recalled almost falling over in the street outside the pub because one of her heels broke suddenly, and that she had to go barefoot, making her way gingerly along the pavement.

What had happened after that? Her memory of the evening seemed to end with her standing alone in a street down by the quayside. She recalled walking away from a taxi rank because the queue was absurdly long; it could take an hour to reach the front. She'd been put off by the raised voices and the pushing in she'd witnessed, the kind of behaviour that always seemed to cause a fight. But, after she had made her decision to turn away, what then?

Rain.

Rain? She had a memory of rain, hard and unrelenting, with large drops falling and drenching her. She had worn no coat that night. It had been a sudden and malicious downpour that soaked her auburn hair and drenched her dress until it clung to her. It was so heavy people were running to take shelter, but Eva was barefoot and the ground was cold, wet and slippery. She couldn't remember anything more after that. Had she been snatched in the street? Had she gone with someone willingly? She couldn't imagine she would ever do that unless it was somebody she knew, but had the combination of the downpour and a couple of drinks made her careless? Would she have accepted a lift from a stranger? It seemed unlikely.

The panic began to rise again in her, along with a clawing sense of despair. Eva had almost reached breaking point when she noticed something scraped on the wall near the foot of the bed: white marks, lots of them – and she thought she understood what they were.

She reached for the handle of the lamp and scrambled down to the foot of the bed, holding her face close and the lamp closer, so she could be sure. Scratched into the metal wall of the box were a large number of little white lines. Four verticals and a diagonal over them, to indicate the number five.

Five days.

Someone had been keeping track of the days, somebody who had been held prisoner here before Eva. Each clump of lines represented five days, and there were many, filling a large space that ran down to the floor of the box then ending abruptly. Eva began to scream then.

Inside the box, her screams came loud and shrill and they went on and on, with a force powered by blind terror. Outside, they were muffled by the thick walls of her metal prison. No one could hear.

Chapter Two

Jenna Ellison always enjoyed the calm that descended at five minutes to six. It was just before locking-up time and her little shop was empty. Everyone knew what time she closed her doors and respected it. Dashing in with a couple of minutes to spare, to grab some washing powder or a packet of sweets, would be thought rude. It was one of the many reasons she never once regretted the decision to swap hectic city living for life in a sleepy village.

It was serendipity: the shop had become available at exactly the right time. She had just enough money, had grown weary of Newcastle and was more than ready for a change. The old lady who had run the place long after normal retirement age finally bowed to the inevitable, selling the lease on the shop and the first-floor flat that went with it, to move away and live with her daughter and her family. Grange Moor needed a shop, so the villagers had given her a cautious welcome, keeping their distance while they waited to see what changes she would bring about. When the stock stayed largely the same but with the addition of products that proved to be popular, when the opening hours didn't alter and she continued to run the villagers' small ads in her windows for free, it stood her in good stead.

Jenna wasn't naïve. She knew she would always be an outsider, but she didn't mind that. As long as the locals bought goods from her and continued to tolerate her presence among them, that was good enough for her. When the shop closed for the day, she felt like she was pulling up the drawbridge; happy to climb the stairs to her flat, feed the cat, cook something in her tiny kitchen and eat dinner in glorious solitude while watching TV in the lounge, with its bay window overlooking the village green, which always seemed to catch the last of the evening sun.

Sometimes she would venture out to the local pub, order a glass of wine and exchange pleasantries with the locals before happily retiring to a corner of the lounge bar. Unlike most women she knew, she had never had a problem going into a quiet pub alone. For the most part, she was happy to be on her own. The men who approached her, especially the married ones, were easily but politely brushed off and she would go back to quietly reading her book. She didn't want a man.

When she thought of her life here in Grange Moor, Jenna felt a sense of serene calm. She had escaped her past, and the memories had slowly begun to fade, even though she knew they would never disappear entirely. Usually, she managed to push them from her mind.

Until she saw the note.

It was on the mat when Jenna went to lock the front door. It must have been pushed through the letterbox, but she hadn't noticed anyone pass the window. There was no envelope, just the handwritten note, with neat writing in block capitals on lined paper.

I KNOW WHO YOU ARE.

Jenna felt heat rush into the skin of her face and a sharp

6

tingle of shock passed through her body. Who had sent this? How could anyone know? It wasn't possible.

There was nothing on the note to give her a clue: no familiar handwriting, no signature or contact number, no indication of what the writer might want from her to keep her secret, just that one simple, devastating fact.

I KNOW WHO YOU ARE.

Chapter Three

Detective Sergeant Ian Bradshaw had been summoned to Kane's office by his boss, DI Kate Tennant. It had been a frosty invitation, consisting of the words, 'DCI Kane wants to see you,' before she pointedly added: 'again.'

Now Bradshaw was waiting in the office – his DCI was late for their appointment – and he had time to ponder Kate Tennant's hostility. He couldn't really blame her. Whenever there was a tricky case with few leads, little evidence and the prospect of newspaper headlines such as 'BAFFLED POLICE STUMPED' becoming attached to it, there were usually only two possible outcomes. The first: the case would be assigned to Durham Constabulary's only female detective inspector, for her team to pick up the poisoned chalice, and even then it would be done reluctantly, with senior officers admitting that this was the 1990s, after all, as if they were being bludgeoned into accepting the intrusion of women into their previously exclusively male environment. The other outcome would be that Kate Tennant's already insufficient workforce would be reduced even further, because DCI Kane would see fit to 'borrow' Ian Bradshaw from her, to provide 'a fresh pair of eyes'. Kane had a grudging respect for Bradshaw's academic record, but he was defiantly old school in his own methods, so he viewed the DS with suspicion. Being called to Kane's office could often feel like a back-handed compliment. Bradshaw knew he was seen as a last resort.

He didn't really fit in. He wasn't a golfer or a mason, didn't always agree with the orders he was given, often relied on his instincts and, to the bemusement of his colleagues, had no particular desire to be promoted. It wasn't exactly true that DS Bradshaw was happy where he was; he just knew he'd be even more unhappy if he rose any further, and his mental health had been too fragile in recent years to add more stress to his life voluntarily.

Bradshaw was hampered by a self-doubt that rarely seemed to plague more senior men. He wasn't sure why he worried about not being good enough when he was often unimpressed by his superiors' abilities, but he couldn't help it. Bradshaw dreamed of a far less responsible life, without murder, with no missing children, abused teenagers, grieving relatives or multiple killers to contend with. On his last foreign holiday he'd seriously considered staying abroad to run a bar or work in a hotel. Wouldn't a world of lemon trees and olive groves be more tranquil than this one?

Bradshaw knew he would never actually do this. His overwrought mind needed the distraction that investigating complex cases provided. He dreaded to think how he would fare if he had too much time alone with his thoughts. He'd already endured counselling sessions to cope with earlier traumas, something he'd found utterly pointless. Kate Tennant was less convinced of the need to suspend the sessions. 'Are you sure about this, Ian?' she had asked when she signed the forms freeing him from regular appointments with the excruciating Dr Mellor. 'You could probably use someone to talk to.'

'Well, I've got mates,' he protested, and she raised her eyebrows.

'Not exactly pub chat,' she said, meaning the time he had spent one to one with a notorious child-killer, trying to get inside the man's mind to solve the disappearance of a missing girl, but she signed the forms anyway, making him feel like a kid getting a note from his mum excusing him from games.

Bradshaw had assured her there were no lasting scars from his repeated encounters with Adrian Wicklow. Of course he hadn't mentioned the bad dreams, night terrors and chronic insomnia. He had also failed to explain another side-effect he'd begun to notice recently: his deadened emotional sense. Almost a year on, the things Bradshaw used to enjoy felt like pale shadows of their former selves. Seeing mates outside the force – not that he had that many – going to the pub, walks in the countryside, watching football, a meal, a drink, a kiss; all of these things felt different now somehow, as if they didn't really matter all that much in the scheme of things.

He was snapped out of these thoughts abruptly when Kane arrived. The DCI greeted Bradshaw with the words, 'Eight detectives!'

Before Bradshaw could react or even stand up, Kane dropped a copy of the country's biggest-selling tabloid newspaper on to his lap. 'Suspended!' he said angrily. 'All eight of them,' and Kane shook his head vehemently, as if he had never heard of such a thing.

Bradshaw looked at that morning's front page. The headline seemed to roar at them:

'BENT COPPERS CAUGHT IN STING'

Underneath was a strapline that helpfully explained

how a TV documentary crew had filmed detectives taking bribes and offering protection to drug dealers.

'Oh Christ,' said Bradshaw, scanning the piece. The documentary in question would be screened in a couple of days and Durham police were being forced to 'clean house' by undertaking a full and comprehensive investigation into the matter, which was likely to recommend a much-needed 'root and branch reform'.

'It's a disgrace!' roared Kane. Bradshaw felt quite buoyed by his DCI's anger at the police officers who had besmirched the name of their force, but only for a moment. 'It's not eight detectives filmed taking bribes. It's just one!'

Bradshaw had to fight the urge to say, *Oh, that's all right, then.* Instead he managed a feeble 'Who was it?'

Kane looked as if he couldn't quite believe it himself when he said, 'DI Peacock.'

'Really?' This was a shock. Peacock had been Bradshaw's boss back when he was an unpromising detective constable. Even though he had given his subordinate a series of often foul-mouthed bollockings, Bradshaw still respected Peacock and had certainly never questioned his integrity. He couldn't say that about some of the other officers in CID. 'What was he thinking?'

Kane shook his head. 'He's been going through a divorce, wanted to keep his house, so I suppose he needed the money. Anyway, he'll lose it now, and a lot more besides, because they've got him bang to rights. He was filmed taking money from a dealer to destroy evidence and let him off the hook.' Kane snorted his disbelief. 'Apparently the dealer was shocked and disgusted to find there were corrupt police officers working on his patch, so he decided to do his civic duty and phone the BBC. They got him to wear a wire and hide a tiny camera in a bag. The shit's already hit the fan. Peacock has been arrested and is looking at proper jail time, unless he gets a lawyer who can perform miracles. The other seven have been suspended on full pay while there's an investigation. I'm not sure how many of them we'll be able to clear.'

Bradshaw couldn't quite believe what he was hearing. 'Is that the aim of the inquiry, sir – to clear them?'

'Of course,' Kane snapped, as if he were an idiot.

'Shouldn't it be to ascertain whether or not they have committed a crime?'

'Don't be bloody obtuse, man. If we find any evidence of corruption, they will receive the proper punishment, but that's what it has to be, proper evidence, not the word of some kangaroo court masquerading as a documentary.' He forced himself to calm down. 'Deputy Chief Constable Tyler has promised a full and unbiased inquiry into all the allegations, but Peacock is the only one who was filmed taking money directly, so an example will have to be made, of course.'

A fall guy, thought Bradshaw. Peacock will get a jail sentence and the misdemeanours of the others will likely be swept under the carpet.

'And some of them might have to go before their time,' Kane said, with some sadness. Bradshaw knew this was a reference to the early retirement so many disgraced police officers took whenever overwhelming evidence of their wrongdoing was presented to them. There really were different rules for the police. 'In any case, it will drag on for months, which means we have lost eight detectives for the foreseeable future.' He looked directly at Bradshaw. 'And some of them had been working on the Disappeared.'

Christ, thought Bradshaw. *Don't give me that case*, but he already knew what was coming.

'I'll need you to take it on, Bradshaw. I'm up shit creek without a paddle . . . or even a bloody boat! I can't spare anyone else and the rest of your team are on this murdered teenager.'

'Everyone reckons it's the stepdad,' said Bradshaw hopefully, praying they would solve that case soon, so he wouldn't be left entirely on his own.

'They do, and I agree with them. I don't think anyone in the country would dispute it, in fact. He's not just the prime suspect, he's the *only* one, but knowing it and proving it are two different things. That's why we've put Katie's team on it' – and in case Bradshaw saw this as Kane giving his DI yet another unexploded grenade to hold – 'because she has proven herself such a fine investigator.'

And if she doesn't get a result, you can throw her to the wolves, thought Bradshaw. There were still a significant number of men in his force who were just waiting for Kate Tennant to make a mistake so they could say, *That's what happens when you put a woman in charge.*

'Anyway' – Kane's voice went up an octave as he tried to sound positive – 'you've proven you can work on your own.'

Not through choice.

'And I reckon this could be just the kind of case to challenge that big brain of yours.'

'I thought we weren't even admitting there was a case, sir.'

'We are not admitting it to the press, yet,' he conceded, 'because it might not be, but we know something is up.

Five women have gone missing in the past six months, and none of them fits the usual profile of a runaway. You know the score: nearly always, when we start digging, we find something; a reason for just running off – among the women, anyway. They're not like the men.'

This was a compliment. Bradshaw knew what he meant – men cracked and left, abandoning wives and family, jobs, homes, even their cars, along with any kind of responsibility, often on a whim. Sometimes there was a reason – debts, scandal, huge pressure of some sort – but often they just couldn't hack modern-day life, so off they went without any explanation. Women didn't usually do that. If they left, they were more than likely fleeing something. It was usually abusive partners or stepfathers, sometimes their own dad. Violence or abuse, either sexual or domestic, figured high on the list of reasons why women were so desperate they chose to run. Rarely did a woman abandon her children, like the men often did – though Bradshaw realized he knew of at least one case where that had happened, because the child affected more than a quarter of a century ago was his friend, the journalist Tom Carney.

'We've found nothing to indicate that any of the women planned to leave,' continued Kane. 'Not so much as a bus ticket or a train timetable. No bank accounts were emptied or cash cards used after they left.' He paused. 'So it's possible they were taken.'

'But how could a man do that without attracting any attention? A woman would struggle. She would scream, surely, unless she knew the man. Were these women linked in any way?'

'Obviously, they looked into that.' Kane meant the suspended detectives he had previously tasked with the investigation. 'And there was no common denominator. They were from different parts of the county and led very different lives. The only commonality is that they are all youngish women from the region. It's hard to imagine how they could have all known the same man.'

'Have we been given any possible explanation from their nearest and dearest?'

'None of them had any reason to go. They vanished abruptly, during nights out or on their way home from somewhere – work, a friend's house . . .' He suddenly grew tired of explaining it all. 'Look, it's all in the case files. I asked Malone to sort them out for you.'

She will have loved that.

Bradshaw thought for a moment. 'You said five women had gone missing. I thought it was four.'

'Another one went two nights ago.'

'And you want me to work this out on my own?' asked Bradshaw.

'Have I not just told you about the eight detectives?'

'Yes, but –'

Kane interrupted him with a raised hand. 'No buts. There is no one else. I can't spare anyone for what could prove to be a wild-goose chase. You have to remember that no demands of any kind have been made, so that rules out kidnap. No bodies have been found, and all these women might simply wind up unharmed in London, or Blackpool, or somewhere. We just don't know. That's why we're not making a song and dance about it in the press. We don't want to panic people unnecessarily.'

Bradshaw folded his arms defiantly. 'I hear what you're saying, sir, but I am still going to need help.'

'I get it.' Kane looked at Bradshaw as if the DS had let him down somehow. 'You want me to hire the princess and the pain in the arse again, don't you?'

'Well, sir,' said Bradshaw more brightly, 'I think it would be a step in the right direction.'

'Norton and Carney?' mused Kane. 'Do you really think it's wise to involve them in this?'

'They're both excellent investigators, and I don't see how I'll be able to do it without them.'

Kane thought for a full minute before answering. 'All right, I'll have a word and see if we can put them back on the pay roll for a bit, assuming they actually want to work with us again, instead of flogging stories to the tabloids for obscene amounts of money. Bloody journalists. They've got the life of Riley.'

At that moment Kane's phone rang. He answered it, listened for a while then threw his DS a significant look. Kane asked, 'When?' then, 'Where?', wrote notes on a pad then thanked the caller and hung up.

'What's that word, Bradshaw,' he said thoughtfully, as he tore the top sheet off the pad, 'the one that means you're the opposite of a lucky mascot?'

'A jinx?' offered a puzzled Bradshaw. 'Or a Jonah?'

Kane handed him the notes. 'A Jonah, that's it. How long have you been on this case?' He pretended to look at his watch. 'About five bloody minutes.' His eyes widened. 'And already they've found a body.'

Chapter Four

Tom Carney turned off the car radio as soon as he heard the words 'Tough on crime, tough on the causes of crime,' from the man widely considered to be the Prime-Minister-in-waiting.

'Why switch it off?' Helen Norton asked him. 'It's the news,' she reminded Tom sarcastically, 'and we are journalists.'

'Because I've heard it all before,' said Tom, 'and any minute now he'll say, "Education, education, education," again; whatever that means.'

'I thought you'd be happy that Blair is going to win the election.'

'Most people *think* he's going to win and I'm not *un*happy about it. I just don't believe he's the messiah, that's all. Because, well, no one is.'

Helen rolled her eyes, even though she knew her business partner in the journalistic enterprise of Norton–Carney was driving and couldn't see it. Tom pulled out into the fast lane of the two-lane A1 and overtook a lorry. A large German car immediately appeared from nowhere, raced up behind them and tailgated their car, flashing its lights repeatedly to shoo them out of the way.

'Tosser,' muttered Tom.

'Are you going to pull over?'

'Because this guy thinks he owns the road? Why should I?'

'I don't know,' she said. 'To prevent the idiot causing an accident, maybe? Just a thought.'

Tom sighed, 'Anything for a quiet life.' He pulled over, and the driver of the German car flew past them, pipping his horn to signal his impatience with Tom's driving.

He turned the radio back on and switched to a music channel. 'Shit,' he said.

'What?'

'The Spice Girls.' He nodded at the radio. 'I'll vote for Blair if he promises to ban them, and fox-hunting.'

'He's promised a free vote on fox-hunting,' said Helen. 'I think it should be a three-line-whip against the Spice Girls.'

'We agree on that, at least.'

'Have you noticed,' Tom asked Helen as they climbed from the car half an hour later, 'that it's either crumbs or a banquet?'

'What is?' They were parked outside a crumbling block of flats on the outskirts of Leeds, and Helen peered up at it.

'Journalism,' he said. 'The freelance variety, anyhow.'

'I'd settle for crumbs right now,' she told him. 'Lately, it's been more of a famine.'

She was right about that. Sometimes the young team of Norton–Carney, aka Helen and Tom, would crack a big story, often while assisting Durham Constabulary to investigate one of its 'unsolvable' cases. If they did blow one of these cold cases wide open, usually with the help of DS Ian Bradshaw, there was a brief honeymoon period while they were courted by every major newspaper and radio station in the land for their exclusive story. Occasionally, an article would be sold for a substantial amount of money, but interest in that case would inevitably wane quite quickly, and they would have to write more mundane stories to pay the bills. Even those were proving hard to come by at the moment.

'This could be a crumb,' he reminded Helen hopefully. 'It was a good spot.' It was Helen who had first read about the woman they were about to visit, in a discarded copy of a West Yorkshire newspaper left on a north-bound train.

Tom pointed to the tower block in front of them. 'What floor is she on?'

'The nineteenth.'

'Bugger,' he said, 'and I'll bet the lift's not working.'

'At least we have a guaranteed sale,' she reminded him. Tom had sounded out one of the women's magazines in advance, because Leeds was a fair drive from Durham and not worth the hassle if there wasn't any money at the end of it. This story was perfect for a low-budget, gossipy publication, the type sold in supermarkets and petrol stations all over the country. They usually focused on celebrities but paid reasonable money for outlandish stories involving real people. The woman they were here to see certainly had one of those to tell, and Mandy Brook was keen to sell her exclusive.

The magazine needed photographs, so Helen had brought her camera and they had endured two hours of stop–start traffic to get here. Tom jabbed at the button on the lift and there was a whirring, cranking sound as it juddered down to them.

'It's working, then,' said Helen doubtfully, just as the doors opened.

Tom recoiled. 'Christ, it smells like a toilet. Do you really want to risk it?'

The prospect of being trapped inside the foul-smelling lift for hours, if it suddenly broke down, was enough to convince them both that climbing nineteen floors was a better option. 'Come on,' said Helen. 'Just think of it as exercise.'

'And so much cheaper than gym membership.'

They arrived breathless, with sore legs, late for their appointment, but Mandy didn't seem to mind or even notice. She was loving the attention and commenced excitably telling her story almost as soon as they were through the door. Tom was forced to cut her off to get her back on track.

'Our theme,' he said forcibly, 'is the possibility of finding love in the unlikeliest places, and that's exactly what you did, isn't it, Mandy?'

'Well,' she said, 'I found it in Leeds.'

'I wasn't talking geographically,' he explained patiently. 'I meant what happened after your wedding.' And when she needed further prompting, he added: 'Which was what, exactly?'

Tom held up his tape recorder to prompt her to speak into it.

'He left me, didn't he?'

'He left you,' repeated Helen, to show Mandy that she was listening. 'Your husband, you mean? And when was this?'

'The day after the wedding.' She said this as if it were a relatively common occurrence.

'The day after,' repeated Tom, when she showed no outward sign of devastation. 'And how did that make you feel?'

'I were gutted, weren't I?' Her Yorkshire accent got broader along with her indignation. 'I were miles from anywhere, on our honeymoon, in the middle of piggin' Thailand. I knew no one, and he just left me. How d'you think I felt?'

'With respect to you, Mandy,' said Tom, 'that's what the readers are going to want to know, but they need to hear it from you, not me.'

'Oh, right,' she said. 'Well, I cried myself to sleep for ages. Anyway, I never saw him again.'

'He just disappeared in Bangkok and never got back in touch?' asked Helen.

'No one knows where he is. I knew he weren't that bothered about getting married, see, but I never thought he'd run off like that. When the honeymoon was over I had to come home.'

'And what happened then?' asked Helen, knowing the answer already but needing Mandy to put it in her own words.

'Well, he were an angel, weren't he?' she said. 'He took my side completely and he comforted me and made me realize my life weren't over at all. In the end, I fell in love with him and he with me. He was everything piggin' Darren weren't.'

'Who was?' asked Tom. 'For the benefit of the readers.'

'Gary,' she beamed happily. 'Darren's dad.'

'Just to confirm, then, so we haven't got this wrong . . .' summarized Tom, because he had no wish to be sued at a later date. 'You were married to Darren for twenty-four hours before he disappeared for good in a foreign country, you came home and were comforted by your husband's father and now you are with him.'

She nodded happily. 'We got married in't registry office as soon as my divorce came through.' She frowned. 'It took two years, you know, because that's how long you have to leave it to prove desertion.' She looked at Helen when she said this. Perhaps she thought it was information that might prove useful to her one day. 'I said to the lass, "He ran away from me the day after our wedding, isn't that proof enough of desertion?" but she was having none of it, the stroppy cow.'

'What a wonderful story,' said Tom, and he winked at Helen while Mandy wasn't looking and she had to try hard not to laugh.

'I'm surprised by how much attention I've been getting about it, to be honest. We've had the local paper round, and that other magazine.'

'Another magazine?' asked Helen abruptly.

Mandy mentioned the name of a rival publication and added, for good measure, 'They were here a few days ago.'

'You've spoken to another magazine already?' – The woman nodded happily – 'but you promised us an exclusive.'

'Yes,' she agreed.

Realizing they were not dealing with an intellectual giant, Tom turned off the tape recorder and put it back inside his jacket pocket. He managed to stay reasonably calm while he explained the definition of 'exclusive'. 'It means you don't give it to anyone else. We didn't realize you'd already sold your *exclusive* story?' he said through gritted teeth.

'Oh, yes,' she said. 'But it's okay, because I'm happy to sell it again, to you.'

'That's not how it works!' protested Helen, who by now could have cheerfully thrown the camera at her.

'It's all my fault,' Helen told Tom as they climbed back into the car.

'It's not your fault,' said Tom, fishing his mobile phone out of his pocket and turning it back on, now the interview was over. 'How were you to know she was so stupid she thought she could sell her exclusive story several times over?'

'There was a clue,' Helen reminded him. 'She *is* currently married to her former father-in-law.' She sighed. 'All this way for nothing. What the hell are we going to do now? For money, I mean. I just wish we had something lined up.'

Tom didn't answer. He was too busy concentrating on the phone, which had rung the moment it kicked back into life, to tell him there was a voicemail. He held it to his ear and listened. The message was a long one.

'What is it?' she asked him.

'Not quite your fairy godmother,' he said when he had finished listening to the message, 'but your wish has been granted. It's our old mate Ian Bradshaw, and he might have a job for us.'

Chapter Five

'Not exactly dressed for the occasion, are you?' The SOCO regarded Bradshaw dubiously as he climbed from his car, which was parked by the end of the footpath that led off into the woods. Bradshaw's suit and smart shoes weren't the most practical clothing for this terrain.

'I was told she was by the side of the road,' explained Bradshaw.

'She's in the trees.' The SOCO nodded towards the woodland at the end of the muddy track.

'Who found her?' Bradshaw guessed it would have been a jogger or a dog-walker, as usual.

'Kids. They were playing in there. I suspect it's a sight that will stay with them, poor bastards. Get your gear on and I'll show you.'

Bradshaw was doing as he was told, lifting protective clothing from the boot of his car, when a second car pulled up not far from his and Detective Constable Hugh Rennie got out. Both he and Rennie normally reported to Kate Tennant. The veteran seemed as perplexed by the sight of Bradshaw standing there as the younger man was to see him. 'Kane sent me,' explained Bradshaw. 'They think this might be one of the Disappeared.'

'Katie Tennant asked me to drive up,' said Rennie. 'In case it's *her*.' He didn't have to say a name. Everyone on Tennant's team was expecting to get a call any day now to say that the young girl who had been missing for more than two weeks had been found. Only then could they really hope to put a proper case together against the man they were already privately referring to as 'Evil Stepdad', such was the suspect's wild-eyed eccentricity during police interviews and press conferences. The stepfather had managed to contradict and trip himself up on more than one occasion and seemed pretty calm, considering his fifteen-year-old stepdaughter had gone missing. As DC Malone succinctly put it, 'He's guilty of being guilty, plain and simple.'

'Left hand, right hand,' said a world-weary Rennie, explaining the lack of communication that had led to them both driving separately out here to check the same crime scene. 'This is the last thing I need when I'm so busy. I've only got a fortnight left, you know.'

Bradshaw did know, because Hugh Rennie had made a point of ensuring everyone was aware how close he was to retirement and just how much he had to tidy up before he went, so no one would have the nerve to give him something new to do. Bradshaw brought his finger to his lips as if shushing the older man. 'Careful, Hugh. You know what happens to cops in films when they only have a couple of weeks to go before retirement? They get killed,' he said solemnly. 'Sorry, mate. It happens every time.'

'Very funny,' said Rennie, who didn't look remotely amused.

They donned their protective suits then put coverings over their shoes and plastic guards across their mouths. The three men trudged along the muddy footpath, Bradshaw trying not to slide in the mud, now that he had lost what little grip his shoes had had. The SOCO led them through a gap in the trees where the ground was a little firmer, and they continued until they reached some yellow police tape that had been used to mark a perimeter. The SOCO lifted it and they ducked underneath. They took a few more steps then went beyond the bushes that had been shielding the crime scene from view.

There was activity all around the clearing. One man was photographing everything in the vicinity, while a number of officers examined small sections of the cordoned-off zone for clues. Bradshaw's eye was immediately drawn to the victim. She was sitting up with her back pressed against a tree. From a distance, it might have appeared she was alive and merely resting. Up close, however, there was no mistaking that she was dead. The sightless eyes bulged wide open, the body was kept in place by the ligature pulled tightly around the neck, a grubby but sturdy length of grey rope that had cut deep into the flesh. Instead of simply strangling the woman by wrapping the rope around her neck, the killer had stretched it all the way around the tree she was leaning against then pulled it taut from behind until she was dead. To Bradshaw it looked almost ritualistic, and he wondered why the woman hadn't struggled. Her mouth was open, as if she had fought for a last breath, but gravity had forced her chin down and her tongue lolled out of her mouth.

Her hair was a greying auburn colour, but her most striking feature was her emaciated body, the bones showing through skin as white as paint. The only contrast to her pale complexion aside from the red markings either side of the rope on her neck was a faded dark strip around her wrist where an old tattoo could still be made out. Bradshaw bent lower and realized it was in the shape of a Celtic band.

'Time of death?' he asked, knowing it could only be a rough estimate at this stage.

'Nothing confirmed yet, but we're probably looking at a couple of days ago,' said the SOCO.

Bradshaw trod carefully around the body and peered at the back of the tree. He saw that the rope had been knotted around a long, thick stick which had been repeatedly turned to tighten the noose. It seemed an elaborate way to kill the victim and he wondered how the killer had achieved it without her wriggling free. Had she been too weak to fight back?

When he stepped back to survey the victim once more, the SOCO nodded towards her. 'That one of your girls, then?'

Bradshaw shook his head. 'No.'

'You're sure?' He sounded surprised. There weren't that many murders in the North-East.

'About twenty years too old,' Bradshaw informed him. By the same reckoning, it couldn't be Hugh Rennie's missing girl either.

'Sorry to hear that.' When they both looked questioningly at the SOCO, he added: 'You know what I mean – you've wasted your time.'

'At least I can rule her out,' said Bradshaw. 'No clue as to the identity yet, then?'

'We were hoping you could shed some light on it,' the SOCO said. 'She had no purse or ID of any kind on her, no door keys or money, no jewellery. All we've got so far in the way of distinguishing marks is a mole on her neck and the tattoo on her wrist.' He shrugged. 'Maybe that will be enough.'

'Someone will know her,' said Bradshaw, then he noticed that DC Rennie had his head to one side and was peering down at the victim with what appeared to be great concentration, even though this could not possibly be the girl he was looking for.

'What is it?' asked Bradshaw.

Rennie didn't answer at first, then he said, 'Nothing.'

'You seen her before?'

'Don't think so,' he said doubtfully, but Rennie continued to peer at the woman as Bradshaw and the SOCO exchanged a look. Rennie was lying, and they both knew it.

Chapter Six

A man of words and not of deeds
Is like a garden full of weeds.
'Gammer Gurton's Garland', 1784

The last thing Eva recalled before waking up inside the box was being incredibly tired. Nothing to explain her presence here.

It was all so unreal.

She couldn't deny the reality of it now, though. Eva had been taken by someone and imprisoned in this box. Surely it couldn't be anyone she knew. None of her ex-boyfriends was this vengeful or unhinged. Eva had no obsessive stalkers or overzealous admirers, so who could have done this, and why? To rape, torture – perhaps even kill her? Eva's mind raced with the possibilities it could imagine, while knowing there might be others it could not. Why would a man imprison a girl except to harm her? Kidnap? A ransom? She barely made enough from her job on the reception desk at the gym to live; her mother was just about surviving financially. It couldn't be that, then, unless it was a case of mistaken identity. Did she look like some rich daddy's girl? Was there another young woman with long, red hair like hers, from a prosperous family somewhere, who the kidnapper was meant to have snatched instead? It seemed impossible, but then so did everything else about her situation. Her anxiety reached a whole new level. It was the thought of her mother sitting at home, frantic with worry, that did it. All that came into Eva's mind now was what would happen if she did not get out of here, and fast.

She sat bolt upright when she heard the door. Someone was unlocking it from the outside and she was torn between conflicting emotions of fear and relief.

Was he letting her out?

Why was he letting her out? To let her go? To kill her? To do something else to her?

Oh God.

She tried to stay calm when the door swung open and light poured through it.

Her captor leaned in and she saw him clearly for the first time.

Then she screamed.

The scream was an involuntary response to the sight before her. A dark face, its features completely hidden by a mask. No, a balaclava, like the ones terrorists or bank robbers wore, but this one was home-made, and all the more disturbing for its shoddy, amateur construction. It hung loosely over the man's head, obscuring his entire face, apart from the eye holes and a thin slit where the mouth was.

Then he stepped into the box and she saw the shotgun. He was carrying it in one hand, pointing it straight at her, his finger near the trigger, and she flinched then pushed herself backwards as far as she could go, until her back was pressed right against the wall. He stood still for a moment, and at first she couldn't take her eyes away from the gun, terrified it would go off. Then, when she realized he wasn't about to fire it, she took in a squat figure in a thick jumper with a padded body-warmer over it. He was average height, perhaps a little overweight, but powerfully built. There was strength here, she could tell. Then she saw that he was balancing a small tray in the palm of his other hand. He set it down next to a book on a packing case by the door. It held a plate of food and a glass of water, along with a plastic container.

He straightened and took a step nearer. Eva felt a growing sense of panic.

'Who are you?' she managed, her voice wavering. 'What do you want?'

'If you do what you're told,' the man said, his deep voice was almost a growl, 'you'll be safe.'

Did he say safe? *It sounded like it, but his voice was muffled by the balaclava.*

'Safe?' she asked.

'If you listen to him, you'll be saved.'

'Who?' she sobbed, her eyes darting around the room, even though she knew no one else was there. 'Listen to who?'

'Father.' And as he said this her eyes settled on the book next to the food. It was well worn and leather bound, with a gold cross embossed on the cover, along with the words 'Holy Bible'.

Was that what he meant by *Father* or was he talking about *his* father? She didn't understand. Eva was about to ask him, but he was already leaving, backing out of the room, the shotgun still pointed towards her.

'Wait. Don't go. Why are you keeping me here?'

'You'll be saved,' the man's deep voice assured her as he left.

'Don't leave me in here!' she shrieked, but his only response was to shut the door and bolt it from the outside, muffling her cries once more.

Chapter Seven

DC Malone greeted Ian Bradshaw's reappearance at HQ with bad grace and a sneer.

'Where the bloody hell have you been?' she demanded, but she didn't wait for an answer. 'Kane dragged me in early to wade through all this shit for you.'

This shit turned out to be the evidence on the Disappeared women gathered by the detectives now on suspension, much of which was on her desk, along with a mug of tea that had gone cold. It had 'You don't have to be mad to work here but it helps!' written on it. Next to the mug was a half-eaten packet of Jaffa cakes. She didn't offer him one.

'Is this everything?' he asked her.

'Nope. Grab some of it and come with me.'

He scooped up a mound of papers then followed the similarly laden DC away from her desk and into a conference room no one was using.

'Oh Christ,' he said, when he saw how many files Malone had been asked to collate for him. 'What the hell is all this?'

She placed a palm on the first pile of papers as she explained its contents. 'Background on each missing woman: height, weight, age, vital stats,' she said dryly. 'Whether she was blonde, brunette, married, single or seeing someone. Did she live alone or with her family? Was she in work or signing on?' Then she added facetiously, 'Favourite food, star sign, sexual preferences – you get the picture.' Malone went on to the next pile. 'All the witness reports from the times they went missing, the last people to see them, and when and where; statements from friends, family, colleagues, bar staff – you name it.' She moved on to another stack of papers. 'Background statements from nearest and dearest – whether they had any problems, worries, stalkers, addictions, mental disorders, or any other reasons for taking off.' She sighed, 'As far as I can tell, the answer to all of those questions about each of the victims is no.'

'Helpful,' he said.

'Yep.' She stopped then, as if tiring of the exercise. 'Obviously, I haven't read every word on every piece of paper. That's your job,' she added ominously, 'but as far as I can see, there is hardly anything in the way of actual evidence here. I mean, otherwise, they would have had a lead to go on, and they didn't.' She thought for a while. 'Unless they were just crap or lazy . . . or too busy shaking down drug-dealers.'

'Allegedly,' he reminded her.

'Allegedly,' she agreed. 'Anyway, I reckon you're more or less starting again from scratch. Who else have you got to help you? And don't look at me. I'm way too busy.'

'Trying to nail the most suspicious step-parent since Snow White bit into an apple? I know. Tough case to crack, that one.'

'We know it was the evil stepdad. It's proving it; that's the hard part.' When Malone had finished admonishing him, she asked, 'So who have you got?'

'At the moment, I am on my tod.'

'You'll be lucky to get out of the building, then, unless you're a very quick reader. What are you going to do?'

'I'm trying to get some outside help, if I can,' he told her.

'Not those bloody journalists again?'

'Why not?'

'In case you haven't noticed, reporters aren't the most popular people round here just now, particularly the investigating kind.'

Bradshaw didn't want to get into an argument about the merits of hiring Helen and Tom. It would have been premature, anyway, as he hadn't been able to get hold of them yet. Perhaps Kane was right and they were too busy working on the glamorous stuff these days. Maybe he really was on his own.

He picked up the nearest file and opened it. Malone left him to it.

Bradshaw started backwards, with the woman who had been missing for just forty-eight hours. He reasoned she was the one most likely to turn up alive. If it was true that she hadn't simply run away, then she could be the latest victim of a serial abductor, and he was surely only doing this for one of two reasons: murder or rape. Often the rape would lead to a murder, to silence the victims. None of the missing women had emerged from their ordeal, so it didn't look good for any of them. True, no bodies had yet been found, and that was unusual, but it could just mean the killer was proficient at disposing of the remains.

Bradshaw went over the details. Eva's height: five feet four; weight; around nine stone; medium to slim build; aged twenty-three; lives at home with her mum and her brother. He examined the photograph of the young woman. Eva Dunbar had a nice face. She was smiling in this photograph, which had been supplied to them by her mother. Eva was on holiday somewhere hot, standing with her arm around a friend, on the terrace of a beach-side bar with the sea in the background. Her face was lightly tanned, which made her smile seem brighter. A note had been stuck to the picture so it was clear which one of the girls was Eva. She had long red hair and bright green eyes and she was leaning forward slightly towards the camera, her face animated. She seemed so full of life, and there was something about her that made Bradshaw warm to her, even though he realized she might very well be dead already.

'Where are you, Eva?' he asked rhetorically. 'Who took you, and why?'

It struck him then that Eva Dunbar had the same colour hair as the woman in the woods.

Chapter Eight

Helen turned the handle of the bathroom door, but it was locked, which was odd, because she was usually up and out of her room in the morning before Tom had left his. As well as his business partner, Helen was also Tom's lodger; an accidental, supposedly short-term arrangement, caused by an attack on her, which they had narrowly escaped but that had resulted in the trashing of her flat. 'Sorry!' she called, loudly enough so Tom could hear her from the landing. Helen was about to go back into her own room to wait when she heard the lock click. The door opened and a face emerged, but it was not Tom.

'Hi, Helen.' The voice was always a little grating to Helen's ear. The younger girl spoke in a perma-cheerful squeak, and she was wrapped in a large towel, steam billowing out behind her from an over-long shower, which probably meant she had used most of their hot water . . . again.

'Penny.' A gritted-teeth smile. 'You stayed over.'

'Yes,' said Penny brightly. 'It's almost like I'm living here at the moment.'

Yes, it is, isn't it?

'I'm done now,' she informed Helen, and padded past her, heading for Tom's room, her long dark hair dripping water on to the annoyingly blemish-free skin of her back, which was barely concealed by the towel.

As Penny reached Tom's door, Helen said, 'That's my towel, by the way.'

'Oh, sorry. I thought it was Tom's.' Penny's face twisted into a regretful grimace she must have assumed looked kooky and endearing. Helen wanted to slap her.

'Hang on,' she said, then she opened Tom's door, shimmied behind it until it concealed her body from Helen, then slipped off the towel and held it out for Helen. Helen had no choice but to walk towards Penny and take the towel from the outstretched hand of the giggling, obviously naked girl. Tom was no doubt enjoying the spectacle from his bed.

Helen didn't feel the need to thank Penny for the return of her very damp towel. 'Tell Tom I'll see him at the café later.'

'Okey-dokey,' chirruped Penny as she closed the door.

Who the hell says Okey-dokey?

Helen could hear laughter from behind the door now as Tom said something to his girlfriend that she didn't catch.

Just as well. I don't want to hear it.

Helen dropped the now contaminated towel into the wash basket on the landing and went to the airing cupboard to get a new one.

It was better this way.

Helen reminded herself of that fact for the umpteenth time as she drove a few yards before halting yet again behind the temporary traffic lights by the 'road improvement' work being carried out in Durham city. The lights seemed incapable of letting more than three cars through

38

at a time before reverting to red, ensuring drivers had a frustrating delay to their daily commute.

Helen and Tom usually went out together in one car, once the morning rush hour was over, but Helen lacked the patience needed to witness the excruciatingly perky Penny draping herself all over Tom, so she'd chosen a peak-time journey to the Rosewood Café for breakfast while she waited for Tom to catch up. It was a place where they often met Ian Bradshaw if they were working a case together, which reminded her that they still owed him a return call.

The lights finally changed to green again. Helen drove her car as close to the rear bumper of the one in front as she dared, willing them both through, but just as the vehicle ahead of hers went through the lights, they reverted to red once more, barring her way.

'Shit,' she hissed, her foul mood exacerbated by the combination of her snail-like progress and the constant presence in their lives these days of Perky Penny. It wasn't that she didn't want Tom to have a girlfriend. She had wished it often enough while she herself had been in a relationship, but, not for the first time, she wondered what the hell he was doing with somebody so young.

'I met someone,' he had announced on his return from his holiday.

'Oh,' was all she could offer in response. She hadn't been expecting that. They had both, almost simultaneously, been through the messiest break-ups imaginable and Tom had, seemingly on a whim, invited Helen to go on the holiday with him. It was already booked and paid for – he had initially intended to go with his girlfriend but that relationship had ended in spectacular fashion. Helen had repeatedly said that it wasn't a good idea and that she wouldn't go with him. Ever the practical one, she had listened to her head and not her heart, despite the obvious mutual attraction between them. What if they fell for each other and started a relationship out there, a holiday romance that couldn't possibly survive the reality of them both living and working together? Helen had known, if she went on that holiday with Tom, she would be running the risk of losing a friend, a business partner and her home.

She kept that stance right till the very last minute, then suddenly changed her mind and did something wildly impulsive for perhaps the first time in her life, driving to meet Tom before he flew out to Crete. Only to discover that he had already left for the airport.

Of course, she never told him. What good would that do?

Helen had put it down to fate, but she hadn't expected Tom to return home a week later and tell her he had met someone. According to him, he spent the first couple of days wandering around listlessly on his own. Then he had gone to a bar and met Penny, who was on holiday with uni pals, and 'her little smile just lit up the room'. Reading between the lines, they barely left the hotel room for the rest of the holiday.

'Well, that's nice,' she had offered when he told her, burying her own emotions. 'I'm pleased for you.'

Was she really, though? She had no claim on Tom. He was single, after all, and she had turned down his invitation, so he must have assumed she didn't want him. Should she be more supportive? She told herself it wasn't that. It was Penny. She was way too young for Tom: he was past thirty, while Penny was barely twenty. It would have been little more than a holiday fling if she had been from any other part of the country, Helen was sure of it. Trust Tom to pick a girl who was studying at Northumbria University. How bloody convenient.

'But does this relationship with Penny have any future?' Helen had asked him recently, alluding to her age.

'I don't know,' replied the infamous commitment-phobe. 'Who cares?'

It'll burn out. It's bound to.

And it's better this way.

Helen told herself she was glad to be single and in no hurry to have another relationship. Peter had called her again the night before and left a long voicemail. Her ex was trying to be calm, as if their last face-to-face conversation hadn't been the one where she called off their engagement and he called her ... what was it? A cold bitch? Among other things. He had also convinced himself she was shagging Tom. Why did everyone always assume she was shagging Tom? She lived with him, but that was just out of convenience for work and their own safety, since there was a gangster out there who wanted them both dead.

Peter's message had included a gently worded request for her to call him back, when she was ready. He explained that it wasn't good to end things the way they had done, and he was probably right. He just wanted to talk. She wasn't sure how she felt about that. Helen didn't want to talk to Peter, but she felt bad. They had been a serious couple for a long time, so it would be strange if they never spoke again. Didn't Peter deserve better than that? She wasn't sure, so she did what she always did when a problem seemed intractable. She slept on it.

After years with Peter and his controlling ways, it was nice to be the only one making the decisions about her life: where to go, what to do, even the clothes she chose to wear. She blanched at the memory of Peter asking her once, 'Are you wearing *that*?' with a frown that had her scurrying to her wardrobe for alternatives. Now she felt angry at her younger, more malleable self for ever permitting that level of control by any man and vowed it would never happen again.

Tom never cared what she wore, but then there were quite a few things he didn't care about. She wondered if he really cared for Penny or whether she would be gone in a few weeks, or months, maybe a year. The girl had lasted a lot longer than Helen had expected.

The lights changed at last, and she was through. Minutes later she reached the café, ordered some tea and toast and waited for Tom. She wondered if he'd managed to track down Ian Bradshaw and speak with him about the missing girls. The detective's lengthy voicemail had been an appeal for help, and it couldn't have been more timely. Missing persons had become something of a speciality of Tom and Helen's, but Ian had explained that this case was different. People disappeared every year, in surprising numbers, often suddenly, but what was missing here, apart from the women themselves, were reasons, and that intrigued Helen. These women hadn't left any clues or explanations behind when they had gone, just a handful of friends and family members desperate to discover the truth.

Bradshaw left his desk and cautiously approached the vending machine, which for once did not have a hand-written

'Out of Order' sign taped to it. He placed his money in the slot, selected a hot drink . . . and nothing happened. Bradshaw examined the slot and saw the edge of his coin: it was jammed. He poked it with a finger, hit the surrounding area hard with the palm of his hand then resorted to rocking the entire machine carefully back and forth in an effort to dislodge the coin but it remained stubbornly stuck.

'Oh, for fu—' He never completed the sentence. Hugh Rennie was standing behind him.

'I've been looking all over for you,' he told Bradshaw. He sounded sheepish. 'I know who she is.'

'The woman in the woods?' Bradshaw turned his attention away from the vending machine. 'Go on.'

'There was something I couldn't quite put my finger on when I saw her, and then it came to me. It was the tattoo.'

'The Celtic band on her wrist?'

'I thought I'd seen it somewhere before, then I remembered. The woman who disappeared, she had a tattoo just like it.'

For a policeman, Rennie was not very good at explaining himself succinctly. 'Which woman?'

'Her name is Cora Harrison.' He corrected himself. 'Or at least it was.'

'Right,' said Bradshaw. 'So when did she go missing?'

'That's the strange part,' said Rennie. 'About eighteen years ago.'

Chapter Nine

Tom arrived at the café late and full of apologies. Helen waved them away because she guessed the delay involved Penny and she didn't want to know the carnal details.

'I can skip breakfast,' he offered, since it was obvious Helen had already eaten.

'No, you can't,' she told him. 'You're hopeless on an empty stomach.'

'You're right.' He ordered a full English. 'Did you call Ian?'

'Me?' she asked indignantly. 'I thought you said you were going to call him?'

'I did, before we left Leeds, remember, but I couldn't get hold of him, so I assumed . . .'

'You assumed?'

'Well, Penny came round, didn't she? So, I thought . . .'

'I would do it for you?'

'For us,' he argued. 'For the business.'

'Well, I didn't, so why don't you just call him now, before your breakfast arrives?'

'Okay,' he said tersely. 'I will.'

Bradshaw forgot all about his cup of tea and the coin jammed in the vending machine. Rennie had his full and undivided attention.

'You're saying this woman was reported missing way back in 1979 and has only just turned up dead now?'

'That's right,' confirmed Rennie.

'Have we any idea where she has been for the past eighteen years?'

'None,' he admitted. 'There was an investigation at the time, of course, but years ago it wasn't taken quite as seriously if a young lass went missing. If no body was found, we tended to assume she'd run away from her parents, gone to London or somewhere, probably with a boyfriend. I mean, a lot of them did, and it was their business. If a girl was over sixteen, there wasn't very much that could be done.'

Rennie went on: 'I remember this particular girl disappearing, and one of our lads asked if there was anything distinctive about her. Her mother said she had a tattoo; a Celtic band thing here' – he put his right hand around his left wrist – 'we mentioned it in our appeal for information at the time. A lot of lasses have tattoos these days, but it was rarer than rocking-horse shit back then, so I remembered it.'

'Just not at first?' Bradshaw remembered Rennie gazing at the body of the woman in the woods.

'No, I mean, yeah, just not at first. Her parents have been dead a while but there's a brother. He was able to confirm it was his sister. That must have been a hell of a shock. He probably thought she'd been killed when she vanished. Now he has to cope with knowing she has been alive all this time.'

'And was only killed recently,' said Bradshaw. 'Poor bastard. It's incredible.'

'Oh, that's not the incredible bit . . .'

Bradshaw was just about to ask Rennie what the

incredible bit was when he noticed Malone standing up at her desk and gesticulating at him. She was too far away to be heard if she called, but she held her hand to her ear with one thumb up and her little finger pointing down, the universal signal for 'phone'.

Cursing her timing, he waved an acknowledgement. Rennie followed Bradshaw back to his desk and took a vacant seat near it, while Malone transferred the call.

'Were you ever planning to call me back?' asked the exasperated detective when he recognized the journalist's voice.

'I'm calling you back now,' said Tom, 'or haven't you noticed?'

'I meant yesterday.'

'I couldn't get hold of you but I asked my people to call your people. Didn't they do that? If you can get down to the Rosewood Café right now, I might even buy you a bacon butty by way of apology.'

'I'm a bit tied up just now but I can meet you later, if you're interested.'

'Let's just say that we'll give it some serious consideration, depending on the terms.'

'The same as always,' said Bradshaw. 'Don't tell me your price has gone up, because we can't afford it.'

'It was worth a try. Just don't go questioning our expenses this time.'

'That wasn't me. It was an officious civilian in Accounts who took exception to your illegible handwriting and crumpled, coffee-stained receipts.'

'Hadn't you better tell me about these missing women?'

'It's easier to explain face to face.' Bradshaw suggested a time for them to get together later. 'That okay with you?'

'Yes,' agreed Tom. 'As long as you can meet us at the Furry Friends Centre?'

'At the what?'

'Haven't you heard of the place? Then you're in for a treat.'

Chapter Ten

Ian Bradshaw was glad he had taken Tom Carney's call – at least now he would have some much-needed help – but he was equally keen to get him off the line so he could hear what else Hugh Rennie had to say about the girl in the woods. They were sitting by Bradshaw's desk in the open-plan HQ and Rennie was keeping his voice low, as if they were plotting something together and not just two colleagues discussing a case.

'There were five of them that fitted the same pattern, all good girls,' explained Rennie. 'Not the kind who would suddenly vanish like that.' He clicked his fingers to illustrate the suddenness of their disappearance. None of them was a tom or an addict, there were no controlling boyfriends or violent fathers, no crimes committed or skeletons in the cupboard, and nothing to be ashamed of – unless all five of them were up the duff at the same time and didn't want to tell anyone, which would be a bit of a bloody coincidence.' He shook his head at the likelihood of that. 'We interviewed everyone around them and all we found were genuinely devastated people who had lost a young woman from their family, suddenly and without rhyme or reason.'

'That we know of,' qualified Bradshaw.

'Everyone has secrets, right?' agreed Rennie. 'And some secrets are darker than others. But we hit a brick wall.'

'Just like now,' said Bradshaw.

'Just like now.'

'This was back in 1979?' asked Bradshaw. 'Five women went missing in quick succession?'

'In '79 and '80,' Rennie corrected him, 'but all within a year or so of each other. Then the disappearances stopped.'

'Until now. What do you think happened?'

'If they were abductions, then we assumed the man behind them either died or got time for other crimes, so he couldn't carry on. Maybe he tired of what he was doing and stopped for some reason – who knows? You can't always work out what's going on in their heads – nutters, I mean.'

'Did anyone follow up on it later?' Bradshaw asked. 'Cross-referencing prison sentences with the dates when the disappearances ceased?'

'There wasn't much appetite for that back then. Remember, we didn't have any bodies, so there wasn't even any evidence that any crimes had been committed. The brass thought we had bigger fish to fry.'

'And none of these women was ever seen again?'

'One was,' Rennie corrected him.

'One of them was found?'

'About a year after she disappeared. She was reported missing on 4 May 1979.'

'You've got a bloody good memory.'

'It was Election Day, when Margaret Thatcher first got into power. Not a date I'm likely to forget. The Tories have been in ever since, but it looks like that might change soon.' Rennie didn't offer a clue as to whether he thought this was a good thing or not.

49

'This woman,' said Bradshaw, to get him back on track. 'What was her name?'

'Sarah Barstow,' said Rennie. 'And when she reappeared she was in a right state.'

'What happened to her?'

'She was half loopy when they found her, wandering up and down an A-road on foot until she got hit by a car. Died in hospital a few days later.'

'Did she ever regain consciousness?'

When Rennie answered it was in a careful and guarded manner. 'I . . . believe she did . . . yes.'

'Anyone interview her before she died?'

'Yes.'

'Not you, though?'

'It wasn't me,' he said. 'No.'

'But someone did. And?'

'It was all pretty incoherent, really, or so I was told later. She made some pretty wild claims, spoke a lot of utter rubbish. She was rambling on about some really quite bizarre stuff and not making much sense, by all accounts. They were saying she was like some hippy chick who fried her brain on LSD. We called her the stoned girl.'

'In 1979? I'd have thought that was more likely in the sixties than the late seventies, wouldn't you?'

Rennie shrugged. 'There are hippies even now,' he said. 'Not many of them, I'll grant you but, whatever she was into, she'd seriously messed up her mind.'

'You said she made some wild claims?'

'She said she'd been abducted by a crazy man who'd kept her underground.' He raised his eyebrows at that. 'She claimed she was held captive for months and that she wasn't the only one. There were others there with her but she couldn't tell us where this was or how she happened to be wandering up and down the road, miles from anywhere.'

'Did she mean she was held in a cellar or basement somewhere?'

'She just kept saying "underground".'

'You never actually saw this young woman personally?'

'Me? No. Like I said, someone else interviewed her.'

'I'd like to speak to them,' said Bradshaw. 'Who was it? Can you remember?'

Rennie shook his head slowly, 'Sorry, mate, can't help you there. It was all a very long while ago.' He added cryptically: 'It would have been a job for an ambitious DS, I shouldn't wonder.' He abruptly changed the subject. 'Listen, you know I haven't got long to go. You are planning on coming, aren't you? To my leaving bash, I mean.'

Bradshaw didn't know Rennie all that well and hadn't given it any thought, if he was honest. He didn't even know when it was.

'I wouldn't miss it for the world, mate.'

Rennie seemed reassured by that, 'Good. Make sure you don't.'

'This Sarah Barstow' – Bradshaw wasn't finished yet and wanted to get more out of Rennie before they started planning his leaving bash – 'was she one of the good girls, you said?'

'Yeah, one of those sweet, innocent, buttoned-down types; butter wouldn't melt and all that. I think she even worked in a library.'

'Yet a year later she turns up stoned and rambling?'

'High as a kite and talking shite,' he confirmed. 'We

reckoned the lass had spent twelve months drugged up to her eyeballs and drunk.'

'Who's "we"?' asked Bradshaw.

'We, us, the team,' said Rennie. 'And we were right because the post-mortem confirmed she'd buggered up her internal organs with drink. She had kidney failure and all sorts wrong with her. The lass had gone from sweet little innocent to raging alcoholic inside a year.'

'Didn't that strike you as a bit odd?'

'Yes, it did, but strange things happen every day in this job. Haven't you noticed?'

Bradshaw had to concede Rennie had a point. 'The woman was lucid enough to say she had been abducted, though?'

'The collective view was that she must have had a guilty conscience and wanted to blame it all on someone.'

'What was your view?'

Rennie just shrugged, as if he didn't have one.

'And you honestly can't remember who told you what happened during her interview?'

Rennie surveyed Bradshaw for a moment then said very quietly, 'I can't, sorry.'

'Who was on the team, then? Let's start with that.'

'All sorts of people. They came and went, and the case never really closed.'

'Give me some names?'

And he did, eventually, but all of them had now left the force, most of them into retirement.

'Is there anyone who is still in this building that might remember working that case?'

'Now you're asking.'

'I am, yes.'

'Not that I can think of,' said Rennie. 'Off the top of my head.'

Again Bradshaw was convinced Rennie was lying, but he let it go, for now. He didn't know the man well enough to call him out and, even if he did, Rennie was hardly going to admit it. 'You said she was on the A1 when they picked her up.'

'Yeah, can't remember exactly where, though. It was such a long while back.'

'Is there a case file, something I could take a look at?'

'Of course. We weren't quite as bureaucratic back then, but we did write things down.'

'So the interview notes should still be there?'

Rennie's face was impassive. 'Should be.'

'Right then. I'll take a look.' Bradshaw got to his feet.

'You going there now?'

You bet I am.

'Yes, Hugh, I think I am.'

Chapter Eleven

Eva told herself it was a good thing he had chosen to hide his face. He must be worried she might identify him later, which meant that, maybe, she would get out of here. If only she knew what he wanted from her.

Was she dealing with a disturbed mind? Nobody normal would do this to another human being. But what did he want? To kill her? Then why was he feeding her? And why go to the trouble of creating this room? If he was a kidnapper who had mistaken her for someone else, what would happen when he found out? Would he just let her go, or . . . ?

It was an hour before she ventured from the bed and walked over to the food on the tray. It was some kind of stew, cold now, and congealed on the plate. Eva was incredibly hungry but didn't dare to eat anything, in case the food was drugged or poisoned. There was a plastic glass full of water next to the paper plate. Again, she was too frightened to drink initially, even though she had never been thirstier. She peeled back the lid on the plastic tub. It contained toothpaste, a toothbrush, sanitary towels, a flannel and a cheap bar of soap.

She picked up the water, raised it cautiously to her lips and took the tiniest of sips. The water felt so good in her parched mouth and, when she suffered no immediate ill effects, she took a grateful gulp. She made sure to keep a third of the liquid in the plastic glass for later. She didn't know how long it would be before he came back – assuming he did come back.

Whatever happened, she would have to eat in order to survive. Tentatively at first, she ate the food. It was cold and didn't taste of much, but she was glad of it nonetheless. Afterwards she lay thinking about her best course of action.

She had to get out of here, and quickly.

Eva got up and walked around the metal box, searching for any weakness in the structure, a crack or a gap, some ragged edge of metal perhaps, but there was nothing. It was entirely sealed, except for an air vent with tiny gaps between the slats that had been welded into the structure, its central point held firmly in place by four large screws that had been painted over, and there was nothing she could do to make them budge.

She went to the door then and banged on it hard with the palm of her hand. Perhaps someone would hear. Maybe *he* would hear and he'd come back and punish her, but that was a risk she had to take. She hammered on the metal door again and again. Then she let out a cry of frustration and shouted, 'Let me out!'

Eva carried on with the banging and the shouting until the palm of her hand was red raw and stinging and her throat hurt so much she had to drink the last of the water.

No one came.

It took Bradshaw an age to find the file he was looking for. He knew he'd be late for his appointment with Helen and Tom and nearly gave up several times, but he hadn't liked the way Rennie asked him if he was going to view the files *now*, and he didn't want to delay his search any longer. In short, he didn't fully trust Hugh Rennie and he needed to see that file.

When he did finally locate it, it was flimsy and only the bare facts were recorded in it. There was no record of any interview with or statement from Sarah Barstow.

'This is bullshit,' muttered Bradshaw to himself. He knew that record-keeping had not been as comprehensive back then but he had expected more than this. Specifically, he had hoped to see detailed notes on the victim's own words, even if they were disbelieved at the time.

Someone has been covering their tracks, he thought, *but why?*

Jenna had tried to forget the note. Then, realizing she couldn't, she had resolved to laugh it off.

When that also failed, she simply hoped. Hoped that it was a sick joke of some kind. Hoped that the person who had written it didn't really know anything at all and just wanted to scare her. Hoped there would never be another one.

It was several days before all those hopes vanished.

Jenna had thought about the note to the exclusion of almost everything else. She recalled reading something about a prank played once on an entire town. Was it a joke or an urban myth, or maybe a horror film she had half watched late one night? Hadn't everyone in town received a note through their door on the same evening, with something like 'I know what you did' written on it? In the morning, half of them had packed up and left because they had a guilty conscience about something.

That's what this must be, right? Just a silly joke.

It didn't seem so silly when the second note arrived. It was waiting for her on the mat when she came downstairs in the morning, and this one had her name on it.

DID YOU REALLY THINK YOU COULD JUST WALK AWAY, JENNA?

THAT'S NEVER GOING TO HAPPEN.

Now she was truly terrified.

Jenna didn't trust men after everything she had been through, and she was pretty certain the person writing the notes was a man. There was something about the taunting tone of the note and the relish taken in the threatening words that screamed *Male*. A woman would be more than capable of writing something like that, as she well knew, but men had been the root cause of most of her problems. Jenna hadn't trusted a man in a long while. There had only been one or two over the years who weren't out to use, control or damage her.

Her thoughts turned idly to one of them and it struck her that he might just be her only chance.

As Ian Bradshaw left police HQ he was surprised to see a journalist running towards the car park with a microphone in his hand and a cameraman trailing behind him. He could hear voices coming from around the corner of the building but he couldn't work out what was going on. Another car pulled up then and a journalist he recognized from the local paper got out and started to walk rapidly in the same direction, then two men he didn't recognize emerged from another car and did the same.

'It's Tyler's announcement,' said the desk sergeant, who was standing next to him, having wandered outside to see

57

what the fuss was about. 'He's making it in the car park. Man of the people, and all that. The PR manager thinks it makes him look more dynamic and accessible if he's standing outside.' He gave a little snort of derision.

Deputy Chief Constable Edward Tyler had been on the TV quite a lot lately. 'What announcement?' asked Bradshaw, who didn't understand the sudden press interest.

'Summat about drugs.' The desk sergeant shrugged. 'They're a bad thing, apparently, and you shouldn't take them. All that bollocks.' And with that underwhelming pronouncement he shuffled back inside.

As he turned the corner of the building, Bradshaw could clearly make out the figure of Tyler, surrounded by a dozen reporters, poised to write down his words or thrust microphones into his face.

'I am Deputy Chief Constable Edward Tyler of Durham Constabulary,' he announced, 'and as some of you already know, I have additional responsibilities for national policing on illegal drug use. I am here to talk to you about a major new campaign to be trialled across our region which is set to change the face of UK law-enforcement policy towards the scourge of drug-dealing in our communities.'

Before the deputy chief could outline his important new policy, he was interrupted. Bradshaw didn't hear the question but he could pick up the irritation in Tyler's answer. 'Well, that is not why I am speaking to you today . . . that is an ongoing investigation and it would be unwise of me to speculate –' He was interrupted by another question and Bradshaw made out a mention of missing women and the word 'body'.

Bradshaw knew they had to be asking about the woman

in the woods. That would explain the press interest. They weren't here to listen to a speech on the perils of drug use. Bradshaw decided it would be a good idea to walk briskly to his car.

The interruptions continued, Tyler floundered and Bradshaw kept his head down and his feet moving. He didn't want to be recognized as the investigating officer on the case and targeted by a gaggle of reporters asking him to supply answers he did not yet have. He'd almost reached his car when a tabloid journalist with a London accent asked Tyler loudly if anyone still had faith in his force, bearing in mind it was 'institutionally corrupt' and 'riddled with bent detectives'. Before Tyler could answer, he followed up with a demand to know why nothing was being done to prevent the disappearances of young women in the area. At that point Tyler swiftly called a halt to his announcement and marched off with an outraged look on his face, closely followed by a harassed-looking PR woman who would surely be made to take the blame for the media ambush.

Bradshaw got in his car and drove off, being extra careful not to accidentally mow down any of the press pack on his way out.

'Are you the detective?' The woman on reception at the Furry Friends Centre was obviously expecting him. 'They're round the back,' she said, and she made a whirling motion with a finger to indicate that he had to go out of the front door and around the side of the building.

Bradshaw did as he was told and emerged into what looked like a school playground with a large pen in one corner that held a number of young Labrador puppies scampering about and playing happily. A slightly older dog on a lead was being trained in the middle of the concrete space, while the animal and its handler were watched by some of the centre's organizers, all of whom wore dark green polo shirts with the centre's logo on it; a black pawprint on a red heart. Bradshaw waved at Helen and Tom, who were standing at the opposite end of the training ground, then joined them so they could watch the spectacle together.

'Blind dogs?' he asked.

'They wouldn't be much use if they were, mate,' Tom told him.

'I'll rephrase that. Are they dogs *for* the blind?'

Helen shook her head. 'The term is "guide dogs" but they're hearing dogs. They're being trained to help the deaf or hard of hearing.'

'What?'

Helen was just about to repeat what she had said when she realized he was joking. 'We can't take you anywhere, Ian.'

'How can a dog help a deaf person anyway? I didn't know they had hearing dogs.'

'If your doorbell rings, the dog will alert you,' Helen explained. 'When the alarm clock goes off it will come and nudge you. More importantly, if it hears the smoke alarm, you can get the hell out of the building.'

'That's amazing.'

'And they give people more confidence to get out and about. These dogs can obey up to forty different commands once they're fully trained.'

'So you're writing about them?'

'We're just helping out,' said Tom, 'with their newsletter and mail shots.'

Bradshaw recalled Helen's sideline in desktop publishing. She could create whole magazines using their advanced but very expensive personal computer. Sometimes that was for paying customers, but they often helped out charities like this one. Tom liked to tease Helen that she was too nice but he never seemed to mind really.

The young girl training the Labrador finished the session, petted the dog, gave it a treat then came over to them. Helen introduced her as Marie, while the Labrador jumped enthusiastically up at Helen, who petted it and told the dog it was 'a *good* girl!'

'It likes you,' said Bradshaw.

'And so it should,' said Tom, 'Helen has been helping them down here a lot. Show him what they taught you.'

When Helen seemed reluctant, Tom told Bradshaw, 'She can do sign language.'

'Only a bit,' she protested.

'Go on, then,' Bradshaw urged her.

Helen rolled her eyes at Marie, pointed at Tom then whirled her hands. The other girl grinned and signed something back to her.

'What did you just say?' asked Bradshaw.

Helen did the actions again and told him the words they represented. 'I said, "My friend here"' – and she pointed at Tom – '"is an idiot," and she replied, "Yes, but what can you do?"'

'Thanks, pet,' said Tom, and he shot a fake frown at the other girl. 'I used to like you, Marie.'

She laughed and walked away with the dog.

'Are you okay to talk now?' asked Bradshaw once she had left them.

'Yes, we're good,' said Tom, and they strolled back to their cars while Bradshaw briefed them about the five missing women and the discovery of the dead woman in the woods.

'Which one was it?' Tom asked.

'Yeah, well, that's the really interesting part,' said Bradshaw. 'It's none of them.'

'I don't understand,' said Helen. 'You said they'd found a woman, but if she hasn't got anything to do with the Disappeared . . .'

'Oh, this woman disappeared all right,' said Bradshaw. 'A very long time ago . . .'

By the time they had reached their cars they knew almost everything he did.

'And none of these women had a reason to run, which leads you to the conclusion that they have been abducted?' asked Helen.

'It doesn't lead me to any conclusion,' said Bradshaw. 'At least not yet. But we can't rule it out.'

'Oh, come on, Ian,' snorted Tom. 'This isn't a press conference. You can tell us what you think.'

'I *am* telling you what I think. There might not be any evidence to back up the runaway theory but there isn't much to support the idea they were snatched from the streets either and, being a detective, I'm not supposed to assume. I'm keeping an open mind and I think you should, too.'

'So, keeping an open mind and working on the basis that they *could* have been abducted,' said Helen, 'do we collectively believe that the disappearance of some women eighteen years ago has any link with today's cases?'

'It seems unlikely,' Bradshaw conceded, 'yet I keep coming back to the similarity of the circumstances and then, there's the number.'

'Five,' said Tom. 'The same as now.'

Bradshaw nodded. 'So far. We won't actually know how many victims there are until he stops.'

'And by then it could be too late,' said Helen.

'For the victims, yes.'

'It is a bit of a coincidence, isn't it?' admitted Tom, intrigued now.

'There's something else. To be honest, I don't know if it's anything at all.' Bradshaw seemed reluctant to come to the point.

'What is it?' asked Helen.

'Eva Dunbar is the most recent woman to disappear,' he said, 'and she's a redhead. She has auburn hair, the same as the woman in the woods.'

He let that sink in, then Tom asked, 'Another coincidence, or there's someone out there with a type?'

Helen asked a question then. 'Are you saying she was . . . ?'

She hesitated, leaving Tom to complete her chilling deduction: 'A replacement.'

Chapter Twelve

Helen and Tom had agreed on the spot to help Ian Bradshaw, and not just because the case intrigued them. The lives of five missing women depended on this, and they wanted to start straight away. Helen suggested that they immerse themselves in the case files at police HQ and it seemed a sensible starting point to Bradshaw, not least because it would free him up to do other things.

Bradshaw had hoped to spirit them into the building without being noticed, but that was always a long shot. They were in a corridor at HQ when he spotted DS O'Brien coming the other way. The man had a face like thunder. His partner, DC Skelton, trailed in his wake. Bradshaw guessed they had been lobbying Kane – unsuccessfully – to get themselves reinstated, since they were among the eight officers who had been suspended on suspicion of corruption. It had long been rumoured that O'Brien and Skelton had a lucrative sideline in shaking down drug-dealers but it had taken the intervention of the newspaper and documentary crew to bring it into the open and force their suspension. Bradshaw had clashed with both O'Brien and Skelton in the past, and so had Tom Carney. They were popular officers, nicknamed the 'Regan and Carter of Durham Constabulary' because their no-nonsense approach led to arrests and convictions; they regarded Bradshaw as a goody-two-shoes.

When they found out he had been receiving counselling, they gleefully told everyone that Bradshaw was bonkers.

As soon as O'Brien saw Tom in the building his nostrils flared. 'What is *he* doing here?'

'Helping me with a case,' said Bradshaw, but O'Brien wasn't listening.

'It's because of you that I've been suspended.'

'Tom had nothing to do with it,' said Bradshaw.

'He's a journalist!' snapped O'Brien. 'And it's their lies that have caused all this trouble.'

'So I am personally responsible for every word written by all journalists now, am I?' asked Tom with a flicker of amusement.

'Journalists lie,' DC Skelton interjected. 'All of them, including you, and there are good coppers who pay the price for those lies.'

'Good coppers? Not all detectives are corrupt,' answered Tom. 'Just some of them. Only you and he know which camp you're in, but I had nothing to do with the article that got you suspended, so back off.'

The two men glared at each other and Bradshaw thought for a moment that Skelton might take a swing at Tom right there in the corridor. He tensed, ready to intervene. O'Brien clamped a hand on his fiery partner's shoulder to restrain him. 'Leave it, mate,' he cautioned. Tom had the impression it was their perilous position in the force he was thinking of and not the reporter's well-being.

'You want to watch yourself,' hissed Skelton.

Tom's response was derision. 'Oh, join the queue,' he sneered.

'Just watch it,' repeated the detective constable, and he deliberately barged into Tom as he forced his way past them, knocking the younger man to one side. O'Brien followed his partner, scowling as he went.

'Nice guys,' said Helen when they were gone.

'They're just a little upset,' said Bradshaw, steering them along the corridor.

Bradshaw showed Helen and Tom into the room where the files were stored, then immediately announced he would have to leave them to it.

'What's so important?' asked Helen.

'Yeah, how come you get to skive off?' said Tom.

'Because I am "skiving off", as you put it, so I can speak to the families of these missing women myself,' he told them. 'And then there's somewhere else I have to be that will be almost as much fun.'

'Where?' asked Tom.

'The mortuary,' Bradshaw told him. 'Want to swap?'

'No, thanks.'

'Then I'll catch up with you both tomorrow.' He nodded at the files. 'Have fun.'

Chapter Thirteen

There was one question that kept coming back to Eva, over and over again: Why?

Why her and not someone else? Why take her? Why keep her here? He hadn't tried to kill her, or rape her, or hurt her. What was he waiting for? Were there other men involved? Was that it – he was waiting for them to show up? Would she be the entertainment for a group of madmen, some criminal gang or ring of sadists who would take delight in her terror?

Would Eva be taken from here and sent off somewhere, perhaps to another country? Was she now a part of a slave trade, something to be sold, like someone's property? Would the real abuse start then? She had heard terrible tales but it couldn't happen in this country, could it?

But if that wasn't the reason, what could it be?

This man was feeding her and bringing her water, but why?

Eva had nothing but time to think: hours – days, in fact – to speculate on and worry about her fate. There were worse things than dying. She believed that now.

The only break from her thoughts was when the man came and opened the container, two, sometimes three times a day; always with the gun, always with his face covered. She was glad about that. If he ever came without wearing his balaclava, she would know it was over. He would kill her then.

Sometimes he would leave food and water for her without speaking. Other occasions she might get a few words, and that deep voice would urge her to eat or drink and maybe add, 'You'll be saved now,' which made no sense to her at all.

The one thing that did make sense to Eva right now was getting out of here and it looked like she would have to make that happen herself. She picked up the lamp and began to examine every inch of the crate again, searching for a weak point in the metal.

Bradshaw visited members of five families that afternoon. Jessica Davies' fiancé said her disappearance was his fault entirely. Bradshaw didn't know if he wanted the detective to agree with him or absolve him. Either way, this was not a confession. The young man had taken a call from Jessica after she missed her bus and would normally have driven from their flat to pick her up, 'But,' he said, 'I'd had a few at the pub that night, hadn't I, and I didn't want to risk it. I need my licence for my job, and I have to have a job if we are ever going to get married, so I said she'd have to wait for the next one.' He looked as if he had been beating himself up over that decision ever since, and Jessica had been gone for three months. 'If I hadn't been drinking, she'd be here with me now.' He glanced up at the photograph of his fiancée that smiled down at him from the mantelpiece. 'If we don't get her back, I'll never forgive myself.'

Bradshaw couldn't think of one crumb of comfort to offer the poor lad.

The parents of Sandra Lane hardly said a word. They

just looked at him as if he'd suddenly landed from another planet and they couldn't for the life of them understand what he was doing in their living room. Their answers to his questions came in monosyllables, and he eventually left the shocked couple with no more information about Sandra than when he had arrived.

Stephanie Evans' husband seemed worried the detective might think he had something to do with his wife's disappearance. Bradshaw didn't, at first, until Bob mentioned it more than once. 'They kept going on about the wedding ring,' he explained, meaning Bradshaw's colleagues.

'Oh, yes, the wedding ring.' It had been mentioned in the file. 'She left it behind when she went out with her friends in Durham.'

'And I was away that night, so they made it sound like a big deal, which it really wasn't. I mean, there are lots of reasons why a woman might take off her wedding ring and forget about it, right?'

You mean other than to pretend she was unmarried while her husband was away, thought Bradshaw. 'Like doing the washing-up?' he offered gamely.

'Oh, no,' he said. 'She wore it when she was doing that.' His face clouded over at that point. 'I meant other reasons,' he added, but it seemed he wasn't able to think of any just then. Bradshaw asked him a series of routine questions and made his own mind up about Bob Evans. This wasn't a man who had killed his wife because he knew she was having an affair; this was a man whose wife had disappeared without her wedding ring, so now, as well as dealing with her loss, he was also wondering if she had been looking for something outside their marriage.

Alice Smith's mother clung to the positive possibilities of her daughter's disappearance with an almost messianic zeal. She knew Alice wasn't dead, she informed Bradshaw, because she would know it if her daughter had been killed. She would have felt it deep inside her. No, Alice must have gone somewhere, with someone, and she couldn't get in touch for some reason, though Alice's mother could offer no possible explanation for this highly uncharacteristic behaviour.

That left one more home and family to visit.

Ian Bradshaw had never seen anyone look as tired as Nancy Dunbar. She had deep, dark grooves under her eyes and the whites were bloodshot. Her hair was almost entirely grey and, when she sat down in the armchair, she looked as if she might not have the energy to get up out of it again. In short, this was not a well woman.

'This is my hour,' Eva's mother said as she gestured for him to sit down on her sofa. 'Simon is at the daycare. My son has autism,' she explained. 'I take him there twice a week on the bus. It gives me a break but by the time I drop him off then get the bus back home and do all the housework, I get about an hour's rest before I'm back on the bus again to collect him. I don't know why I'm rambling on about that.'

Eva's mother had been talking to him non-stop from the moment he confirmed he had no new information as to her whereabouts. Was it relief because her daughter's body had not been found or the crushing realization that Eva was still missing that had led to her nervous chatter?

'I don't know what I can do to help you,' she said. 'I told your colleagues everything I can think of. Eva's a good girl. She wouldn't just run off, she wouldn't . . . leave us.' She said this haltingly, as if there were a tiny scintilla of doubt in her mind, just for an instant, before she banished it. 'It's been hard, I'll admit that, but she loves Simon and he loves her. She wouldn't just go. Please believe me.'

'I do,' Bradshaw told her, and he could see her become less tense, as if him believing her were half the battle. But what else could he offer this distraught woman? Not much.

'You'll want to look round,' she said. 'Isn't that what they do on the telly?'

'If you don't mind.'

'If you think it will help.' Before he answered, she got up and led the way out of the room, and he followed her, because it was a small thing to do and it might make her feel a little better, even though he knew the house had already been searched and nothing had turned up.

She guided Bradshaw upstairs and showed him Eva's room. He took a look round while she stood by the door, watching. Was she expecting him to make some significant breakthrough from evidence gleaned by looking at the contents of her daughter's room?

There wasn't much to see, just a single bed, a chest of drawers and a wardrobe, all in white, but surely Eva would have outgrown the pink-patterned wallpaper by now. They probably just didn't have the time or the energy to redecorate. There was a simple black dress hanging from the wardrobe door but no jewellery or make-up on the dressing table, just a hairbrush and a deodorant. A poster of Uma Thurman as Mia Wallace in *Pulp Fiction* adorned one wall and another had a clip-framed photo of Leonardo DiCaprio in *Romeo + Juliet* hanging on it. There was barely anything else to see, barring a couple of photo albums and a CD player. It was neat, unfussy and lacked the usual clutter he had seen before in young girls' bedrooms. Eva did not seem to value possessions all that much, and Bradshaw warmed to her because of it.

'Everything all right?' Nancy asked.

'It's very tidy.' He smiled. 'No make-up or clothes.'

'I haven't touched anything,' she told him, as if it were a crime scene. 'She was never that bothered about getting dolled up.'

Perhaps it was the sight of a detective standing in her missing daughter's room that did it, but suddenly she was wiping tears away. 'You *will* find her? You'll do everything you can?' she managed.

'Yes, we'll do everything we can. We have some really good investigators working on it. I promise you, they're the best.'

Chapter Fourteen

'I'll admit it,' said Tom. 'Right now, I haven't got a bloody clue.'

They were standing next to each other, surveying the photographs of the five missing women which were face up on the table. Between them, they had read as much material in the case files as possible.

Helen regarded the photographs closely. 'He doesn't appear to have a type.'

One of the women had dark hair tied back off her face; one had brown hair with a fringe; two were blonde, but one looked natural, the other as if the colour came from a bottle. Then there was Eva Dunbar, who had long, auburn hair that reached below her shoulders. It made a striking contrast to her pale and delicate face.

It wasn't just the hair. When you examined their facial features or skin tone, it was immediately clear that the women were all quite different. The files revealed they were of different heights and weights, and their ages spanned ten years: the youngest was twenty; the oldest was just over thirty. Their backgrounds varied; one was a student from a reasonably well-to-do middle-class background, one a young woman with impoverished parents who was working two jobs (cleaner and supermarket cashier), to support herself and them.

None of the women had children, but was this just a

coincidence? If they were abducted, had he been stalking them for weeks, or had he known nothing about them, acting impulsively and dragging them from the street?

'Not a type, then,' agreed Tom, his tone thoughtful, 'except they are all youngish women. But is there any pattern to this that we're missing somehow?'

'They all disappeared when they were returning home from work or an evening out,' said Helen, 'but the times vary and so do the locations.'

They had marked the last-known whereabouts of each woman on a map. The sites were in County Durham or into Northumbria but there was no defined area with a specific location at its centre, and even the places themselves were markedly different. One disappeared after a night out in Newcastle,' continued Helen. 'Another went missing following a friend's birthday drink in Durham city, one after she missed a bus home to her village, another was last seen coming out of an office she had been cleaning at the end of a working day, and the first victim had been shopping.'

'And there is no known link between any of them,' he recounted. 'They didn't attend the same school, work near one another or go to the same gym. They had no shared friends or boyfriends and their political or religious views, hobbies and interests varied. Not one of them had any history of stalkers, troublesome ex-boyfriends or overbearing families. I can't see a single link here, can you?'

'No and nor could any of the officers that worked the case before us. There's nothing.'

'So, he likes to take women,' concluded Tom. 'Not too young but not too old, and he's very careful about it. The pattern is there is no pattern. He must have covered some miles to do all this and my gut feeling is that he takes advantage of any opportunity spontaneously when he spots someone who fits the bill. That way, no one is expecting him. The police can warn women to be careful when they're walking home at night in a rural location, say, but then he grabs a woman right off the streets of Newcastle. It's chilling.'

'Every woman's nightmare,' said Helen.

It wasn't like it was on the telly. It was never like it was on the telly. On the TV, hard-nosed detectives walked into autopsies like they were a matter of routine. Young, freshly minted detectives might throw up in a corner, to the irritation of their older superiors, but you weren't meant to bat an eyelid once you'd been doing this for a while. You were supposed to take it in your stride, ignore the evidence of your own eyes, disregard the overpowering smell of chemicals and the sight of carefully extracted internal organs and somehow ask intelligent questions about the cause and time of death, then go home and have your tea like nothing had happened. But Bradshaw hated this part of the job.

He didn't relish the idea of going to the mortuary to pick up the results of the post-mortem on the woman in the woods. He hoped there wasn't a fresh cadaver on the slab when he opened the door and was grateful for that small mercy when he found the pathologist making notes at his desk in a corpseless room.

'Yes?' The pathologist looked irritated by the disturbance.

Bradshaw introduced himself and explained why he was there.

'You too? I do have other things to be getting on with.'

'Who else has been down here?' He knew it wasn't Kane, who preferred a few sentences in summary from a subordinate.

'It's been like Piccadilly Circus,' harrumphed the pathologist, but it seemed that was all Bradshaw was going to get in the way of an answer. Maybe the old grump wasn't referring to the same case. Who knew how many other bodies he was working on, even if it was only to rule out foul play? There were usually a few on the go at any one time and Bradshaw always wondered what it did to your mind to be constantly surrounded by reminders of your own mortality, to be poking into corpses of people who had been walking around just a few days or even hours before, until a crime or a traffic accident, a heart attack or a brain tumour, suddenly and prematurely ended their life without warning. 'I'm assuming you want the top line?' He peered over his reading glasses at Bradshaw.

'Yes, please.'

'Cause of death was strangulation, obviously,' he said, 'but there were other factors that were' – he searched for the word – 'noteworthy.'

'How so?'

'There was a lot of damage to the internal organs.'

'Which ones?'

'All of them to an extent, but it was particularly noticeable in the liver and kidneys.'

Just like Sarah Barstow. What had Rennie told him about the stoned girl? *She'd buggered up her internal organs with drink.*

'Cause?'

'Could be a number of things.'

Why would these pathologists never nail their bloody colours to the mast? But Bradshaw knew why. It was mainly because they didn't want to be picked up on it in court if one of their assumptions turned out to be wrong.

'Off the record, what do you think it might be? It would be bloody helpful to get an expert's opinion, to help me narrow it down a bit.' Bradshaw had learned that a combination of flattery and a plea for help was often surprisingly effective when dealing with figures of authority.

'It could be alcohol abuse over a sustained period. That would eventually wear out the liver and kidneys.'

'Thank you,' said Bradshaw.

'And there was one other thing,' said the pathologist. He dangled this tantalizingly in front of Bradshaw and waited for his response.

'What was that?'

'The lady in question had rickets.' The pathologist looked troubled at the recollection. 'And I have to say, in all my years of doing this job, that has to be a first.'

Chapter Fifteen

When they pulled over by the side of the road, thirty or forty yards before they reached the gate at the bottom of their drive, Helen looked questioningly at Tom, sensing danger. He pointed ahead and she saw the reason for his caution. Someone was standing on the street outside their home, evidently waiting for them to return, even though the rain was coming down hard now. She understood Tom's concern. Their job meant they lived with the permanent prospect of someone seeking revenge, and they knew from the bitterest experience that this wasn't paranoia on their part.

The house they shared, which doubled as their office, had every conceivable security measure, from a CCTV camera and alarm system to barred windows and electronic gates that blocked the driveway. Bradshaw joked that they lived in Fort Knox, but at least they could sleep at night.

'I'm going to keep driving to the gate,' Tom told her. 'If I don't like the look of him, we won't stop.'

Helen nodded in agreement and Tom eased the car out from the side of the road and began to drive towards their home. Helen kept her eyes locked on the figure, but he had his back to her. She could make out a man in a raincoat but little else. She found herself clenching her fists as they drew closer, a nervous reaction to the tension.

Then the man turned towards them, hearing the sound of the car. 'Bloody hell,' said Tom. It was part relief, part exasperation, and Helen knew why. The mysterious figure was Ian Bradshaw, but why was he standing outside in the rain? The answer lay with the phone he was holding. When he saw the car, he stopped dialling and put it back in his pocket.

Tom pulled over, Helen wound down the window and the sopping figure took a step towards them. 'About time,' he said. 'Can't you just leave a key under the mat for me?'

'Ian, what are you doing standing out here in the rain?' Helen asked him.

'I've only been here two minutes. I rang the bell then tried to call you ... again. Do you never switch those phones on?'

'Sorry,' said Tom. 'I turn mine off when I'm driving and Helen always forgets to charge hers.'

'I do not,' she protested. 'At least not always.'

'Well, you're here now,' said Bradshaw.

'But why are you here?' asked Helen, because they weren't due to meet up again until the following morning.

'There's been a development.'

Once they were inside, Helen offered Bradshaw a cup of tea, but the offer became redundant when Tom came back from the kitchen with a bottle of beer for each of them. The detective took his gratefully. Then he explained why he had felt the need to come here straight from the mortuary.

'Rickets?' asked Helen. 'In this day and age?'

'Remind me what rickets is?' said Tom. 'It rings a bell,

79

but I thought only poor people got that, you know, back in Dickens' day, chimney sweeps and the like.'

'Not quite,' said Bradshaw. 'But not many people get it these days and, yes, it is usually a sign of poverty and malnutrition.'

'But in this case it could have been caused by long-term imprisonment?' asked Helen.

'If we accept the theory that she was abducted eighteen years ago and has been kept a prisoner ever since – a staggering thought – then it could.' Bradshaw looked at his notebook. 'There was also a noticeable degradation of the teeth and muscles, as well as the bones.' He raised his eyes. 'Rickets is caused by a lack of vitamin D. It weakens the bones and makes them go soft.'

'How do you get vitamin D?' asked Tom.

'It's in fresh foods like tuna and cheese, so her diet must have been lacking in those.'

'Sunlight,' said Helen abruptly.

Tom smiled. 'You can't eat sunlight.'

'No, but you also get vitamin D from the sun.'

'How does that work?' asked Tom.

'Just by walking around,' she said. 'I'm not making this up: we need sunshine to touch our skin to generate vitamin D.'

'I thought sunbathing was bad for you,' said Bradshaw.

'Too much sun is,' she agreed. 'You can get melanomas. You don't have to lie on a beach all day to get enough vitamin D, though. You just have to go for a walk every now and then and your skin will soak up the sun's rays.'

'How do you know all this, Helen?' asked Bradshaw.

'She went to a posh school down south, remember,'

teased Tom. 'Not like the crumbling shit-tip you and I attended.'

'The same way you know things,' Helen told Bradshaw. 'I read.' She turned to Tom. 'And I did not go to a posh school. It was a state school.'

'When I saw her in the woods,' said Bradshaw, 'her skin was unnaturally pale. I've seen a few bodies in my time, but she was ghostly white.'

'No sunlight,' said Helen.

'Because she'd been kept prisoner all this time?' Tom speculated.

'And the other woman from years before, Sarah Barstow – the stoned girl. Her internal organs had been damaged, just like Cora Harrison's.'

'Did she have rickets, too?' asked Tom.

'No, but Sarah claimed she was held prisoner by a man for more than a year and there were other women there too,' Bradshaw told them. 'And here's the thing: she said he kept her underground.'

'Right,' said Tom. 'But how could he possibly do that?'

Chapter Sixteen

1972

By his own admission, John Dent was only interested in two things: beer and fanny. He told Samuel he couldn't wait for the shift change so he could get away from this bloody bunker and into town, where he could openly pursue both these obsessions. For now, though, he seemed content merely to prolong his ongoing campaign of harassment against his fellow aircraftman, calling Samuel a stroppy bastard and asking if his idea of a good time was 'a mug of Ovaltine and a night in with the Bible'.

Dent had not been getting the usual rise out of his fellow hostage to the Cold War that day. Samuel had learned to turn the other cheek, for now. He'd been a fool to fall for Dent's goading before. It wasn't going to happen twice.

When they had first been assigned to the two-man listening post in the bunker at ROC Observation Post Bamburgh, Dent had conned Samuel into believing he had an interest in learning more about the good book. They were alone and deep in the heart of the Northumbrian countryside, just a few hundred yards from the famous castle which dominated the horizon, but they were underground and unable to enjoy the view. Nothing much ever seemed to happen for them to report back on either, so having each other for company mattered. For

Samuel, the hours would go much faster if he was able to discuss his deep commitment to the Scriptures, which wasn't something he normally felt comfortable talking about in the RAF.

When Dent had explained to his fellow airman that he really wanted to change because, deep down, he was unhappy with the way he was leading his life, he was telling Samuel something he really wanted to hear. 'Repentance is the first act on the path to redemption,' Samuel had assured him solemnly, and Dent seemed to be listening.

He had managed to keep the act going for around ten minutes while Samuel counselled him earnestly, before he asked, 'But I still get to drink, smoke and screw, right?' Then he collapsed into laughter and got a murderous look from Samuel, who warned him not to mock God again.

Dent had agreed to this condition, but only 'as long as I am allowed to mock you instead, you God-bothering idiot. Christ, could I not have been put in this bloody hole with someone else?' he pleaded. '*Anybody* else?'

Samuel had made a point of not saying a single word to the man for the rest of the shift, because he knew Dent didn't want to sit in silence for hours, whereas Samuel was disciplined enough to take it.

'Sulking, are you?' taunted Dent. 'Is that it?' but Samuel could sense the irritation of the other man and derived some slim comfort from it.

Samuel wasn't sulking. Sitting in silence was the only way he could contain the murderous fury he felt at being mocked for his religion. He was so angry at Dent, for the rest of their shift he had fantasized about killing the man.

Chapter Seventeen

They ordered Chinese food and tucked into it at the kitchen table. 'I'm starving,' Tom said, spooning a helping of Kung Pao chicken on to his plate before passing the foil tray to Helen.

'You're always starving,' Helen said, taking it from him.

'Well, I burn off a lot of calories.'

'I don't want to know.'

'That's not what I meant.'

'Do you two spend all day bickering?' asked Bradshaw, putting some egg-fried rice and crispy beef on his plate.

'Not all day,' said Tom, his mouth half full, 'but Helen likes to tell me where I'm going wrong.'

'If I did that, we'd never have time to get anything else done,' retorted Helen. 'Can we get back on track?' They settled down to eat while they reviewed the case, helping themselves to more food when they wanted it. 'We have two investigations here, eighteen years apart. They could be linked,' Helen admitted, 'but what if they aren't? It does seem pretty incredible that someone could abduct a number of women in a relatively short period of time, stop offending entirely then start up again nearly two decades later.' She looked at Tom for confirmation. 'Doesn't it?'

'It does,' he agreed, 'but it is possible.'

'Under what circumstances?'

Tom thought for a while before answering. 'Suppose the

perpetrator had had his fill of killing, or whatever it is he does with these women? Suppose he decided to turn his back on it all and try to fit in with society – perhaps he married, had a family, buried his true nature and lived a lie. He might have been able to do that for a while.'

'He might,' concurred Bradshaw. 'It has been known.'

'For nearly twenty years?' asked Helen. 'And why suddenly start again now?'

Tom shrugged. 'Wife left him, or died? His family grew up and went away? He grew tired of living like that, or he just felt the urge again. We simply don't know, do we?'

'What about a copycat?'

'Anything is possible,' said Bradshaw, 'but it's not like it's a famous case. The earlier disappearances weren't ever linked in the newspapers, so how would a copycat know anything about them?'

'What if the man was caught for something else and jailed?' asked Helen. 'That might explain the gap.'

'It could,' admitted Bradshaw. He and Hugh Rennie had had the same thought.

'And the copycat theory could work that way, too. Maybe he told someone in his cell what he'd been up to.'

'Confessed to crimes he wasn't even doing time for?' said Tom. 'If he did that, wouldn't the person he was telling be more likely to report his cell mate and gain some privileges? No honour among thieves, remember?'

'That's more likely, I admit, but perhaps we're dealing with two disturbed individuals . . . I don't know. I'm just fishing here.'

'We all are, but we have to start somewhere. A copycat is the less likely scenario, but a killer stopping because he was imprisoned for something else is a possibility and I think we should check it out.'

'It's certainly a line of inquiry,' conceded Bradshaw, 'and worth pursuing.'

They finished their food and Bradshaw suggested they went to the pub. It had been a day of surprises but none of them was more shocking to the detective than Tom's answer.

'I can't, sorry.'

'Did you just turn down a pint?' asked Bradshaw in disbelief.

'I did, much as it pains me, but I already have plans.'

'Do you hear that?' Bradshaw asked Helen. 'That is the sound of the world spinning on its axis.'

'Wonders never cease,' she said, 'but he mustn't keep his fans waiting.'

'Watch it, you,' warned Tom, as if she were about to betray a secret. Bradshaw could tell that, whatever this was about, Tom wasn't keen to talk about it.

'Looks like it's just you and me, then, Helen.'

Chapter Eighteen

The two men had settled into an uneasy truce, possible only because they had orders to obey and a job to do. Samuel and Dent had to cooperate since they were part of the early-warning system that would alert the country to impending nuclear attack from a hostile foreign power, namely the Soviet Union.

'But what's the point?' asked Dent, yet again.

'It's an experiment,' Samuel told him, 'to see if professionals would do a better job compiling data than the usual volunteers from the ROC.' Samuel couldn't help thinking that Dent wasn't a particularly good representative of the professional armed forces.

'But what good does it do?' moaned Dent. 'Estimated blast radiuses, weather averages, projected fallout zones. I mean, it's all bleeding pointless, isn't it? We're like those blokes on the *Titanic* who carry on playing their violins while the ship goes down.'

'How about we just obey orders?'

'Oh, I intend to,' Dent assured Samuel. 'I don't want a court martial, which is why I stay in this place and put up with you.'

Samuel considered Dent to be the worst kind of philistine. Even when they walked across the fields together, as they did at the beginning and end of each of their shifts, the other man seemed to barely notice the imposing castle or the sea stationed behind it. Dent didn't give a shit about the view, or anything else for that matter, and Samuel had to spend twelve hours at a time with the man in that tiny underground bunker.

'What do you reckon?' Dent chided him as the clock ticked slowly towards the end of their shift. 'The four "S"'s, then out on the town?'

'The what?'

'You know,' said Dent. 'Shave, shit, shower and shampoo. Then off for a few pints and chat up some dolly birds down the local – tell them we're fighter pilots or something and we might even get our end away.' Samuel ignored him. 'Oh, I forgot. You don't do that, do you? You don't drink and you don't screw. So, what exactly do you do?'

No answer.

'Why are you even here? Answer me that. Everyone says your family is loaded, so what are you doing in the forces when there's no national service any more? Are you mad or something? Why would anyone choose to do this if they didn't have to?'

'Don't talk about my family.'

'Why not? What's wrong with them?'

'I'm warning you, Dent.'

Dent shook his head. 'God help me if they do drop the big one and I have to stay in here with you for months on end.' He sighed theatrically. 'I'll either kill you or myself, haven't decided which yet.'

'What do you know about God?' Samuel's voice was so low Dent barely heard him.

'What did you say?'

'I said, "What do you know about God?"' He gave Dent such an evil look that the gobby airman even shut up for a second, but he soon recovered.

'You're strange, you know that?' Dent told him. 'The lads all said you was a weirdo. Well, if you believe in God so much, then why do you even care about any of this? He'll save you, won't he, and he'll send non-believers like me to eternal damnation. Isn't that what your lot think? Even if the Russkies do drop the bloody bomb, it won't matter. You're off to heaven anyway.'

Dent didn't understand. How could he? He was too stupid and he didn't believe in anything, except getting his end away.

'This is a bloody waste of time,' Dent suddenly announced. 'What we're doing here is pointless. This whole listening post is obsolete, has been for years. We're supposed to be the last line of defence, so they can scramble fighter jets to intercept the enemy, right? Well, when did you last hear of the Russkies using big bombers to drop their nukes? Not for years. It's all missiles now. The first we'll know about the ICBMs is when they're heading right down our throats. Two-minute warning is right! That's about how long we'll have before they light up the whole country. It's stupid. The only thing I've detected lately is haemor-rhoids, and if war ever comes we'll hear about it only a few precious seconds before anyone else.'

'It's coming,' Samuel said flatly.

'How do you bloody know? This Cold War's been going on for years. What makes you think anyone wants to make it any hotter?'

'All it will take is one madman with his finger on the button,' Samuel assured him. 'Nixon wants to do it, you can tell just by looking at him. Mao and Brezhnev can see it, too, so they might just do it first. These crazy old men are so used to death they have become death.'

'What are you banging on about?' asked Dent. 'Is this your religious shit again? You think this is the apocalypse? Doomsday? Is that it?'

'How else will Judgement Day come? If the whole of mankind is to be judged together, then it must destroy itself.'

'They won't be able to kill everybody, will they, no matter how many bombs they drop. There's too many people, and too many bunkers, like this one.'

'"Then said one unto him, Lord are there few that be saved?"' Samuel said softly.

'What? Is that in the Bible? Do you actually think it works like that? You reckon God saves the good people? No, mate. Most of the good people don't have a bunker to go to. It's only the bloody politicians that have those, and the ones lucky enough to protect them. Oh yeah, and people like us.' He laughed. 'Shame we'll only get a few minutes' notice. A day would be good. Then we could get a few cases of beer in and some proper food, not this army-ration shit they've given us. A couple of women, too – each, I mean. It would be the best chat-up line ever invented. *Come back to my bunker, if you want to live!*' He smiled. '*But you've got to earn your place, love; cooking, cleaning and screwing from now on. It's not much to ask when all your friends and neighbours are about to be turned into kindling.* We could audition them all and keep the best ones . . . or the dirtiest.' He laughed obscenely.

Samuel knew what he would do if that attack ever came. As soon as he reported it, he would kill Dent with his bare hands. Then he would throw the man's body outside, climb back in and seal the hatch before the warheads struck. He'd just say the man went mad and bolted. No one would care, even if they didn't believe him. They'd be too busy by then anyway, watching the world end.

There'd be no place for Dent. He belonged with the others, blown to pieces or dying in flames or from sickness caused by radiation. Get rid of Dent and he'd have the place to himself. He could stay down here on his own where it was safe. When the purging fires had stopped and the plague had finally ceased, he would open the hatch, emerge and inherit the earth.

On his own.

All on his own.

That's how he had imagined it since the first day of his posting here but something Dent said had made him reconsider. If you took away the stupid jokes and the crudity, somehow this moronic man had a point. Samuel believed he would be on his own but Adam had not been alone. When the Lord God began the world, he made man in his own image. Then he fashioned a companion for Adam.

Eve.

Adam needed Eve.

Chapter Nineteen

The White Horse was a quiet, homely place with a wood fire that wasn't needed on a fine spring evening like this one. The customers were mostly regulars, so Helen and Ian stood out and they took their drinks away to a quiet corner.

'What's Tom up to tonight, then?' he asked.

'Library talk,' she said. 'About his books.' Tom's latest non-fiction crime book was about the notorious serial killer Adrian Wicklow and the disappearance of young Susan Verity, who had been missing for twenty years before they had solved the mystery. *Without a Trace* had been published to the usual lack of fanfare and modest sales but Tom had been invited to do a talk about it that evening.

'They'll be queuing round the block,' said Bradshaw. 'All those old ladies fighting for his autograph.'

'He was being really funny about it.'

'It's a North-East thing,' Bradshaw told her. 'The biggest crime imaginable round here is if you start thinking you're *it*.'

Helen knew what he meant. She'd interviewed enough local success stories to know the score. Millionaire businessmen were always quick to tell you that they started out in the roughest city streets, rock stars ensured you knew they came back to see their old mates whenever they could and actors told you they used to have a season ticket for Newcastle United until just a couple of years back and only lived in London now because that was where the work was. It was as if they felt they were being judged by an entire community on whether their boots still fitted them or not.

'So, how are things with you?' Bradshaw asked.

'Good. We've been busyish. Not always the most glamorous work but enough to keep our heads above water, just.'

'I meant . . . erm . . .'

'You meant my short-lived engagement?'

'I actually meant you generally, outside of work, but I suppose the engagement qualifies.'

The memory of Peter's surprise proposal still had the ability to send a chill through Helen. He had sprung it on her in the most public manner imaginable, at a huge party to commemorate his parent's twenty-fifth wedding anniversary, giving her no easy option. If she had turned him down flat, it would have ruined their big day and made him look ridiculous in front of their families and all their friends. As it was, she took the path of least resistance and accepted before undergoing what alcoholics term *a moment of clarity*, following a nearly fatal assault on her person by a murderer she was pursuing. Helen's narrow escape left her with a lower than usual regard for other people's feelings, particularly Peter's. He'd been devastated at first, then angry and resentful, putting most of the blame on her, and the rest on Tom. Since that emotionally draining day, however, Peter had calmed down and decided to keep pursuing Helen until she finally came back to him.

Helen could have told Bradshaw some or all of this but chose not to. His concern for her was genuine enough but she was never very comfortable sharing her true feelings with anyone, except perhaps Tom. They'd had one or two wine-fuelled late-night conversations about her former fiancé and she'd shared her view that they had simply become two very different people.

'I'm good, thanks,' Helen told Bradshaw brightly. 'And just now I'm more than happy being on my own.'

Tom was much less happy being on his own. Right then, he could have done with a couple of friends to go for a pint with. As he was leaving the building a librarian followed him to the door. 'I'm really sorry,' she said. 'It doesn't normally go like that.'

'No problem,' he told her. 'It was probably the bad weather.' At least he hoped that was the reason.

The librarian frowned. 'It was absolutely pouring down last week but loads of people turned up.'

'There are so many demands on people's time these days.'

'I just don't understand it,' she went on. 'We told all the local book groups and we had posters in the window for ages.'

Tom sighed. He knew she wasn't trying to make him feel worse but he wished she would stop going on about it. Only four members of the public had come to his talk. He'd thought there were at least ten until he spotted the lanyards six of them were wearing and realized that embarrassed library staff had padded out the audience out of sheer pity for him.

'We should have contacted the newspapers.' She seemed intent on beating herself up.

'It's no one's fault,' he told her. 'Really, I'm fine.' *At least I will be if you stop talking about it.* Christ, one old lady had actually fallen asleep in there. She probably only came into the library to stay warm, poor cow.

'We'll have to invite you back,' the librarian finished brightly. 'Some other time.'

'That would be great, thanks.' He was edging out through the door.

Tom let it close behind him, took a deep breath now that he was on his own, muttered, 'Christ,' in frustration and headed for his car, just as a very attractive woman was walking up the path towards him. Was she there to see him speak? It seemed unlikely. He didn't know if he was annoyed because he'd cut the talk short and would not now get to meet her or relieved she hadn't witnessed him slowly dying in there. He stepped to one side to let her walk in.

She stopped and turned to face him. 'Tom,' she said brightly, and he blinked at her in confusion.

'Yes?'

'Oh no, I haven't changed that much, have I?'

She slowly came into focus. A tastefully made-up face framed by an expensive haircut full of blonde highlights had initially deceived him, so he concentrated on her eyes. It took a second.

'Jenna! Oh my god.'

'Correct.' She smiled at the mention of her name. 'It took you a while, though. You're not supposed to forget your first love, Tom.'

Chapter Twenty

The noise of metal scraping against metal made Eva start. A bolt had been drawn back. The door was opening.

She realized it was dark outside. She'd lost track of time. It had little meaning in here. Day and night hardly mattered. She didn't even know how long he had kept her in the box. Perhaps she, too, should have recorded the days by scratching marks on the wall.

Eva couldn't see outside clearly; the light from the lamp was hampering her night vision. She could feel her breathing quicken and become more ragged and her whole body trembled. She had been fed already, so why had he opened the door? What was he going to do? Fearful, she instinctively moved further away, until her back was pressed right against the metal wall and she could go no further.

He pointed the shotgun at her then jerked it to show he wanted her to step out of her metal prison. It was the first time. He gestured again then stepped outside. Slowly, she rose then tentatively followed, wondering if he would kill her as soon as she was outside.

Eva stepped through the door of the shipping crate and looked around her. Her eyes adjusted to the gloom, helped by a half-moon. Her captor was standing before her with the shotgun poised in case she tried to escape, but there was nowhere to run to. She was standing in a field somewhere, her bare feet on the cool grass, and she realized the crate was in a hollow. Even in the dark she could make out the outline of others nearby. Was anyone in them or was she alone here? One was old and rusted; the others looked comparatively new, with just a slight discolouration of the metal. Weeds were trying to grow up their sides.

Eva couldn't see anything else except the outline of some trees on the high ground at the top of the hollow. The land was too low to afford a view of the area around her but she had a strong feeling of isolation. There were no buildings visible from here, no overhead wires, or telegraph poles, or sounds of traffic. There were no roads, no cars, no other people. Her captor was standing close by but she had never felt more alone.

What if he chose to pull the trigger and finish her nightmare? She probably wouldn't even hear the blast from the gun before it was all over. The stark realization that he had the power to end her life at any moment hit her fully then.

Eva heard fumbling behind her. What now? She started when she felt the rough cloth being put on the top of her head and let out an involuntary whimper as the bag was pulled down over her face. She could barely breathe and she couldn't see anything; the absence of light was terrifying. Then she felt a strong grip on her arm and she was being propelled forwards. God, he was strong. Her limbs had stiffened from being confined in the box. Eva forced herself to concentrate and put one foot in front of the other. She was moving across the field and he was holding her upright, but she kept stumbling because she couldn't see where she was meant to plant her feet. Each time Eva lost her balance he straightened her. Her arm began to throb from his grip.

97

The journey went on for minutes, but where was he taking her? She recalled the numerous scratches on the side of the wall in the container, each one representing a day, and wondered why she was being taken out of it now. To be freed? To be killed? For some other purpose?

'Please don't hurt me,' she begged, but he ignored her plea.

He finally stopped her with a jolt. His grip on her arm tightened further, hurting her now. The next stage was terrifying.

'Put your foot on the ladder and climb down,' he ordered her.

What ladder? She couldn't see anything. Before she could ask how she could possibly do this, he pushed her firmly on. Her left foot went out instinctively ahead of her, but the ground was gone. Eva felt only air beneath her and she pitched forward with a little scream, one foot on the ground and the other dangling in space, convinced she was about to fall, and with no idea how far. He held on to her fast. It was like some stupid, childish prank where you pretend to push someone but grab them before they can fall.

'Put your foot on the ladder,' he ordered again, but she still couldn't see one. She couldn't see anything. Blindly, she pushed her foot out further until it touched metal – this must be it. Immediately he levered her forward so that her weight went on to that foot and her other foot left the ground. He was still supporting her and pulled her forwards until her whole body moved and her second foot landed next to the first. Now she had two feet on the first rung of the ladder and he was preventing her from falling over it or backwards into the hole.

'Climb down.' The voice was impatient and she wanted to comply, wary of the punishment that might follow if she did not obey. She felt with her hand and found nothing. Still supported by him, she crouched down until her hands connected with the top of the ladder, which was sticking a couple of feet out of a hole in the ground. It felt cold and hard and solid, and there was a hatch behind it. Panic seized her. He was putting her into a hole in the ground. The claustrophobia she had battled to contain in the shipping crate suddenly overwhelmed her. What if it was a tiny space and he closed the hatch on her, sealing her in? She'd rather die now than experience the terror of that.

'Go down,' he demanded, and Eva, petrified, began a slow and unsteady descent of the ladder, not knowing how far she had to go or what was waiting at the bottom when she got there. Would he follow her down or simply shut her up in there? Had she just given up her tiny prison for one that was even smaller?

He let go of her then and she had to use all her concentration to handle her blind descent of the ladder. Almost instinctively, she counted the steps as she descended: one . . . two . . . three . . .

It was a long way. How long could it go on?

. . . seventeen . . . eighteen . . . nineteen . . .

Wherever she was going, it was deep; very deep and as quiet as a graveyard.

. . . twenty-six . . . twenty-seven . . . twenty-eight . . .

Eva had reached thirty when her feet abruptly touched concrete. She stayed on that spot, not daring to move, hands still gripping the ladder tightly, even though she had got to the bottom.

She could hear his feet as they lightly touched each step of the ladder in turn. He was moving quickly, with practised ease, even with the gun in his hand. How many times had he done this before? As she felt his feet come close to her head she let go of the ladder and drew back. He reached the bottom and spun her round with a hand on her shoulder then on her back, which halted her.

He pulled the cover off her head. All she could see before her was blackness. The dark was completely impenetrable; any light outside was too far away to reach them. She prayed he wasn't going to leave her here.

He must have moved from her side because there was a loud click and then a mechanical whirring noise as if a switch had been pulled and a generator activated strip lights in the roof, which blinked on and illuminated a tunnel directly ahead of her.

This wasn't some ramshackle creation with roof props and rock walls like a mine, this was a real building that had been built deep underground, with white-tiled walls, a cement floor, a roof with light fittings and long corridors that disappeared around a corner and continued who knew how far?

Oh god, what was this place?

'Move.'

Chapter Twenty-one

The barman was doing his rounds of the room, picking up ashtrays and upending their stale contents into the metal bin he carried in his free hand. He took the empty glasses from Helen's table on his way past, just as Bradshaw returned from the bar with a second drink.

'Is Tom still seeing that girl he met on his holiday?' he asked.

'Young Penny?' She nodded.

'You sound as if you don't approve.'

'I don't *dis*approve,' she countered. 'What makes you think I do?'

'The way you call her *young* Penny. How old is she again?'

'Twenty,' she said. 'Just.' And she laughed. 'So she was nineteen when he met her.'

'What's funny?'

'Back then he told me she was "nineteen and a half".' She smirked. 'When did you last add *and a half* to your age? Only kids do that, right?'

'Kids and guys dating girls much younger than themselves. It's a bit early for a midlife crisis.'

'It's not a midlife crisis. Tom just doesn't like commitment.' *Although he offered it to me once*, she recalled, and immediately felt guilty. 'Nineteen-year-old girls are not very demanding on that front. All that matters is that he can afford to buy the drinks.' As she said it, she realized what a bitch she sounded. Worse, Bradshaw might think she actually cared who Tom was dating, which she didn't, of course.

Jenna and Tom were virtually alone in a pub at the other end of town. Tom wondered how the place managed to stay open. The barmaid was reading a book; there was no one else to serve.

'Sorry I missed your talk. I got held up,' said Jenna. 'How did it go?'

'Great,' he told her. *Great* was definitely stretching it. 'I can't believe you're here, Jenna. It's lovely to see you again after all this time.'

'And you.' Her warm smile told him she meant it. 'So how are you, Tom Carney? Married, kids, enormous mortgage?'

'No, no and yes,' he replied. 'I don't know why I've got one without all the others but the house doubles as our office.'

'*Our* office? You've got people working for you? I'm impressed, Tom.'

'One person, and she doesn't work for me. She's my partner.'

'Your partner. Oh,' she said, as if she understood what that meant.

'Er, no, Helen is my *business* partner. She's a journalist, too.'

'So she's not –'

'No, she's not,' he interrupted her.

'But you must be seeing someone?' she probed.

'Why must I be seeing someone?'

'Because I remember you, and I know what you're like.'

'Do you now?' He skated over that. 'I am seeing someone, kind of.'

'Only kind of? Sounds deep.'

'I met her on holiday.' He shrugged. 'She's from the area, we see each other, that's all.'

'And how long has this been going on, Mr Carney.'

'A few months,' he said, though it was closer to nine.

'And what does she do?'

'Studies,' he said dismissively.

'Post-grad?' She raised an eyebrow.

'Undergrad,' he admitted.

'You cradle-snatcher! How old? Eighteen?'

'Twenty.'

'Corrupting such a young girl?' then she added the word: *again*.

'As I recall, it was the other way round,' he told her. 'I'm fairly sure you led me astray.'

'That's not the way I remember it.'

'Anyway, what about you, Jenna? Married . . . all that?' He hadn't spotted a ring. She shook her head. 'Happily single,' she said, then leaned forward and picked up her wine glass, but her eyes only left his for a moment. 'For the time being,' she added.

'And what have you been up to,' he asked, 'since we last met?'

'What have I been up to?' she repeated, as if she didn't know where to begin. 'Well, recently, I've taken on a shop in Grange Moor.'

'What do you sell?'

'The usual: household items, groceries, sweets.'

'Sweets? Can I get a ten-pence mix-up, then?' he smiled. 'In one of those little paper bags?'

'You can, but it will cost you more than ten pence nowadays and the little bags are plastic.'

'What price progress?' he asked. 'I'm pleased for you, even though I can't imagine you doing that.'

'What can you imagine me doing?'

'Something less quiet, I suppose. You couldn't wait to get out and see the world.'

'Well, I did,' she reminded him. 'And now I'm back. How about another drink, my shout?' She put her hand on his knee and squeezed it momentarily as she got to her feet. She wriggled through a gap between two tables and Tom watched her as she walked to the bar.

Chapter Twenty-two

It was beyond her comprehension. Eva walked dumbly along the corridor, trying but failing to make sense of her surroundings. Where the hell was she? The corridor seemed to go on for ever and every few yards she passed a locked door, all dark green, numbered and made of metal. The only sound that accompanied her and her captor, apart from their footsteps as they progressed along the tunnel, was the low murmur of the generator and the buzzing of the neon strip lights.

Finally, the man in the balaclava ordered her to stop, then he waved the gun so she knew to step away from one of the doors. He unlocked it and pushed her inside. He must have flicked a switch because a light came on and she was confronted with a bare tiled room with a bench bolted to the far wall.

'Take off your clothes,' he said, his voice emotionless, and a chill went through her. It was going to happen. It was actually going to happen now, and there was nothing she could do about it. The man was much stronger than she was and, even without the gun, she could see no way to overpower him. He was going to force her to strip, then he would rape her, down here where no one could help. Terror quickly morphed into the survival instinct. If he wanted her to strip, he wanted her body, so perhaps there was a slim chance he wouldn't kill her.

People would be out looking for her: friends, her family, the police. They might have leads or an idea of what had happened to her. Perhaps they even knew who this man was and their investigation would eventually lead them to him, and then she'd be freed and he'd be the one to rot in prison for years. Until then, though, she had to stay alive.

Eva told herself there was another option. Escape. If she went along with it now, if she avoided angering this man, if she kept as calm as she could, then maybe the madness in him wouldn't yet show itself and she could survive long enough to find a weak point in her prison. Then she could break free.

'Strip!' he commanded. His voice was loud and harsh in the small room, his anger and impatience obvious in the single barked word. He pushed her in the back and she stumbled towards the bench. She walked forward until she could go no further and faced the wall, her mind racing. She told herself that she had to endure.

Eva brought her hands to the material at the bottom of her thick woollen top and began to lift it. She tried not to think of the view the man had of her as she pulled the top up and bared her back, slid it past her breasts then over her head. She stood there topless in the cold room, holding the shirt uselessly in her hand.

Eva knew there was no way to stall things now, so she became resolute and hooked her thumbs into the elasticated waist of her jogging bottoms. They were loose anyway and came free easily. She stepped out of them and placed them on the bench. There was no sound from the man behind her.

She hooked her thumbs into her knickers and pulled them down, too, stepping out of them and dropping them with the rest of her clothes on the bench. She had never felt more vulnerable. Eva braced herself for what must surely come but for a time nothing happened. She stood there for a full minute, hands covering her nakedness as best they could, but the man did not advance on her and she began to wonder what he was doing. Was he savouring the sight of her? She realized she was holding her breath.

That breath left her suddenly as the shock of the noise hit her all at once and she rocked forward on her heels. It took her fevered brain a moment to understand what it was but something cut in and then she understood.

Water.

Fast-running water.

A shower?

When nothing further happened, she dared to turn her head. The man in the balaclava was standing watching her as she slowly turned to face him, determined to cover as much of her nakedness as possible for now. Because of his mask, it was impossible to tell whether he was surveying her with lust or simply regarding her dispassionately. In one hand, he still held the gun but in the other was a bar of soap.

There was an opening to the right of the thick metal door she had walked through and she could hear drops of water hitting the ground inside it. A tiled step led up to the opening, which was the size of a doorway, and the man jerked his head to indicate she should go through.

'Wash.'

So he wanted her clean first.

Reluctantly, Eva advanced, and the man thrust out his hand to offer her the bar of soap. She had to take her hand momentarily from her breasts to grab it then she quickly moved across towards the opening.

Inside the alcove was a shower and she got under the running water. It was only tepid and the water fell slowly compared to the shower at home but it still felt good after being imprisoned in that shipping crate for days.

Eva tried hard to ignore the man standing behind her, presumably still watching every move she made, and began to wash herself. The cheap unperfumed bar of soap helped to ease away the grime and she soaked her hair and tried to wash the strands as best she could, always conscious of him watching her but not wanting to rush things because she knew what he had planned for her.

When Eva had finished, she paused for a moment to steel herself, preparing her mind so she could accept and endure her fate. Then, resigned to it, she turned off the shower and turned to face the man, but he was no longer there. Cautiously, she walked out of the tiny shower block and back into the room. He was sitting on the bench, waiting, cradling the gun in one hand and her dirty clothes in the other. On the bench was a large, rough-looking blue towel and next to it lay a pile of plain functional clothes: tracksuit bottoms, another cheap practical top and what she might have described in an earlier life as boring underwear.

'Get dry,' he told her, 'and dress.'

She dried herself hastily and self-consciously then dressed quickly, the clothes sticking to the parts of her body that were still damp in her haste to cover herself once more. All the while she wondered why he hadn't touched her or bothered to watch her while she showered. Was he somehow repelled by her nakedness or trying to keep himself under control? She got the impression her state of undress didn't interest him very much. Then why take her in the first place? Why keep her here?

When she was dressed he walked up to her, spun her round to face the wall and pushed her out through the door then back down the corridor to the ladder. He stopped her there and put the rough bag back on her head again. Then he made Eva climb the ladder, prodding her with the gun barrel if she hesitated. At the top, she climbed out and waited silently for him to catch up, wishing she could find the courage to kick out at him or try and lift the heavy hatch and smash it down on his head, but she knew he would be expecting that and the gun would fire before she could make a move against him. She lacked the strength, the speed and, she had to admit, the courage for such a suicidal attempt at escape. She would bide her time instead, relieved for now that she'd not been raped or killed.

Moments later she was back in the shipping crate with the door closed and bolted, a prisoner once more. Eva let herself fall back on the bed and wept, her tears a combination of relief, fear and frustration. She was still no nearer learning her fate than she had been before.

While she lay there it slowly dawned on her that her captor might not return to the crate for a while. This might give her the time she needed. She rose from the bed and picked up the lamp. She walked towards the one vulnerable spot she had discovered when she searched the crate. The panel that was welded to the opposite wall which contained the small metal vent that let in enough air for her to breathe. It was fixed solidly and permanently but she had noticed earlier that the central portion which contained the slats of the vent was only kept in place by the four large screws that had been painted over and were partly hidden in the gloom. The central part of the vent might just be wide enough for a person to wriggle through. Even though Eva had no idea how to even begin to move those screws to create that gap, the thought that it might be possible was enough to give her hope.

Chapter Twenty-three

'Why ever did we break up?' she mock-sighed after Tom had made her laugh for the umpteenth time that night. Jenna had a point. They still found each other easy company and the chemistry between them made Tom feel as if they had picked up almost where they left off. He had to remind himself he was seeing Penny.

'You don't remember?'

'Not really.'

'You went off to university, wanted a clean break, so you' – he almost said *dumped me* but thought better of it – 'ended it. You said you wanted to see other people.'

'Oh, did I? That wasn't very nice. I'm sorry.'

'I was devastated,' he said with a straight face, then he smiled. 'For a couple of weeks.'

'Until you sought solace elsewhere.' She grinned. 'You see, I do know you.'

'What made you look me up now?' he asked.

'I don't know,' she said absent-mindedly. 'I saw the event in the local paper, so I thought I'd pop by. See how you were doing, you know, for old time's sake, but don't worry, I wasn't planning on rekindling an old flame. I'll leave you to your sixth-former.'

'She's at university,' he chided, but he was enjoying the teasing. 'So that was the only reason, just a catch-up?'

There was a moment then when he thought Jenna might let her guard down and tell him it was something more. She even opened her mouth to form the words, but after a second or two she simply said, 'Yep,' closely followed by, 'So who do you still see from the old days? I've lost track of everyone.'

They spent another pleasant hour talking about old schoolfriends, teenage parties and their struggles to get served in pubs while they were still underage, though it was always much easier for girls. Then, a little too soon, the barman called time and they walked out of the pub together, agreeing they should do this again properly, and soon. Jenna suggested a pub lunch.

She kissed him then, not on the cheek but on the lips. It was a quick kiss and could be dismissed as merely affectionate but it triggered something in him, even if it was only a memory. She was about to leave when he said, 'It wasn't in the local paper.'

She turned back to him. 'What?'

'My talk. It wasn't advertised in the paper. The librarian forgot to tell them.'

'Oh,' she said, 'then I must have heard about it from somewhere else.'

He reached into his pocket, took out his wallet, removed one of his business cards then handed it to her. 'If you ever need anything,' he said, and when she seemed reluctant to take it, 'or if you just fancy that pub lunch . . . ?'

Jenna took the card, read the details then said, 'Norton–Carney? That has a certain ring to it. Is she pretty?'

He was a little taken aback by the question but said, 'Helen? I suppose so, yes.'

'Prettier than me?' She was being deliberately coquettish, enjoying the game.

'How could anybody possibly be prettier than my first love?'

'Is the correct answer, Mr Carney! Now why did I ever let you go?'

He drove a long way to buy the newspaper. He didn't want anyone to see him. It was always better to have no contact. Out of sight was out of mind. He lived four miles from the nearest village.

The service station stayed open late, mostly for the truck drivers who parked their lorries in the car park and dozed in their cabins. They pulled curtains across their windscreens or blocked them with pieces of cardboard. It was the best place to buy a paper. Newspapers were important. They told people things, but not always the truth. Some people liked to lie, even though lying was a sin, unless it was in the service of God or for a greater good, but sometimes they just got the truth wrong because they knew no better.

He picked up the newspaper and paid wordlessly, using the exact amount in change so he didn't have to interact with the woman behind the till. He read the report slowly but avidly in the front seat of his truck, tracing the words with his fingers and letting his mouth form them because he had never been very good with his letters and this always helped him to get over the big words. That was why he read the newspaper in the truck. No one could see him when he parked it amongst the lorries at the back, facing the hedges. There hadn't been a word about it the day before, but here it was.

Woman Found Strangled

A post-mortem has confirmed that a woman found dead in County Durham woodland had been strangled. Though the police are yet to publicly name the victim, she has been formally identified and her relatives informed. A murder inquiry has now begun.

And that was it. It wasn't much for a life. He wasn't sure how he would feel when he read about the woman in the woods. She had been the last of them – the rest had all died long before her – and he had known her for a very long time. He had helped to take care of her and had wanted to save her but she had made it clear by her actions that she didn't wish to be saved. She was old now, she was ill and dried up, and as the good book said about Abraham's wife, 'The way of women had ceased to be with her.'

In the end, Cora must have preferred death to life, and he had been forced to comply, for he was God's servant and if you hated God then you loved death. That was in the Scriptures, too. She had gone willingly in the end. He didn't want to do it there, in the bunker, so he'd driven her to the woods. Cora was so weak he had to carry her from the vehicle, then he leant her against the tree. She didn't say a word while he did it. He couldn't look at her face, so he wrapped the rope right round the tree then tightened it with the stick till her strangled gurgling ended.

He knew he was supposed to get rid of her body. That was what you were meant to do but, now that she was dead, he couldn't bring himself to touch her again, so he left her there and hoped that God would confound and confuse his enemies.

And she had been replaced. The new woman was young and unadorned, she had red hair like the painting, she would be fertile and, according to the plastic cards in her purse, her name was Eva, which was almost like 'Eve'. This had to be the Lord's will.

He drove home with his mind at rest, reassured that God was helping him.

Chapter Twenty-four

Kane insisted on regular morning briefings so Bradshaw began with the results of the post-mortem. The DCI listened intently to the part about the victim having rickets, then said, 'Yeah, well, let's not jump to any conclusions, shall we? If she was a drug addict or an alkie, then she might not have seen much sunlight, and if she was funding a habit she probably only went out at night, if she was working as a prozzie or something.'

'There was no evidence of her doing that,' countered Bradshaw.

'All I am saying is, be . . . moderate when considering your findings.'

'Moderate, sir?'

Kane was getting frustrated with Bradshaw's inability to read his DCI's mind. 'Moderate, man – you know, the opposite of the tabloid journalists we have to put up with who take a crumb of evidence and turn it into a sensationalist theory that has little bearing on the truth. Just . . . tread carefully, all right.'

'Sir, is there something I should know about this case?'

Kane sighed. 'It does seem to be attracting a lot of the wrong kind of interest.'

'From the press?'

'Them, too,' Kane said, 'but I'm talking about interest from senior officers.'

'I see.' Maybe that explained the pathologist's words. *Like Piccadilly Circus here this morning.*

'No, you don't,' Kane assured him. 'It's even more delicate than usual.' By way of explanation, he added, 'You know that Chief Constable Newman is going at the end of the year?'

'I heard he was retiring a little early.'

Kane nodded. 'He is off to tend to his garden, or whatever it is that the top brass do once they're gone. Of course, his deputy, Edward Tyler, wants the job and is shadowing his boss until he goes.' So that explained why Tyler was always on the telly these days. 'He won't want anything to go wrong on their joint watch until the successor is announced.'

'And is he likely to get the top job?'

Kane snorted. 'Call yourself a detective?'

'I don't tend to keep up with the gossip at senior level, sir.'

'Well, you should. It's called self-preservation. Tyler has the backing of the current chief constable. The alternative for the powers-that-be is to defy the existing incumbent, a man who is considered to have been a success' – he paused then added significantly – 'by the press and general public, at any rate, and risk passing over his deputy in return for an outsider.'

'Who might make a mess of things,' said Bradshaw. 'They prefer a safe pair of hands.'

'In my experience, they always do. No one wants to get the blame for appointing a loose cannon.'

'It's pretty rare for anyone above the rank of superintendent to even put their head round the door on a case.'

'It is, but rest assured they are always watching us from

on high, especially when there's any press coverage that might harm their careers. In this particular case, Tyler has already been asking questions at AC level.' This meant that Kane would have an assistant commissioner keeping an eye on him because the deputy chief constable was keeping an eye on the AC.

'What's he like?'

Kane almost seemed to wince. 'Tyler has a certain reputation. Doesn't take prisoners, won't cut you any slack, has very high expectations of his officers and never forgives even a hint of disloyalty, so I've heard.'

'Why has he taken an interest in this case?'

'Press reports about the missing women. Then we have a body turning up and it's someone who has been missing for a long time . . . it has all the makings of another bloody exposé, doesn't it?'

Bradshaw knew that if there was any suggestion that Durham police had been negligent when the woman had gone missing eighteen years earlier, this would be used against them by the press during their current investigation.

'Just be careful, that's all.' Kane gave him a thin smile. 'You know what they say, Bradshaw, anyone who gets above a certain rank has to be a complete and utter bastard.' There was a glint in his eye.

'And what rank would that be, sir?'

His DCI showed an innocent face when he said, 'Detective Chief Inspector, of course.'

First she scratched the blue, dried-on paint away from the centre of the screw, at the cost of a fingernail, which broke off painfully, right down to the quick, but at least Eva was left with a groove in the screw that she could work on, if she could just find something hard enough to make it turn. Each of the screws had been deliberately clogged with the paint to make them hard to undo. The vent was the only bit of the crate that wasn't originally part of it. It was high up on the wall and the dim light from the table lamp couldn't reach it, so Eva's handiwork would be obscured from any eye that did not peer too closely. Her captor might not spot it at all, unless he examined the vent, and this gave her more hope.

If she could remove the dried paint from all four screws then find something to undo them, she might be able to remove the central part of the vent. She couldn't be certain the whole section would come entirely free but if it did she was almost sure she could wriggle through the gap it would leave and get out of the container. What she would do on the other side once she was clear of it, she didn't know, but Eva resolved to worry about that problem once she was out of her prison.

But what could she use to undo the screws? It would have to be something metal, which discounted virtually everything in the crate. She got down on to the floor and examined the frame of the camp bed. It was made from strips of metal that had been welded into place: no loose screws here. Then she noticed a piece of metal hanging down at the far end of the bed and crawled towards it for a closer examination. It was a steel clip that would fasten the two halves of the bed together when it was stored. The end that was furthest from the bed looked too thick for her purposes but it narrowed considerably as it got nearer the point where it joined the frame. If she could somehow sheer this piece of metal off the bed, this edge might prove thin enough to fit inside the centre of the screws and enable her to turn them.

Eva tugged at the clasp then tried bending it, but it went only so far before meeting the point of resistance. She put all her weight into it and thought she felt it give a tiny amount. But had it really bent slightly or was it just her imagination? She tugged and bent it again. There was definitely a slight movement and, if she could worry away at it for long enough, maybe she could pull it free. She tugged at it again and again, stopping only when her hand began to throb with the pain. She surveyed the clasp. It was a little looser. Eva swapped hands and began to tug at the metal once more, bending it back over and over again.

Tom's phone was ringing, but he couldn't remember where he'd left it. He kept still so he could try and trace the ring tone and realized the sound was coming from the living room, but when he went in he couldn't see the phone anywhere. Then he remembered he'd left it on the coffee table under a newspaper and grabbed it before the caller rang off.

'Hi, Tom. It's Jenna.'

It was good to hear from her so soon after their drink, but it heightened Tom's suspicion that Jenna might want something from him. If she did, she hid it well, her tone matter-of-fact.

'I'm calling about our pub lunch,' she said. 'I reckon if we leave it, then we'll never get around to arranging something and that would be a shame, so how about tomorrow?'

'So soon?'

'Tomorrow is good for me. It's early closing.'

'I could probably get away for a while,' he said, wondering what he would tell Helen. Then he remembered she was his business partner, not his wife, so he could tell her what he pleased.

Eva's hand was swollen and the skin on it red raw. There were blisters forming, she could barely flex her fingers and she was exhausted from her exertions, but she was nearly there. Once more, she swapped hands and began to pull on the clasp, back and forth, the pain transferred to her left hand.

She had to listen intently as she tugged at the clasp in case the man returned and opened the door before she could get back on to the bed. If he caught her now, all her efforts would be for nothing.

She knew she would have to stop soon, rest and let her hands heal for a while. Eva had been worrying away at the metal for ages. The last time she surveyed the clasp there was just a thin sliver of metal keeping it attached to the bed, and that had turned white from being bent repeatedly.

Exhaustion threatened to overcome Eva and she told herself to stop so she could rest and go at the task again later. She just wanted to sleep now but almost mechanically and without willing to she continued, a few more tugs that grew more and more half-hearted.

Suddenly and without any sound or warning the metal snapped and broke loose. Eva looked down at the thin strip of metal she was holding in her blistered hand and almost cried with relief.

Chapter Twenty-five

Helen was deep in conversation in the hallway when Tom came down the stairs that morning. It was probably the idiot-ex-boyfriend, so he walked past her and left her to it. He made two cups of coffee in the kitchen and when he emerged again she was saying goodbye.

'Who was that?' he asked.

'Ian,' said Helen as she hung up the phone. 'He was calling with an address. Sarah Barstow, the stoned girl, she had a brother. He lives in Newcastle these days. I thought it might be worth going to see him.'

'Maybe.'

'Don't you think it's a good idea?'

'I do,' he agreed. 'I just can't do it today.' He hadn't had the chance to explain about his lunch with Jenna or, more accurately, he had been putting off telling her.

'Why not?'

'I've got plans.'

'What plans?'

'Just plans.'

'Are they to do with the case?'

'Not really, no.'

'Care to enlighten me?'

'Not really, no.'

'Are you deliberately trying to wind me up?' And when

he opened his mouth to say the same phrase a third time, she said, 'Don't even think about it.'

'Look,' he said, 'it's no big deal and I'll be back in a few hours.'

'How about I just go and do it on my own then?' Her tone told him how unimpressed she was.

Tom wondered what was expected of him. If he said it was okay for her to go on her own, would she be annoyed at having to visit Sarah Barstow's brother while he was elsewhere? If, however, he protested, was that likely to annoy her just as much, because it might imply she didn't know how to do her job without him?

He knew he couldn't win either way but he had an appointment to keep so he just said, 'Fine.'

The pain in her hands was the first thing Eva noticed when she opened her eyes. She had slept fitfully but now she ignored the burning sensation and the blisters and went back to work. First she retrieved the metal tool from the hiding place she had fashioned for it in the side of the mattress. Then she got to her feet and removed the lamp from the makeshift bedside cabinet. The packing case was sturdy enough for her to stand on and just tall enough so she could reach the vent. She took the metal clasp and wedged its thinner end into the head of the screw, all the while desperately hoping the man wouldn't suddenly come back to the crate and catch her doing it.

Bracing, Eva turned the clasp against the screw and silently prayed that it would give. It was stuck fast. She tried again and the clasp slipped, dislodging itself from the screw head and hitting the packing case by her feet and at the same time tipping her off balance. The case wobbled alarmingly and she almost fell, but she managed to regain her balance at the last moment and avoid crashing down.

Eva straightened up and tried once more. She put the end of the clasp into the screw and tried to turn it. Still it didn't budge. She did it again and, before the thin metal slipped once more, she thought she felt it give just a little.

She tried one more time. She put the clasp into the head of the screw and pressed down hard, trying to keep it in place, then forced it to one side. The screw slowly began to turn.

'You're a very long way from home, pet.' The man who opened the door to Helen seemed quite surprised by this.

She was used to this kind of comment. Helen only had to open her mouth for people to know that she was 'not from round here'. The absence of a Geordie accent in Newcastle was still worthy of comment. A lot of people left the North-East for new opportunities down south. It was very rarely the other way around. Helen loved the city and the region but knew she would always feel like an outsider, no matter how friendly most of the natives were to her.

Phil Barstow listened patiently and silently while she explained her reason for visiting him. 'You're going to catch him, then?' he asked. 'Finally?'

Clearly there was no doubt in his mind that his sister had been abducted all those years ago.

'That's our aim, yes.'

He considered this for a moment, nodded once and

invited her in. Then he put the kettle on and made Helen the darkest mug of builder's tea she'd ever had.

'Not too strong for you?' he asked when they were seated in his living room.

She shook her head, even though you could have stood a spoon up in it, and made a point of sipping the tea while she asked him to recount the events following Sarah's disappearance. He was scornful about the police's theories.

'I kept telling them she didn't do drugs and she wasn't a drinker. It didn't make any sense to me. I knew my sister but the young detective who talked to her was so cold and arrogant. He just said, "No one really knows anyone." And that was that. I said to him, "She had a pretty wild life for a librarian!"'

'She was working in the library when she disappeared?'

Phil nodded. 'She liked books, always had done, ever since she was little.' He sighed at the distant memory. 'When she got the job at the library she was so happy. She'd been there for a couple of years when it happened.'

'Could you tell me about the day she went missing?'

'She did her shift at work then went to see a film in Durham with one of her friends.'

Helen was making notes. 'This was someone from her town?'

'No, it was a girl she worked with. They went to the film all right; it was that *Quadrophenia*, the other girl described it clear enough, and she had the ticket stub from the cinema in her purse when the police asked her. They were seen going in together, too.'

'What happened after the film?'

'They went their separate ways home, had different

buses to catch, but Sarah didn't get on hers. No one saw her after that. Not for more than a year.'

'And it was uncharacteristic for her to just go off on her own? I mean, she was over eighteen so . . .'

'My sister didn't have a boyfriend or any wild friends. She was a quiet soul. She didn't even like pubs.'

'Did you alert the police?'

'Not straight away,' he admitted. 'I just thought maybe the bus had broken down or something. Then, when it got very late, I drove up into the centre of town to look for her, and after that I drove to Durham and all around it to see if I could see her. My mother and father waited at home in case she came back.'

'And you had no luck, so what did you do then?'

'I went home,' he said, 'fully expecting to find her sitting there with some story about a bus cancellation or getting on the wrong one. There were no mobile phones back then. People couldn't just call each other if there were traffic jams or breakdowns.'

'And phone boxes weren't exactly reliable either,' she said.

'Nearly always vandalized,' he agreed.

'But you weren't too worried at first, though you reported it?'

'My father did. He spoke to the police that night but because she was over eighteen they didn't take it very seriously. They said they would look out for her but I don't think they did anything at all, to be honest.'

'And the next day?'

'We went to see them and tried to explain this was not what my sister was like but even then it was, "We'll make inquiries but let us know when she walks back through your door" – not *if*, but *when*.'

'They thought she was with someone?'

'It didn't matter who we spoke to or how many times we said it, the police just assumed she was a typical teenage girl – you know, irresponsible, probably got drunk at a party, crashed there and didn't come home, sleeping off a hangover somewhere or too embarrassed to phone or return to her family.' He shook his head at their idiocy. 'It was a Wednesday. Who has a party on a Wednesday night?'

'When did they start to take it seriously?'

'We lost three or four days before they began putting out appeals on the local news. By then we were all frantic. We knew something terrible must have happened to Sarah but they kept asking about boyfriends she might have run off with. They were fixated with the idea that she had got bored with small-town life and run off to London without telling us, as if we would have disapproved of it.'

'Would you?'

'If she had wanted a new life somewhere, she could have come and talked to us about it. My dad wasn't an ogre. He probably would have tried to talk her out of it but, like you said, she was over eighteen and could do what she liked. I'm telling you, though, she never once talked about a different life. She was happy.'

'What do you think happened?'

'We know she didn't get on that bus,' he said emphatically. 'The driver remembered a couple of blokes getting on it, an old lady and a woman with a young kid who he thought was out well past its bedtime, which was why he recalled a routine pick-up at Durham station. There was no young lass on his bus that night. We spoke to the cinema and they told us the time the film ended. Sarah would have just missed her bus, leaving her an hour to . . .' Did he pause because he was he about to say *kill time*? '. . . hang about. That bus station in Durham is bloody freezing when the wind rolls through it. She probably wouldn't want to have stayed there all that time.'

'What do you think she did?'

'We don't know but, like I said, she wasn't into pubs. Maybe she walked up the high street and thought about a taxi.'

'That would be an expensive end to the night,' Helen said, 'for a young girl on a librarian's pay.'

'I've thought of that, and she was careful with her money.'

'Would she have accepted a lift from someone?'

'From a stranger? No chance.'

'What about someone she knew?'

'I've thought about that, too, but she didn't know any maniacs. Who from our village or her library is going to imprison a lass all that time she was gone?'

'In my experience, most killers look perfectly normal until they are caught.'

'When Sarah finally showed up,' he said hesitantly, 'she hadn't been in a normal place . . .'

'And you have absolutely no idea where she might have been?'

'None,' he said. 'I've spent years thinking about that, trying to work out what she must have gone through' – his voice cracked then – 'my own sister, my poor baby sister.'

Chapter Twenty-six

Only when they had finished their pub lunch in a sunny beer garden did Jenna turn to the matter on her mind and even then it was in a roundabout way.

'It's been lovely to see you again, Tom. I know we're both older but it doesn't seem as if so many years have gone by. I still feel like we are the same people inside, deep down.'

'Me, too.'

'I thought you would still be like the old Tom and I'm so glad you are' – she hesitated – 'but I have to admit that wasn't the only reason I got back in touch with you.'

'I know,' he said calmly.

'You know?' She regarded him thoughtfully. 'How could you know?'

He shrugged. 'Little signs,' he said, and when she did not appear content with that: 'You were very keen to meet up again so soon after the last time, you came to the talk at the library just when it was scheduled to end, you couldn't have read about it in your local paper like you said, so I figured you must have heard about it from the leaflets in the bookstore when my book came out, which means you've seen the book. So you know I try to find missing persons and I help the police to solve murders. I don't peg you for a murderer, so who's gone missing?'

Jenna looked a bit startled. Was she was struck by the

tone in his voice? He hadn't meant it to sound so cold, as if he thought this whole thing had been one big charade staged by Jenna to get him to help her.

'No one,' she said, 'and nobody has been murdered either.'

'Then how can I help?'

'I don't know if you can,' she said, 'or if I even want to ask you now. I don't want to spoil this but the truth is I didn't know what else to do.'

'About what?'

She fished into her handbag and brought out the notes. 'About these.' She handed the pieces of paper to Tom.

'What are they?' he asked, and when she did not answer immediately he looked at each one in turn, starting with the first note she received.

I KNOW WHO YOU ARE.

Tom looked at her for a clue, but none was forthcoming. He slid that note to the bottom of the pile and glanced at the second one.

DID YOU REALLY THINK YOU COULD JUST WALK AWAY, JENNA?

THAT'S NEVER GOING TO HAPPEN.

He glanced up at her but she seemed to be willing him to continue.

There was a third note.

I KNOW WHO YOU USED TO BE. I'LL TELL EVERYONE.

'And I got this one today.'

The final note read:

YOU'RE GOING TO PAY.

'I'm sorry, Tom, but I need help and there's no one else I can ask.'

'You're being blackmailed?'

'Yes,' she said, 'and I don't know what to do.'

'But how ... I mean, what could you have possibly done that's so bad someone could blackmail you over it?'

She shook her head violently. 'I don't want to talk about that.'

He thought for a moment. 'But how can I help you if you won't say what it is?'

'Can't you just give me some advice on what to do? That's what I need. I'm going out of my mind here.'

'This thing you did?' he probed gently. 'It would be bad if it came out? You can't just tell him to do his worst' – he corrected himself – 'if it is a *he*, of course, but then it usually is.'

'No,' she said. 'Nobody can ever know about this.'

He let that sink in, wondering what the hell she could have done that was so bad her life in the village would be irreparably damaged if it came to be known. While his mind raced, he tried to give her the advice she craved.

'Well, my first instinct would be to go to the police, but that's assuming you can actually tell the police. If you're a serial killer, for example, I'd advise against it.'

She didn't laugh at that. 'I don't want to involve the police.'

'Because you did something illegal?'

She didn't reply.

'Have you had a demand for money?'

'No,' she said. 'Not yet.'

'You'll get one,' he assured her. 'Unless it's someone being malicious, messing with your mind. I'm saying, everybody has secrets, Jenna. Are you sure this person really knows yours?'

'Yes,' she said. 'I just know it.'

'Okay, well, you could wait until they make their demands and pay up –'

'You think I should pay them?' she interrupted.

'But there is no guarantee that that will be the end of the matter. Pay them once and they'll be happy for a time but you'll have proved you're desperate to keep whatever it is a secret. When they've spent your money, they're very likely to come back to ask you for more and then you'll never be free.'

She seemed to slump then, 'So I can't pay and I can't go to the police. What *can* I do?'

'I don't know,' he said, and she looked at him as if he was no help, 'because I don't know any of the circumstances. Look, Jenna, I'd love to help you, genuinely, but if you're not prepared to trust me with whatever it is you've done, I don't see how I can.' He let that sink in. 'And there is a chance that, even if you do, I won't want to.'

'What?'

He shrugged. 'If you killed a kid in a hit and run, say, why would I want to let you get away with that?'

She snorted. 'It's nothing like that. I haven't done anything evil.'

'But it's still bad?'

'For me personally, yes, and in the small community I live in it would be . . . devastating. It can't come out.'

'All right.'

'Then you'll help me?'

'Jenna, if I don't know what you did, I can't work out who might know about it,' he said, 'so how can I possibly help you?'

Jenna thought for a long while. She kept looking at Tom, as if she was wondering whether he would judge her, then she sighed and said, 'Maybe you can't.'

Chapter Twenty-seven

The screw was six inches long. The part nearest the head had been congealed by the paint then, further in, it had rusted, which impeded her progress. Each full turn of the screw was a tortuous process that took several attempts and caused Eva considerable pain. Her hands burned in protest every time she leaned in to twist it. Finally, after what seemed like an eternity, the first screw came out.

Eva's first sensation was elation, but it quickly turned to fear. The man could not find her doing this and it might not be long before he returned. If he caught her unscrewing the vent, it would all be for nothing. Tentatively, she tried to reinsert the screw and she was relieved when it went back in smoothly then came out again without too much effort. The sensible thing would be to bide her time, so she could be sure of not being found out before she tried to escape. Undoing all four screws would take a while, if it was possible at all, and it would be better if she tried to get through the hole left by the vent after he had been in with her food. That would give her precious hours to break out and get away from this place, wherever that was.

She put the screw back in then waited for her captor to visit once more.

*

It had seemed like such a sensible notion, but now he realized why nobody else had bothered to try it. Ian Bradshaw had spent hours wading through old cases and had got precisely nowhere. He was looking for anyone who might have been put in prison within a few months of the disappearance of the last woman to go missing in 1980 and released not long prior to the latest batch of disappearances.

The first thing he realized was how hard it was to narrow the list down and find a feasible suspect and how easy it was to eliminate vast numbers of men from his inquiries. He could rule out anyone too old or infirm upon their release, and he didn't bother to pursue criminals who had committed crimes with a financial motive, such as fraud or armed robbery, no matter how violent, because these were acts unrelated to the crimes he was investigating. Instead he concentrated on murderers or those who had been convicted of crimes against women such as rape or serious assault. There were one or two promising possibilities but then, one by one, he ended up ruling them out, because the dates weren't right and they had been in prison when the abductions had occurred.

In short, after spending the best part of a day reading about a great many former jailbirds, he hadn't come up with a single plausible suspect who was worth tracking down for questioning. He couldn't be sure of it of course, but the more Bradshaw thought about the man who was behind these crimes, the more he became convinced that he was unknown to the authorities, and that would make him so very much harder to catch. He had the feeling he was completely off the radar.

*

There was a padded envelope waiting for Helen on the mat when she opened the front door. She recognized Peter's handwriting and took it to the kitchen table. Ever the cautious one, he'd used Sellotape to reinforce the opening but far too much of it, and she needed scissors to get it open. A small item wrapped in plastic dropped out on to the table, along with a little note that said, 'I saw this and thought of you,' next to a heart, a kiss and his initials. It might have been unoriginal to use the Royal Mail's long-standing advertising slogan but at least the item he'd sent showed he'd been thinking about her and the gesture was a kind one. Helen unwrapped a chrome keyring with a picture of Bagpuss on it; a shared private joke because the old cloth cat had been the star of her favourite TV programme as a child. She found herself smiling at the memory now.

Helen heard Tom's key turn in the lock and quickly put the keyring back in the envelope then stuffed it into her bag in case he asked her about it.

'Hi,' he said. 'How did it go?'

'I'm not sure I really learned all that much,' Helen admitted, 'but Phil Barstow was convinced his sister was abducted and never believed the police theory that she had been drinking and doing drugs. He said she was too straight for that. Anyway, I thought starting with Sarah's brother might be a good idea,' she said pointedly.

'And I agreed with you,' said Tom. 'I just couldn't go to Newcastle because I was busy.'

'That's suitably vague,' she said. 'Worryingly so.'

'Why should you be worried about what I do?'

'Because you are normally an open book, Tom. You tell me things,' she reminded him, 'so now I'm wondering why you won't say where you went.'

'I had to meet someone.'

'Who?'

'A friend.'

'Just a friend? It's a woman, isn't it, and you haven't told Penny. You're worried I'll drop you in it by accident.'

'If I was worried about you dropping me in it, it wouldn't be accidental.'

'Ouch.'

'I know you don't like Penny.'

'Rubbish,' Helen lied, 'but let's not get off the subject. Who is this woman you don't want her to know about? Are you having an affair, Mr Carney?'

'No, I am not,' he protested, 'but I would appreciate it if you didn't mention it to Penny because she does get a bit jealous and this is a little delicate.'

'Deal,' she agreed, 'as long as you tell me what you're up to. Who is the lady in question?'

'She's kind of . . . an old flame.'

Helen laughed. 'Penny will love that. Not that I would tell her, obviously. Was she a serious old flame, then? I never knew you had any.'

'There's a lot you don't know about me. Jenna was my first.'

'Your first *love*?'

'No, just my first –' He laughed at her reaction. 'Actually, that's not quite true. I was . . .'

Helen waited to hear some declaration of love from him.

'. . . very fond of her.'

'Fond of her?' she scoffed. 'You make her sound like a family pet.'

'What do you want me to say?'

'Did you love her?'

'I' – he hesitated and was obviously weighing the word – 'probably thought back then that I was more or less *in* love with her, but it was teenage stuff, you know?'

'And how long was it before you fell out of love with her?'

'She dumped me, actually,' he said. 'I knew that would amuse you.'

'I'm not amused,' she said, stifling a smile. 'Poor you.'

'Well, it was a very long time ago, when I was young and foolish.'

'So, why were you meeting your old flame? Trying to rekindle it?'

'Not at all. It was just lunch.'

Helen looked as if she was still waiting for an answer.

'Why do you have to know everything?'

'You're supposed to be my partner, helping me with an investigation,' she said. 'Instead you're off having lunch with an ex-girlfriend you're not trying to get back with, so there must be something going on.'

'So now you won't let it go?'

'I'm an investigative journalist,' said Helen. 'It does tend to come with the territory.'

'It's no big deal,' said Tom dismissively, 'but she might need some help.'

Helen frowned. 'With what?'

'I think she could be in a spot of bother, that's all.'

'Oh, here we go again.'

'What's that supposed to mean?'

'You,' she said. 'You're doing your Sir Galahad act, aren't you? I can tell.'

'It's not like that,' he protested. 'She came to me for . . .' For what? He didn't want to tell Helen the truth: that Jenna was being blackmailed but wouldn't tell him why, that he wanted to help his former girlfriend but might not be able to, that it was possible he would never hear from her again. He was desperate to play it down but suddenly he was struggling to find the words to appease her. 'I'm not exactly sure why she came to me.'

Helen gave him a withering look.

Then he snapped, 'What do you want me to do?'

'I want you to avoid becoming distracted when we are working a case for which we will actually get paid.'

'I won't get distracted.'

'You did once before.' She meant Lena, and he immediately flared at the allusion to his ex-girlfriend and the havoc she had caused.

'This is different.'

'If you say so,' she said softly and left the room.

'Bollocks,' he said in frustration.

The process of removing the screws was fraught. Each one took an age to turn until it was free from the vent and there was the constant fear her captor might return while she was working on them. Her hands were now a mess of bleeding blisters and she had to clench them when he came into the crate in case he spotted the damage and wondered what she had been doing. Despite the pain and the lengthy process, she had managed to undo three of the painted-over and rusting screws.

Only one more to go, then she could remove the centre of the vent from the wall and attempt to squeeze through the gap. She refused to contemplate what she would do if she couldn't wriggle through it or how she would feel if the fourth screw proved more stubborn than the previous ones. What if it was stuck fast and she couldn't budge it? It didn't bear thinking about. There was no plan B.

She had been waiting on the bed for an hour, too afraid to attempt to remove the final screw in case he came in and caught her. He had to be due to bring her some food, but there was no sign of him.

Eva still didn't know why he was holding her captive. If she tried to engage him in conversation, the man would simply demand her silence at the point of his gun. He only ever spoke to give her instructions: his deep voice would issue short commands – eat, drink, strip, wash – and she would comply, because she wanted to contain the rage that bubbled up inside him. He would get angry if she didn't eat all her food, so she learned to finish it and to drink all of the water. Then he was calmer.

When the door finally opened it was not to bring her food. Instead the man ordered her out of the crate and gestured towards the bunker. It was daylight, but she couldn't see anything around her that would help her gain her bearings when she escaped, only fields. The shipping crate was on low-lying land so she couldn't see far beyond it.

He put the bag over her head and marched Eva towards the bunker. He was taking her for another shower and she was glad of that. She needed one; she'd make sure to wash some of the dirt from her damaged hands. They went through the same routine and, when Eva had finished in the shower, he gave her a set of clean clothes then marched her back into the corridor but, instead of taking her back to the hatch, he steered her in the opposite direction, deeper into the bunker. Then he opened a door and made her walk into a room. It was sparsely furnished – a camp bed, a bedside cabinet, a sink in one corner and a single armchair – but there were some books: a Bible and some historical romances, plus a few children's stories – some of Enid Blyton's Famous Five and Secret Seven series, and a single Nancy Drew mystery. Was this some strange way of trying to make her more comfortable? Was it a reward, a punishment or a treat? Would she be back in her crate in an hour or two? She had to be, or there would be no way of escaping. All the work she had put in to break the metal clasp and loosen the screws would be for nothing. She wanted to weep in frustration but managed to hide her emotions while he was in the room with her. He closed the door and locked her in.

Chapter Twenty-eight

1973

She was smoking outside the NAAFI at RAF Gütersloh when Samuel first saw her. He wondered who had let her into the base and what she was doing there on her own. You'd have thought security might have been tighter here. It was the closest RAF base to the border between East and West Germany and the two squadrons of Lightning fighter-interceptors based here were meant to be first-response aircraft, if the Cold War became hotter and Soviet forces streamed over the border into NATO-controlled territory.

She could have been anyone but here she was, calmly smoking, and no one had moved her on. The wives who went into the NAAFI-run supermarket barely gave her a glance, but he noticed her. She was about sixteen years old, still a kid, really; a skinny, sad-eyed, bare-legged German girl from the town, with dirty-blonde hair, dressed in a short skirt and a T-shirt, and her cigarette had been smoked almost down to the filter. There wasn't much there but he saw something in her.

He stood next to the girl and reached for his own cigs. He liked to smoke the American brands, Camels or Lucky Strikes, because they seemed more exotic, and he offered her one. She accepted it without a word. He lit it for her with his Zippo and watched as she took a drag. 'Friends left you?' he asked.

She nodded.

'Cold?'

She gave a non-committal shrug that he took as an affirmative. He left her then and went into the café over the road. He ordered two hot drinks, waited till the waitress walked away then took the china cups outside, crossed back over the road and handed one of them to the girl. 'Hot chocolate,' he told her, and she held the cup gratefully in both hands to warm them.

She didn't say anything for a while, then she took a sip and said, '*Danke*,' before correcting herself: 'Thank you.'

Samuel guessed it had been a while since anyone had given her anything. Maybe it was the reassurance of his uniform but he got the impression the girl trusted him already. She was so young; she shouldn't be out there on her own. She was lucky he had chanced upon her and not someone like Dent. He wondered how her parents could let her hang around a military base like this. Didn't they care? This girl was so young and trusting she was like a blank canvas, and that was why it was not too late for her.

'What's your name?'

'Ingrid.'

Samuel stood outside the NAAFI with her while they finished their drinks and smoked his cigarettes, then he said, 'Come on, Ingrid. I'll get you something to eat.'

She trailed after him like an obedient dog. He knew then that he would save her.

Chapter Twenty-nine

When she called, Tom was watching the TV news while eating a ham roll that passed for a late lunch. He'd just faxed a story through to a magazine about mobile army catering units; one of those everyday features whose modest fees helped keep them afloat. Apparently, squaddies weren't too fussy what they ate, as long as it came with chips.

His mobile rang and he hit the mute button on the TV and put the ham butty to one side.

'Tom? It's me.'

'Jenna?' He waited for her to say something further.

It took her a moment and he heard her let out a breath before she spoke. 'All right, I'll tell you,' she said, 'but not over the phone. Can you come over tonight?'

'Er, yeah, maybe,' he said, though he knew he would have to cancel on Penny if he did and he wasn't sure what he could tell her about this, other than that it was work, and was it really *work* when he was helping a former lover? He decided not to think about that too deeply and instead promised Jenna he would be there.

Penny didn't sound too impressed when he phoned to explain he was busy that night. Though she told him it was *fine*, he suspected it was anything but.

Tom drove to Jenna's village at the agreed time and automatically parked a street away from her shop. He knew there was a certain amount of risk for Jenna in his visit. How would she account for Tom, if he was seen, when she couldn't tell the truth about their meeting? As an old friend, perhaps, or a former lover? Tom had grown up in a village and had always hated the lack of anonymity. He far preferred city life, where people didn't feel like they always had to know everybody else's business: who they were seeing, who else they had been seen with. He never wanted to return to that smaller world, but Jenna seemed to love it here. She was certainly keen to preserve her life in the village.

She showed him upstairs to her flat. Jenna made coffee and they sat together at a little table by the bay window, which looked out on to the main street and the village green. There was no one out there now; even the bus shelter was empty.

'So quiet, isn't it?' she said with relish, as if the silence instilled a calm in her.

'It is,' answered Tom. He wasn't sure he could cope with it.

It took her a few moments to start and he realized she was steeling herself or perhaps trying to get the story straight in her own mind before she could explain it to him. 'When I graduated,' she began, 'I really wanted to stay in the North-East, but there weren't many jobs.'

'There never are,' he agreed, noting that most of the people he knew who had left school with any qualifications had almost immediately ventured south, some through choice and others by necessity, seeking work that was unavailable in their region.

'It wasn't easy, but I finally got a job in marketing for a food-and-drink wholesaler in Newcastle. It was hard work but I enjoyed it most of the time and the pay was pretty good. Not quite good enough for me to afford the flat I fell in love with, though.'

Tom began to feel apprehensive. Had Jenna stolen from the company, or from someone else?

'I'd saved enough money for the deposit, but I couldn't get the right mortgage on my salary. Then I met a broker who said I didn't have to worry about any of that. I could just exaggerate what I earned and no one would bother to check the forms, they would sort me out a mortgage without asking any questions. So that's what I did. I added a few thousand on to my declaration of earnings, I got my mortgage and moved in. All good.'

Tom frowned at this. 'But how did you make the payments if you weren't earning enough?'

'With difficulty,' she admitted. 'There was very little left at the end of each month, but I just about managed it. I juggled credit cards to survive but I knew I was robbing Peter to pay Paul. I loved the flat, though, and I figured if I could just get through the early years, maybe get a pay rise or a better job, then I'd be okay.'

'But that didn't happen?'

'No,' she said grimly. 'I lost my job, quite suddenly.'

'You were fired?'

She shook her head. 'Made redundant. It seemed that, just like me, the company had been living beyond its means. They'd been borrowing a lot of money to keep going and, in the end, it wasn't sustainable. They got rid of four people and I was one of them.'

'What did you do?'

'I panicked.' She laughed, but there was no humour in

it. 'I got some money when they made me redundant but I knew it wouldn't last. I applied for dozens of jobs in the area, and beyond, but I got nowhere. I had enough to pay my mortgage for three or four months but after that . . .'

'You'd lose your flat.'

'Unless I found a way to make some money.'

She let that sink in. Tom thought he was beginning to understand.

She exhaled. 'Then I saw an advert for an agency. They were looking for young, attractive women. It was discreet, the money was . . .' She shrugged, as if to highlight the irresistible nature of it. 'I figured I was young and attractive. I wasn't seeing anyone, so there were no complications on that score, and I was desperate, so . . .' She still couldn't quite find the words.

'You started working as an escort?' He kept his voice deliberately neutral. He didn't want her to think he was judging her and, in truth, he wasn't, though he was a little shocked to discover that his teenage sweetheart had been having sex with men for money.

'Yes,' she admitted.

They both needed a moment to let it sink in.

'This agency, what was it called?'

'Angels.'

'And how did it work?'

'They advertised in some newspapers and in men's magazines. Guys would call them up and arrange to see a girl for a set time – an hour, an evening, sometimes overnight, though that was rare. They'd ask the man what kind of girl he was looking for – her age, height, vital statistics, hair colour, that sort of thing – then they'd call one of us and book us in.'

'Where did you meet them?'

'Hotels, sometimes,' she said. 'That was an outcall. They'd be guys on business, staying in the city, mostly. Then there were incalls.'

'You'd meet the guy in his flat or yours?'

She shook her head. 'Never in my flat. I wanted to keep that life very separate from the work I was doing.'

It struck Tom how odd it was to describe sex as work, even though it was meant to be the oldest profession, along with spying.

'And I didn't like to go to their homes either. It didn't feel quite as safe somehow.'

'What did you do?'

'Angels rented an apartment in the city. They'd book us in and we'd show up before the client so we could meet him there.'

'It was only supposed to be for a little while – a few weeks, a month or two maybe, to make enough to cover the mortgage until I got a proper job again, but I just couldn't get anything in the area.'

'How long did you do this kind of work?'

'Four years,' she said, and he could see the admission cost her.

'Wow.'

'Don't,' she cautioned.

'Don't what?'

'Do the maths,' she said. 'I can tell you're doing it in your head. Thinking about how many weeks it was, then working out how many men I've slept with.'

'I genuinely wasn't doing that, Jenna.'

'Good, because I didn't keep score,' she told him a little sharply.

'I was actually thinking it must have been difficult for you.'

'It was,' she admitted. 'Some of them men were nice – most of them were okay, in fact – but some were very far from nice. In the end, I couldn't keep doing it. I just couldn't.'

'That's understandable.'

'So I quit.'

'What about your flat?'

'It had gone up a bit in value and the irony was that, once I realized what it was costing me to keep it, I didn't like it so much any more. I wanted to get away – from the apartment, from the city, from the lifestyle. I sold it and put the proceeds and all my savings into this shop.'

'And it's going okay, is it, the business?'

'I'm getting by. It's taken me a while, but I feel like I'm established here now. You know what a village is like. They reserve judgement until they get to know you, but I provide what people need and they drop by.'

'But the villagers might turn against you if they knew about this?'

'I should imagine a lot of people will no longer want to shop here if they know what I used to do.'

'And there might be some blokes who'll get the wrong idea.'

'And think I'm still open for business? That had crossed my mind.'

'So this can never come out,' he reasoned. 'But how

could someone know what you used to do unless they were a former client?'

'I've been thinking about that – wondering about it a lot, in fact.'

'And, if they are, surely they wouldn't want anyone to know about it, so blackmailing you would be counter-productive.'

'It is possible it's someone from the village,' she said, 'but I don't think so.'

'What makes you say that?' he probed. 'Why do you have that feeling?'

'Well, I've never experienced that shock of recognition from anyone, you know, that look in someone's eyes when they have a previous, embarrassing connection with you. I never even had that when I lived in Newcastle, let alone here, with its tiny population, and you're right – why would someone blackmail another person if the secret would be just as damning to them? Even if they're single, it would be humiliating if it came out that they had been paying for sex with an escort; more so, if they're married, of course.'

'Someone from the agency, perhaps?'

'Maybe, but I didn't have too many dealings with the people there. I went for one interview before I started. That's all.'

'This interview, was it with the owner, was it like . . . er . . . an audition?'

She laughed. 'No, they didn't make me sleep with any-one to get the job. The person who interviewed me was a woman. She explained that the agency's role was to pair up girls with clients, and they took a cut. All they prom-ised was that clients would have *time* with the girls. What we did with that time was our business, but they obviously explained what was required of me.'

'Sex?'

'Yes, and the various things men expect from a professional, but it wasn't anything that men don't want in general,' she explained. 'I didn't do any kinky stuff. I left that to the girls who specialized in those things.'

'Do you remember the name of the woman who interviewed you?'

'Only her first name, I'm afraid. Amanda.'

'Well, it's a start. What about an address for this agency? You said it was called Angels?'

'It no longer exists. It was closed down. Actually, it was raided.'

'Really?'

'This was after I left, about a year ago. I read about it in the paper. Some people were fined and got suspended sentences; only one did prison time. He got a year for living off immoral earnings.'

'Do you have his name?'

'Yes,' she said. 'I kept the newspaper cutting.'

She went to a drawer and opened it, rummaged for a moment, withdrew the cutting and gave it to him. Tom read the report of the trial. Francis Walker was 'a parasite who lived off the immoral earnings of a number of young women he preyed on, tempting them into a life of vice, cloaked in a veneer of respectability', the judge had said. 'Because of this and his previous convictions, I have no hesitation in passing a custodial sentence. Time is what he offered his clients, and time is what I am going to give him – to reflect.'

'The judge did have a sense of humour,' said Tom, 'as well as one of his own self-importance. This bloke got a year. If he kept his nose clean, he might have been out months ago.' He gave her a meaningful look. 'Could it be him?'

'Blackmailing me, you mean? I don't know. I suppose it could.'

'If he was just out of prison and no longer had a business, and he could trace the girls he used to employ, then he might resort to something like this.'

'He might,' she said. 'I know better than anyone what people are prepared to do if they're desperate.'

'Then I'll see if I can track Francis Walker down,' he told her, 'and have a word with him.'

'Are you sure it's a good idea to approach a man like that?' Her tone told him she wasn't convinced it was.

'How else will we flush him out?'

Chapter Thirty

Throw out the worthless slave into the outer darkness.
— Matthew 25:30

He examined every inch of the shipping crate by torchlight. Even in daytime it was a gloomy, windowless room, and it was easy to miss things unless you used the torch and shone it into every dark corner. He had learned to be careful and not rush these searches. It was amazing what they were capable of, especially in the early days, before they had learned to accept things, so he would systematically examine every inch of each crate and every room to make sure he missed nothing. One had even escaped once and had to be replaced by a far less suitable girl, a parentless teenager who nobody seemed to miss. That could never be allowed to happen again.

It didn't take him long. The missing paint and the bare metal on the head of the screw were a dead giveaway. What had she been up to, and how had it been possible? She was a cunning little one. It took him a few more minutes before he found the tool, hidden in a gap she had made on the blind side of the mattress. His anger threatened to take control of him then. Unknowing, ungrateful, treacherous bitch. After all the work he had put in, after everything he had done for her.

He was going to kill her and he was going to do it now. He reached for the shotgun and set off to do it immediately, while she was still locked in the underground room, with no possible means of escape.

Then he stopped. He couldn't do it. Not yet.

There had to be five.

Newcastle was nearly always a great night out, until the end. Then it was a pain to get away from, when you were competing with so many other people for a taxi and many of them were mullered after a night – sometimes a whole day – on the drink.

You could usually get a cab in the underpass, though, if you didn't mind trekking down there, and it was better than waiting at the rank, which would involve hanging about for ages, being pestered by drunks who thought you were fair game just because you were on a night out or your skirt was a bit short. Kelly didn't want to walk too far either, because these bloody heels were killing her, so she chose the underpass.

It wasn't official or anything, but they were *sort of* cab drivers, blokes who hadn't bothered to fill in all the paperwork for the licence and were probably dodging the tax on the income – but who could blame them if they were skint? Anyway, she was very tired and a bit too pissed to worry about it. When she got there she was surprised to see only one car waiting. She knew why, though. Bloody police had moved everyone on again. They were buggers like that. Instead of going out and solving real crimes they spent their time coming down hard on working blokes who were only trying to add a bit of cash on to their social. It wasn't like they were real villains or anything.

It wouldn't work. They'd just lie low for a bit and be back again after a few weeks, when the police had lost interest in the area. It was the same everywhere in the city. If there was a spot that became notorious for hookers or dealers, the police would eventually bow to the public outcry, swoop down, make a few arrests and keep an eye on the place for a week or so, then they'd go off and do it somewhere else. Sure enough, as soon as their eye was off the ball, the prozzies and smackheads would return and it would be business as usual.

At least there was one car. Thank fuck for that. She didn't know the make but it was quite an old vehicle, a bit square and clunky, like something you'd see on TV in an old cop show when there was a car chase, but she didn't care. Kelly didn't need a limo, just a cheap ride home.

She walked right up to it, but the bloke had his window wound up, even though it wasn't cold, and the glass was dirty so she couldn't make him out too well. Plus, he had dark glasses on and an old man's cap, but that didn't freak her out. Her uncle wore dark-lens prescription glasses because he had scars around his eyes from the time he went through a windscreen when he'd been drink-driving.

She thought she'd better check he wasn't just waiting for someone, so she ducked down and peered in then gave him a thumbs-up to see how he'd react. He couldn't have misunderstood her intention because he jabbed a finger towards the back seat. She got into the car gratefully.

Maybe he was a proper cab-driver, after all, because he had one of those heavy-duty plastic screens between the front and back seats and it fitted so neatly it filled every inch of the space between them.

'Can you tack uz to Benwell?' Kelly sounded slurry even to her own ears. 'They usually dae it for a fiver.'

He just nodded, and she took the movement of the back of his head to be a binding agreement on both the fare and the destination.

Kelly settled back to enjoy the ride.

It only took a second for the doubts to form. She realized something was wrong even before he turned the key in the ignition. It was the sound that did it. It wasn't like the noise of a normal car, particularly one without its engine running. There was a tiny hissing sound.

The car wouldn't start at first. The engine turned over hopelessly so the driver switched off the engine and gave it another go. The fear Kelly felt was purely instinctive, but then she saw the little plastic pipe jutting out on the floor beneath her feet and knew straight away that the hissing she could hear was linked to it.

'I've changed me mind,' she told him, and sat bolt upright.

He ignored her and turned the key in the ignition once more.

'It's all right, I don't want to go,' she told him sharply, but the engine had started this time and the car began to move forwards. 'I've got no money!' she called out, but even that did not deter him.

She banged on the screen. 'Did you hear me? Stop the car! I want to get out!'

He couldn't have failed to hear that but he wasn't going to stop, and what normal man would drive off with a woman knowing she didn't want to go with him and had no money for the fare?

Kelly panicked, and that panic rose when the car picked up speed. Soon it would be out of the underpass and on to the main road, where he could drive off at full pelt and there'd be nothing she could do about it. And the cab's rear-seat windows were tinted, so no one would see her or hear her. The car would soon be moving too fast to do anything. She knew this was her only chance. Kelly opened the door and flung her whole weight against it.

She shot out of the car and hit the concrete with a sickening impact and, as her body rolled, her head bounced against the hard ground. The pain was intense. It seemed to sting every part of her body from her head to her knees. The wind was knocked out of her and she felt physically sick from the blow to her head. The last thing she recalled was watching the back of the car as it carried on, it's open rear door colliding with the side of the narrow underpass. As she tried to avoid drifting into a shocked unconsciousness, Kelly tried very hard to remember one extremely important thing.

Chapter Thirty-one

Ian Bradshaw knew he shouldn't do it. It was at best irregular and possibly a sackable offence, or one that could get him into even more serious trouble . . . but he did it anyway. Tom Carney seemed very keen to get the address of a man who had been released early from a prison sentence for living off immoral earnings. Since he was on parole, the man had to register his current address with the police. It turned out he was living at his sister's flat in Tynemouth.

Bradshaw wrote the address on a slip of paper then phoned Tom to pass it on, and add a note of caution: 'You didn't get this from me.'

'Of course.'

Then Bradshaw lowered his voice to almost a whisper so nobody at HQ could hear him. 'I won't ask why you're going to knock on the door of a pimp, because I don't want to know, but please don't end up brawling with him in the street or causing any kind of incident that might lead people to wonder how you found out where he lived.'

'I'll try not to,' said Tom dryly. 'All I want is a quiet word.'

'A quiet word?'

'Cross my heart.'

Bradshaw had been off the phone for less than a minute when DC Malone called his name shrilly across the room. When Bradshaw turned to look at the source of the sound, she said, 'There's a woman you might want to talk to about a cab-driver who tried to pick her up.' She seemed to have just taken the call and was still holding the phone.

Malone was always crap at explaining herself, and this was no exception. 'That's what they usually do, isn't it?' he called back.

She failed to hide her exasperation. 'But this guy wasn't a real cabbie and she got wind of it somehow, so she got out of the car.'

'Right.'

'While it was bloody moving.'

'Christ,' said Bradshaw. 'Where is she now?'

'At home watching *Cold Feet*?'

'Eh?'

'In the bloody hospital, man. Where do you think she is?'

'Who's on the line?' he snapped.

'Northumbria,' she told him, meaning the police force.

He almost wrestled the phone from her and when he put it to his ear he was greeted by a familiar voice. 'The next time that bloody woman screams across the room at you,' DC Argyle told him, 'tell her to take the phone away from her mouth first. She almost deafened me.'

Bradshaw frowned at Malone. 'You should try working with her every day,' he said, and she slunk away to the coffee machine with a scowl on her face.

'So, tell me about this woman.'

'Well, it's an odd one,' said his Geordie counterpart, 'and I thought it could be linked to your missing girls. She was found lying on the pavement. That, in itself, is not so strange on a night in Newcastle, but she had multiple injuries and was only barely conscious. As the ambulance drove her away, she told them she threw herself out of a cab because the driver was trying to abduct her. The place is a known pick-up point for fake cab-drivers but they're usually only in it for the undeclared income. This sounds very different – I thought you might like to talk to her.'

'I would,' said Bradshaw. 'I definitely would.'

Francis Walker looked like a man who had been defeated by life but still had a long way to go before he could formally surrender. In his early forties, he had no job nor any prospect of one. Neither did he have a home, and when Tom knocked on the door of the apartment in Tynemouth he shared with his sister, he found a man who acted as if he was expecting the Grim Reaper and wouldn't have minded all that much if his time had been up.

Tom explained why he was there. 'One of your girls has been experiencing some trouble and we thought you might know something about it.'

'Why would I know anything?' he protested. 'I haven't seen anyone since the day you arrested me.' He clearly thought Tom was from the police. Tom knew it was unethical not to reveal who he was, but he wanted to see if Francis would let something slip so he played along.

'You've had no contact with any of them since you got out of prison?'

Francis almost flinched at the word 'prison' and Tom surmised he'd had a hard time in jail. He looked like a classic white-collar criminal and they always struggled.

'I've not seen any of them. Why would I? I hardly had any contact with them when they worked for me, so why should I see them now that it's all over?'

Tom gave a little shrug. 'Blackmail.'

'Blackmail?' Francis looked genuinely confused. 'How could anybody blackmail anyone? We were all arrested together.' He was trying to keep his voice low, to avoid being overheard by a neighbour, perhaps, but this apartment block was like all the others: virtually empty during the day, while everyone was at work.

'They were arrested,' Tom conceded, 'but you were the only one who was sent down. That must have made you bitter?'

'I've had a bad time lately,' he conceded, 'but it doesn't mean I want a bunch of lasses I hardly knew to have a shit time, too. It was a business arrangement, and none of us deserved jail.'

'I heard you got sent down because you had rivals in the city who didn't like what you were doing. They knew powerful people and they whispered in the right ears so you got a stretch.'

'Look, I did the crime and I did the time. Am I happy about it? No. But what am I going to do?'

'What *are* you going to do?' asked Tom. 'Now, I mean.'

The question flummoxed Francis. 'I don't know,' he mumbled. 'I have no idea.'

'You could use some cash, presumably, to start again. Some people think you might be trying to get that money by threatening your former employees with exposure. They didn't get the attention you got in the newspapers so they can get on with their lives, but you can't. Perhaps you deserve a little slice of what they've got. Is that it?'

Francis was starting to become unnerved now. 'Sorry, who was it that sent you? I've never seen you before. Are

161

you even with the Northumbria force? Do I look like I'm back doing what I was doing? I'm skint.'

'Did I inadvertently give you the impression I was a police officer?'

'Who are you, then?' Francis looked scared. Maybe it was Tom's mention of a business rival. Perhaps he feared he was about to be put out of business permanently. 'I'll slam this bloody door in your face,' he said, but he didn't do it. Maybe he was worried Tom would turn violent. Francis looked as if he'd seen more than his fair share of that lately.

'Relax, Francis. I'm an investigative reporter and I work with the police on a number of cases.' That part was, of course, true, even if it was misleading. Tom didn't want to admit he was here on his own bit of private enterprise. 'I've taken an interest in your girls because one of them is being blackmailed.'

'Well, if she is, it has nowt to do with me, and I don't want to talk about this any more.' He put his hand on the door to close it.

'Then I will naturally assume you have something to hide and that will simply increase my interest in you.'

Francis hesitated at that.

'Or you could try helping me out, and maybe you'll convince me you had nothing to do with it. Your call.'

Francis looked like he was weighing up these unattractive options. Tom could tell he was conflicted. Above all, though, it was weariness that he saw in the man. He didn't have the energy to fight. 'I'll talk to you,' he said, 'though it will be a waste of your time and mine. Not that I've got much else on right now.' And with that he retreated into the apartment. 'Not here, though. It's my sister's flat and I'm just crashing for a while.'

Tom waited outside. The TV was silenced and he heard the scraping sound of keys being picked up from a wooden table. Francis returned and said, 'Let's go for a walk.'

Chapter Thirty-two

Tell tale tit
Your tongue shall be slit
And all the doggies of the town
Shall have a little bit.
— Traditional nursery rhyme

In the fall from the car Kelly had broken her collarbone, her wrist and two ribs and she'd fractured her skull. Bradshaw found her conscious, lucid but adversarial and got the impression she might just be like that all the time.

'I've already been through this once. The other fella just left. He wore a uniform.'

He wondered if she had been more impressed by his predecessor's appearance. 'I'm following up on another case, which might be linked to yours,' he explained, 'so I'd be grateful if you could take a few moments to answer some of my questions.'

'Go on, then,' she told him impatiently, as if there was somewhere she had to be, instead of lying in her hospital bed recovering.

'So you went down to the underpass to get a cab?' asked Bradshaw.

'Yes.'

'Why didn't you use the normal rank outside the railway station?'

'Have you ever tried that on a Saturday night?' she snapped. 'It's like queueing for free money. I'd've been there ages. I've got more sense, man.'

'You've got more sense than to queue up at the rank, so instead you went to a dark underpass and climbed into a strange man's car and he tried to abduct you?'

'Yeah, well, when you put it like that it sounds stupid but . . .' She reacted to his questioning look: 'All right, maybe it *was* stupid, but I'm not the only one who does it. There are never enough cabs at the weekend at kicking-out time. It's usually just unemployed guys who can't get by on the social, so they do a bit of driving on the side to make some money, or it's people with shit jobs who aren't earning enough to survive. The proper cab-drivers don't like it, but it's not as if anyone is robbing business from them. They can't cope with demand as it is. Look, it's no secret that it goes on. Your lot must know all about it. Where's the harm?'

'There is no harm,' he told her. 'Apart from the rapes and the robberies. We haven't had a murder yet, but it's only a matter of time. You could have been our first.' Her face fell. 'We do know about it, yes, mainly because we get reports of people being driven from city centres and, instead of being taken home, they're taken to rough estates full of high-rises, where they're robbed of everything they have and left to walk home. The lucky ones aren't badly beaten up as well. Women sometimes get raped by these bogus drivers. That's the harm in it.'

'Then why don't you warn people?'

'We try to. We put posters up in libraries and community centres and place stickers in genuine cabs warning people not to get into strangers' cars, but they still do it. Explain that one to me.'

The fire seemed to go out of her. 'Okay, all right, it was stupid. I was drunk and I didn't think.'

'You're not the first,' he said, 'and I'm afraid you won't be the last.'

'But you reckon I was one of the lucky ones, don't you?'

'Well, we don't know this man's intentions, but only because you were brave enough to throw yourself out of a moving car.'

'I said I'd changed my mind. I told him to let me out but he just ignored me and the car started to move. I panicked. I didn't know what to do.'

'So you opened the door and jumped.'

'I did open the door, then I sort of . . . fell, I think.'

'What made you do it?'

'I just said . . .'

'I meant, what made you suspicious of this guy in the first place?'

'Well, a couple of things. First, it was the way he was.'

'And what was that?'

'He was . . . strange . . . odd.'

'In what way?'

'He didn't speak.'

'Not at all?'

'No. I got to the underpass and he was there and he must have realized I wanted a ride home. I stopped right by him and he indicated I should get in the back, so I opened the door and got in.'

'What did he look like?'

'I don't know. The front window was filthy and he was wearing dark glasses and an old man's cap.'

'An old man's cap?'

'You know, not a baseball cap, a flat one with a tartan pattern on it.'

'Any idea how old he was?'

'Impossible to tell.' She seemed to reconsider. 'Though I don't think he was all that old.'

'What makes you say that, if you didn't get a good look at him?'

'His face,' she said. 'From what I could see of it, it didn't look old.'

'Fair enough. What did you say to him?'

'Not much. I just asked him to take me home and said it was usually a fiver.'

'And what did he say to you?'

'I told you, he didn't say anything. He just nodded his head, so I assumed he was okay with it. Then I noticed it on the floor.'

'Noticed what?'

'I've already told your mate,' she said wearily.

'Which mate?'

'The one in uniform,' she said. 'And he didn't believe a bloody word I told him, I could tell. You won't either.'

'Try me,' he said, and when she didn't respond he added: 'I don't know who you spoke to, but he wasn't my mate. He's with Northumbria Police and he probably thinks you're just a daft girl who had too much to drink . . .'

'Oh, thanks very much.'

'. . . but I'm with the Durham force, and I'm investigating the disappearance of a number of women. I think you can help me. So, the question is, can you?'

She regarded him for a moment and realized he was serious. 'Someone's taking women?'

'Maybe.'

'Okay,' she said. 'I just happened to look down and I noticed this bit of plastic piping sticking out from under the passenger seat. It was black and there was a mat covering it, like it wasn't meant to be seen.'

'What do you think it was?'

'I don't know, but it didn't look right,' she said. 'That, and the screen.'

'The windscreen?'

'No,' she said. 'The car had one of those big, hard plastic screens that keep the driver separate from the passenger. It was all sealed off.'

'A lot of cabs have those,' he observed.

'Yeah, but he wasn't a cab, was he?' Not if he was picking people up from the underpass like that and his car had no markings.'

'So, he's got a normal car with a big plastic screen between the front and the back and a strange plastic pipe sticking out, and that made you suspicious?'

'That and the hissing.'

'The hissing?'

'You could barely hear it, but he had the engine turned off when I got in and I could hear a very faint hissing sound.'

'Then you put the pipe, the screen and the hissing together and you thought . . .'

'*Get the fuck out of there* is what I thought.'

'And you told him that?'

'I said, "I've changed me mind," but he just started up the engine and I knew he was about to drive away so I banged on the screen and said, "Stop the car! I want to get out!" but the car started to move off.'

'There was no way he could have misunderstood what you were saying?'

'I told you, I banged on the screen,' she repeated. 'Hard. I even said I had no money. He deliberately ignored me and just drove off. I thought, *I've got to get out of there*, so I did.'

'And he didn't stop, even then?'

'No, and it's not like he didn't notice I'd opened the door and chucked myself out of his car. He didn't even stop when the door hit the wall as he drove out of the underpass.'

Bradshaw had been busy making notes and he remained quiet while he finished them.

'So, do you believe me or what?'

'Of course,' he said. 'Why would you make something like that up? Plus, your injuries are consistent with that kind of fall.'

She seemed satisfied with that but immediately went on the offensive again. 'What you going to do about it, then?'

'Find him, I hope,' he told her. 'With your help. Tell me about the car. What was the make and model, do you know?'

She shook her head. 'No, but it was silver . . .'

'Silver? There are a lot of silver cars in the North-East. Can you tell me anything else about it?'

'Only the reg number,' she told him.

'You got the reg number?' He was amazed she had had the presence of mind to try to remember it after landing so heavily on the ground from a moving car.

'Yes, I bloody did,' she said, 'because I want you to catch the bastard!'

Chapter Thirty-three

They sat on the steps of the Collingwood Monument on the hill looking out to sea. It was a pleasant morning and there was no one else around except a handful of dog-walkers who were far enough from them for Francis to feel he could talk without being overheard.

'I didn't do anything,' he said, 'not really. I just got sick of the office job. I was doing long hours with loads of pressure and taking home just enough to survive.' Then he added: 'Like just about everybody else, I suppose. Anyway, it was a shit job, so I started thinking about ways I could earn a bit of money on the side and I came up with my bright idea.'

'Prostitution?'

'All I had to do was borrow some money to put down on a flat in Newcastle and advertise for women looking for work as escorts. As long as you don't actually say that it's sex work, you can get away with it. As soon as I had three or four lasses keen to do it, I put an advert in one of the porn mags and we started getting punters. The women got their share and I got mine. I had an older lass running things on a day-to-day basis and I just carried on with my life in Durham. As far as anyone who knew me was concerned, it was like the Newcastle place never existed. I just took my cut every month. It was incredible.'

'But you were exploiting the women,' Tom reminded him.

'How? No, seriously. They were all volunteers, they all knew what they were getting paid for. I provided them with a place to ply their trade in a safe environment, and that was all there was to it. No one got hurt.'

'Until the police raided you.'

'I wasn't expecting that,' he admitted. 'We'd been going for ages with no problems. I didn't think anybody really minded. Everyone knows that it goes on. Christ, they even advertise in local newspapers in some parts of the country. I couldn't believe it when all those police burst through the door.'

'You made one pretty fundamental mistake,' said Tom. 'You didn't pay off the right people.'

'How could I,' he asked, 'when I don't know who they are? Offer money to the wrong copper and you get arrested for bribing him.'

'That's the dilemma but, if you didn't know who they were, you probably should have left that life to the professionals.'

'Well, I know that now,' Francis reminded Tom, as if the reporter had forgotten about the prison sentence.

'What have you been doing since you got out?'

'Nothing. What can I do? I've got a record that prevents me from getting any kind of job, even though I never hurt anyone. It was a victimless crime, for Christ's sake.'

'You must feel desperate.'

'I do. Every day I have a knot of anxiety that I just can't get rid of, right here.' He pressed his fist to his chest.

'If I was that desperate, I'd be tempted to contact some of my old girls and ask them to give me a few bob, just to get me back on my feet.'

'Oh really, you think?' he scoffed. 'Do you reckon I

want to go back to prison? I'm never going back! I only just got out of there alive.' He shook his head. 'So, no, even if I was the kind of man who wanted to blackmail women, which I'm not, I wouldn't do it because it wouldn't be worth the risk. Whoever is doing this thing, it isn't me.'

'Who, then?'

'I have no idea.'

'Who knew the girls' details apart from you? The woman you hired to be your' – he was trying to think of the right phrase for a brothel-runner – 'housekeeper?'

Francis shook his head. 'She knew the girls by their chosen working names and had a mobile number for each of them, but that was all, so how could she trace them?'

'How could anyone?'

'I really don't know . . . unless . . .'

'Unless what?'

'Unless they had the ledger.'

'What ledger?'

'I kept one with the girls' details in it. It had their real names, their fake names, their age, address and contact details and a few bits and pieces like their vital statistics and what they were prepared to do so we didn't get any disappointed customers wanting stuff the girl wouldn't provide, and a photo.'

'You kept a photo of the girls?'

'One of those passport ones. And I made them sign an agreement, too, to say they weren't coerced. The photograph was clipped to the document, but it was strictly confidential.'

'Who else but you and the girls could have seen these agreements?'

'No one. I kept it under lock and key at my house in Durham.' He added, needlessly: 'When I had a house.'

Tom thought for a moment. 'Where is it now?'

'I haven't got it.'

'Who has?'

'Who else but the police?' he told Tom. 'They took it away when I was arrested. It was one of the main pieces of evidence against me.'

'The police. Have they still got it?'

'I assume so. They were hardly going to give it back to me.'

While Tom contemplated the implications of this, Francis continued, 'Look, I don't know who's blackmailing the girls, but it isn't me. I daren't risk anything that is going to land me back inside. I wouldn't be able to cope with going back. Maybe it was those people you mentioned,' he offered, 'the ones who put me out of business. Perhaps they got bent law to give them my ledger and are using it.'

'Perhaps,' Tom replied, though he could have added: *but I doubt it.*

'Do I look like I'm living off the proceeds of blackmail?' Francis asked then. 'Look at me. I have no life, and nothing to look forward to.'

'You do have a life,' Tom reminded him as he got to his feet, 'and you should remember that, because I know some people in Newcastle who wouldn't have taken the trouble to shut down their business rivals with a police raid. They would have left you floating face down in the Tyne with your fingertips missing.' When Francis looked alarmed, Tom said, 'Think about that the next time you're feeling sorry for yourself.'

Chapter Thirty-four

Bradshaw dialled them from the hospital. When Helen answered, he said, 'A man tried to pick up a woman in an unmarked cab and he wouldn't let her go. He drove off with her and she jumped out of it.'

'Oh my god,' said Helen. 'Was she badly hurt?'

'She's in pretty bad shape, but she'll heal. She's conscious and talking. She wanted to tell me all about this guy. I think he could be our abductor, and guess what?'

'What?'

'She got a reg number. Somehow, this amazing woman forced herself to look up from the road she had just fallen on to and she clocked his reg number. I think we've got him, Helen.'

He watched Eva through the hatch in the door. She was asleep. The young woman looked so peaceful, so devoid of sin. Eva Dunbar would never know how close she had come to dying. If the crazy woman in the underpass hadn't thrown herself out of the car like that, almost killing herself in the process, then she'd have been Eva's replacement and she would have been saved instead. The flame-haired girl would have been punished for her failure to obey the rules.

Not trying to escape was the most important rule.

It had happened before, years ago, and almost brought

catastrophe down on them. When a girl who'd looked close to death had been left unattended for just a moment, she'd somehow found an ounce of extra strength and managed to break free. The whole thing could have been over then, but fortune had been on their side. Sarah Bradshaw was so far gone no one had believed her story. It was as if she was claiming she'd been abducted by aliens. Instead of the newspapers reporting her kidnapping and imprisonment underground, they told the story of a missing woman who died after she was struck by a car.

They were blind and could not see. Thank God in His mercy.

But it could never be allowed to happen again. Every lock, every key, every door had to be checked and secured before bed, the keys left in the locks from the outside, so the keyholes were blocked and could never be picked. Always the shotgun had to be on hand in case it was needed, and every inch of every room had to be searched regularly. Vigilance was the only way, and it was that vigilance which had led to the discovery of the tampered-with screw in the vent and the tool she had used to loosen it. Eva had been meant to stay locked in the underground room only while he searched the crate, but she couldn't go back now.

Did she think he was stupid? It seemed so, and the discovery that she was no good caused him pain. She had been perfect. The hair, the plain dress, the lack of jewellery or any other adornment – all hinted at qualities within her that could be nurtured.

A shame she had to die and be replaced, but the failure at the underpass had made him think again. He'd almost been exposed. Why risk it, when he already had five and it would be safer to give her another chance? She looked perfect. She could perhaps be trained to be perfect, if he was tough enough, if he could break her will. After all, this was for her own good.

And then there was her name. He remembered when he had opened her purse and seen that name on all the cards she carried to pay for things. Eva.

So much like Eve. The first woman.

She was a sly one, but he could be sly, too. He wouldn't tell her he had discovered the tool and the loose screw. That would make her even more careful and deceitful. He'd let her think he wasn't watching her so closely, the better to catch her if she tried to fool him again.

He'd give her another chance, then, but she would have to stay underground for good.

Bradshaw arranged to meet them at police HQ. He had already phoned his information into CID. As soon as he had brought Helen up to date, he left the hospital and went there.

DC Malone came back into the room as he entered it. 'We ran that reg number,' she told him, 'and we have a match. It's registered to a Charlie Hamilton.'

'What have we got on him?'

'Not much yet, but we do have an address and I've checked with Northumbria Police. They're happy for us to pick this one up, since there might be a link to your case.'

'Great,' he said. 'I'll head down there now.'

'What about me? Am I not coming?'

'I need you to get me everything you can on this guy then call me up before I go in there.'

'What about back-up?' she asked, because she wanted in on this one, too. 'Kane said to be careful with this and not just go barging in on your own.'

'Get Jack Gibson to meet me there.'

'Who's Jack Gibson?'

'A specially trained officer.'

'Specially trained in what?' asked Malone.

'Firearms.'

Chapter Thirty-five

'*Warum?*' she asked him, before quickly correcting herself. Ingrid knew how much he hated it when she used her old language. She knew it, but she still did it. Careless, stupid bitch. 'Why?'

He greeted this with the same stony silence that followed every word his wife had uttered to him in the past three days.

'Why won't you speak to me, Samuel?' Her voice was high, the tone pleading; she was desperate now, he could tell. Ingrid needed human contact more than he did, which meant he was winning.

Good.

'What have I done?' she demanded. 'Can you not tell me that, please? What have I done?'

If she didn't know, he certainly wasn't going to tell her.

It was the ingratitude that hurt him the most. He had saved Ingrid from her home, from her parents, from herself and her own sinful nature. If it hadn't been for his act of charity, she'd be lying down with squaddies every night for a packet of cigs. Instead she was safe and warm in her own home with food on the table, all provided by him, but it wasn't enough for her. He just wanted Ingrid to stay here in their apartment and avoid the corruption of the outside world. He would spare her that. She didn't have to work or shop or meet anyone at all. He took care of everything. All he asked from her in return was just a little bit of obedience, for the girl to understand and obey his rules. Was that really too much? It seemed it was, for Ingrid.

She started sobbing uncontrollably then and, as the tears fell, her voice was distorted by her crying until it became the snotty, whining protest of a child. '*Ich bin so einsam,*' she said.

The words seemed to cut him.

Ich bin so einsam.

Of all the ungrateful, hurtful, selfish . . .

It was no use. He was going to have to lock her in again.

Ich bin so einsam.

I am so lonely.

Chapter Thirty-six

In the end, three armed officers descended on 17 Mercer Road, as well as DS Bradshaw and two other uniformed policemen. They parked in the main street so they could not be seen from Hamilton's two-up two-down.

'You'd better wait in the car,' Bradshaw told Tom and Helen, and when Tom bridled he said, 'In case there's any shooting.' He shrugged. 'Wouldn't want any journalists to come to any harm.'

'Too much paperwork?' asked Tom.

'Exactly, and the chief constable hates to pay compensation.'

'We'll stay here on one condition. If you get anything juicy that can be used in a story, you give it to us and no one else.'

'I'm a respectable officer of the law,' said Bradshaw. 'I never leak information to journalists.'

'Not you, no,' Tom assured him. 'But an anonymous police source might.'

'Yes,' said Bradshaw quietly. 'I suppose he might.'

Moments later, Bradshaw led the way towards the house, at the head of a column of policemen who were moving swiftly but quietly down the street. There wasn't much light from the streetlamps, just a dull yellow glow that left most of the street in darkness, and that suited their purpose. The curtains were all drawn, so there was little danger of them being spotted before they got there, and men were sent round to cover the back of the house.

Only when they reached the front door did DC Gibson and his colleagues produce the handguns they were carrying. They held the Smith & Wesson .38s low and pointing down until they were needed, ready to raise them and fire if necessary. They had debated whether to try a knock at the door first but had discounted that idea. If the owner of the house was the man who had tried to abduct the girl, he would surely be expecting them. Better to have at least an element of surprise by breaking the door down.

The officer with the battering ram stepped forward between his armed colleagues, who stood either side of the doorframe, tensed in readiness. He took a step closer then swung the battering ram back to get some momentum and crashed it against the door. There was a bang and the wood splintered, but the door did not give way and a dog started to bark incessantly from a neighbour's house. It took two more smashes of the battering ram to break it down. The armed police rushed inside, pointing their guns out in front of them.

As they were going in, a pale, gaunt figure was rushing towards them, presumably panicked by the sound of his front door coming off its hinges.

'Armed police!' the men yelled at once and the terrified man slid to a halt, his eyes wide. 'On your knees! On your knees!' Then someone shouted, 'Drop it! Drop it now!' Bradshaw could see the man had something in his hand, but he couldn't tell what it was through the gloom and his partially obscured view.

Oh Christ, don't shoot him if he's only carrying a newspaper.

He strained to look over his colleague's shoulder and saw the man let go of something. It hit the floor and rolled away.

A teacup.

Bradshaw was mightily relieved they hadn't opened up on him. That would have taken some explaining.

The man was petrified, rambling, 'What are you doing? What's going on? I haven't done anything!'

Bradshaw walked right up to him as another officer pulled the man's hands behind his back and cuffed his wrists.

'Charlie Hamilton?' asked Bradshaw.

'Yes.'

'Have you got a cellar?' he asked. The man looked at him as if Bradshaw had lost his mind. The detective repeated his question slowly and clearly: 'Have . . . you . . . got . . . a . . . cellar?'

'Yes,' the man managed.

'Where's the entrance?'

There was nothing in the cellar, just a meter cupboard, a lot of cobwebs and an ancient lawnmower rusting in a corner. There was barely room for anything else. If this man had been abducting women, he must be keeping them somewhere else. They searched the rest of the house and found nothing.

When Bradshaw returned to the man he seemed to have regained a little composure and was trying to sound indignant, though he still looked scared and guilty. 'This is out of order,' he told the detective. 'It was only a bloody pamphlet.'

Bradshaw ignored this, read the man his rights and the other officers bundled him into a car and took him to the station.

Bradshaw briefed Tom and Helen on the way back there.

'Nothing incriminating, then?' asked Helen.

'The place is a mess, but apart from that . . .'

'Sign of a guilty man,' quipped Tom.

'When did you last use a Hoover?' Helen asked him.

He considered this. 'I think it was 1992.'

Eva had lost hope. Just when she thought she might be about to break free from the prison he had made for her inside the crate, he had placed her in another one. This time, she was far below ground, behind a solid metal door that could not be opened from the inside. He had left her there with nothing but her own mind for company, her own thoughts to torment her, and she still had no explanation as to why she was here.

He continued to bring food on a little tray and water but he barely spoke to Eva. Had he worked out what she had intended to do with the air vent? Did he realize she was planning to escape? It seemed likely. Were the silences another form of punishment, designed to slowly drive her mad? If they were, then it seemed they would succeed, for Eva had started to believe she might be going crazy.

The markings didn't help. They were on the pipes that ran across the room just below the ceiling, and there was another one on the door.

MOD.

That was Ministry of Defence, wasn't it? Could this place

be owned by the government? Was Eva part of some terrible secret experiment they were conducting on their own people, to see how much they could take before they could endure no more? No wonder she hadn't been rescued. Her thoughts grew more paranoid, drifting between the notion that she might be part of an enormous government conspiracy and the idea that she had been imprisoned by some solitary madman. None of it made any sense, but she knew that, somehow, she had to keep on trying to get out.

Eva had explored every inch of her new prison and found no structural weakness to exploit. The solid brick walls were thick and there was no window. There was an air vent but it was high up on the wall and the gap behind it tiny compared to the one in the crate. There was no way she could crawl through that, even if she could remove the cover, which was impossible without a tool of some kind, and she lacked one here, since the bed had no clasp and there was nothing else she could use.

Eva tried not to panic but every time she considered her situation, two things became clear: she could not escape and no one was coming to save her.

Kane was pacing his office restlessly. 'Tell me about this man,' he demanded of Bradshaw.

'Charlie Hamilton is a forty-one-year-old council employee working at Green Lane, processing admin. His car has the registration number the victim gave me but –'

Kane interrupted impatiently. 'Christ, there's always a "but". What is it?'

'His car isn't silver like she said. It's more of a light metallic blue.'

'Well,' said Kane, 'in that underpass, with not much lighting, maybe it looked silver.'

'Perhaps,' said Bradshaw. 'There's no plastic screen in it either.'

'So he took it out,' said Kane, by way of explanation, 'when he knew the woman would put us on to him.' Then he asked, 'Has he got a wife?'

'He's never been married and currently lives alone.'

'A woman-hater?' asked Kane, almost hopefully, as if Bradshaw could possibly know this purely from the man's marital status.

'There's no record of any violence towards women. However, he has been arrested on a number of occasions.'

'Has he now?' Kane seemed to brighten at that. 'What for?'

'Obstruction, mostly, and one instance of assaulting a police officer.'

'Obstruction?' Kane was puzzled by this. 'But Assault – so he's violent?'

'I'm not so sure about that,' said Bradshaw.

'What do you mean?' snapped Kane. 'He assaulted a fellow officer. Normal people don't do that.'

'It happened at a demo,' Bradshaw explained. 'Some anti-capitalism thing outside a meeting of world leaders up in Scotland. He was on the front line, seemingly, it got a bit heated and he was bundled away. It has happened to him before but, on this occasion, he was charged with assaulting the arresting officer. However, the CPS didn't prosecute him in the end, due to insufficient evidence.'

'What's your point, Bradshaw?'

'Reading between the lines, it looks like the officer who

hauled him out of the demo decided to throw the book at him and might not have had good reason.'

'You think he fabricated it? Go on, say what you mean. You should be a bloody social worker, not a police officer.'

'I'm not saying that at all. I'm just thinking that a struggle between a PC and a demonstrator at an anti-capitalism rally proves nothing about this man. He just doesn't believe in the world order.'

'And wants to bring it down,' argued Kane. 'Violently, if necessary. A man like that could very well be capable of abducting a woman for his own pleasure. Now, go in there, Bradshaw, and get him to admit it.'

'Yes, sir.'

Chapter Thirty-seven

They stuck Charlie Hamilton in an interview room on his own and left him there for a while to make him sweat. Tom and Helen had no involvement in his questioning. This was police business.

'Thank you for agreeing to speak to me,' Bradshaw told him at the beginning of their interview, 'without legal representation.'

'I don't believe in lawyers,' sneered Hamilton.

'For the record, I would like you to confirm you are refusing legal representation.'

'I don't need a lawyer. I haven't done anything. This whole thing is entirely political.'

'Do you know why you are here, Mr Hamilton?'

'I have a pretty good idea.'

'Do you?'

'Yes.'

'Care to enlighten me?'

'Police harassment.' He folded his arms in an aggressive, almost triumphant gesture.

'Police harassment? You're serious?'

'Perfectly. What other reason could there be? I'm a thorn in your side and you will never allow me to carry on with my work.'

'And what work is that? I thought you had a job at County Hall. You work as an administrator, is that right?'

'That's my day job.' He was defensive. 'I've got to eat, but it's not exactly my calling.'

'And what is your calling?'

'I'm an anarchist.'

Bradshaw frowned. 'An anarchist . . . who works for the council.'

'I have to pay my rent, otherwise I'd be homeless, wouldn't I? But all my spare time is devoted to subverting the state.'

'Hence your reference to the pamphlets.'

'Which is why I'm here.'

'I've not seen any pamphlets and we didn't find any when we searched your home.'

'No shit, Sherlock.' The man spoke as if he was still a teenager. He looked like the kind of politics lecturer who routinely calls the police fascists in front of their students to make themselves sound trendy. 'I've handed them all out. They're gone. They're not much use if I keep them in my home, are they?'

'Some would argue they're not much use once you've handed them out. Where do you do that, exactly, so we can find out if you are telling the truth?'

'Lots of places – political rallies, outside the football ground in Newcastle, at Grey's Monument.'

Bradshaw had witnessed numerous men with megaphones shouting at passing shoppers beneath Grey's Monument in the centre of Newcastle. It was ironic that the enormous statue of one of Britain's former prime ministers seemed to attract anti-democratic extremists from both left and right, as well as God-botherers, rainbow warriors and the occasional anarchist like Charlie

Hamilton, all of them wasting their breath as shoppers and football fans swiftly walked by without breaking stride, barely sparing them a glance.

'Right,' said Bradshaw, 'and how do your employers feel about the being-an-anarchist thing?'

'They don't seem to mind.'

'Really. How tolerant of them. You want to bring down the state while working for it. Is that it? You're the enemy within?'

Hamilton scowled at Bradshaw, 'It's a crumbling edifice anyway. I'm just giving it a little push.'

Bradshaw could have argued longer with Hamilton about his political views and the effectiveness of a few pamphlets, but it would have been a waste of time, 'Okay, so now we know how you regard the state, but how do you feel about women?'

'Women?' he asked, as if he had never heard of them.

'Women, yes – you know, females, the opposite sex.'

'I don't feel anything for them. I mean, nothing unusual. What do you mean?'

'Do you have a girlfriend?'

He folded his arms defensively 'You mean, am I a homosexual?'

'No,' said Bradshaw, 'I mean, do you have a girlfriend?'

'Not currently, no.'

'Why not?'

'Is that any of your business?'

'Perhaps not,' admitted Bradshaw, 'but I'm trying to find out a little more about you, Mr Hamilton, because a serious allegation has been made against you, and it has nothing to do with a few pamphlets.'

'Oh, here we go,' snorted Hamilton, and to Bradshaw's surprise the man added: 'What's she been saying?'

Bradshaw looked at Hamilton's scornful face and decided it was time to get to the point. 'That you tried to force her –' Bradshaw was going to add the words *to come with you* but before he could do this Hamilton interrupted him sharply.

'Oh, for fuck's sake. That is ludicrous. That is not what happened. It's not what happened at all.' He was jabbing his finger at Bradshaw now, but he looked rattled.

'Why don't you tell me what happened, then? Let's hear your side of it.'

He seemed reluctant to continue. 'I knew this would happen.' He was staring at the table in front of him, then he looked up and caught Bradshaw's eye. 'I don't wish to sound intolerant of people with mental health problems,' he informed Bradshaw, before adding: 'But she is bloody crazy.'

'Tell me more.'

'Look, we were both drunk . . . way too drunk. She came back to my house and things got a bit out of hand. I thought she wanted to . . . ' He was struggling to find the words.

'Have sex with you?' offered Bradshaw when the pause seemed never-ending.

'Yes,' agreed Hamilton, and Bradshaw realized he was describing an entirely different incident, one which he now assumed had been reported to the police. Bradshaw could have stopped him at that point and got him back on track but he wanted to learn more about Hamilton and just why the man thought the police might be interested in his treatment of another girl. 'And she did sleep with me, in a literal sense. We shared a bed and I thought that meant that she was, you know, up for it.'

'But it turned out she wasn't?'

'Sort of, well, it's not always easy if you don't get a yes or a no.'

'It is easy,' said Bradshaw. 'If you don't get a yes, you can assume it's a no.' He regarded Hamilton closely. 'So what happened? You raped this poor girl?'

'God, no! No, I never did.'

'Then what did you do? It must have been something for you to assume she'd reported you to us when I never even described the incident.'

'I only . . . I just touched her . . . that's all.'

'You touched her?'

'That's all, I swear.'

'You touched her while she was asleep.'

'I'm not sure she was really asleep.'

'But you certainly weren't sure she was awake,' said Bradshaw, 'and you sexually assaulted her?'

'Is that what she's saying? It wasn't like that!'

'What was it like? Did she wake up at that point? Was she distraught? Did she threaten to report you?'

'What has she been saying?' He shook his head violently from side to side. 'I'm not saying anything more. I want a solicitor.'

'Do you? I thought you didn't believe in lawyers. What's the name of this girl?'

He opened his mouth to answer then stopped. 'Well, you know her name, if she made a complaint about me.'

'I never said anyone made a complaint about you

committing a sexual assault on a sleeping girl who was incapable of giving consent,' said Bradshaw, and Hamilton looked sick as he realized his error, 'but we will of course be investigating that. So, tell me her name.'

'I'm saying nothing. It didn't happen, not like that. You're making it up to confuse me. I'm admitting nothing.' Bradshaw watched him for a while and allowed the silence to oppress the younger man, who began to look more and more uncomfortable until finally he managed to say, 'Why did you bring me in here, then? If it wasn't that?'

Bradshaw told him.

'That wasn't me!' Hamilton was wild-eyed. 'How could you think that was me?'

'You're an anarchist,' Bradshaw reminded him. 'You hate the police and don't believe in the rule of law. Why would I assume you believe that any of the rules apply to you? Why is it such a stretch to imagine you just decided to take what you wanted, even if what you wanted didn't want you?'

'It's not . . . that's not what being an anarchist means. I want everyone to live in peace. It doesn't mean grabbing people off the street.'

'And yet you previously committed a sexual assault,' Bradshaw reminded him.

'I did not.'

'Your own words on the tape.' Bradshaw nodded at the recording device that was whirring away quietly in the background.

Hamilton panicked then. 'I said I touched her, not that I assaulted her, and I never said where I touched her. I didn't even give you a name.'

'I'm sure she'll come forward when she learns you are suspected of abducting another woman.'

'What other woman? Who?'

'The woman who fell out of a moving car and clocked your reg plate before you sped away. We found your car in a side street, by the way. We'll get Forensics to look at it, so you might want to think very carefully before you answer my next question. Did you pick up a woman in your car last night in an underpass in Newcastle? Because if you say you didn't and we find traces of her – prints, fibres, DNA – then you'll have a very big problem on your hands. If you did pick her up and there was a row or something and she fell out, then perhaps you can admit that and we'll take it from there.'

'An underpass! What the fuck would I be doing in an underpass? When was this, exactly?'

'I told you – last night. Around eleven fifteen.'

'I was round at my mate's house then.' And he gave Bradshaw a name and address.

'Really? That's handy. You've got a mate who can give you an alibi, have you?'

'Yes! Well, no.'

'Which is it?'

'I went round to see him but he'd fallen asleep on the sofa with his music on and he didn't let me in.'

'High, was he?'

'Just tired.'

'So what did you do?'

'I knocked a few times but when he didn't open up I got back in my car and went home.'

'One of your anarchist mates, was it? Someone else who hates the police and the state? I'm sure they'll believe you both in court when you come up with that story.'

Hamilton looked really scared then. 'I want a lawyer,' he demanded.

Chapter Thirty-eight

It took a couple of hours to equip Hamilton with a solicitor, before they could reconvene. Bradshaw decided to use that time to check out Hamilton's alibi, weak as it was. He drove down to the street in question and knocked on some doors, got what he needed then came back to HQ to examine the evidence before Hamilton's solicitor arrived.

When Bradshaw returned to the interview room he virtually ignored the solicitor. He was holding one of Charlie Hamilton's pamphlets. 'We found this in the boot of your car.' It had an image of a CCTV camera on it with the face of Big Brother, from the film version of George Orwell's *Nineteen Eighty-Four*, looking on approvingly.

'I'm saying nowt more,' Hamilton told him.

'Fine,' said Bradshaw. 'Not a big fan of modern technology, are you, Mr Hamilton?'

'Eh?'

'Big Brother is watching you, and all that.'

'Closed-circuit television, you mean? No, I'm not.' He seemed to have forgotten his claim that he wouldn't say anything more.

'And why is that?'

'It's against ancient civil liberties to be spied on by the state. A man should be able to walk freely around his town without those bloody cameras pointing at him and noting his every move.'

'Most people don't mind it,' said Bradshaw. 'In fact, it usually makes them feel safer to know they are less likely to be attacked in the street by some random drunk.'

'Random drunks don't tend to worry about CCTV before they attack.'

'Nevertheless, violent crime is decreasing in our city centres and it's a trend that's directly attributable to the presence of these cameras, yet you say that's a bad thing.'

'Freedom and liberty are not values to be lightly traded in exchange for the reassuring myth of benign surveillance by a police state.'

'Like I said, most people don't mind them, but then most people haven't got something to hide, have they?'

'I haven't got anything to hide. Not in the way you mean. I just don't like everyone knowing my business.'

'And you didn't try to abduct that girl,' Bradshaw prompted, 'because you were somewhere else at the time, even though she gave us your reg number?'

'How many times have I got to say it? I didn't attack any girl. I was bloody miles away.'

'Yet you can't prove that.'

Hamilton sounded immensely weary. 'No, I can't,' he admitted.

'So, it's your word against hers,' said Bradshaw. 'As it stands.'

'I don't know what else I can do.' He looked defeated. He was out of options and he knew it.

'Okay,' said Bradshaw, 'it's fine. You're free to go.'

'What?' Hamilton was astonished. The solicitor shot a questioning look at the detective sergeant but Bradshaw's face betrayed no emotion. It took Hamilton a moment to digest what he was being told. 'You're saying I can go?'

'Yes.'

'But . . . why? I thought –'

'CCTV,' said Bradshaw, 'on the high street near where your friend lives. You said you went round there and parked up, knocked on his door but, crucially, he didn't let you in, so he wasn't able to corroborate your story. Frankly, even if he had been, he's your mate so we would have remained sceptical.' Bradshaw gave the man a beatific smile. 'However, I managed to obtain the tape from the CCTV camera by the off-licence in that street and I've been through it. Around the time you said you were there, lo and behold, the camera picked you up, parking across from the local pub, getting out of your car and heading down the side street, just like you said.' Bradshaw let that sink in. 'So, thanks to the power of closed-circuit television, you are vindicated and can leave here a free man without a stain on your character. Good old Big Brother, eh?'

First Hamilton looked confused, then he appeared conflicted, but he soon turned resentful. 'I should never have been arrested in the first place.'

'Well, you see, we had reason to believe you may have committed a crime, so we brought you in for questioning. That's how our legal system works. However, because of my diligence, you're off the hook. But there's no need to thank me. I was only doing my job.'

'Enjoying yourself, aren't you?' sneered the man.

'I'm beginning to,' said Bradshaw.

Chapter Thirty-nine

He watched her all the time. Not every moment of the day, perhaps, but he came back far more often now than he had done before, when she was locked in the crate. Did he know she had tried to escape? She had been thinking about that a lot.

Now that Eva was down in the bunker, she never knew when he might come to her. She'd be startled by the sudden sound as the key forced the lock back, and he would walk in unannounced, checking up on her, not that there was anything she could do about her imprisonment, trapped underground like this. Even if there had been a way to escape from the room, she couldn't attempt it when he was likely to appear at any moment.

She was allowed out only to shower. This was her one chance to confront him outside the room. He would march her to the shower room at gunpoint, always a few paces behind her so she couldn't suddenly turn, grab the barrel of the shotgun and struggle with him. They never paused until they were in the shower room, and straight away he would order her to undress. That was the only time his eyes weren't directly on her. Eva sensed that her nudity made him uncomfortable somehow. He didn't entirely disregard her. It was as if he was watching Eva just enough to ensure she didn't do anything. She would walk to the shower, hang the rough towel on a peg at the entrance to the alcove then step inside.

Those were the only moments where he didn't supervise Eva outside of the room. When she was standing in the shower and the water was coming down over her she had a modicum of privacy, but there was nothing she could do to take advantage of it. There wasn't anything of use in the tiny alcove, just the shower screwed to the far wall and the bar of soap he gave her. Being underground, the shower room was windowless and there was nothing here that could be taken and used as a tool or a weapon.

Nothing.

Or so she thought.

Then, one day, when Eva held the shower head tightly in her hand and leaned on it to support herself, as she lifted a leg to soap the soles of her feet, suddenly, she felt it give. Was it loose?

The shower had a slide bar fixed with a bracket. The water supply came from pipes with valves attached that were securely fastened to the wall, and the only part of the shower she could move was the head, but, as it swivelled in her hand, a thought came to her. It was old, it was made of metal and it was heavy.

The shower head was attached to the end of the long metal shower hose and perhaps it was possible to unscrew it and detach it completely.

Eva turned her head and looked behind her, but she couldn't see him. He was usually off to one side while she showered, sitting on the bench by the wall, the shotgun next to him, waiting for her. Did she have enough time? She'd already been in there a while, but she had to risk it. Eva faced the wall and straightened, gripping the shower hose in one hand and taking the metal shower head in the other, then she tensed and twisted both hands in opposite directions.

Nothing happened.

Not at first.

Eva put all her strength into it and tried once more, twisting the shower head, which slowly gave way and began to turn. It was coming loose. She kept on turning until it had done one full rotation.

'What are you doing?'

Eva immediately stopped turning the shower head. Her body was shielding it from view. She pulled the attachment up a little, so the water hit her full in the face.

'Why are you taking so long?'

She half turned to face him and pretended to squint in discomfort. 'Soap in my eyes,' she said, letting the water run down her face as if she had just been rinsing them.

He didn't reply. He just looked at her appraisingly, the balaclava blocking any clue to his thoughts and mood, rendering him expressionless. He wasn't holding the shotgun.

If he didn't believe her now, he might want to examine the shower. She needed to distract him. Her body was side on to him still and she deliberately turned until she was facing him directly and he could see her clearly. His body immediately straightened and he mumbled, 'Be quick,' before sloping away.

Eva turned her attention back to the shower head and quickly screwed it back into place so no one would notice it had been moved.

Next time, she told herself as she left the alcove, sweeping the towel around her.

*

While Bradshaw had been getting nowhere with Charlie Hamilton, Tom had been thinking about Jenna's situation. The desperation and weariness he had seen in Francis Walker's face was not an easy thing to fake, and he genuinely believed the man had nothing to do with this. He'd already come to a very different conclusion, in fact, but it was one he wanted to share with Ian before he spoke to Jenna. They agreed to meet for a pint in the centre of Durham because Bradshaw had a leaving do to attend that night.

Tom was already seated in the Shakespeare pub when Bradshaw walked in. It was a place they both favoured because it was tiny and traditional and the antithesis of the chain pubs that seemed to be springing up everywhere these days.

'Did you get any joy with that ledger?'

'It's not there. I looked for it myself,' Bradshaw assured him. 'Then I called Newcastle, and they haven't got it either.'

Bradshaw sipped his beer and listened intently but without comment while Tom recounted the conversation at the Collingwood Memorial. When he had concluded, Tom said, 'I only really have one question and I think I know the answer already.'

'Go on.' The detective was grim-faced.

'Is there any way that ledger could have been taken from the evidence store and been' – he paused while he searched for the right word – 'misplaced?' He spread his arms to show he was not simply being gullible. 'I'm searching for an innocent explanation here.'

Bradshaw didn't waste their time on a lengthy reply. 'No.'

'That's what I thought.'

'Once it has been sealed as evidence, it wouldn't just be released or thrown in a bin.'

Tom nodded. 'So, really, that just leaves two possible explanations. Someone either sold the ledger to another person who is using it to blackmail the girls or –'

'They are doing it themselves and, either way –'

'They must be a serving police officer,' concluded Tom.

'Exactly.'

Tom's theory did not go down well with Jenna when he dropped by her flat later that evening.

'You think I'm being blackmailed by a policeman?'

'I'd say, having ruled out the only other man who knew you all because he is terrified of ever going back to prison, that yes, on the balance of probability, you are being blackmailed by a police officer.'

'But how?'

'The ledger that was discovered during the raid on Francis Walker's home was used as evidence in court against your former employer, then sealed and placed back with the case files in an evidence store. It should still be there, but my contact in the force asked to take a look at the files and there is no ledger. It's gone. Only someone with access to that evidence could have removed it and it's the only way I can think of that the person who sent those notes could have got details of the women involved. The girls were only picked up by police if they were working that night and most of them were cautioned or given a slap on the wrist. There was no big reveal in the newspapers. The court, the police and even the press were only really interested in the man running the operation, not the girls he had seemingly exploited, so their real names weren't even read out in court.'

'I can't believe it,' Jenna said. 'He's a policeman?'

'Probably.'

'But they're supposed to *catch* criminals.'

'And most of them do,' said Tom. 'The vast majority of them, in fact, but every now and then you get one who is bent and only in it for themselves.'

'But that's terrible.' She seemed utterly bewildered. 'So what do I do?'

'Pay him,' said Tom, and when she looked shocked he told her, 'How else are we going to catch him?'

Chapter Forty

Hugh Rennie's leaving do was a traditional affair, befitting a man in late middle age who was neither especially popular nor unpopular. He was just a regular guy who kept his head down and got on with it for thirty years and was now retiring on a full pension thank you very much. He wasn't an ambitious man – he'd been a DC for as long as anyone could remember – and his lack of drive seemed to extend to his retirement. Asked what he was going to do with his time, he'd merely reply, 'Oh, we'll wait and see,' as if he hadn't even thought about it, though the day had been a long time coming and he'd had ample opportunity to plan for it. There was no job in the private sector lined up, or a scheme to buy a retirement home or go on a world cruise. He seemed happy enough to take each day as it came, just as he had done while on the force.

Even his leaving bash was unambitious. Police parties were notorious for epic lock-ins and hard-core strippers – as long as they picked the right pub and a landlord they knew, then made sure nobody on duty from Uniform turned up to break up the gathering – but this didn't suit Rennie. He'd even ruled against a pub crawl, electing instead to stay put in his favourite city-centre pub. Some of his fellow officers could put in an early appearance then quietly slope away, citing young families at home or an early start the next morning as an excuse. There'd be handshakes and the odd pat on the back, statements about what a lucky man he was, but few would stay till the bitter end, just a couple of fellow old-timers and some of his current squad, who'd feel obliged to ensure he got a good send-off.

When Bradshaw put his head round the door after his pint with Tom, quite a few had already been and gone, though he was surprised to see Kate Tennant propping up the bar, in earnest conversation with DC Malone, a large glass of white wine in her hand. Was this a bit of female solidarity or informal career counselling? More than likely his DI was letting her hair down for probably the first time in a while, and who could blame her?

He crossed the bar to say hello and was immediately intercepted by Rennie, who had already had a few leaving drinks, judging by his flushed complexion and the way he invaded Bradshaw's personal space to give him a man-hug. 'Hey, big fellah!' he called as he clasped Bradshaw to him. 'Didn't think you were going to make it.'

'Wouldn't miss it for the world,' Bradshaw declared. 'Had to make sure you were really leaving.' There was laughter at this from the retiree and some of his peer group, who seemed to communicate to one another almost entirely through banter.

To Bradshaw's general incredulity, he had a bloody good night. He almost always felt like an outsider in this team, and the force in general, but there was an air of frivolity that evening, with petty squabbles and long-standing differences of opinion largely put aside once the drink flowed, as everyone got high on the jovial atmosphere caused by Hugh's escape. No one wanted to put a damper on things, so office talk was unofficially banned. Instead it was all about what they would do if they were in Hugh's shoes. Bradshaw couldn't even imagine being a police officer for another twenty years, or being in his fifties; it seemed like such a distant prospect. There was a bit of talk about football, too, and how Newcastle United were bound to finally win something now they had the world's most expensive player in Alan Shearer, and as always there was lots and lots of piss-taking.

Bradshaw stayed till closing time, which he hadn't intended to do, and Kate Tennant was also one of the last ones standing, along with DC Malone. who was way more drunk than her DI, and considerably louder, incapable of expressing herself at all by the end without shouting.

Kate Tennant said she'd called a cab to get her and DC Malone home safely and she told Bradshaw he could cadge a lift with them but to keep it to himself. She meant she didn't want half a dozen drunken old relics competing for a free ride home. 'Hopefully, Malone is throwing up in the toilet *before* we get her into the cab.'

Bradshaw took that moment to congratulate Rennie on his retirement, so he could leave without any delay. He knew that trying to extricate yourself from a lads' night out, when the lads in question don't want you to leave, could be a protracted affair, involving the refusal of further pints ('Just have one for the road!'), challenges to his manhood ('What are you, a man or a mouse?') and most probably a few barbs about him leaving with not one but two women this time ('Well, lads, someone has to keep them out of trouble.')

Rennie was, predictably, drunk, as you would expect,

since he had bought everyone in the bar a drink and they had all insisted on buying him one back. At one stage he had three full pints lined up on the bar while he struggled to finish the one he was drinking. He was still on his feet, though, and able to talk fairly clearly, if a little loud and unsteady on his feet.

'Listen, there was something I was going to tell you.' He was leaning heavily on Bradshaw's shoulder now and the detective sergeant was worried, in case Rennie was going to say he had always hated the younger man then start an argument, or even a fight. It wouldn't do to knock a man out in the car park after his own leaving do.

'When you asked me the other day' – his hand gripped Bradshaw's shoulder more tightly, but instinct told Bradshaw this wasn't aggression, it was more like a confession – 'who had questioned the girl who claimed she had been kept prisoner for a year, I said I'd forgotten, and I had.' He nodded significantly. 'But for some reason, now that I am officially retired, well, let's just say it's all starting to come back to me.'

'Right, mate,' said Bradshaw, who understood what Rennie was saying completely. 'So what exactly has come back to you?'

'The name of the man who questioned her, all those years ago.'

'Who was it? Hugh?'

'Edward Tyler,' said Rennie.

'Oh, Jesus Christ,' said Bradshaw, immediately recalling the furious senior officer surrounded by journalists in the car park.

'Not quite,' slurred the retiree. 'He just thinks he is.' And he picked up his pint glass to make a mock-toast. 'To Deputy

Chief Constable Edward Tyler, who was just a young prick back then but is now . . . a complete and utter bastard.'

'Bloody hell.' Bradshaw couldn't believe it.

'Good luck, my friend.' Rennie smiled at him and slapped him heartily on the shoulder. 'You're going to need it.'

Police Vendetta Could Cost Lives

BY OUR CRIME CORRESPONDENT

A political activist has lashed out at police for showing a 'reckless disregard for human life'. Charlie Hamilton, 32, is suing Durham Constabulary for wrongful arrest and is demanding damages and an apology. He claims he was picked up by the force because of his personal views, which had nothing to do with the case they were looking into.

Police arrested Hamilton following a report of an attempted abduction of a young woman in a Newcastle underpass. He was detained for hours and repeatedly questioned about a crime he could not have committed because he was miles from the scene when it happened. His version of events was proven by a simple examination of CCTV footage in the area.

'The police wouldn't believe me and kept going on about my political ideology, as if that somehow made me a potential killer,' he said. 'The whole thing has been a scandal and a complete waste of my time and theirs. Why aren't they out there looking for the real culprit? Unlike the police, I am concerned he might strike again. That's why I am making this claim. It's not about the money.'

Chapter Forty-one

'*Why aren't they out there looking for the real culprit?*' DCI Kane read the accusing words from their former suspect to his slightly hungover DS. 'Well, Bradshaw, why *aren't* you out there looking for the real culprit?'

'To be honest, sir, it hadn't crossed my mind,' he said dryly.

'We'll be sure to thank Mr Hamilton for his expert advice when this case is over,' and he rolled up the newspaper and dropped it into the bin.

'It won't actually go anywhere, will it?'

'Years ago, we'd have told him to piss off, but I had a meeting with the top brass and a lawyer, and they're talking about offering him thirty grand to drop the case, as long as he signs a gagging order.'

'They can't be serious?' Bradshaw could tell by Kane's face that they were.

'I'd gag him all right,' mumbled Kane, 'then beat him with a bit of lead piping. Let's hope they eventually come to their senses but, frankly, your approach didn't help.'

'How do you mean?'

'Smashing down his door and bursting in like that with guns.'

'Hang on. You told Malone we had to be careful and not take any risks. What if it had been the right man? Nobody would have minded then.'

'They wouldn't,' admitted Kane. 'But he wasn't, so they do.'

'I can't bloody win.'

'Of course you can't, Bradshaw,' said Kane. 'You're a police officer. We never win, you should know that by now. We have shit dropped on us from above and in the newspapers no matter what we do, but there's no point sulking about it. You've got to get on with it. Just don't kick any more doors in or haul suspects out at gunpoint, you hear? Not unless we have a bloody good reason to suspect there is someone armed standing behind that door. Softly, softly from now on, lad.' Then he noticed the slight look of apprehension on Bradshaw's face. 'What is it?' he asked.

Bradshaw had slept on it, but the problem hadn't gone away, which is why he had come to see Kane. The one man who could recall the questioning of the stoned girl was now not just top brass, he was the deputy chief constable, a man with a savage reputation for utter ruthlessness towards anyone foolish enough to cross him, by accident or by design. Worse than that, the man was a hair's breadth from the top job, which meant he would soon be all-powerful and very unlikely to permit anyone to dredge up a potentially embarrassing episode from his past. But Bradshaw had no choice if he wanted to find the truth. Edward Tyler was the witness he needed to question. However, to even speak to the deputy chief constable about this case would be putting his own career on the line, a fact that was swiftly confirmed by Kane when he broke the news to his DCI.

'You *are* kidding me,' said Kane. 'Of all the people.' He shook his head for emphasis. 'Of *all* the bloody people. It couldn't just be a long-retired DS or someone even halfway up the food chain, it had to be the right hand of God Almighty Himself, didn't it? Bloody hell, what are you going to do?'

Bradshaw was taken aback by the question. 'Well, that's why I came to see you, sir.'

'It's your decision, Bradshaw. It's your case, and you must choose the direction you take it.'

This was news to Ian Bradshaw. In the past he had been given the distinct impression that, when it came to awkward moments in difficult cases, he didn't have the authority to sneeze unless he asked permission from an adult first. Now it appeared he was suddenly on his own, and all because he had mentioned the chief constable-elect. In the second or two before he answered his senior officer, Bradshaw had worked out the politics involved. Both men knew that it was an obvious move to question or at least informally speak with Edward Tyler. In some instances, this might have been a relatively easy thing to arrange and would probably be well worth it. Even if it ruled out a link between the cases it would free them up to concentrate on other leads. That would have been fine if Tyler had been a different kind of man, instead of the rapaciously political figure he actually was. Kane did not want to tell Bradshaw to drop it, in case it later turned out that the deputy chief constable's information proved vital and the DCI could be accused of hampering his detective sergeant's investigation. However, neither did he want to be seen as the driving force behind a decision to question such a senior figure in case the man took offence and then a personal interest in sabotaging both their careers further down the line. He wanted Bradshaw's intervention to look as if it was entirely his own idea.

'Well, sir, I do think that, despite the political implications, it would be useful to interview the deputy chief constable about the events of that day.'

There was a short pause while his DCI surveyed him with an emotionless stare, giving nothing away.

'Right then, lad,' he said eventually. 'You'd better set that up.'

'Er . . . how would I go about doing that, sir?' He had assumed his DCI might have been the best person to approach the senior man.

'Put a request in to his office – politely, of course – and make sure it's in writing,' said Kane. 'That way, it can't just be ignored.' Bradshaw guessed that what he really wanted was a paper trail that had someone else's name on it. 'Then, if you're lucky, they'll get back to you with a slot in his diary.'

'How do you want me to handle this?'

'With kid gloves, obviously. There has to be a very careful balancing act between finding out the truth and not scuppering your own future in the process. You'll be out on a limb.'

Bradshaw was beginning to feel entirely isolated already, and he didn't like it. 'I would appreciate it, sir, if you would back me.'

'It doesn't make any difference whether I back you or not.'

'Of course it does,' said Bradshaw, then he added the word: 'sir.'

'You clearly don't understand, so let me spell it out for you. The deputy chief constable is a fucking great killer whale who could rip me apart as a snack.' Kane let Bradshaw digest that. 'If you upset him for no good reason, if you, God forbid, derail his career in any way, we won't have to imagine the worst thing he can do to us because it will happen; that, I promise you.'

'But how is that allowed to occur?' protested Bradshaw. 'If I ask him a few legitimate questions and he gets upset about them, how is he allowed to demote me or ship me out somewhere terrible as a punishment for trying to find out the truth? There are rules, aren't there, that even he has to follow?'

Kane sighed at his naivety. 'Of course there are rules, Bradshaw, which is why, when it happens, no one will be able to point a finger and prove he was behind it or why. It'll be something else that gets you busted to DC or put back in uniform – an expenses form you filled out carelessly; a complaint from a member of the public that wouldn't normally be upheld; medical grounds, from those counselling session you've had.' He shrugged. 'It could be anything, and I'm telling you, you'll end up in Siberia if he wants you to.' He took a deep breath and checked to see if Bradshaw was taking him seriously. 'So I suppose the question is, what are you prepared to do in order to get this information you need and just how far do you really want to push it?'

Bradshaw contemplated this for a time then said, 'Is he really as bad as they say?'

'Oh no' – Kane was dismissive – 'he's way worse. His nickname used to be the Rottweiler, and not just because it rhymed with Tyler.'

'Used to be?'

'Then someone pointed out that a pit bull would be a more accurate comparison. You see, they're every bit as vicious,' Kane reminded him, 'and they never let go.'

Chapter Forty-two

They were married days after her eighteenth birthday and it was a matter of weeks before Ingrid became pregnant. God's will, he had to assume. Maybe it was for the best. It would settle her down, he thought at the time. When she announced she was going to have a baby he went out and bought her a silver chain with a cross. He placed it around her neck and told her, 'This is to remind you that God will always be with you. He sees everything and knows all.' He said he hoped the necklace would enable her to remember that, whenever she grew restless. He himself hoped that the responsibility of a child would help to banish the old Ingrid, but it didn't, at least not entirely. She loved the child, or so it seemed to him, but she quickly grew bored being at home all day and kept wanting to go out, which she couldn't do on her own. He wouldn't permit it. He needed to keep her and the child safe; away from other people who might try and influence her. He made sure she had no money. Every few weeks he would take her somewhere, but it was never enough and he grew angry with her. Why did she want other things when she had a home, a husband, a child? What possible reason could she have to miss the old days, the unsuitable friends?

Sometimes he would return home to find her crying,

and he couldn't understand why she wasn't happier or more grateful that he had saved her from her former life, from herself in fact, because he knew she had it in her to be wicked.

That was why he chose the new life for them both. When he left the air force he brought her back to England with him to start again. He knew just the place.

But Ingrid got worse. Her English was good enough for her to make friends and fit in, but he didn't want her to. He needed them to live away from other people. How could you form attachments to anyone when you knew they were all going to die soon? He tried to explain it to Ingrid but she became more argumentative and troublesome. He knew she was going to leave him then, one day. It was inevitable. It was only a question of what he would say to the child when she was gone.

Chapter Forty-three

There were pieces of paper and bits of white card all over Tom's kitchen table, along with pens and pencils. He looked like a particularly disorganized kid trying to complete his school homework, an image that was heightened by the half-drunk mug of cold tea he was using as a paperweight. Helen had let Bradshaw in but Tom continued with the task that was occupying him.

'What are you doing?' asked the detective.

'The woman who jumped from the car in the underpass,' Tom recalled, 'had the presence of mind, despite being quite badly hurt, to remember the reg number as it drove away at speed.'

'That's what she said, but she did forget it, evidently,' said Bradshaw, 'because we traced the car and the owner and we know from the CCTV footage that he wasn't in the underpass when she fell from that vehicle, and neither was his car. It wasn't even the right colour.'

'And there's no way to have two cars with the exact same registration plate.' It was not a question, more a statement of fact.

'It's not impossible,' conceded Bradshaw in a tone which said he didn't buy it, 'but it's highly unlikely. Criminals usually steal plates rather than try and fake them, and his plates definitely weren't stolen, since they were still on his car.'

'So, she forgot the number she saw, which could easily happen if you've had a bit to drink or suffer a bang to the head after falling from a speeding car?'

'That's looking like the official line on this one.'

'Or she was mistaken,' said Tom, and he let that thought hang without explaining himself further.

'What's going through that devious mind of yours?'

'I don't know,' he admitted, 'but do you think we could have a look down there?'

'In the underpass? I've already been,' explained Bradshaw. 'With the Uniform who found her.'

'Can you meet me there tonight at the exact same time the incident took place, do you think?'

'Well, I was going to stay in and wash my hair,' said Bradshaw, 'but okay.'

Chapter Forty-four

1977

Wives, submit to your husbands as to the Lord.
— Ephesians 5:22

'Why do you make me do it?' he asked her, not for the first time. 'Why do you *always* make me do it?'

Ingrid was lying on the floor like a dog, one hand pressed hard against the bruise that was already forming on the side of her face, a red welt that marked her punishment. She wasn't sobbing this time, though. Perhaps she knew it would make no difference. Samuel was resolute and would never let weeping prevent him from chastising her or correcting her behaviour.

'Why don't you ever learn?' he asked her. 'Why are you so incredibly stupid? Don't you realize where you would be without me? Don't you understand that you are' — he searched for the right word then found it – 'nothing?'

She moved her hand. There was blood on her cheek now, and a large red mark. It looked bad. He didn't recall hitting her hard enough to cause that, though. It must have happened when she fell to the floor, so it couldn't have been his fault.

None of this would have happened if she just listened

to him and did as she was told. Had he not already told her the words of the apostle Paul, who said about wives, 'And if they will learn anything, let them ask their husbands at home.' He taught her this passage because she told him he had no right to keep her prisoner.

Prisoner? What a ridiculous notion. He would perhaps let her go out one day, if she could be trusted, but Ingrid was very far from that point. It seemed as if she had learned nothing since they had come here. He was trying to leave a crazy and doomed world behind them.

'Well?' he demanded again. 'Why don't you ever learn?'

She moved then, but slowly, and winced in pain, holding her arm tight in to her ribs, where he had first struck her when she questioned him. The memory of it came back to him and his anger increased. *I do not permit a woman to have authority over man, she must be silent.* That was St Paul, too, but Ingrid wanted to defy the words of a saint. Who did she think she was?

'Answer me,' he told her. 'Why are you so stupid?'

She climbed unsteadily to her feet then and glared back at him, but she no longer looked like the cowed woman he had seen following previous corrections. When she spoke, she almost spat the words and there was defiance in her. 'I don't know. Maybe I'm crazy . . . or maybe it's you!'

Their eyes locked and she looked as if she wanted to kill him. He could see the hatred there. He was about to hit her again but thought better of it when he noticed the look in her eyes. Samuel would have to sleep at some point and he no longer trusted her. He focused his attention on the cross that hung around her neck and wondered why she could not be inspired by it to obey him, as God intended.

The silence between them was broken by a piercing wail.

He challenged her with his eyes but she didn't move.

'The child is crying,' he said in disbelief. She wasn't even fit to be a mother.

She bared her teeth at him, exposing bleeding gums, and it made him recoil from her.

Finally, she went to the child.

When she was gone he considered the problem of Ingrid. Their Bible study wasn't making her better. If anything, she was getting worse. What was he supposed to do with her? She hadn't learned: Ingrid was not modifying her behaviour, nor was she an obedient wife. He wondered now what he had seen in her. Was there really something special hidden inside the skinny girl he had met outside the NAAFI, something which spoke to him of redemption, hers and his? Had he been blinded by the desire to save her and deliver her from evil or was there a darker reason? Had Ingrid tempted him, using the promise of the sins of the flesh to lead him away from the path to true righteousness? Had she seduced him with those same eyes that were now so full of hatred for him? Had he in fact been bewitched?

Another Bible verse popped into his head: *Do not allow a sorceress to live.*

Immediately he banished the thought from his mind, the sound of their crying child racking him with guilt. Perhaps if she just left and went away somewhere? Surely that would be for the best.

As long as she left him the child. The future depended on the child.

Chapter Forty-five

When DS Bradshaw drove into the underpass, Tom was already waiting for him on the pavement by the side of the road. There were no other vehicles there. The unlicensed cabdrivers had heard about the recent police operation and been frightened off.

Bradshaw parked and got out of his car and Tom asked to see the exact spot where the woman had fallen. Bradshaw showed him, and the journalist glanced down at the pavement then looked towards the exit, which was some way off.

'She must have good eyes,' said Tom, 'to see a reg plate from this distance.'

'She does, apparently.'

'But this place is gloomier than a Goth's wardrobe.'

Bradshaw saw that he had a point. There was some lighting in the underpass, but it had been neglected. One or two of the lamps had no bulbs and the ones that still worked shone without giving much illumination. Their plastic covers were filthy and the dirt masked the light. 'You don't believe she could have seen it?'

'I believe she could have,' said Tom, 'just that it might have been difficult with a moving car and the impact from her fall.'

'She was adamant.' Bradshaw reminded him. 'But it seems she was wrong.'

'What are your eyes like?'

'Do you see me wearing bifocals? I've got perfect eye-sight.' Bradshaw realized he sounded a little defensive, possibly because the last resort of a desperate lawyer in a courtroom was often to question what the arresting officer had actually seen and whether he might have been mistaken.

'Let's give it a go, then.'

'Give what a go?'

Tom took some long thin pieces of card from his ruck-sack. 'You are the girl and I'm the speeding car.'

'Okay.'

Tom walked a few paces away from Bradshaw towards the exit then stopped, turned around and looked back at the detective. 'What?' asked Bradshaw.

'That's not how it was,' Tom reminded him. 'She wasn't just standing there.'

'Oh, for God's sake,' moaned Bradshaw. 'I'd have put old clothes on if you'd warned me.' With a sigh the detec-tive lowered himself till he was on one knee, then he lay down on the pavement, feeling foolish. He twisted round so he was on the ground but facing towards the exit, in a loose approximation of the woman's position that night.

'What exactly have you got there?'

'The reg number,' Tom told him. 'Hang on.' He walked the final yards to the exit and stood at the point where the car would have had to slow to take the bend on to the road. He then held the reg number he had scrawled on to one of the pieces of card at approximately the right height.

'The letters are exactly the same size as a number plate,' he assured the detective. 'Now, what can you see?'

'I can see the reg number she gave us,' Bradshaw informed him. 'Clearly, even in this light.'

'All right.' Tom switched the card for another one with a different registration number on it. 'What do you see now?'

Bradshaw read it out. It wasn't easy, but he took his time and felt he had picked out every letter.

'Good,' said Tom. He tried another card. 'What do you see now?'

'Same number as the reg plate she gave us . . . but you've changed it by one letter. There's an A where there should be an E.'

'Well spotted.'

'I *am* a detective,' Bradshaw reminded Tom. 'Are you done?'

'Almost.'

Twice more Tom held up a different card with a new reg number and got Bradshaw to recite it, then he held up a third card, which had the same reg number as the one the girl had identified. Bradshaw was able to correctly read them all.

When he did it again, Bradshaw became impatient. 'Come on, it's hacky on this floor.' He wanted to get up and brush the thick grey dust from his coat and trousers.

'Last one!' called Tom, and he held the final card up.

It was the number the woman had given the police and Bradshaw impatiently informed Tom of this. Then he got to his feet and brushed his coat with his hands as Tom came towards him.

'I knew it,' the journalist told him.

'You knew what?'

'I've been playing around with that reg number, examining the letters, considering the possibilities, and that last one . . .'

'What about it?'

'You got it wrong.'

'What?' snapped Bradshaw. 'No, I didn't.'

'You did.' Tom held it up. 'But only by one letter, and it is an entirely forgivable error.'

Bradshaw peered at the final card and realized to his astonishment that Tom was right.

'Down here, in this gloom, lying on your back and twisting your head to stare at a moving car, it would be very easy to make the same mistake. When you look at a reg plate the letter X looks very like the letter K and, under these circumstances, it's almost identical.' Tom let that sink in before adding: 'Which means that we have been looking for the wrong car.'

Chapter Forty-six

He stood facing her as Eva removed her clothes, holding the shotgun loosely. She walked naked to the shower and hung the towel on the peg. She turned the dial and the water came down, cold at first, as usual; it would gradually rise in temperature until peaking at tepid. She didn't wait for that, though. She gasped as she stepped under the cold water, ignoring the discomfort as she went to work on the shower head, which turned slowly as she began to unscrew it from the hose. Eva imagined him sitting there on the bench, shotgun by his side, waiting impatiently for her to finish washing. She had to be quick.

It took five full turns before the shower head gave way and came free from the hose, the water shooting out on to her in a torrent instead of a measured flow. She hoped the change in sound wouldn't alert him. She took the hose out of the slide bar and let it fall so the water would flow straight down, then placed the head on the floor by her side. If she finished washing too soon he would be suspicious, but if he came in now she could say it broke free. She washed herself as she normally would, sticking to the usual routine, then, when she was finished, she turned the shower off and picked up the heavy metal shower head.

Eva reached around for her towel with one hand and wiped her face with it while holding the shower head in the other hand, hidden from view by the alcove wall. She dried her body quickly before wrapping the towel around the shower head, which she now held parallel to her arm. It might look as if she was simply holding her towel over one arm when she stepped out and she was gambling he wouldn't scrutinize her naked form too closely. He didn't like to do that and he had no reason to suspect anything.

Eva stepped out of the shower, her heart thumping. He was sitting on the bench waiting, the gun next to him, her clothes close by. He picked up the gun and placed it over his lap so he could level it at any moment, but he didn't point it directly at her. She kept the towel that was hiding the shower head on her right side so it was partially hidden as she walked towards the bench and made as if to pick up her clothes, but as she bent to do this she removed the towel from her right hand with her left. This was it.

Everything happened very fast. The towel fell on to the bench then slipped on to the floor; Eva turned towards him and raised her right arm. He must have seen it then, the shower head she was clutching. He had hardly any time to react and she brought it crashing down on the top of his head with a cry. The blow rocked him and he seemed to sway on the bench, but she could tell he was still trying to lift his gun. She couldn't let that happen. Eva knew she had to be strong. She hit him again, putting everything she had behind a sickening blow, and he dropped the gun, pitched forward and fell on to the floor.

He lay still then and she thought of picking up the gun and shooting him where he lay, but if he was unconscious, would that be self-defence, or murder? In any case, he had fallen across the gun and she didn't think she could roll him off it. All her senses were screaming at her to just get out of there as quickly as she could and call the police. They could deal with this madman.

Eva grabbed her clothes, ran out into the corridor and started to pull them on. If only there was a lock on the shower room and she had the key. She could have locked him in there then, but she couldn't dwell on that impossibility. As soon as she was dressed she ran all the way back down the corridor, revelling in the feeling of her bare feet slapping against the concrete floor, powering away from him.

Had she killed him? Would she care if she had? Maybe she should have finished the job while she had the chance? Was she capable of such a brutal act, even against her captor? He was unconscious now, but how long for – a minute, ten, longer? The uncertainty made her run even faster.

She reached the bottom of the hatch and started to climb the ladder. Almost as soon as her foot touched the bottom rung she heard it. The sound of the shower-room door being wrenched open. Oh God, so soon. How could he have got up again so quickly? Was he not human?

Eva reached the fourth step, but in her haste her wet foot slid on the rung and she slipped, falling straight back down to the bottom and banging her chin hard against one of the higher rungs in the process. Ignoring the jarring pain, she climbed again, as fast as she dared; she could not afford to slip again.

She could hear the sound of a man running and she tried to focus on the ladder and her climb to the hatch. She could see it clearly above her now. It was tantalizingly close.

She reached the top a moment later, grabbed the wheel that turned the hatch then twisted.

Nothing happened.

The hatch was locked somehow, but how? She looked for a padlock or a space for a key, but there was nothing. Perhaps it was just too tight for her. Eva strained against the hatch and put everything into it. Slowly, it began to give.

Once she had broken its resistance, the wheel began to turn. A surge of hope went through Eva and she kept on twisting the wheel until the hatch felt loose enough to be opened. With a surge of exhilaration that gave her strength, she pushed hard and the hatch moved upwards then fell back. A burst of cold fresh air hit her.

She was free.

'Don't move!'

Eva froze, not daring to look down. She could tell from his voice he was directly below her. He sounded determined, confident even, in control, and she knew why. He was pointing the shotgun right up at her. His words were a warning as well as a command.

She had a choice to make. Submit and go back down inside to her underground hell and an almost certain death or try to make a break for it and hope he didn't fire? He could hardly miss from this range. Would it be better to die that way? He would surely kill her now anyway – or was there a chance he would let her live if she gave in to him? She thought back to the blows she had administered to his head and how tough he must be to have got up so quickly and chased after her. She could only guess the pain he was in. He'd want revenge.

Run for it, Eva. Run.

And then he would shoot her. It would be over, at least,

but what if she didn't die immediately? What damage would that shotgun inflict on her? What terrible injuries and horrific disfigurement would she have to endure?

She forced herself to look down. He was standing there, right below her, aiming upwards.

'Get down.'

Make your choice, Eva. Do something!

But she knew what she had to do already. He was too close and the gun was aimed straight at her. She wouldn't be able to take another step before he fired. There was no hope of escape. Eva took one last gulp of cold fresh air and a final glance at the sky above her then made her decision. Slowly, reluctantly, she climbed back down into the bunker, knowing this might be the last thing she ever did.

As soon as her feet touched the ground at the bottom of the ladder the air was knocked out of her. All it took was a jab in the stomach from the shotgun and she collapsed like someone had just pulled the plug on her. As she lay groaning on the cold, hard ground she told herself she was still alive. He hadn't fired the gun.

He picked her up by grabbing the back of her shirt then hauling her upwards and dragging her along. She managed to stagger back down the corridor until she reached her room. He gave her a final thump in the back with the butt of the shotgun which propelled her forwards to the bed. He pushed her on to her back then pinned one of her arms at the wrist with one hand and clamped the other around her throat, hard, as he climbed on top of her. His grip was so strong Eva started to choke and she instinctively grabbed at his arm with her free hand but the muscles felt like iron and she couldn't budge him. He was so close she could smell the sweat from him. His balaclava had a dark stain on its side and she knew it must have been blood from the blow to the top of his head. He squeezed harder, until she thought her eyes were about to pop out. She could feel the fury in him. She tried to wriggle free but she couldn't break away from his grip.

Eva's hopes ended then. He'd only brought her back in here to kill her, but without using the gun. He'd strangle her here instead. It was all over.

She couldn't fight. She couldn't breathe. She felt her throat compressing as she fought for a last breath. Then she gave up. It had all been for nothing.

He let go of her suddenly and let out a snarl of frustration, releasing his grip. There was a great gasping sound as she exhaled, the pressure on her throat released all at once, then she took in great breaths, fighting for air between choking coughs that racked her whole body.

'No, no, no!' He was shouting the word over and over, but not at her. It was as if he was berating himself, not Eva. 'There have to be five!' He brought his hands up to his head, as if he was in turmoil.

Then, abruptly, he went to the door. 'I'll be back for you!' he shouted as he stepped through it. 'Maybe I'll put you back in the crate for good!' He slammed the door behind him and locked it from the outside, while Eva gasped and coughed and tried to breathe in great lungfuls of the stale air around her as she attempted to take in the most surprising and unlikely part of it all.

Somehow, she was still alive.

Chapter Forty-seven

Jenna had been downstairs for a while when she remembered the milk delivery. She always got up early and enjoyed the calm before the working day in the shop began. She had glanced at the mat by the door as soon as she came down the stairs and, thankfully, there was no new note waiting for her there. She opened the door, picked up the milk bottles and straightened up. That was when she saw him, leaning nonchalantly against the wall on the other side of the road, staring right back at her.

She almost dropped the milk. She wasn't sure how but she knew instantly that this was her tormentor. Maybe it was the way he was looking at her, with a faint trace of amusement on his face, because he knew the real Jenna, or possibly it was the unforgiving demeanour of the man. He looked so big and powerfully built, which added to her sense of helplessness. How the hell could she stand up to someone like this? When he spoke, his words were accompanied by the sneer of the bully.

'Come on,' he told her, and jerked his head to one side to indicate she should follow him. 'We've got things to discuss.'

Bradshaw did not expect to be convinced. He was hugely sceptical, in fact, until he ran a check on the number plate the next morning. Then he called Tom with the results.

'That registration' – he explained himself further – 'the one you came up with, I mean.'

'What did you find?'

'It's from the region. The first letter in a reg plate is the age identifier, which gives us the year of registration; the last two letters are the area identifier, and those have stayed the same. The letter you are querying gives the vehicle its unique identity, along with the numbers. The registered owner of the car is a Mr Joe McEwan, and he lives in the area.'

'Do we know anything about him?'

'Ex-serviceman, fought in Iraq in '91.'

Tom knew this might be significant then instantly felt some guilt. On one level, an ex-serviceman had selflessly volunteered to put himself into danger, risking his life to serve his country in a war zone. The man was a hero, obviously. There was a flip side to this, though, and both he and Ian Bradshaw knew it. The vast majority of armed forces personnel could get through a war, return to their families and go on to lead very normal lives. Others were adversely affected by the experience. Killing changed a man, no matter what the circumstances, and many struggled to live with what they had done. Some, however, actually enjoyed the experience or had perhaps already been a bit unhinged before they signed up. This was not just a prejudice Tom held. He had known a lot of army veterans, having interviewed survivors of the Korean and Falklands wars and the Second World War during his career as a journalist. Every one of them was a good man but each had stories to tell of less fine ones who had fought alongside them. Then there was the ten per cent of the prison population who had served. That meant around six thousand former members of the armed forces had been convicted of crimes serious enough to put them in jail. It was a sobering thought.

'Anyway, I wanted to let you know that we are bringing McEwan in.'

Jenna left the milk on the doorstep and closed then locked the door behind her. She had to move quickly to keep up with the man as he walked briskly along the high street. She hoped no one would see him and ask her later who he was.

She drew alongside and waited for him to say something, her heart thumping in her chest, but he remained silent. She couldn't abide it. 'Who are you?' she blurted out. 'What do you want?'

Was this really a police officer? He looked more like a criminal or a hooligan; a big thug of a man. He didn't even look at her. 'I think the real question, Jenna, is who are you?' He said it airily, as if it was just a little matter he was keen to clear up. 'Nice little place, this; good, decent folk with polite, well-behaved kids, mostly. I can see why you might want to make a home here. It's a world away from the . . . *life* you knew.'

His words pierced her, each one wounding and weakening her, robbing her of the will to stand up to him.

'It would be terrible if they found out just who had been living among them. Imagine their shock when they learn the truth about the woman who serves sweets to their kids or sits near their husbands in the pub, all on her own, pretending to read a book while secretly' – he turned to look at her and raised his eyebrows significantly – 'it's what they'd think, isn't it?'

It *was* what they would think, she knew that.

'I've been looking for you,' he told her. 'You took a bit of tracking down. The others were easier, but you' – he shook his head – 'you went further afield. These days, though, who can disappear for long, eh? And what did I find' – he smirked at her then – 'a pillar of the community; the lady who sells groceries to the villagers and has bar meals in the pub of an evening. I bet she even goes to church on Sundays?'

Jenna could not speak at this point, even if she had wanted to.

'No? That's a bit much, I suppose, even for you, Jenna. I suspect your confession might take quite a while.' He chuckled to himself at that.

'Don't worry. I'm the only who knows your little secret, and I might even be prepared to keep it that way.' He beamed at her. 'For a small consideration.'

He told her the figure then. It was far from small but not as bad as she had imagined. 'Then you'll go away?' she asked hopefully. 'You'll leave me alone?'

He snorted. 'You're joking, love. That's not a flat fee. I expect to see it every month from now on.'

It was too much.

'I . . .' she began, but faltered.

'Tell you what I'll do,' he said brightly. 'I'll leave you alone for a while so you can make up your mind. I'll be back in touch. I'm pretty certain you'll see things my way.' Then he was striding ahead of Jenna, but he turned back before he reached the corner. 'The others did.'

Chapter Forty-eight

The former soldier wasn't exactly cooperative, nor did he resist them when they knocked on the door of his home, a static caravan in a holiday park not far from Seahouses. Bradshaw had uniformed officers with him, to assist with a search of the surrounding area. There wasn't much in the caravan apart from the basics needed to survive: food and cooking pots, a pillow and a bed roll that was tied and tucked into a tiny wardrobe so the bed could be folded away to make more living space. The man led a spartan existence that aroused some suspicion. Bradshaw asked him to come in voluntarily for questioning and he complied.

Joe McEwan was another man who was convinced he didn't need a solicitor. Bradshaw had barely come across anyone who had turned one down before being questioned. Now he found himself talking to a second suspect within days who had waived his rights, even if Charlie Hamilton had changed his mind pretty quickly, once he knew he was in trouble.

McEwan sat impassively before him now, a tall, stocky man with long, unkempt hair and an unshaven face. His hands were dirty, the nails filthy, as if he had been fixing something before they brought him in.

'Let's be clear for the tape that the right to a solicitor has been declined,' Bradshaw said. 'Against the advice given.' He added that part in case anyone tried to claim

McEwan had been bullied into turning down legal representation.

'I don't need a solicitor.' The tone was dismissive.

'Because you haven't done anything, is that it?'

The face that looked up at him was so calm it was almost saintly. 'We've all done things, Detective, but none of it matters in the end. We are all just meat.'

'We are all just meat? That's an unusual thing to say.'

'But it's true. All flesh is weak and all flesh must die.' He shrugged, as if this was likely to happen at any moment, not at some far-off point in the future.

'You are saying it doesn't matter what we do, just to clarify that?'

'I'm saying what we do doesn't matter in the long run, since none of us will be here to talk about it and the world will keep on turning without us. In the meantime, we should probably try to help one another. It would be a grim old life if we didn't do that.'

'So, you'll help *me*?' asked Bradshaw. 'With my inquiries?'

'If I can,' said the ex-soldier.

'You haven't even asked me what they're about. People usually want to know why they are being questioned.'

'Figure you have your reasons. Misguided ones, obviously,' he said. 'Go on, then – what are you inquiring about?'

'A woman was abducted.' Bradshaw gave the soldier the briefest possible account. He had the right to know why he was being questioned, but Bradshaw didn't want to give him any details he didn't have to, in case the suspect revealed something under questioning that only the culprit could have known.

'Well, I haven't abducted anyone.'

'Let's start with where you were that night.' And he told McEwan the date and time.

'At home.'

'Can anyone corroborate that?'

'No.'

'No one living nearby saw you around that time?'

'I live in a static caravan on a caravan park. Most of the caravans are empty unless it's peak season, especially during the week. There aren't many of us here all year round. People who live in a place like this tend to want to keep themselves to themselves. They don't socialize.'

'Why is that?'

He shrugged. 'Some move here to get away from people, and some have very little money. That tends to make them grumpy and possibly a little embarrassed about their predicament.'

'That include you?' asked Bradshaw. 'Do you want to keep yourself to yourself?'

'Yes.'

'Why is that?'

'I'm not very fond of people. It doesn't make me a murderer.'

'Now who said anything about murder? I didn't.'

The two men looked at each other for a while, as if appraising each other. Finally, McEwan spoke. 'You used the word "abducted". Why would any man want to abduct a woman, unless he was going to kill her?'

'I think the question should be *Why would any man want to abduct a woman at all?*, but you tell me.'

'Are you serious?'

'Perfectly.'

'You're a police officer, you know there are men out there who like to harm women, but I'm not one of them. I'm sure you've come across it before.'

'Do you like women, Joe?'

'I don't dislike them.'

'But you said you didn't like people.'

'No, I never . . .'

Bradshaw read from his notes: 'I'm not very fond of people'; then he looked up at McEwan. 'Aren't women people?'

'Very clever,' he sneered. 'You asked me why I liked being on my own, I gave you a flippant response.'

'You do like women, then?'

'From time to time.'

'But you don't force yourself on them?'

'Of course not.'

'You don't drive around posing as a cab-driver, picking up drunk lasses after closing time?'

'Not a hobby of mine, Detective,' said McEwan. 'Who's said that it is? You might want to ask them about their whereabouts because I think they have been leading you down the garden path.'

Bradshaw ignored his question. 'So you haven't abducted anyone?'

He shook his head.

'Could you please speak,' Bradshaw asked him, 'for the benefit of the tape.'

'No,' he said, then added: 'that's a *no* to ever having abducted anyone, not to speaking on the tape.' And he gave a grim smile to show his cooperation. 'Look, I'm assuming you are very short of leads and are just picking up a bunch of people for questioning, is that it? Am I just the latest in a fairly long line? Is it because I'm ex-military and I live alone? Does that tick a couple of boxes on some psychological profile? I bet it does, but if that's all you've got . . .'

'Have you ever killed anyone?' asked Bradshaw, purely to see what reaction he would get from the enigmatic figure before him.

'Yes,' he said quietly, 'I have. I've killed people.'

'Are you referring to your time in the army, Mr McEwan?'

'Yes. Sorry,' he said facetiously. 'Were you talking about more recently?'

'You were in the Gulf War back in 1991?'

The man nodded, then he remembered the tape and said in a loud, clear voice, 'That is correct,' before adding: 'Though I don't really consider it a war.'

'What do you consider it to be?'

'Mass murder.'

'Infantry?' asked Bradshaw.

'Artillery. I was a gunner in a tank. We had a Challenger but they mostly had old T-72s. That's a Soviet-made seventies model. A bit of a mismatch, like having an airgun versus a Magnum. One of our guys blew up an enemy tank from just short of three miles away. I think he still holds the record.'

'Why do you consider it mass murder?'

'Not many people were killed in the Gulf War, if you recall.' He looked grim. 'At least not on our side. Tens of thousands of their lot were, of course, but nobody really cared about that, did they? Just so long as we marched on and kept mowing them down, usually from the skies, sometimes on the ground, but they didn't have to see it. Do you have any idea what it's like to see so many corpses up close or to pass line after line of burnt-out lorries or tanks with the crews still in them, already cremated? Their own families wouldn't be able to recognize them. It wasn't what we trained for.'

'But it was better than dying,' offered Bradshaw. 'Wasn't it?'

McEwan didn't answer that, just said, 'If that's soldiering, I don't want any part of it.'

'That why you left?'

'After a while. I kept my head down because I still had time to serve, but as soon as the redundancy was offered I took it. They were disbanding whole regiments by that point, so no one minded when I crept out the back door.'

'Were you angry when you left?'

'Most soldiers are angry for one reason or another.'

'Have you worked since?'

'Yes.'

'Have you been working lately?'

'Not recently. I seem to struggle to keep jobs.'

'Why do you think that is?'

He took a long while to answer, as if he was contemplating it for the first time, but Bradshaw reasoned he was probably not used to explaining himself.

'Nothing seems that important,' he said finally. 'Not compared to what I've seen. If some boss gets a strop on because he isn't going to hit some stupid sales target, I just find it amusing. If a customer gets het up about something not being to their liking, I just think they're ridiculous. I can't take any of it seriously.'

'Are you in a relationship, Mr McEwan?'

'That's none of your business,' he snapped. 'How is it relevant?'

'Sometimes it's relevant and sometimes it isn't, but it might help me to save time if you were to answer the question, unless there's something about your relationship status that you're keen to hide from me.'

'Let me ask you something, Detective Sergeant. If I answer yes or no, which one of those would make me more likely to abduct a woman?' When Bradshaw said nothing, he said, 'If I say I'm single, you're going to tick another little box in your head, aren't you, until you've ticked enough to make me a prime suspect? That's right, isn't it?'

Bradshaw stayed silent.

The ex-soldier continued, 'Hasn't got a job: tick! Moves around: tick! Ex-army: big tick! Don't try and pretend that it isn't. You civilians all love the army, don't you, until you actually have to deal with soldiers. Not so proud of us, then, eh? Finally, is he single? Another big tick.'

'Well, are you?'

'Yes. I'm single. Happy now?' He held out his hands. 'Why don't you just slap the cuffs on me?'

'Do you own a car?'

'No.'

'You don't? You don't own a car?'

'Are you deaf?'

'I'm giving you the chance to correct yourself. You just said you don't own a car.'

'That is correct.' His tone was laced with sarcasm.

'That's funny,' said Bradshaw, 'because we have you down as the owner of a car.' Bradshaw recited the registration number.

'My car?' he asked. 'Is that what this is all about? My car?' His voice was shrill, but he sounded more upbeat.

'Yes. Your car. The one you just said you didn't own.'

'I don't have a car.' He said that with some satisfaction. 'I sold it two bloody years ago.'

'You sold it?' asked Bradshaw in disbelief.

'Yes.'

'Then why is it still registered in your name?'

'What? Oh, I dunno. I don't think I ever really told anyone about it. I didn't think it mattered.'

'You didn't think it mattered?'

'No, not really.'

'Why not?'

'He only wanted it for scrap.'

'Who did?'

'The bloke who bought it off me,' said McEwan. 'He had one of those trucks with a hook on the back to take it to the yard. No one was going to be driving it again.'

'I meant, what was his name?'

'Oh, I see.' He looked thoughtful, as though he wanted to help. 'I dunno.'

'You sold your car to some bloke and you didn't even take his name? Who are you trying to kid?'

'No, I did take his name.'

'Well?'

'But that was two years ago. I don't think I kept it. Why would I?'

'Why did you sell your car? If indeed you did sell your car.'

243

'I was broke. The guy gave me a few quid for it. I needed the money.'

'But hang on, how did this mystery man know it was up for sale, if you didn't advertise it?'

'I stuck a hand-written cardboard sign with "For Sale" on it in the back window. I'm no detective, but I guess that must have been a clue.'

'You realize that failing to report the sale of a motor vehicle is an offence.'

'Oh,' said McEwan. He sounded as if he couldn't be less interested. 'Better haul me up before the judge in the morning, then. I expect he'll want to throw away the key.' Then he snorted. 'Or possibly give me a fine, which I won't be able to pay.'

Bradshaw was lost for words.

'Are we done?' McEwan asked. 'Or are your mates still searching my caravan for missing women?'

Chapter Forty-nine

1982

It was Father's job to protect him. That's what he had told Chris over and over. It was Father's duty to do what was best for them both, no matter how hard that might seem at the time, especially when Mother had left them both for good.

It was the way other people thought that was the problem and, if Chris was exposed to it, who knew how damaging it could be? That was why Father had bought the land out here and set up the business, to deceive the outside world about the true purpose of the site. Father wasn't really building a business, he was creating a sanctuary, and he couldn't let non-believers in to destroy it before the end of the world came.

So, there would be no school. Instead there would be books to learn things from, but the main book was the good book. There was nothing you couldn't learn from the Bible, except perhaps how to strip and rebuild an engine, but Father could show Chris how to do that. Father had always been good at making things.

No other children could come here because they would have been poisoned already. The words of their parents would be enough to do that and soon they would become just like their mothers and fathers. Chris had to be protected from others. His father would do that, but Chris could never leave.

He need not worry, though, because Father would do all the thinking and he would keep Chris safe from the Apocalypse when it came, which it inevitably would, because there was a cowboy in the White House called Ray Gun and he wanted to start a war.

Father told Chris how God had come to him one day and had told him what to do, just like he had done before with Noah. Chris asked him if God had come to him in a dream or did he walk up to him in the street? How did Father come by this idea that the world would soon be destroyed? Father would always wave that question away.

'It doesn't matter,' he would say. 'Just know that he came to me one day and that God does indeed move in mysterious ways.'

Chapter Fifty

Bradshaw was late for their breakfast meeting. He blamed the traffic, but it wasn't the real reason. The previous night he'd been hit with a bout of crippling insomnia that kept him awake until long past the early hours, no matter what he tried to do. He'd read a book, watched some middle-of-the-night TV and even gone for a drive, but none of it got him even halfway to sleep until an hour before his alarm went off. It was a very tired DS Bradshaw who walked in to see Tom finishing off a bacon butty while Helen ate the last of her tea and toast. He managed to summon the energy to fill them in.

'Are you just going to let him go?' asked Helen when he explained about Joe McEwan's car.

'We've let him go already. We can't hold McEwan on suspicion of attempting to abduct a woman just because he's a pain in the arse, Helen. While I was talking to him we had Uniform scouring the land around his caravan and searching inside it. They didn't find anything, much less a car. The only thing we have is the reg plate, and that's just Tom's theory. Imagine if we had to explain in court that it wasn't even the one the woman gave us.'

'Can't she identify him?'

'The guy who was driving had a cap and sunglasses on and she was in the back of his cab. I could have been driving it, for all she knew.'

'I can't believe he can just go back on to the street like that.'

'Helen, there's no evidence, none at all. He hasn't done anything except sell his car without telling the DVLA. I had to let him go.'

The waitress finally spotted him then and came over. 'Can I get a cup of coffee in a takeaway cup?' he asked her.

'You've only just got here,' said Tom.

'And I've got to leave now,' Bradshaw told him firmly. 'I've an appointment this morning and I really can't be late for this one.'

He hadn't been back for two days. There had been no food or water; the empty plate and plastic glass taunted her now. He hadn't gone through with his threat to put her back in the crate or even checked up on her. So this was her punishment for trying to escape, but how long would it go on for? Another day? Two? Perhaps he would never come back and she would starve to death or die of dehydration.

At first she was filled with despair at her failed attempt to escape and the certainty that he would never again allow her an opportunity as good as that one. Eva had been given one chance and she had blown it. Now, all she could think about was food and water. The hunger cramps in her stomach were agonizing and they would get worse if he didn't bring her some food soon. Was this deliberate, or had he simply disappeared? What if he had been in an accident and been injured and was lying unconscious in a hospital somewhere? What if he had been killed? No one would ever find her then. She would starve to death and this room would become her crypt. Her disappearance would never be solved.

Had that blow to his head been more serious then she had thought? Perhaps he had gone back up to the surface and collapsed. Maybe even now his body was lying in the fields. She wished she had shot him when she had the chance or struck him harder with the heavy shower head, then she would be free. She cursed herself for her weakness.

Hours later she started hearing voices – one voice, at any rate, a high-pitched, whispered, keening sound, but it was so soft the words were inaudible. The sound was inside her own head. She was hallucinating due to dehydration. That was the only explanation. There was no one else in this room, nobody else down here with her. Or so she had always thought.

Eva shook her head to clear it and sat up on the bed. When the sound continued she began to question her sanity, then she started to entertain the slim possibility that it was real – but where was it coming from? She walked unsteadily to the door and pressed her ear against it. She could hear something, but it wasn't coming from the corridor. Where else? Eva forced herself to concentrate and scanned the room. The pipes in the ceiling were too solid surely? The air vent, then. It had to be.

She walked over and stood beneath it. Was the inaudible sound clearer here? She couldn't tell; the vent was too high up for her to listen clearly. She went to the armchair and used what was left of her strength to drag it towards the vent. Once the chair was in place, with its back against the wall, she stood on it then climbed higher by placing a foot on one of the arms, which wobbled alarmingly, then she put her other foot on the highest point at the back of the chair, stabilizing it with her weight, and reached for the vent. There was no way she could remove it, and it was far too small to climb through even if she could, but she could place her ear against it.

It was like opening a window. Now she could make out the sound far more clearly. It was reverberating down the air vent towards her but she still couldn't understand what was being said. Then she realized it wasn't words at all but screaming. Someone was crying. Somebody was in a room nears her and they were crying out in despair. Someone else had reached breaking point.

Despite the awful, gut-wrenching sound, Eva's heart lifted. She was not alone.

'Hey!' she called down the vent, not knowing if the other woman would be able to even hear her above the sound of her own cries, which must have been loud and insistent to carry all this way. 'Hey! Heeeeyyyyyyyy!'

She called for more than a minute but got no reply. She belatedly realized the sound of the screams had stopped. Eva stopped, too, then she waited and listened.

The sound was very faint and some way off, but she could make it out: a muffled, distorted, echoing reply of 'Hey.'

Even though this changed nothing – she was still a prisoner, couldn't do anything about it and was starving and dying of thirst – the presence of another woman, a prisoner like herself, filled her with a burst of hope and energy, just from the simple fact that she was not the only one down here. She wasn't even sure why it gave her hope, but it did.

If another woman was missing, she reasoned, then people must be looking for her too. She wasn't the only one, and perhaps this other woman was not the only other one?

'What's your name?' Eva called.

The reply was lost in the vents but at least the other woman had tried to tell her. 'I am Eva!' she called back, her dry throat cracking through lack of water. 'Eva! My name is Eva!'

She called it again, as much for herself as the other woman, who was trying to call back to her, but the words were echoing in the air ducts, rendering them inaudible. 'Eva!' she called.

I am Eva and I am still here.

To Ian Bradshaw's considerable consternation, another very familiar figure was standing next to Deputy Chief Constable Edward Tyler. It was Chief Constable Newman himself. It was like being summoned to the headmaster's office.

'Detective Sergeant Bradshaw reporting, sir,' he told the deputy chief constable. 'Thank you for agreeing to see me.'

'Ah, yes,' said Tyler. 'DS Bradshaw.' His eyes narrowed, as if he was committing the detective's face to memory as well as his name, to make it easier to enact his future revenge. 'Now, what's this all about, eh?' He let out a humourless chuckle. 'As you know, I'm rather busy at the moment.' The allusion to his imminent confirmation as Chief Constable was offered at the earliest possible point in the conversation, Bradshaw noted.

'Sir,' said Bradshaw, but he didn't go any further. He was waiting to see if the current chief constable was going to vacate the room and leave them on their own.

'I've asked the chief to stay,' Tyler explained. 'I try not to keep anything from him, since we work so closely together.'

'Don't mind me, Bradshaw,' said the chief constable. 'I'll just sit in and hear what you've got to say.' Bradshaw wondered if that was meant to sound as threatening as it did, then decided it was. They were closing ranks already. Siberia was looming.

'Very well, sir.' Somehow he managed to compose himself long enough to explain the reason for their appointment, then to ask his deputy chief constable if he recalled Sarah Barstow, the woman he had interviewed years earlier.

'I do recall her, yes,' said Tyler, and he directed the second part of his answer to his chief constable: 'Bit of an odd case, to say the least.'

'I understand she claimed to have been abducted?'

'She did.'

Bradshaw tried to choose his words carefully. 'But that claim was not considered . . . credible?'

'We had no evidence to support the accusation that she had been kidnapped.'

'Apart from the state she was in,' countered Bradshaw.

'The state she was in,' bridled the deputy chief constable, 'was the reason why she wasn't taken seriously. She was rambling and incoherent and we had concerns about the state of her mental health. Look, you have to understand this wasn't a woman who was rescued from somewhere who could then explain how she had been abducted or why. There were no witnesses who could corroborate her story, no one who saw her bundled into a car or anything like that. She was missing for a year and yet no one was approached for a ransom. There were no signs of physical assault on her person or any marks to indicate that she had been forcibly restrained. Her injuries could be accounted for by the fact that she walked out into a busy A-road and received a glancing blow from a car. She received multiple fractures, but it wasn't that which led to her death. The physical symptoms that did the most damage, and ultimately finished her off, were quite damning, but only against her.'

'How do you mean, *against her*?'

'She was very pale, extremely undernourished and talking utter nonsense, then she lost consciousness, and drifted in and out for a while before dying quite suddenly. The post-mortem revealed hepatic and renal failure. You know what that is?'

'Her liver and kidneys gave out.'

'Exactly,' said Tyler. 'Which means she was a bloody alkie, amongst other things.'

'What do you mean by *amongst other things*?'

'We had very strong reason to believe she was also a druggie and possibly even a prostitute, living on the street for the previous twelve months. She probably invented a story to explain this to her family. It was just a shame she couldn't come up with something more plausible. I felt sorry for the parents. They got her back, but only briefly, and they couldn't face the truth. She had completely lost her way in life. They couldn't accept the evidence we gave them from the post-mortem. When we told them about the liver damage they said she was teetotal. If that ever was true, she must have gone through one hell of a transformation in twelve months, as well as a lot of booze.'

'Didn't you ever entertain the thought that she might be telling the truth? About being abducted, I mean?'

This was too much for the deputy chief constable. 'She was talking utter rubbish, man. She kept saying she'd been trapped in a box' – he paused to let Bradshaw contemplate the sheer lunacy of that statement – 'for a whole year, and when we asked her how that could be possible, she told us a man with no face had held her underground and that there were others down there, too, though she didn't actually see any of them. She heard them, apparently. When we asked where this was, she couldn't tell us. Instead, she started banging on about lions in his garden and fields full of pink trees. Do you see what we were up against?'

'Pink trees?' queried Bradshaw.

'Pink trees,' snapped Tyler. 'She might as well have been talking about pink elephants or Pink bloody Floyd, the amount of help that was to us. How do you even begin to investigate something like that?'

'And lions walking round the garden?'

'In the North-East of England! This from a woman who swore blind she'd been kept underground the whole time,' he protested, 'so how could she have seen trees and lions, unless they were inside her addled mind?'

'When she escaped?' offered Bradshaw.

'Escaped from whom? Escaped from where? A circus, perhaps, or a zoo? No, it was all nonsense. We all thought she'd had a bust-up with a boyfriend, she'd run off and was too ashamed to come home with her tail between her legs, so she made up this cock-and-bull story about being held captive underground.'

'When you say *we all*, what exactly do you mean by that, sir? Were there others who interviewed her?'

'I reported my findings back to my superiors at that time and they agreed with my assessment.'

'That she was perhaps hallucinating? As a result of drugs?'

'What else could it have been but acid?'

'You think she'd taken LSD?'

'Well, if you can come up with a better explanation, then be my guest. Her brain was fried.'

Bradshaw nodded slowly at this. The deputy chief constable must have thought he was agreeing with him. 'But then she died. Wasn't that suspicious?'

'Not under the circumstances. Whatever chemicals she had been imbibing affected her body as well as her brain. When they cut her open afterwards her internal organs were a bloody mess. That young woman had been partying hard, and I defy anyone to come to a different conclusion.'

By that, he clearly meant he was defying Bradshaw to. Even if he could have, at this point, Bradshaw probably would not have attempted it.

'Thank you so much for your time, sir,' he said, then nodded towards the chief constable and said, 'Sir,' again. Christ, he was like some nodding donkey. Neither of them said a word and the deputy chief constable didn't bother to disguise the contemptuous look he gave his DS as he departed.

As soon as he was in the corridor Bradshaw felt his whole body sag. The Siberian chill followed him all the way along it.

Chapter Fifty-one

The voices continued long after Eva was forced to stop because of dehydration. Were there two of them now, maybe more? The sound travelled down the air vents like whispers on a breeze. Although the actual words were lost and all she could make out were the high-pitched pleas from the other woman and her screams, at least she knew she was no longer alone. What was it her captor had said? 'There have to be five.' Which meant there might be four other women just like her trapped down here.

The desperate sounds went on so long she began to fear he might come back and catch them trying to communicate with each other. What would he do to them then? Finally exhausted and weak through hunger, she had just enough energy to slide the chair back in place, then she fell down on the bed and slept for a while.

When Eva awoke he was standing over her, his masked, emotionless face like something out of a nightmare. She started. When he made no move towards her, Eva managed to compose herself, and her spirits lifted when she realized the reason for his visit. He was not here to strangle her or shoot her. There was a tray on the table with a plate of grey lukewarm food and a large plastic bottle of water.

'Eat, drink,' he commanded sullenly, as if he really didn't want her to do either. And she willingly obeyed. He stayed in the cell watching her. Eva had never been more grateful for anything, even though she was horrified to admit she was relieved to see him, even to herself.

When she had finished he gestured for her to stand away from the tray and picked it up in his free hand – the other still held the shotgun – and he made to leave.

'I've been reading the Bible,' she told him instinctively, and he stopped and stared at her. She wasn't lying. There had been nothing else to do for days so she had examined all the books to try to take her mind off her hunger – the children's stories and then the ragged, much-thumbed copy of the King James Bible. She had been surprised to see notes in the margins on many of the pages. The scrawl was spidery and almost impossible to decipher but it looked as if someone cared enough about the Bible to attempt to understand certain passages. If she could convince the man to sit with her and teach her about the Bible and his twisted world view, maybe she could make some form of connection with him. Then perhaps he would lower his guard or, at the very least, see her in a different light and then he might be less likely to kill her when it came to it.

'And I'm sorry,' she said, trying to look earnest and contrite, 'that I tried to leave. I should never have struck you. That was bad, sinful. God will judge me. I know that now. I can only beg for His forgiveness . . . and yours.' She was winging it, hoping he would appreciate her contrition and respond positively to it. Wasn't the Bible always going on about women being obedient and repenting their sins? Was that what he wanted from her?

He straightened at this and seemed to be regarding her more closely. She braced for the onslaught that would likely follow if he thought she was lying or committing some form of blasphemy by invoking his precious Bible, but he didn't move. Was that uncertainty she could sense? Did he really believe she had somehow seen the light?

'I read lots of it,' she said eagerly, 'but I didn't understand it all, though I want to.' It made her feel sick to be talking to him on this level, like a little girl seeking guidance from a wiser person rather what she actually was – a prisoner who hated her captor – but she would do anything to get away from here, and maybe this is what it would take.

Absolute silence while he watched her.

'Perhaps you could help me to understand,' she pleaded.

More silence from him, and she cursed the balaclava that hid all his emotions from her.

'Please,' she urged him.

No reaction. Was he thinking this through?

Make a connection, Eva, she willed herself.

'Rest.' That deep, unnatural-sounding voice betrayed no emotion, then the man looked towards the Bible and said, 'And read the good book.'

Before she could even ask what passage of the Bible she should focus on, he turned and abruptly left the room, locking her in once more.

It was Tom's turn to cook. They ate together because it saved money and were meant to do it on alternate nights so that every evening one of them would get a night off from the chore. It didn't always work out that way, though. Sometimes Tom would be out with Penny, so Helen wasn't expecting the pan of Bolognese sauce that was gently bubbling on the hob when she got in. Tom had even bought fresh, crusty bread to go with it. Meals together at his kitchen table were always a good time to catch up and she was glad he had made the effort.

Then Tom said, 'Great timing. Sit down, Helen. I've made enough for everyone,' and she heard the toilet flush and the sound of the bathroom door being opened and closed upstairs. A moment later Penny appeared. There would be three of them for dinner tonight.

'Hi, Helen,' Penny greeted her.

'Hello, Penny.'

The younger woman joined Helen at the table and they watched Tom drain the pasta. 'He's quite domesticated, isn't he?' beamed Penny, as if Tom had prepared a banquet.

'I suppose he is.' Despite herself, Helen couldn't suppress a smile at the sight of Tom dutifully dishing up dinner for them both before sitting at the table himself.

That smile vanished when Penny said, 'Tom's been telling me all about the latest case.'

'Has he now?'

'Well, mostly just what's in the public domain,' said Tom quickly, 'and Penny's not going to tell all her mates, is she?' Then he added: 'I always think it's useful to have a different perspective, in case we miss something.'

Helen bridled at the notion they could somehow miss something that Penny might be able to spot.

'It's really creepy,' said Penny, 'isn't it?'

'Yes, Penny,' replied Helen, 'it is.'

'Those poor women.'

'We've been talking about Sarah, the woman who got away,' said Tom, recalling Bradshaw's chilling briefing to them following his meeting with the deputy chief constable. 'How she said she knew there were other women with her, even though she didn't see them.'

'Maybe she heard them,' said Helen. 'Perhaps it was a big basement, with separate rooms? A very large house in the country maybe, or an abandoned office of some kind. We could look at plans for buildings like that?'

'Needle in a haystack, wouldn't you say?' said Tom. 'Where would we start?'

'Within a few miles of where the woman was found. She was weak – she can't have got far.'

'Inquiries were made in that area,' Tom reminded her. 'According to Ian, they found nothing, though I'm assuming the inquiries might have been half-hearted, if the woman's story wasn't believed.'

'I'm starting to believe her now, though,' said Helen, 'since we have a second victim, who has only just turned up after all these years.'

'You couldn't keep people underground for months, unless there was water connected and a power supply. It would have to be secure and insulated somehow, so no one hears them or ever sees them. I don't see how you could do it.'

'You could if . . .' Penny blurted out the words then stopped mid-sentence when they both turned and looked at her. 'Never mind.'

'No, come on,' Tom urged her. 'What were you going to say?'

Helen braced herself for Penny's theory. 'Well . . . I was going to say . . . you could if it was a bunker.'

'A bunker?' repeated Helen. 'You mean, like a nuclear one?'

'Or an old one from the Second World War,' said Penny.

'Where did you get that idea from?' asked Tom.

'It was just a thought.' She flushed. 'A stupid one, probably.'

'No,' Helen said firmly, 'it's a good one.'

'It is,' agreed Tom, 'but what made you think of it?'

'My ex,' she began, 'the first guy I went out with when I came to uni; he used to explore them.'

'Really?' asked Tom, and Penny misunderstood his tone.

'Everyone has a past, right?' she said, as if she had just made him jealous.

He smiled at her. 'I just meant it's a very unusual hobby.'

'Tunnel rats,' she said, 'that's what they're called. They go off at weekends and explore bunkers and tunnels on old bases. That sort of thing. He wanted to take me with him.' She grimaced at the notion. 'I think that's one of the reasons why I dumped him.'

'And how did he manage to find these bunkers?' asked Helen. 'I don't suppose they're on any maps in the local library.'

'They're not,' said Penny, 'but word gets round if someone finds an old abandoned place and people go down and explore them in little groups. He used to say it was safe, but I don't see how it could have been. They're all pretty much derelict.'

'How many underground bunkers are there?' asked Helen.

'My ex said there were at least a thousand in this country.'

'Bloody hell,' Tom said. 'Even if we're only dealing with this region, that's way too many and we don't know where they are either. That's the problem with secret bunkers – they tend to be secret.'

'And wouldn't that make them an appealing prospect for a man who wants to take women?' said Helen. 'A fall-out shelter is the one underground building you wouldn't want to be on any map or survey. You would have to keep it secret even from your closest neighbours.'

'In case they all wanted to join you in there?' said Tom.

'Exactly,' agreed Helen. 'There are companies that still build them, even now, with the Cold War long over.'

'There will always be paranoid survivalist types inter-ested in buying stuff like that, in case a nuclear war gets started by accident by some fourteen-year-old computer hacker.'

'And people who think order is going to break down like the idea of a strong room to hide in.'

'Maybe it's the Zombie Apocalypse they're scared of,' said Tom, and Helen frowned at him. 'What?' he protested with a shrug. 'It could happen.'

'The point I'm making is that these companies make secrecy a virtue,' she said. 'It's one of their big selling points.'

'Sparing their customers the anxiety of having to tell their next-door neighbours to sod off and die of radiation poisoning.'

Helen considered it further, 'But Sarah was under-ground for a year and Cora missing for eighteen. Were people really purchasing private fall-out shelters back in the late seventies?'

'Not many, I should imagine,' admitted Tom, 'but a lot of places would have been decommissioned when they became obsolete and just left to crumble away. I've read about them. Some were little places for observation or communications purposes and others were really big, designed to keep local government going after a nuclear strike. We built them during the Second World War, in case the Germans invaded and we had to fight on. Thankfully, they were never needed.'

'It explains how he could keep people underground for years without anyone knowing,' said Helen. 'In fact, it's starting to look like the only plausible explanation.'

'Well done, you,' said Tom, and Penny flushed again.

So, Penny had a theory, thought Helen, and it turned out to be a good one.

Chapter Fifty-two

The desk sergeant told Ian Bradshaw that a woman had come forward with some information for him. She'd read all about the case in the newspaper and needed to speak to him urgently, so could he come down? Was this about the body in the woods or the missing women? Both had been written about in the tabloids lately. There was only one way to find out.

The young woman before him looked tense and worried, so he steered her into a side room and offered her a cup of tea, which she declined. He got the impression she had been fretting about coming to see him. When she didn't immediately explain her presence he opted to make the first move. 'Can I help you?' he asked.

'I'm Rachel, and I've decided to come forward,' she said, as if it hadn't been an easy decision. 'I wasn't going to. I was just going to move on and try and forget about it, you know.'

'Right,' he said.

'But then I realized he can't be allowed to get away with it, and not just because it could happen to another woman, though that's what I'm worried about. It's the arrogance, you see, and the fact that he doesn't seem to have learned anything from it. He still thinks he's important.'

'I see,' said Bradshaw, trying to contain his excitement. Was this another woman who had escaped the clutches of the rogue cab-driver? Would she be able to identify the man who had attacked her?

'When I saw it in the paper,' she continued, 'I just had to come in and talk to someone. He sounded so entitled. I know he'll do it again. I just know it.'

'Who is he?' Bradshaw asked, leaning forward in his chair.

'Sorry.' She shook her head as if to clear it. 'I'm sorry, it's hard for me to . . . I'm talking about Charlie Hamilton, the man who wants to sue you. He assaulted me.'

Bradshaw was momentarily stunned.

'A few months back I stayed over at his house. I can give you the exact date. I fell asleep next to him and I woke up because he was touching me. I didn't consent to it,' she said, then looked forcefully into Bradshaw's eyes. 'I never consented to it. He will say that I did, but he's lying. You have to believe me, even though I know he'll deny every word I say about it.'

'Oh no,' said Bradshaw, slowly piecing things together. 'I do believe you, and he can't deny it.'

'Why not?' she asked abruptly.

'Because he has already admitted it,' said Bradshaw. 'On tape. We just didn't know who you were,' he said, then he gave a supportive half-smile. 'Until now.'

'He's going to regret going to the newspapers,' said Kane hours later, once Bradshaw told him about the woman who had come in about Charlie Hamilton. 'Is there enough to charge him?'

'You may be very surprised to hear that he has copped for it,' Bradshaw told him.

'Really? I am.'

'Well, we had his partial confession on tape and now we have the victim's identity and her account of that night, so I suppose he felt he had nowhere else to go. I think he is hoping a judge will reckon it's all a bit of a drunken misunderstanding, but I doubt that.'

Kane frowned. 'You never know with judges. They're an odd bunch. Either way, whatever the sentence, if he pleads guilty, at least it's a start.'

'He's going to,' said Bradshaw, 'and we've charged him.'

'Suing the force is a non-starter.' Kane was gleeful.

'He's dropped that idea,' Bradshaw confirmed.

'Not that it is my prime concern, obviously,' said Kane. 'It's the victim that counts. Still, I think his disgrace deserves as much attention as his sanctimonious rant about police victimization, don't you? Give this one to Carney. Might as well make the most of the fact that we have a journalist on the pay roll, and he'll be happy because he'll make a few bob out of it.'

'Let me get this straight, sir, you're ordering me to leak the details of an ongoing case to a member of the press?' Bradshaw pretended to be shocked.

'I am,' smiled Kane, 'but of course it didn't come from me or you.'

'He'll understand that without being told.'

'Bradshaw' – Kane's tone was firm – 'make sure you tell him anyway.'

When Bradshaw called Tom with the news he found the whole situation amusing, particularly Kane's assertion that he might need telling that the crucial information about Charlie Hamilton's arrest didn't come from his office, but he assured Bradshaw he would tell no one his source. Grateful for the tip-off, he spent some time writing up the story of Charlie Hamilton's arrest for sexual assault and the withdrawal of his claim against Durham Constabulary, then he faxed the story to one of his contacts at the *Daily Mirror*. They promised to make it a page lead, which he saw as a form of justice after Hamilton's widely read criticisms of the local police.

He'd barely finished when there was a buzz from the gate, and he glanced at the monitor to see Jenna on the CCTV, standing outside his home. He pressed the buzzer to let her in and spent the next half-hour listening as she explained how her blackmailer had made contact with her in person.

'What did this guy look like?' he asked, and when she described the man in detail he realized that he could be anyone.

'I don't know what to do,' she said.

'I can help you, Jenna, if you really want me to, but it won't be without risk. You could pay him instead. It's your choice.'

'But you don't think I should?' she probed.

'Pay him once and you'll be paying him forever.'

'Then what choice do I have,' she asked, 'except to trust you?'

When he was convinced she was certain, Tom said, 'Okay, then, so this is what we're going to do.'

Chapter Fifty-three

Your beauty should not come from outward adornment, such as elaborate hairstyles and the wearing of gold jewellery or fine clothes.

— Peter 3 3:4

The first few weeks were a test. If they passed, they could stay and be saved. If they failed, well, it made no difference, because they'd die soon in the outside world even if he let them go, and he could never do that. It gave him some consolation to know that he wasn't killing them, not really. If anything, it was a mercy, because strangulation was far less painful than being burnt alive or slowly dying of radiation poisoning. He was sparing them that fate at least.

He tried several young ones at first, all runaways, and this had its advantages. They would climb into his vehicle willingly and trustingly, because his offer of a lift gave them a hope of escape. They wanted to believe everything would be okay, and wanting that made them careless.

He soon learned that the really young ones were a bad choice and gave up on them. The teenagers were troublesome, like his wife had been, and wouldn't accept his rules, even when he told them the alternative. Perhaps they didn't believe he was serious, so they learned the hard way. He buried three of them before he gave up and looked elsewhere. No one even noticed.

The next time, Samuel went for a modest woman. No revealing clothes or gold chains, no dyed hair or make-up on her face. Not a harlot or a painted woman. Just a red-haired girl in a simple black dress.

He didn't spot the tattoo on her wrist until she was already in the crate.

Chapter Fifty-four

'Thanks, Tom,' Jenna told him, when they had finally finished going over every option available to her and had settled on a plan of action that was, if not appealing, perhaps the least worst option she could take. 'I don't know what I'd do without you.'

'No problem,' he told her. They left his house and went out on to the driveway together. She turned back to face him then.

'You're an absolute diamond,' she said, and caught him by surprise by leaning forward and kissing him. It was only brief, but it was another one on the lips, not the cheek, and that meant something, because of their history. Every time she did this it rekindled a spark in him and he reckoned she bloody knew it. Still, he wouldn't have minded that half as much or even given it any further thought if it wasn't for the sight that greeted him when they broke from the kiss. With impeccable timing, Penny was standing at the foot of the driveway, staring straight at them. She seemed to be frozen in the act of pressing the buzzer and it was obvious she had seen the kiss.

'Tom?' She looked hurt and confused.

'Penny!' he called, far too brightly, and realized too late that his efforts to look innocent had merely made him appear more guilty.

Jenna immediately understood and gave a little laugh. 'Whoops.'

Penny did not look impressed.

Tom had to go back into the house to release the gate and let Penny in. He returned as quickly as he could, but the two women were already standing next to one another.

'You must be Penny,' said Jenna, and he could see the confusion in his girlfriend's eyes. *Who is this woman?* she must have been thinking, and *How come she knows who I am yet I don't know about her?* 'Don't mind me,' said Jenna. 'I'm far too tactile and Tom and I go way back. We're very old friends.'

'This is Jenna,' Tom told Penny, but he couldn't think of anything else to add at this point that wouldn't make things worse. His girlfriend had just seen him kiss another woman. In actual fact, *she* had kissed *him*, but it probably hadn't looked all that different from a distance. Now Penny looked as if she wanted to hit Jenna – and stab him.

'Well, I'll leave you to it,' said Jenna. 'Thanks again for your help, Tom, and it's nice to meet you, Penny.' She breezed away. Penny didn't say a word till she was gone.

'What does she mean by *very* old friends?'

The conversation started badly for Tom and went rapidly downhill from there.

'Are you cheating on me?' she demanded.

'God no!' he protested. 'How would I find the time?' This attempt to defuse the situation backfired so badly he was forced to backtrack swiftly then explain how Jenna had called round to see him because she needed his help.

'With what?'

His first instinct was to tell her to mind her own

business. Tom didn't like to be challenged, bossed or ordered around by anyone, and certainly wasn't used to relationship rows of this kind, or even relationships at all, if he was honest. 'I can't tell you that,' he said. 'It's private.'

Penny wasn't having that. 'How do you know her, then?'

At that point, Tom decided honesty was the best policy. He could have lied and said they were old friends, colleagues or school mates – anything at all, really, but if he admitted Jenna was an ex-girlfriend, if he was honest about that much, then perhaps she would believe the rest of his explanation.

After he told her, he wished he hadn't.

'You mean you used to sleep with her?'

'Well, er, yes, but everybody has a past, right? I didn't ask you about your ex-boyfriend.'

'He doesn't come knocking on my door for help then kiss me goodbye afterwards,' she snapped, and she had a point there, even if he still didn't believe he had done anything wrong.

'Look, it's a complicated situation. I'm just helping her with a problem, that's all. I'm sorry she kissed me, but it's not as if I kissed her back.' When she didn't come up with a counterargument he continued, 'Now why we don't calm down and just stop rowing about this? How about I take you for a pizza?'

He was taken aback when she said, 'I'm not hungry. Why don't you ask your old girlfriend instead?'

Chapter Fifty-five

Helen drove out to the local hospital to fulfil an appointment she had been unable to confirm over the phone.

The gastroenterologist was a very busy man. Helen knew this because she had been told it repeatedly, at every stage of her pursuit of the doctor and his expert opinion. She had phoned the hospital on several occasions and each time she had listened as she was told just how busy Dr Hemming was and how he was probably in far too much demand to phone the journalist back.

'Did you tell him I am working with the police on an important case?'

'Yes.'

'But he still hasn't called me back. I wonder why?'

'I told him you were interested in his opinion on a dead person. He said he was rather too busy caring for the living.'

Helen had to concede that this was a fair point, but she wasn't going to give up that easily. She drove down to the hospital and found Dr Hemming's private parking spot, which was helpfully marked with his name. His car was still there. Helen waited. And waited. Then she waited some more.

She wondered if people ever realized how much of her time was spent waiting for people. There wasn't a lot of glamour in professions most people considered glamorous. Police, private detectives, investigative journalists – all of them seemed to spend a great deal of their time sitting around waiting for something to happen. She listened to the radio and read the bits of the newspaper she'd had insufficient time for that morning while people started to leave the hospital for the day, until there were only two vehicles remaining in that section of the car park: Dr Hemming's expensive Mercedes and her own car.

Finally, a smartly dressed figure emerged. He looked tired and not a little formidable. Helen decided to intercept him before he reached his car.

'Helen Norton,' she called cheerfully, and shook the man's hand, as if the doctor had been expecting her all along. 'Did you get my messages?'

'I did, but –'

'You're a very busy man, I know,' Helen said, in a tone designed to placate the doctor, 'which is why I thought it best to drive down here and meet you, so I could perhaps steal just a moment of your time now, then I could finally leave you in peace.'

The doctor frowned at her. 'I quite like the sound of that last bit.'

'I'm working on a case with the police. I want to talk to you about renal failure; in particular, its causes.'

The doctor jerked his head to indicate Helen should follow him and indicated the pub across the road. 'You can buy the drinks.'

It cost Helen a large gin and tonic, but at least Hemming knew his topic.

'There are a number of causes of renal failure, but in our society one of the most common is excessive alcohol consumption,' the doctor told her.

'I thought alcohol harmed the liver, not the kidneys?'

'It can affect both,' he said, then he held up his glass with a grim smile and said, 'Cheers, by the way.' He took a sip of his G&T and continued: 'Drinking too much can damage the liver, which places an additional burden on the kidneys. Liver disease impairs the rate of blood flow to your kidneys and hampers their ability to filter the blood of impurities. Taken to extremes, it can cause organ failure.'

'Is there any way to get that kind of organ failure that doesn't involve alcohol or drugs? One of the women we're trying to find out about wasn't known for that kind of lifestyle, so it was a shock to her family when the extent of the damage was revealed.'

'There are lots of way. Trauma, for one, such as a heavy blow, for example.'

'One of the subjects was hit by a car, but it wasn't a fatal blow. I don't think the impact damage destroyed the internal organs. That was more of a long-term condition.'

'I see.'

'So what else could cause renal failure?'

'Diabetes, perhaps, or a genetic predisposition.'

'Okay,' said Helen, discounting both of those, since none of them had been mentioned by Sarah's family as a possible explanation. 'How about drugging someone?'

'Drugging someone?' repeated the doctor. 'Or do you mean someone taking drugs voluntarily?'

'Possibly either,' Helen admitted, 'but I'm interested

in any drug that could be used on a person being held against their wishes in order to make them compliant or knock them out all together for sustained periods of time. Would the long-term effect of something like that be enough to cause kidney failure?'

The doctor thought for a while. 'Well, there are some drugs that, if taken in sufficient quantity, and regularly enough, could damage the kidneys.'

'Such as?'

Helen was expecting something dramatic but instead she was told, 'Paracetamol.'

'Paracetamol?'

'Yes,' said the doctor, 'and Ibuprofen.'

'The headache tablets?'

'Yes.'

'I can't see a kidnapper forcing large quantities of paracetamol down his prisoner's throat, can you?'

'Er . . . no,' admitted the doctor.

'There's nothing else out there that someone would use to subdue another human being that might cause kidney failure?'

'I can't think of anything offhand, but then I'm not used to being questioned about kidnappings. I'll have a think about it and if I come up with anything I'll call you back and let you know.' He drained his drink. *Of course you will*, thought Helen, knowing she would probably never hear from the overworked doctor again. 'Now I really must be getting home.'

The Bible passages were turgid and often used a lot of words while saying very little, but she read large passages anyway, focusing on the ones that had been highlighted, hoping to find some way to communicate with the man the next time he came to her room. Eva had had nothing to do with the Bible since she was at primary school, when sanitized passages about the baby Jesus were read aloud in class at Christmastime. She didn't have a religious bone in her body and struggled to take any of it seriously but she read as much as she could and thought of it as important homework which might help her to break down the barrier between herself and her captor but, really, how could you believe any of this was the actual word of God?

There were too many contradictions, for one thing. The Old Testament Lord was a frightening vengeful God and the one from the New Testament was apparently loving and merciful, except where he seemed to be instructing his followers to tell everyone that women were inferior creatures who should be left uneducated and at the mercy and instruction of their husbands. Then there were adulterers, all of whom should be killed.

That's half our street executed, then.

It was all a load of old bollocks, in Eva's opinion, but it would help her to reach out to her captor, so she was determined to play the wide-eyed, repentant sinner and made sure the Bible was close to her at all times so she could scoop it up as soon as she heard the key turn in the lock and it would look as if she had been reading it avidly.

It was a long wait but finally she heard the sound she had been waiting for. Immediately she sat up as the door swung open and grabbed the Bible and opened it, like a schoolgirl pretending she has been doing her homework all along. The masked man stopped just inside her room and seemed to be staring at her. Was he impressed, or had he caught her in the act of picking it up?

When he made no move towards her she found a passage she'd picked out earlier. ' "I wait patiently for God to save me; I depend on Him alone," ' she read. She stopped and looked at him. 'But that's not right, is it?' she asked him earnestly. 'Because you can save me, can't you?'

He did not react to this. Instead he seemed to stare right through her.

'You said you would. Isn't that right? You said if I believed in *Father*, I would be saved.'

Silence from the masked man.

'But how,' she asked him, 'how will I be saved? Can you explain it to me? I want you to. I think you want to tell me, too.'

Was he wavering? It was so hard to guess what he might be thinking when he was wearing that bloody balaclava.

'Why don't you come and tell me?' She moved along the bed a little and patted the mattress where she had just been sitting.

She didn't have to see the look on his face to know she had gone too far. His whole body stiffened, then he marched right up to her.

He didn't point the gun at her but there was no doubting the anger and aggression in the words, which came out a little higher pitched than usual. 'Without faith it's impossible to please God.' His tone was a rebuke. He didn't believe her. 'And who can forgive your sins but God alone?'

Chapter Fifty-six

1983

'Women can't be trusted. I'm sorry, Chris, but that's just the way it is,' Samuel had told him when Chris was still very young. 'Remember Eve and how she gave in to temptation and led Adam into it, too?' Chris nodded earnestly. 'That's women for you. Too easily tempted, too weak to avoid temptation in the first place. Not strong like men. Men have to be strong to take on the burdens of the world. Women are just not built for it, you see? Women are weak, Chris. I'm not just talking about their bodies. It's their minds, too.'

'That's what happened to your mother. It's why she went away, see, cos she met someone else and didn't have the strength not to give in to temptation, so she abandoned us.'

Chris nodded, but he didn't ask further about Mother, even though he did want to talk about her. He knew curiosity wasn't good. Curiosity killed the cat. His father was always telling him this, though he didn't really understand exactly how the cat had died. He knew better than to ask.

Chapter Fifty-seven

Helen was already in a bad mood. She was home alone and had no idea where Tom was. She had wasted hours waiting for the gastroenterologist and come away with next to nothing for her troubles, then she'd spent even more time on some additional research that might prove to be equally fruitless. She'd barely walked through the front door when the phone rang. It was her mother, who she'd apparently failed to call for a fortnight. It was lecture time, and the subject was Peter.

Could he not be given a second chance? Had he not earned the right to at least be heard out by his ex-girlfriend? Then, most depressingly of all: was Helen getting any younger?

'You do want a family one day?'

'Of course.'

'Well, how exactly are you going to achieve this, if you're living with that journalist? He's hardly a long-term bet, is he?' And before Helen could either defend Tom or deny she was sleeping with him, her mother staggered her by lowering her voice to a conspiratorial whisper. 'No one is saying you can't have a bit of fun while you're young, Helen, but really, is this the father of your future children?'

'Oh Mother, you're impossible!'

The call eventually ended with a rapprochement of

sorts, where Helen agreed to at least think about speaking to 'poor Peter' in return for her mother ending her ill-informed speculations about Tom.

Thoroughly worn out by her day, Helen decided to cook some food and pour herself a very large glass of wine. Then the buzzer went and she was surprised to see who was standing by the gate. She pressed the entry button then opened the door to Penny. 'Oh, it's you,' Penny said. 'Where is he?'

'Tom?' Helen didn't have the energy for Penny right now. 'I don't know. Out.'

'He's with her, isn't he?' Penny hissed.

'I don't know where he is. I just said.'

'Don't lie for him, Helen.'

'I'm not lying for him! I genuinely don't know where he is.' Then she realized what Penny had said a moment ago. 'Who is he with? I mean, who do you think he is with?'

Helen didn't like being accused of lying and she wasn't happy with Penny's tone. Her sense of loyalty to Tom kicked in immediately and she was keen to protect him from the younger girl's accusations, even though she couldn't guarantee Tom hadn't actually been up to whatever Penny was about to accuse him of.

To Helen's surprise, Penny did not lash out or start a row. Instead she burst into tears.

'You'd better come in,' sighed Helen.

Yes, he's cheating on you, with his ex. He's still in love with her, apparently. I'm sorry you had to hear it from me, Penny. I'll be sure to tell him to go to hell for you. It's been nice knowing you. Bye.

Helen was tempted to say all of that and more to Perky Penny but instead she bit her tongue and listened while the younger woman poured her heart out.

'I'm sorry, I know I'm being stupid, but I really, really, really care about him, Helen, and I think I've ruined everything.' Helen put aside her journalistic criticism of Penny's use of the word 'really' three times in the same sentence and realized she might have to be the shoulder to cry on, which was not a role she relished. It was quite obvious to her that Penny and Tom were not right for each other, even putting aside her own feelings for Tom. They were about as ill matched a couple as she had ever come across and she felt compelled to gently offer this up as a possible reason for their lover's tiff, but then she looked into Penny's teary eyes and knew she didn't have it in her. Instead she listened while Penny told her everything: how Tom had spent less time with her lately, how he'd been helping an ex-girlfriend; how she'd seen them kiss in the driveway and the row that followed it.

'Tom has a good heart,' Helen told her. 'Sometimes it's easy to forget that. When an old friend comes to him for help, he'll always try and give it, even if that extends to an annoying ex-girlfriend.' Penny let out a half-laugh, half-cry at this. 'But that is all he is doing. I happen to know he didn't tell you about it because he was worried you might be jealous, ironically enough. He cares about you, he really does. He should have told you, Penny, he messed up, but he did it for the right reasons. Tom does everything for the right reasons, even when he is wrong, which is why we both put up with him. I'm sure he'll be fine with you the next time he sees you.'

'Thank you, Helen,' sniffed Penny. 'Please don't tell him I've been round here.'

'I won't,' Helen assured her.

'You're so lovely and I'm such an idiot. I wish I was as level-headed as you are. You take everything in your stride.'

'I really don't.'

'But you do,' protested Penny. 'The way you called off your engagement like that. I really admired you for not going ahead with it when you weren't happy. Not everyone is brave enough to do that, but you did.'

'And now look at me,' said Helen dryly, then, worried she might disillusion the younger woman, she added: 'I mean, I'm fine, it's just . . .' And Helen had no idea why but she started to tell Penny all about Peter, including the shocking moment of his unexpected proposal and the fallout when she rejected him, even the recent excruciating phone call with her mother (though she didn't mention the part about Tom or his suitability as her future husband). The two women started to have a long and honest conversation and Penny confided to Helen that Tom had come along at just the right time for her, following a disastrous, confidence-sapping relationship that had left her 'in bits'.

'I didn't like myself until I met Tom,' Penny admitted. 'I've never told anyone that before.' Helen realized that the over-confident, oh-so-perfect girl she thought she knew had actually been a bundle of insecurities until she had started seeing Tom, who had simply made her happier.

'What are you going to do?' asked Penny when their conversation was drawing to a close. 'About Peter, I mean.'

'I don't know,' said Helen, and for some reason she laughed. 'I really don't.'

Chapter Fifty-eight

1986

For nation will rise against nation, and kingdom against kingdom.

— Matthew 24:7

You couldn't save them all. He hoped Chris would understand that. Only a few, and they would have to earn it first. They would have to prove that they could obey, otherwise there would be no point putting them in the safe place, not if they didn't deserve it. That would be like casting seeds on rocky ground, pearls before swine. Undeserving people were like weeds and had to be plucked out. There wasn't room for many down there. Five was the right number. Modest, unadorned women were best and most likely to obey. A select few who would outlive the coming retribution and survive to start all over again following God's judgement.

'Like the Ark?' asked Chris.

'Yes.' Father's smile was almost triumphant when he realized Chris understood. 'Exactly like the Ark.'

'Only without the water?'

Father nodded. 'Without the water,' he agreed. They were walking across the fields because Father had something important to show him. 'For His judgement this time will be fire. It's coming, Chris, and it is coming very soon, so we must be strong and prepared.'

'Strong and prepared,' he repeated, because he knew Father liked that. It showed he had been listening.

'They call it the H Bomb, and it makes a huge ball of fire up in the sky. They say they will never drop it, but why make those bombs if you are never going to use them? They can't wait to drop them, and they've done it before. Whole cities destroyed in Japan. We can't trust them, not the Ivans or the Yanks – and do you know where we are?'

Chris shook his head.

'We are right in the middle, stuck between the bear and the eagle. The bear wants to kill the eagle, but he can't catch it. The eagle wants to destroy the bear, but the bear is too strong. Do you understand?'

And he did understand. Chris could see it in his mind's eye: a thrashing, clawing bear and a diving, swooping eagle locked in a deadly combat, tearing up the woods as they tried to destroy each other and ruining everything around them.

'We have to be like the fox – clever, sly and cunning. That's the only way to survive.' And that was when Father first showed Chris the bunker.

Chapter Fifty-nine

Penny hadn't been gone long when the buzzer went again and Helen was forced to abandon her attempt at preparing a meal for a second time.

'Where the bloody hell have you been?' asked Bradshaw cheerfully once she let him in.

'Working,' she snapped.

'Well, I wish you would turn that phone of yours on occasionally,' he chided her gently.

'It *was* on, Ian!' The vehemence of her reply shocked him. 'It was on, okay. I just forgot to charge it. Again! All right, happy now? Why don't you tell Tom about it and you can both have a laugh at how stupid I am?'

Ian Bradshaw looked like someone had cast a spell on him. He seemed to freeze and just stared at her. 'What?' she demanded, but she knew what. He had never heard her lose her temper like this before.

'Are you okay?'

'Why should I not be okay?'

'You don't sound okay,' he offered cautiously. 'Sorry if I upset you.'

She forced herself to calm down. 'That's all right,' she said. 'I'm sorry for shouting.'

'Bad day, eh?'

She nodded firmly and he decided it was best to move on. 'You said you've been working. What on?'

'Scrapyards,' she told him, grateful that he sensed she didn't want to talk about any of her problems. 'I didn't think your Gulf War veteran was very likely to come up with that name, so I've been looking up scrapyards in the region. There are eleven of them, at least,' and she handed him a piece of paper with names written on it.

'Christ,' muttered Bradshaw. 'Maybe we can rule one or two of them out before we go trudging round them all. Kane won't want us to raid eleven scrapyards, so we'll have to check them all out first before we start turning up and asking questions.' He stopped to think. 'I'll take a look for any suspicious characters, though people who run scrapyards tend to be a bit odd already. It comes with the turf. Once we narrow it down we can inquire about the make and model of the car and give them the reg number, then ask to have a look around.'

'And we can look out for any place where women could be hidden away,' she said, 'particularly anything that looks like it might lead underground – a tunnel, a cellar or a bunker of some kind.'

'Sounds like a plan,' he said. 'Good work, Helen.'

The next morning Helen couldn't find her phone, despite the fact that it was ringing. She realized she had left it in another room, but which one? She followed the noise, unsure at first if it was coming from upstairs or somewhere towards the back of the house.

'Your phone's ringing!' called Tom from his bedroom.

'I know!' she yelled back at him. Did he think she was deaf? She found it in the kitchen next to the kettle. Worried the caller might ring off, she grabbed for the phone, almost dropped it and answered impatiently.

'Yes?'

'Helen Norton?'

'It is.'

'It's Dr Hemming.' Helen was surprised to get the call back, even though he had said he'd phone if he thought of anything. 'I've been thinking about your case, the kidnapper and his victims.'

'Oh, right.'

'And I think I might have come up with something.'

'Great.'

'Methoxyflurane,' said the doctor.

'Come again?'

'I was contemplating what you said about someone keeping another person drugged and compliant, and I did a bit of research for you.'

'Thanks,' said Helen, 'so what is Meth-oxy–?'

'Methoxyflurane, otherwise known as Penthrane.' Helen grabbed a pencil and wrote the words on the side of a cereal box. 'It's an anaesthetic. Primarily used on trauma victims by paramedics and the like. It's an effective way to treat patients suffering severe pain sustained in traffic accidents, for example, but only in small doses. Larger ones would render a person completely unconscious, which might appeal to a kidnapper, and here's the thing that might interest you: it's nephrotoxic.'

'Sorry?'

'It means that too much of it would cause liver and kidney failure as a side effect, which is why it hasn't really caught on over here.'

'You could be on to something there, Doctor. I'm assuming this Methoxyflurane is not available over the counter.'

'Oh no,' he said. 'You couldn't just get it from the chemist's.'

'Well, that ought to help narrow down the suspects. So where would I get it from? A hospital?'

'Nowhere in the UK,' said the doctor.

'It's not available in this country at all?' Her heart sank.

'No, it's banned here now, because of the side effects. They still manufacture and use it in Australia, though,' he said, as if this might be helpful in some way.

'I thought we might have made a breakthrough, but I doubt anyone is going to be able to bring drums of that stuff in without someone flagging it up. It's not normal to ship in quantities of a banned general anaesthetic, is it?'

'No, it's not.'

'Oh, well. Nice try, Doctor, and I do appreciate your efforts.'

'My pleasure. I'm only sorry it's not what you are looking for. I wish I could have been more help.'

Then a thought struck Helen. 'How come you've heard of this stuff, if it's banned in the UK and only used in Australia, I mean.'

'It wasn't always banned.'

Helen thought about that for a moment. 'When was it banned, Doctor?'

'A long time ago.'

'How long?'

'Hang on, I'll get my notes.' Helen heard him put the phone down while he retrieved them. After a short while he returned. 'It was 1979, I think.'

'Thanks, Doctor. Thank you very much indeed.'

*

There was a lot to discuss at their latest breakfast meeting, where Helen shared her knowledge of the banned anaesthetic, then the subject turned to the list of scrapyards.

'We may have something,' Bradshaw told them. 'I've been checking out the owners of the scrapyards to try and narrow them down a bit. Most of them seem normal enough for that line of work, but there are three that stand out.'

'How do you mean?' asked Tom.

'The registered owners ring bells,' said Bradshaw. 'Sometimes alarm bells.'

'Go on,' Helen urged him.

'The first one is owned by a Mr Keogh. That name ought to be familiar to you.' He was looking at Tom when he said it.

'Not the bus people?'

'The very same. The Keogh family ran half the buses in our area when we were little. Old man Keogh also had money in haulage and some construction projects. I'd say he was one of the wealthiest men in the county back then.'

'Agreed,' said Tom. 'But he can't still be alive.'

'He isn't. This place is owned by one of the sons. He had three, the eldest being the black sheep of the family. He stormed out on his dad when he was a young man and never looked back.' He snorted in amusement. 'Until the old fellah died and the will was read.'

'Did he get anything?'

'A third. Old man never cut him out of the will. Apparently, the business had to be carved up and sold off to settle everything. According to one of our lads who has worked the area far longer than me, the break-up of the Keogh empire was quite big news twenty years ago. One of the sons kept the bus company, another one the lorries and the eldest took his share in cash and bought the scrapyard.'

'Seems a strange thing to spend your inheritance on,' said Tom. 'It can't be worth much, flogging bits of old engines and car body parts from wrecked motors. Who else is on your list?'

'The second owner is interesting,' said Bradshaw. 'A former pastor of a non-episcopal church, would you believe.'

'Why did he leave his church?' asked Helen.

'Had to. A prison sentence. Not a long one, though, and it was for good, old-fashioned fraud. Pastor Belasis stole church funds and money destined for charity, though there was also a scandal involving a young girl . . .'

'You said there were three sites that made you suspicious?' said Tom.

'I'm saving the best til last.' Bradshaw's face turned grim. 'The third scrapyard is owned by a Mr Sean Draycott.' He looked at them meaningfully and when they did not react he said, 'The registered owner of that other scrapyard where the burnt girl was found a couple of years back.'

Helen shuddered at the memory of that gruesome case.

'And we all know the real owner of that place.'

'Jimmy McCree,' said Tom. 'Jesus Christ, if he's behind this . . .'

'I'm not saying he is. All I'm saying is he owns more than one scrapyard in the North-East and he has made women disappear before. I think we should start with him.'

Chapter Sixty

Finding Draycott's scrapyard was something of a challenge. It was situated in a dip between steep hills in the Northumbrian countryside. If you wanted to open a business in a quiet spot no one would be likely to stumble upon by accident, then this was the ideal place.

Ian Bradshaw knew it wasn't right from the very beginning. As soon as he set eyes on it he could tell there was something badly wrong here, besides the fact that no one had ever set eyes on the fictitious owner. The gates were high and wide and held together by a thick chain which seemed designed to ensure nobody could enter the property easily. You couldn't sell car body parts if your customers were denied access. A single sign advertised the site's purpose, but it was small and low down, as if trying to avoid eye contact. There was a bell at the front gate, but he had been ringing it repeatedly and, so far, no one had bothered to come and see what he wanted.

Bradshaw had experience of dealing with fronts for organized crime and, at first glance, this scrapyard strongly resembled one. A business like this was very useful, because money could be laundered through it without too many questions being asked. People usually paid cash for bits from an old car and cannibalized parts weren't subject to much of an inventory or any kind of stringent record-keeping. And there was another reason why owning a scrapyard could be handy for a crime firm. Vehicles used in robberies or drive-by shootings against a rival could be taken here and crushed into small pieces and, if there happened to be a body in the boot, too, well, it would save the bother of disposing of it separately.

He was about to give up and come back later, possibly with a warrant, some colleagues and cutting gear for the fence, when he saw a man wander nonchalantly across his line of vision from some way inside the perimeter. The man made no attempt to come towards him and showed no sign of having even noticed Bradshaw.

'Hey!' yelled the detective, and the man spun on his heel and stared at Bradshaw as if his presence there was an unexpected inconvenience. Bradshaw waved him over.

The man took his time. 'We're closed.'

'Oh, really?' said Bradshaw. 'When are you open, then?'

'Depends.'

'On what?'

'What we got going on.'

'So if I was looking to buy the bonnet from a Mk 2 Escort, when should I come back?'

'Look, don't bother, all right. Just try somewhere else, eh. There's a good lad.'

'And what if I was to ask you about some missing girls?' Bradshaw reached into his jacket pocket and produced his warrant card. 'Would you ask me to come back then?'

'Yeah,' said the man, who was taking all this completely in his stride. 'Unless you've got a warrant.' He shrugged. 'And even then I ain't got a key for the gate.'

'Really? How did you get in?'

The man ignored that question. 'I don't know nothing about any missing girls.'

'What about Mr Draycott?' asked Bradshaw. 'Would he know anything about them?'

'Who?'

'Sean Draycott.'

'Never heard of him.'

'You've never heard of the registered owner of this scrapyard.'

'Name does ring a bell.' The man pivoted effortlessly from one lie to the next. 'But he ain't my boss.'

'Who is your boss?'

'I ain't really got a boss. I'm my own boss.'

'Who pays you, then?'

The man shrugged again.

'What's your name?'

'I don't have to give you my name.'

'You do if I believe you have committed an offence.'

The man smirked. 'And what offence do you believe I've committed?'

Bradshaw looked at the scrapyard. 'Money-laundering, false accounting, tax evasion, kidnap, possibly.'

'David Anderson.' He conceded it lightly in the end, as if it really didn't matter.

'That's your real name?'

''Course.'

'Now then, David Anderson, I'd like to come in, if I may?'

'Why?'

'Because I wish to question you about the missing women I mentioned.'

'You can't come in. Not unless you get a warrant, and

even then it ain't really down to me. I'm just looking after the place for a friend of a friend.'

'You're not being very cooperative, Mr Anderson. That makes me suspicious.'

'Does it?'

'It does.'

'Listen, Copper, I don't like the law, I don't trust the law and I don't help the law, got it? If you want to traipse back to the rock you crawled out from and type up a warrant to search this place, then good luck to you, but you won't find nothing and you'll only get a magistrate to approve that warrant if you've got evidence that a crime's been committed. Until then you can just fuck off.' And with that calm dismissal he turned and sauntered back to his office, seemingly without a care in the world.

At first it appeared that Tom and Helen were going to have even worse luck with the Keogh scrapyard. When they drove to the address, between two isolated County Durham villages, there was no sign of the yard.

'I assume,' said Tom, 'that this is not the place.' They were standing by the locked rusted gates of an abandoned farmhouse that looked as if it hadn't seen a tenant in years. 'You sure you wrote it down right?'

'Of course I did,' said Helen. 'The electoral roll said 115 Magnolia Lane.' She pointed to a stone marker post not far from the gate which had that same number carved on it.

'And this is definitely Magnolia Lane,' he conceded. 'Well, the electoral roll must be wrong, because this place is uninhabited and it's a farmhouse not a scrapyard. I suggest we keep looking.'

They got back in the car, but they didn't have to drive far. They went down the hill and around the corner then caught their first glimpse of a cottage, and beyond it they could see the piles of wrecked cars that made up the scrapyard. As they drew closer they spotted the number 117. Tom knew Helen well enough to have more faith in her than the records she had lifted the address from, so he had to assume the electoral roll was wrong.

Tom drove into the scrapyard, which was open and seemed to be a functioning business, though there was no office, not even a prefab building or caravan, just the old stone cottage to one side of the yard. They parked, got out of the car and went up to it. There was no bell but there was a metal knocker and Tom banged on the door hard.

They stood silently waiting, then Tom banged again. When no one came they exchanged looks, reluctant to admit defeat, having come this far. Tom tried for a third time and was about to suggest they give up and come back later when they heard a sound from within. Someone was moving about and seemed to be making progress towards the front door. A bolt was drawn back, then a second one, and at last the door was pulled open by a young woman.

'Miss Keogh?' Helen asked, since she did not know her first name. This woman was not listed on the electoral roll, though she was certainly well past voting age. Helen made an assumption that she was a family member, but she looked too young to be the wife of a man of Keogh's age.

'What do you want?' she asked them.

Helen explained who they were and why they were there and the woman gawped back at her, seemingly uncomprehendingly. The lights are on, thought Tom, but no one's home. Even Helen was modifying her explanation to keep it very simple for the dowdy woman in front of them. It was hard to tell her age but she looked well shy of thirty. Her hair was cropped short and she wore a woolly hat that covered most of it, and her figure was obscured by the stained dungarees she wore over a plain white T-shirt.

She didn't say a single word until Helen finished explaining that they were looking for a particular vehicle then handed the woman a scrap of paper with the registration number on it. Helen told her approximately when this car might have been purchased and the woman frowned.

'I don't write things down,' she offered eventually.

Tiring of her lack of response, Tom asked, 'Is Mr Keogh in? Can we speak to him about it?'

She blinked at Tom and retreated into the house without a word and he wondered if she had gone to fetch the owner of the yard. He exchanged glances with Helen and decided to follow her inside. The hallway was a long, thin corridor that went right through the house, with rooms on either side of it, but before Tom could decide whether to proceed or to wait for the woman to return, Helen said, 'Tom, look at this.'

He turned back to the old framed embroidered messages on the walls he hadn't noticed and read aloud the one Helen was looking at.

> *Since all is well*
> *Keep it so*
> *Wake not a sleeping wolf.*

'Is that from the Bible?' he asked.

'It's Shakespeare, I think.'

'But not one of his greatest hits,' said Tom, who had only a passing knowledge of Shakespeare's plays. He walked further into the hallway and glanced at the portraits of young women on the walls. They were prints of paintings done in an Impressionist style but Tom could never tell Monet from Manet and he turned back when Helen called him.

'What about this one?' she asked, and she read the next embroidered quote aloud – '"Being darkened in their understanding, excluded from the life of God because of the ignorance that is in them, because of the hardness of their heart"' – and peered at the smaller print below it. 'This one is from the Bible. Ephesians, apparently.'

'Very cheerful,' he said, and at that moment the woman returned and Tom asked, 'Church-goer, are you?'

The woman shook her head.

'Your dad, then?'

He realized she had a newspaper cutting in her hand and she gave it to him to read. It was from the local paper's obituary column and dated more than a year ago. Here was a death notice listing Keogh Senior's age, place of birth, date of death and, finally, its cause: a suspected heart attack. The man they had come to see was long gone and certainly died well before the newest group of women had gone missing. They had hit another brick wall.

The woman leaned forward slightly. It looked as if she was about to tell Helen something in confidence. Instead she just said, 'You smell nice.'

Taken aback, Helen replied, 'It's just a body spray.'

And she could see Tom widen his eyes at the strangeness of it all.

'That was weird,' said Helen as they drove away.

'Certainly was,' said Tom. 'But then there are a lot weird folk about. Believe me, I've interviewed most of them.'

'Those religious quotes on the walls were a bit eerie.'

'They weren't all religious. You said one was Shakespeare.'

'I think it was,' she corrected him. 'What did you make of her?'

'She was odd, but then I suppose she lives alone in a cottage on a scrapyard, miles from anywhere, so what did we expect?'

'She hardly said a word,' continued Helen.

'I'm guessing she doesn't get out much.'

'She didn't even mention he was dead, just trotted out with that death notice. What was that all about?'

'Proof, I suppose. You told her we worked with the police. Maybe she thought we wouldn't believe her unless we saw it with our own eyes. At least we now know it can't be Keogh, and she doesn't look like a killer.'

And Helen couldn't argue with that. 'Maybe Ian's having better luck.'

Chapter Sixty-one

Ian wasn't having better luck. Former Pastor Belasis received him unenthusiastically into his home, a dilapidated caravan at the edge of a yard filled with wrecked cars, opposite a Portakabin office. Then he listened to the detective's reasons for calling.

When Bradshaw had finished, Belasis handed Bradshaw a folder. 'Every registration number I've taken in the past six months,' he said.

'What about before that? What about two years ago?'

'Oh, I don't keep records that long,' he said. 'Why would I? The cars here are old and used for parts. They won't drive anywhere again. If I bought the one you mentioned, then it would have been for just a little cash so I could strip it down.'

'Ever sell a reg plate?'

The accusation seemed to sting the man. 'I'd never do that.'

'Because it wouldn't be legal?' It was almost a taunt, but the former pastor didn't rise to it.

'Because it wouldn't be right,' Belasis assured him.

'And how did you get this business in the first place?'

There was a second's hesitation. 'Through a former parishioner.'

'Purchased from the man in question?' asked Bradshaw.

'Or did you con him out of it? Did you tell him it was the Lord's will? Should I ask him, perhaps?'

'You could try asking him,' he answered, 'but only through prayer. I'm afraid he passed away some time ago. This was a legacy, bequeathed to me by a man who was grateful for my many visits to his bedside during a long and debilitating illness.'

'While you were still with the church?' clarified Bradshaw. 'The one you left under a cloud, shortly after a large amount of its funds went missing?' He locked eyes with Belasis, and added: 'Before spending some time in another institution.'

Bradshaw expected excuses or protestations of innocence but instead Belasis just said, 'Are you trying to shame me, Officer? I sinned.' He spread his palms in a gesture of admission. 'I paid for those sins. Am I to be punished for the rest of my life, or should I now try to make an honest living and a positive contribution to society? What would you have me do?'

'A little bird told me there was a girl involved.'

The pastor glanced away from Bradshaw then, as if he did not want to talk about that.

'A very young one. The daughter of one of your congregation. I heard she got pregnant. I also heard she disappeared.'

'The rumour of her pregnancy was malicious gossip originating from a jealous member of the congregation . . .'

'Jealous of her or jealous of you?'

'. . . and she didn't disappear. She ran away from home. There's a difference. Quite a big one.'

'Not been seen or heard of since, though,' the detective reminded him. 'Run off to the big city, has she? That's convenient.'

'She was a wilful girl,' he said, as if this was sufficient explanation in itself.

'Was?'

'When I knew her,' clarified Belasis. 'And very probably still is.'

'That what made you fall for her?' asked Bradshaw. 'Even though she was barely fifteen?'

'I was bewitched,' said the pastor, then he quoted, '"Do not desire her beauty in your heart, nor let her capture you with her eyelids."'

'That an admission or some sort of justification?'

'I don't have to justify myself to you, only to God.'

'That depends on what you've been up to lately.'

'Selling parts from old cars, nothing more.' His tone was wistful then, as if he truly missed sinning. Bradshaw didn't believe him for a second. Belasis had the air of someone who would always have something crooked on the go.

'Bit of a comedown, though, isn't it? Not tempted to move away and set up another church somewhere where no one has ever heard of you? I think I would if I was in your shoes.'

'I'm through with all that. I live a simpler life now.'

'Really? Well, if I hear even a whisper that you have anything else to confess, I'll be right back here, Pastor.'

'You are welcome any time, Officer. We could pray together.'

As he was leaving Bradshaw glanced over at the Portakabin and a sudden movement from inside it caught his eye.

'What's going on over there?' he asked.

Belasis couldn't hide his discomfort. 'Nothing.'

'Who are you hiding in there, Belasis?'

'No one.' But he looked worried.

Bradshaw ignored his protestations and made his way across the yard towards the Portakabin. Belasis followed, struggling to keep up with the other man's strides.

'There is nothing there that need concern you. I give you my word,' he said, which only made Bradshaw more determined to get to the bottom of it.

He reached the Portakabin, yanked open the door and walked in on a small gathering of downtrodden-looking people who sat in rows of chairs facing the opposite wall of the cabin, as if waiting for something to begin. Hearing the door open, they turned as one and looked at the newcomer vacantly. The former pastor smiled benignly at them. 'There's no reason for concern. I'm merely helping this gentleman,' he said, and with that they all turned back and stared straight ahead once more.

'What's this?' asked Bradshaw as the pastor ushered him outside.

'My flock.'

'Oh, I see,' said Bradshaw. 'Not much of a church, though, is it, unless you like to pray in a Portakabin?'

'The church is inside us,' Belasis protested, and he brought a clenched fist up to his heart and tapped it. 'These are true believers, some from my old congregation, who recognize that I was not entirely lost to sin.'

'You brought these mugs with you, in other words? Fleecing them again, are you? How much is the weekly collection plate worth? Not much, by the look of them.'

Belasis could not completely hide the look of superiority that briefly flitted across his face before it went blank again and Bradshaw wondered if a lying narcissist like him could ever be truly harmless. He had already caught the man out in one lie about his scrapyard church and he wondered how many more the former pastor had told him. Bradshaw remembered the young girl, then, who had fallen for this supposedly religious man before she abruptly disappeared. He wondered whether he could find her.

Chapter Sixty-two

'I say we focus on the yard supposedly owned by Mr Draycott to begin with,' said Bradshaw when they met that evening at Tom's house to share their findings. 'And I'm making some inquiries to see if we can trace the girl from Belasis's flock. Your Miss Keogh sounds more than a little unusual, but I doubt she's a kidnapper. McCree's site is the one that's intriguing me the most, though, since they wouldn't even let me inside the place, but I won't be able to get a warrant unless I can provide some evidence that a crime has been committed.'

'Can we at least watch the place for a while?' asked Tom, 'without being seen, I mean.'

'Not from the road outside. You'd be spotted immediately and you wouldn't be able to see into the place in any case from there but . . .' Bradshaw stopped to think for a moment. 'There are some large hills overlooking the yard and they're quite overgrown. We could probably get a good view from there, but we'd need binoculars and, ideally, some way of recording what we see so I could show the evidence for a warrant.'

Tom nodded. 'Leave that to me.'

It took Tom twenty-four hours to deliver on that promise and the two men were then able to return to the land around the scrapyard. 'You promised to do what?' asked

Bradshaw as they trudged up the hill together, Tom carrying a large video camera in a padded case.

'Film the raid,' said Tom, 'but only if there is one.' He had called in a favour with a television news producer who had often needed his help, either when he had no good stories for the evening bulletins or he had them but little of the inside track. Now the reporter was cashing in that debt.

'Jesus Christ.' Bradshaw was well aware of how embarrassing that could be. 'What if the raid does happen and we end up with nowt?'

'Then he gets nothing,' Tom assured him, 'and he won't be able to use it, will he?'

'He'd better not.'

They climbed further until they were on high ground and could see miles of lush green Northumbrian countryside beneath them. Only the tiny scar of the scrapyard far below disturbed this picture-postcard scene. They sought the shelter of the dense gorse bushes and Tom started taking the camera out of its case.

'Keep your bloody head down,' hissed Bradshaw, gesturing for Tom to sit.

'No one could possibly see us all the way up here,' protested Tom, but he joined Bradshaw on the grass, landing heavily on his backside as he tried to keep low.

'You sure you know how to use that thing?'

'You'd better hope so' – Tom had been given a brief lesson with the camera, but he was certainly no expert – 'or this will be one monumental waste of time.' He placed the camera on his shoulder and aimed it at the yard down below.

'Looks pretty light to me, for a TV camera. Isn't technology amazing? It's only about the size of a ghetto-blaster.'

'Got a bloody good zoom, too.' Tom smiled, 'I can see right into the compound.'

'And?'

Tom scanned the scrapyard for a while. 'Nothing,' he said. 'Not a thing, or even a person. If the place really is bent, then this could take a while.'

'Great,' said Bradshaw.

'Cheer up, Ian. Ten more minutes and it will be your turn to hold the bloody camera.'

'You have a think about it and let me know,' he had told Jenna, but how could she do that when she had no way of contacting him? He left her to stew until he got in touch with her again.

It happened early one morning, just like before. She came down to the shop and saw him through the window, leaning on that same wall.

'You made up your mind, love?' he asked when she joined him outside, and once he was sure she was alone and not wearing a wire. His hands had lingered on her as he checked and she was glad there was no one else around at this hour.

'Yes,' she said. 'I'll pay.'

'Right,' he said. 'Not here, not now. I hope you're listening, because here's how we are going to do this. 'When you come to meet me, don't bring anyone else. If I see anyone, the deal is off. I'll walk and you won't get another opportunity to keep your past hidden.'

'I understand.'

'Don't go calling the police, because I'll know. If you involve them, it'll be the word of a prozzie against mine, so who are they going to believe, eh? Think about that if you get scared, because I don't want you panicking and doing anything stupid. When we meet, if you're wearing a wire or have any kind of recording device or camera on you, I will leave without a word. Don't try and rig anything up there, because I'll find it. I want small bills, nothing over a fifty, and I want them in an unsealed envelope so I can see it's only the money that's in there. When you give me the cash I'll leave and you'll wait for ten minutes before going back to your car. Do you understand?'

'Yes.'

'I bloody hope you do, because I'm not playing games, Jenna. If you mess this up – if I even think you've broken any of my rules – then I'm gone, and the very next day letters start to arrive here. Not everyone will get one, just the landlord, the headteacher at the school, the vicar, the head of the parish council – the people who'll be shocked to hear about the woman with the dirty little secret who lives here among them. That'll be the end of you and your little village shop. Now, do we understand each other?'

She nodded.

'Any questions?'

'Just one,' she said. 'Where do we meet?'

They had been taking turns pointing the camera's zoom lens at the scrapyard for more than four hours and had talked about giving up more than once. They were only still there at all because both of them were reluctant to concede that their whole afternoon had been a complete waste of time. Bradshaw was on the verge of finally accepting the inevitable when Tom's phone rang. The journalist picked it up and said, 'Jenna?' then listened for a while and asked, 'What did he say to you?'

Tom listened again and when he received a questioning look from the detective he held up one finger and mouthed, *One minute*, at him. A moment later Tom asked, 'So where's the meet?' and when he received his answer he said, 'Yeah, I know it, and it's not going to be easy, but leave it with me, Jenna. I'll think of something.'

When the call was over, Bradshaw asked, 'A problem?'

'To add to all the others,' was all he received as an answer. He took the camera from Bradshaw and began to train it back on to the scrapyard once more. Bradshaw lay down in the grass, the back of his head resting in the palms of his hands and closed his eyes for a while. Just when he felt he could almost have dozed off, Tom jabbed him in the ribs and said, 'A woman.' Bradshaw sat up and Tom pointed towards the scrapyard. 'And a man.'

'What are they doing?' asked Bradshaw, who could only make out the tiniest of shapes far below them.

'They just got out of a minibus that pulled in to the yard and now they are walking. She's in front of him and he's following. He just pushed her.' When Bradshaw sounded agitated he said, 'Don't worry. I'm filming.' Tom kept up a steady stream of commentary on the woman's movements. 'He just shoved her again but I can't tell if it's a domestic of some kind or he's trying to get her to go somewhere. Either way, it doesn't look good.'

A moment later Tom said, 'Oh Christ, he just knocked her to the ground and I think he may have aimed a kick at her.'

'Jesus, is she all right?'

'She's back on her feet and walking again, stumbling along. This is definitely something dodgy. She's being herded towards something. Oh my god.'

'What is it?'

Tom didn't answer immediately. He was too absorbed watching the man, who was steering the woman towards a large metal cover to one side, by the edge of a steel-roofed barn. The metal sheet was pulled away to reveal an entrance underneath and, with one last shove, the woman was sent into it and down she went.

'It's a staircase of some kind. It goes down.' He watched until the woman disappeared and the man slid the metal cover back in place.

'That's your underground prison,' he told Bradshaw. 'Right there.'

Chapter Sixty-three

The flowers caught Helen off guard and on a bad day. Maybe if she had been feeling less vulnerable she would not have welcomed them, but the words on the card attached to the bouquet were kind and the accompanying letter which landed on the doormat that same morning was long and thoughtful. It seemed to have been written by a very different man to the one she had argued so fiercely with when they broke up. Perhaps people can change. Maybe Peter had done some growing up.

Although Peter's letter was an obvious attempt to re-engage with Helen, more importantly it was also an admission that he was at least partly responsible for the death of their relationship. He conceded he had been dismissive of her career and too wrapped up in his own job, managing the carpet stores his father owned, to fully consider her needs. He should have been more tolerant of the strains placed on them both due to the long-distance nature of their relationship. He finished by urging her to remember the good times – and there had been some, she had to concede that – when they first met at college and during the early years of their relationship, when she had genuinely considered he might be the one she was going to spend the rest of her life with.

What the hell am I doing, getting sentimental about an old relationship that's well past its sell-by date? Then she countered that thought with another one. *What am I doing here, miles from home, living in a friend's spare room, obsessing about missing girls? Where will it lead me?* Her mother's lecture had annoyed her, perhaps because it had struck a chord. You did have to keep one eye on the future. She folded the letter and put it in her bag so she didn't have to tell Tom about it and she took the flowers up to her bedroom. Then Helen came back down and surprised herself by dialling Peter's number.

They debated attempting to hit the place there and then, but Bradshaw pointed out the obvious: he couldn't even get through the gate. And as well as that physical barrier, he had no warrant. What if they tried to force their way into the scrapyard and they couldn't find the woman or she was whisked away before they reached her? What if they found her but she denied everything, as she might under duress, and they were forced to leave her there? Despite her fairly rough treatment, she didn't appear to be in imminent serious danger, so they reluctantly agreed to wait.

It was the footage that did it. As soon as the magistrate learned about it, along with Bradshaw's ongoing inquiry into the missing girls, he granted the warrant to raid the premises. Bradshaw knew he was taking a risk and that his reputation hinged on whether they found any of the missing girls in the scrapyard and not simply the down-trodden girlfriend or partner of a thug.

They decided to go in early. Bradshaw was far from the senior man but he was expected to take the lead when the team went in, since the raid was his responsibility. More than twenty officers had been summoned, some armed, and Bradshaw felt under huge pressure.

At dawn, the locks and chains on the gate were cut by police and they went in hard, catching the half-dozen men who ran the place unawares and dragging them from buildings across the site, then lining them up against a wall for questioning while the place was thoroughly searched. Bradshaw took some satisfaction from the presence against that wall of the man who had told him to fuck off.

Tom watched it all unfolding from the same spot on the hill where he had witnessed the mini-bus pull in to the scrapyard. He recorded everything on the camera so he could repay his debt to the TV news producer. He could clearly see the officers scatter round the compound while they searched for the girl.

To his astonishment, the officers nearest to the metal cover that had been placed over the hidden staircase went straight past it without stopping or even noticing it. 'Come on,' he said to himself, as they certainly couldn't hear him from this height. He wondered if the bird's-eye view he had was more effective than the one they were afforded at ground level and that was why they hadn't seen the suspicious cover by the barn. He sat tight and waited for more officers to come by, but none did. They were all busy elsewhere or taking suspects away from the premises.

Then the first two officers came back, and once again they went straight past the metal shutter. What did they think it was? Perhaps they couldn't see it at all from that angle. Tom cried out in frustration.

'Well, that was an absolute bloody waste of time,' the detective superintendent who had insisted on accompanying the raid told Bradshaw. 'They didn't find a thing.'

'No, sir,' said Bradshaw, who couldn't believe it. Tom had recorded a woman being physically abused on the site, and now there was no one here.

'This has been a farce,' the most senior uniformed officer chipped in, damning Bradshaw even further.

'What the bloody hell have you been playing at?' barked the detective superintendent, who was clearly smarting from the sarcastic comments from his uniformed counterpart.

Just then Bradshaw's mobile phone began to ring. He let it, because he was in the middle of a bollocking from a detective superintendent and didn't want it to look like he wasn't listening to the man. Unfortunately, it rang and rang.

'Well, answer it then!' roared the DS, so Bradshaw did as he was told.

'Hello,' he said, then he listened intently and hung up.

The DS was still waiting for an explanation, and the head of the uniformed squad was looking decidedly smug.

'It seems your men have been looking in the wrong places,' Bradshaw told him with relish. He turned to the detective superintendent. 'Perhaps you'd like to follow me, sir.'

Bradshaw set off for the location Tom had described on the phone and prayed to all the gods that they would find something when he pulled back the metal cover. It took him a while to find it because it was set back and on lower ground, but he knew it was there, which gave him an advantage over the uniformed men. He found it, lifted back the cover and saw the steps leading down. That wasn't all that he found. Two scared Chinese faces were staring back up at him from the foot of the staircase, and there were other people lurking behind them down in the shadows.

The DS peered down as well. 'Er . . . well done, Bradshaw,' he said, then he turned on his uniformed opposite number with some ferocity. 'Care to explain how your men missed this? Not bloody good enough, is it?'

Tom witnessed it all from the hilltop and a sense of relief flooded through him. One by one, the figures emerged from the covered staircase and he watched as other officers joined Bradshaw and led the victims away from their place of captivity.

He had promised to phone Helen as soon as he knew the outcome and she answered on the first ring. 'We got a result,' he said. 'I reckon there are thirty people down there, at least.'

'And the missing women?' she asked.

'Don't know yet. Let's keep our fingers crossed.'

Was it over? Perhaps it was. Even if the missing women had not yet been found, no one could deny their intervention here had paid off. Perhaps thirty lives had been saved. That was something.

'Listen,' she said. 'While the dust is settling, would you mind if I went home tomorrow?'

'Sure, no problem.' Then he asked, 'How long will you be?'

'Only a couple of days. I'll be back in time to vote.'

'What have you got planned?'

'See my mum, see my dad,' she said, and then because she remembered how much she hated it when he was evasive, 'I promised I'd have a chat with Peter.' There was a long silence on the line. 'Hello?'

'Are you serious? You're not actually thinking of getting back together with him, are you?'

'It's only a talk.'

'To what end?'

She almost told him it was none of his business but had to admit he was only being as intrusive about her personal life as she was about his. 'I promised to hear him out, that's all.'

'Yes, but he's trying to get you back, Helen,' Tom reminded her, 'And he's an arse.'

'He's changed,' she said, 'since we broke up. Even my mother says so.' It sounded so weak now that she was saying it out loud, but how could she admit her true feelings? Helen was in her late twenties, hadn't met anyone she liked in ages and the one man she really did care about was dating a twenty-year-old. Helen was living in his spare bedroom and felt like she had nothing in her life except work. How could she explain that all this was making her scared and that, for that reason alone, she was willing to hear Peter out? Perhaps she would be settling for less with Peter, but maybe that was what everyone did, in the end.

'People don't change,' said Tom, and before she could react he mumbled, 'Look, I've got to go,' and abruptly hung up.

Chapter Sixty-four

The next morning Ian Bradshaw ordered three crispy bacon rolls from the waitress at the Rosewood Café. 'They're on me,' he declared, and was surprised by the muted atmosphere at their table. Tom seemed sullen and was sitting back in his chair with his arms folded. Helen lacked her usual warmth and he noticed she had an overnight bag on the ground by her feet.

'What's the matter with you two?' he asked.

'Nothing,' they both chorused at once.

'You're like an old married couple.' He only meant the way they gave the same reply at exactly the same moment, but they both shifted uneasily at his comment so he decided to change the subject. 'Thirty-two people,' he told them with a smile. 'Men and women. That's how many they lifted out of the bunker, as it's being called, though really it's just the lower level of the old barn. The evil bastards dug it out and bricked around it, then they put a brand-new barn on top of it. You wouldn't know the underground part was there at all unless you saw the people going in.'

'Where are they from?' asked Tom.

'China, mostly, but there are also a number of Eastern Europeans, several of African origin and at least one from India. We've got translators coming in to try and work it all out.'

'It looks like a classic trafficking operation,' he continued. 'The people being held there were brought into the country illegally, for a fee they had to stump up themselves, and forced to work as slave labour. The criminals behind this scheme were getting money from their victims up front then profiting from their misery. We've seen this before: they invent false debts the immigrants have incurred and say they have to pay them off before they can be released.'

'What were they using them for?' asked Tom.

'Unpaid labour,' said Bradshaw. 'Slaves, basically. They worked on farms or in factories, and some of the women, well, you can guess where they were made to work.'

'That's horrific,' Helen said, 'but was there any sign of our missing women?' She knew he would have mentioned it by now if there had been.

He shook his head. 'There is a theory that they may have been through there, though.'

'Why would anyone think that?'

'You could describe the site as being underground. You said that yourself,' he reminded Tom. 'One of the senior officers reckons they might be part of some reverse white-slave trade deal that's going on.'

'Seriously?' asked Tom.

'I'm not saying I fully agree, but in the meantime everyone is pretty happy that we got so many people out of there.'

'What does that mean?' Helen demanded. 'They're not just going to give up on finding the other women, surely?'

'Not giving up, no,' said Bradshaw.

'Just winding it down?' said Tom, and his tone made it clear he was unhappy.

'Not even that,' said Bradshaw defensively. 'Look, we never had much in the way of resources to start with, did we, and now we are no worse off. You two are still on the payroll. It's just a question of where we go from here. When they both seemed unconvinced, he added: 'So if you have any bright ideas, now would be the time to air them.'

'I'm stumped if I know,' admitted Tom, 'but you're right. Getting those people out of there was a real result.'

'It was,' said Bradshaw, 'and one we shouldn't take lightly.' He had even enjoyed winding up DC Malone on her lack of progress with the 'evil stepdad' case, while he had been busy freeing the migrants from the scrapyards. 'Maybe we'll get something more from the men we arrested.'

'What about Jimmy McCree?' asked Helen. 'Will they give him up?'

'Don't hold your breath.'

'But we know he's behind this,' she protested.

'We do, but proving it is another matter and, so far, no one is grassing him up to save their skins. Would you, if it meant you'd probably be stabbed on remand? I suspect they will all quietly serve their time instead. They may not even know they're working for Jimmy. He has cut-outs. You know, middlemen.'

'So he gets away with it,' she said coldly. 'Again.'

'Perhaps, but we'll get him one day, Helen, and in the meantime we just saved thirty-two people from a life of slavery. The cup is half full.'

'I suppose it is,' she admitted. 'It just doesn't feel like it.'

Jenna had to drive more than thirty miles to meet her blackmailer. He'd chosen the village of Warkworth in

Northumbria for the handover, and she'd spent a good part of the journey wondering why. Maybe nobody knew him there, and perhaps they would go unnoticed in this pretty little village, so used to strangers visiting its medieval castle, which dominated the horizon and towered over its shops and houses. She parked halfway up the steep hill road which doubled as the main street then walked back down it, away from the castle, until she passed the Church of St Lawrence and reached the bank of the River Coquet, its muddy waters, swelled by recent rains, flowing swiftly by.

Jenna scanned the riverbank for any sign of her tormentor. He wasn't on the first bench or the second, but she soon spotted him a little way off, sitting on his own, staring straight ahead as if placidly watching the ducks as they floated down the river. Such a calm scene for a meeting of huge importance.

Jenna had her instructions: *Tell no one, come alone, don't wear a wire.* She'd also been told what would happen if she broke any of those rules. It didn't bear thinking about.

When she drew closer to the bench he stood up abruptly. 'Take off your coat,' he said.

She obeyed and handed it to him. He passed his hands through its folds and invaded its pockets, touching and squeezing the contents until he appeared satisfied and placed it on the bench. 'Now the shirt,' he said, as if this was a simple matter.

'You want me to take my top off? Here?'

'Lift it up,' he said impatiently, and when she widened her eyes: 'I need to know you are not wearing a wire.

There's no one around,' he snapped. 'That's why I chose the place. No one can see us, no one can hear us.

'Come on, love,' he hissed. 'I haven't got all day. and it's a bit late to pretend you're shy now, isn't it?'

Jenna glanced quickly left and right then did as he ordered. She grabbed her shirt and pulled it up over her stomach and bra then lifted her hands higher until they touched her chin. He took a long look and seemed to enjoy the view.

'Happy?' she asked, once it was obvious she wasn't concealing anything.

'Very,' he smirked, and she wanted to hurt him then, really badly. Jenna let go of the bottom of her shirt and it fell back down to cover her once more.

'Can we at least sit down?' she asked. 'My feet are hurting.'

He glanced at her shoes. 'Should have worn something more practical. You could have had a walk round the village afterwards.' He said it as if that was what people did once they had paid off a blackmailer.

He sat back down on the bench and she joined him so they were a foot apart, both looking out across the river, a father and daughter, perhaps, out for a stroll.

'Did you bring the money?' he asked. 'Is that what I felt in your coat pocket?'

'I brought the money,' she confirmed. 'Just like you asked . . . or should I say demanded.'

'There's no need to get shirty.'

'Oh really? I'm supposed to be polite, am I, when someone blackmails me?'

'Shut up and give me my money.'

321

'No.'

'No? What do you mean, *no*? You know what will happen if you don't.'

'Yes,' she admitted, 'I do. You told me. You'll tell my whole village I used to be an escort, ruining my life in the process.' Then she took a breath, stealing herself. 'But how do I know you won't do that anyway, after I pay you?'

'Well, that's the beauty of our little arrangement, isn't it, darling? If you continue to pay, I'm not going to tell, am I? There would be no incentive for me to.'

'So, I have to keep on paying you the same amount every month for ever, to buy your silence?'

'That's how it works and I'd say it's a good deal, for you and me both. Now hand over the money like a good little girl and I'll be on my way, until the same time next month.'

She hesitated then said, 'All right,' and reluctantly reached into her coat pocket for the envelope with the money. She held it out for him and he frowned as if she was being indiscreet doing it that way, but there was no one nearby to witness anything. He snatched the money and put it in his inside coat pocket.

'Right,' he said. 'Got to go. There's somewhere I have to be.'

'How many?' she asked.

'How many what?'

'How many more of the women,' she demanded, 'have you blackmailed like this?'

He snorted. 'I told you, love. All of them.'

Chapter Sixty-five

The theory that women from the UK might have been sent back to impoverished areas in some form of reverse white-slavery deal made no sense to Helen. Why would you go to all of the trouble of doing that if you were a criminal looking to make money? You wouldn't need to kidnap British women and send them east when there were plenty of girls already in the area who could serve the same purpose. The reward wouldn't be enough in a weaker local economy to go to all the risk and inconvenience. She just couldn't see it.

So, if the women weren't at that scrapyard, they had to be somewhere else, but where? Helen's thoughts went back to the abandoned farmhouse she had visited with Tom and the name and address on the electoral roll. It was the wrong name, or so they had thought when they went out there, but what if the document wasn't wrong? What if the farmhouse had been owned by Keogh, too? As soon as that thought struck her, it made her want to go back there and take a closer look at the building to see what was behind it. The scrapyard backed on to the same land as the farmhouse and Keogh was a loose cannon who had stormed out of his family home when he was still a young man. He might be entirely harmless, but perhaps he wasn't. The daughter he left behind hadn't struck Helen as normal either, but of course that didn't mean her father had been capable of abducting women all those years ago. The link with the present was trickier, however, and that's when Helen's intuition immediately fell down. If he was dead and had left only a daughter to run his business, how could she have any involvement in this? That was when she saw it.

If he was dead.

What was it Tom had said? 'Maybe she thought we wouldn't believe her unless we saw it with our own eyes.' And how did she prove his death? With a scrap of paper from a newspaper column that anyone could have placed. All Helen and Tom had seen was a death notice. That alone did not constitute proof.

Helen still had a couple of hours before her train back home. *Why not?* she thought.

'Detective Sergeant O'Brien,' Bradshaw greeted the older man as he entered the conference room at Police HQ. 'It's been a while since we've seen you in here.'

'I was suspended, as well you know, on full pay, with nothing proven and without a stain on my character.'

'That why you are taking early retirement today? To avoid any awkward questions?'

'When people throw enough shit, some of it is bound to stick. Mostly, *they* are on my side' – he jerked his thumb to indicate the roomful of detectives working in the office outside – 'but there's always some who like to cast aspersions.' He narrowed his eyes at Bradshaw as he said this, to make it clear he felt the younger man was one of them. 'I've had enough. What you doing here anyway, Sherlock, and where's the woman from Personnel?'

'They call it Human Resources these days,' Bradshaw told him, 'and I'm here to formalize things.'

'Bloody hell.' He shot Bradshaw a look of disgust. 'I'd have thought Kane might be here at least, or is he too bloody busy to see off a man who is heading for well-earned retirement?'

'It's a very timely retirement,' observed Bradshaw, 'with those misconduct charges hanging over you.'

O'Brien smiled. 'Yeah, well, they can't touch me now. I've done my years, pretty much, and I've got a full pension, as near as damn-it, so as far as they are concerned, I'm Teflon. Nothing will stick.' And he gave Bradshaw a humourless grin.

'But what will you do?' asked Bradshaw. 'How will you live? A pension is all very well, but is it really enough, and how will you fill those hours?'

DS O'Brien looked incredibly smug. 'Oh, don't you worry about me,' he said. 'I'll be just fine. I've got a few plans and I know how to make a bob or two.'

'I bet you do,' said Bradshaw amiably, then his tone changed. 'Blackmailing hookers, presumably.'

O'Brien froze and the colour seemed to drain from him. He tried hard to recover. 'What did you say?'

'You heard me.'

O'Brien took a step towards the door. 'Don't try and leave,' Bradshaw told him. It's not going to look good if I have to wrestle you to the ground.'

O'Brien turned, gritted his teeth and advanced on Bradshaw.

'Go on, then,' said Bradshaw. 'Throw a punch. I'd love that.'

O'Brien stopped in his tracks and seemed to be evaluating whether the younger man was serious. When it appeared he was, O'Brien changed tactic. 'I've got no idea what you're talking about. Just because some prozzie has been saying stuff about me, it doesn't mean it's true. They'll make up anything to get coppers into bother.'

In answer, Bradshaw went to the large TV set at the end of the conference room. He bent towards the VCR and hit play. A videotaped image appeared on the TV and O'Brien walked towards it and peered at the screen. What he saw was a clear image of himself and Jenna sitting on a bench looking outwards towards a camera that had been secreted a long way back from the opposite bank then zoomed in on them from a distance. Tom Carney had used the good will he had mustered from the TV news producer from the footage he got of the police raid on the scrapyard to borrow the camera again. Then he had gone to the riverbank where Jenna had been ordered to meet her blackmailer and waited.

The picture was at a slight angle because Tom could not have known which of the benches O'Brien was going to choose for his meeting with Jenna and he had to set up the camera in a spot where he could survey them yet not be seen, which was far from easy. Thankfully, the powerful zoom lens had made it possible.

'Are you saying that's not you, extorting money from a former prostitute?'

O'Brien's face betrayed him; it was filled with panic, anger and fear. 'That's not why I met with her,' he said. 'She approached me and said she had information . . . about a crime, an ongoing investigation.'

'Really? That's not what she says.'

'Then it's my word against hers,' O'Brien hissed. 'Isn't it?'

He turned back to the screen and realized there was no audio to accompany the video pictures. 'What have you got here anyway?' He sounded triumphant now. 'Nothing. Just a bit of film of me sitting with someone. We could have been talking about anything.' He was right. The pictures alone were nowhere near enough to get a conviction.

'Now, are you done, Bradshaw? Because I'm not. I'm going to put in an official complaint about you. So help me, I'll make sure everyone in this force hears what you tried to do to me. Everybody already knows you ain't right in the head. You're not one of us and you never will be.'

It was then that the door opened and Tom walked in, accompanied by a young woman. 'What's he doing here?' O'Brien demanded.

Tom ignored him. 'Sorry I'm a bit late,' he told Bradshaw. 'Got held up downstairs when we signed in. I got the impression the desk sergeant isn't that keen on journalists.'

He turned to O'Brien. 'This is Marie. You could say she's a friend of a friend. I've brought her here today to take a look at the film I shot of you blackmailing my old friend Jenna.' Before O'Brien could react or say another word, Tom said, 'Okay, Marie, do your stuff.'

The young woman walked closer to the TV set. She moved to within a few yards of it and stopped, peering at it intently as the video tape continued to roll, then, in front of a disbelieving O'Brien, she began to speak along with the tape.

'*Did you bring the money? Is that what I felt in your coat pocket?*'

'*I brought the money, just like you asked . . . or should I say demanded.*'

'*There's no need to get shirty.*'

'*Oh really? I'm supposed to be polite, am I, when someone black-mails me?*'

'*Shut up and give me my money.*'

O'Brien looked like he was in complete shock. It was as if he was witnessing sorcery. 'What the fuck is this?' he managed.

'That, O'Brien, is lip-reading,' Bradshaw informed him.

Chapter Sixty-six

Helen had to drive past the farmhouse and park on a grass verge just before she reached the corner that separated it from the Keogh cottage. She got out of her car, walked back and went to the locked, rusty gate. The house still looked abandoned – it was grubby and the net curtains were old and dirty. There were no lights on inside.

Helen examined the yard beyond the gate. The ground was dry and there was no fresh mud on the concrete where a vehicle might have driven across it. The whole building had the air of a place long abandoned, but what might lie beyond it? Were there outbuildings or barns? Were there places on the land around that might have been mistaken in some victim's overwrought mind for an underground dwelling?

Helen knew she couldn't ask the police to search the place without good cause but she didn't fancy the idea of exploring the land around it without Tom and Ian at least knowing where she was, so she decided it was best to call them. She reached for her phone and, for once, was grateful that Tom's chiding about the blooming thing never being charged had led her to take more care to plug it into the socket in the kitchen at night. Helen hoped she'd be able to get a signal in a rural spot like this, then, to her consternation, she realized the battery indicator was showing only a tiny amount of life.

How could that be? She had definitely plugged it into the socket on the wall by the toaster. Then she remembered

Tom's other annoying trait. He was always turning off the power switches next to the sockets, rendering them useless, because he had once written a story where some people had died in a fire caused by a shorted electric circuit triggered by a ghetto-blaster that had been left plugged in. She cursed Tom for being so bloody anal and chided herself for forgetting about it. She tried to call him anyway but the phone died immediately.

'Shit,' she hissed. Helen knew she had to make a decision. She wanted to check the place out in case it held secrets beyond its stark building and she would have preferred people to know where she was going. Fate had robbed her of that opportunity, however, and she really didn't want to leave here and waste more time driving back on another day, possibly for no reason.

It was the lack of life in the building which convinced her to just do it. Helen told herself she would take a look, no more than that, then she would head back. If she saw anything even slightly suspicious, she could let Ian know and he could come back mob-handed with a warrant.

Helen put a foot on the lowest part of the fence, placed her weight on it then climbed over the gate before carefully dismounting and standing in the farmyard.

She didn't move at first. Instead she waited to see if anyone would react to her presence by calling out, or whether a dog might start to bark at the intruder. But there was no sound and no sign of anyone in the farmhouse, not even a twitching curtain. She told herself that even if there was someone there she could explain her presence, though in truth she wasn't sure how. Helen would knock on the door, just to make sure, then if no one answered she would take a look around. No harm in that, surely?

She did feel a little uneasy now that she was on the wrong side of the gate, and she had to tell herself not to be so foolish. There really didn't appear to be anyone living here. She walked up to the door of the farmhouse and knocked firmly then waited. After a few moments she knocked again, harder this time, but there was still no answer. She tried the door and it was locked.

She walked round the side of the building and began to explore the farm.

There was some shouting and a bit of a struggle at the very end but not as much as Bradshaw was expecting. DS O'Brien didn't go quietly, but his eventual arrest wasn't as violent or noisy as any of them had feared. Admittedly, some onlookers came towards the conference room once the raised voice of the DS reached a certain volume, but all they heard as he was led away from the room was a loud but surprisingly half-hearted protest that 'This is all bullshit and she is some kind of bloody witch!'

To begin with, the problem had kept Tom up at night. How could he record a conversation with a man who was bound to check his victim wasn't wearing a wire and savvy enough to avoid specifying a particular spot for a bug to be planted there in advance? He could have picked any one of a number of benches along the riverbank or simply chosen to have walked along it with Jenna while he talked.

The idea of filming him from a distance came to him after the raid on the scrapyard. The footage Tom provided to his producer friend of large numbers of migrants being rescued had gone down a storm and the promise that there might be more footage he would be interested in involving police corruption and blackmail had been persuasive. But there was no way to clearly record what they were saying from that distance. All Tom would be left with was a film with no dialogue.

It was thinking about silent films that had done it, those old movies where people mouthed the words and the dialogue appeared on the screen in the form of subtitles. That was what he needed. Magical subtitles that could communicate the meaning of lips that moved silently. Then he realized there was a better and far less fanciful idea. He needed someone who could look at those silent lips and read them for him.

Marie from the Furry Friends Centre had been an absolute star, never questioning her involvement and accepting the word of Helen, Tom and later DS Ian Bradshaw that she was on the side of right. What really impressed Tom was how unfazed she had been when she was face to face with DS O'Brien. She had merely concentrated on the job in hand and read every incriminating word from the screen, even as the accused man had begun to first question then rant at her.

Tom phoned Jenna with the news and broke off from her repeated, relieved thank-yous only because Marie was patiently waiting for a lift back. He took her to lunch first then dropped her off at the hearing-dog centre before heading home so he could write a piece about a detective sergeant being arrested for corruption then sell it as an exclusive.

'That's another one we owe you, Tom,' said Paul Hill,

Tom's long-standing contact at the *Daily Mirror* when he phoned it in to the tabloid.

'It's actually money that you owe me Paul, not favours, so I would be grateful for prompt payment.'

'You got it, mate.' The spectre of Tom's outstanding bills began to slowly recede.

Finally, he returned to Bradshaw at police HQ. 'I don't suppose we're too popular right now,' he said, 'with the rank and file.'

'Normally, you're not,' admitted the detective, 'but I don't think O'Brien has many friends left. They're all in shock. It's not as if your lip-reader was going to make any of it up. Jenna played her part as well, by the way, coaxing the incriminating words out of him, though I suppose some of that was your doing?'

'I gave her a few pointers but she still had to hand him enough rope to hang himself. She did a great job – there was a lot resting on it for her.'

Bradshaw shook his head in something resembling disbelief. 'I still can't quite believe he did it. I mean, I never liked the guy, we'd had our tussles in the past, but what the hell was he thinking?'

'The usual,' said Tom. 'That the rules don't apply to him, that he would get away with it.'

'Do you really think he'll go down for this? Won't they want to give him the benefit of the doubt one last time?'

Bradshaw shook his head. 'They just searched O'Brien's house. They found the ledger with the girls' names in it. Why would he have that except to blackmail them? He's finished, Tom.'

Chapter Sixty-seven

Two stone animals flanked the back door of the farmhouse, as if guarding it. The statues were old, weather-beaten and quite small, each one the dimensions of a medium-sized dog, and they glared out, as if warning trespassers not to come too close. Helen couldn't make out exactly what they were meant to be. They were a bit like domestic cats, though fierce-looking. Could they be pumas or jaguars? Could they perhaps be the lions that Sarah said she saw when she escaped her captivity? It was possible, but was this even a garden? Not really. It was a farmyard backing on to fields.

At the far end of the yard were a number of metal drums. Three were stacked next to one another vertically and a fourth was lying on the ground, having presumably fallen over at some point and never been righted. Grass grew around them and the metal on the drums was rusted. It looked as if they hadn't been moved in a while. Perhaps they were empty or, like the farmhouse, no longer of use to anyone. Helen drew closer and noticed writing on the side of each drum. She had to bend low so that she was almost down on one knee in order to read it. There was white lettering on a blue background and it gave information on the contents of the drums. The largest word was presumably the name of the company that supplied them, then there were some chemical symbols which meant nothing to Helen.

$C_3H_4Cl_2F_2O$

Followed by a product name: Methoxyflurane.

Outlawed in the UK since the late seventies, according to Dr Hemming, but it could put you to sleep and damage your internal organs. Now Helen was staring at barrels of the stuff on a farm in rural County Durham. How could there be any innocent explanation for this?

Helen turned and looked about her. No one there, nobody staring out at her from the farmhouse windows, even though for a moment she was convinced she was being watched. She switched her attention back to the barrels then, determined to record the information written on them. Helen reached inside her jacket pocket for her notebook and a pen, bending low once more to write down the chemical symbol, name and address.

When she was done, she straightened once more and her eyeline went beyond the barrels to the fields behind them. This was grazing land that been allowed to fall fallow, so it was littered with weeds and wildflowers that were blooming now that spring was here. It was a colourful spectacle, so at odds with Helen's creeping sense of dread, and complemented by a large clump of trees off to one side of the field which had broken into bloom. They stretched all the way down the hill. Their branches were thrusting outwards proudly now that they were full of colourful blossom. So that's where the street name came from. These were magnolia trees and there were dozens of them with pretty pale flowers at the end of their branches.

Pink flowers.

Pink trees, thought Helen.

Helen was so shocked by this realization that she opened her mouth to actually say the words, but then she heard a loud click. Someone was standing behind her. Slowly and reluctantly, she turned to face her fate. There was a man there, standing between her and the gate of the farm, preventing her from returning to the safety of the open road and her car. He was wearing a balaclava and carrying a large double-barrelled shotgun, which he pointed right at her.

'Please don't shoot me,' she said quietly, because she was certain now that he would.

'I knew you'd come,' he told her.

Chapter Sixty-eight

1990

*Then when lust has conceived, it gives birth to sin; and when
sin is accomplished, it brings forth death.*
— James 1:15

Chris was fourteen when he finally worked out the secret of
the big house. The sense that his father owned it, too, was a
vague one till then and never discussed between them, but
no one else lived there or appeared to have the right to come
there. His father went into the building unaccompanied, its
fields bordered the garden of the cottage and he used to
roam them freely, and the adjacent woodland.

The first night that Chris followed Father, first to the
farmhouse then, after he emerged from it, across the
fields, he was driven by more than simple curiosity. He
knew about the bunker and his father's plans for it but
instinct told him there was something not quite right in
the world and that his father was a part of it somehow. He
felt compelled to discover just what the man was up to
after dark while Chris was tucked up in bed.

He watched as the door to one of the big metal boxes
swung open. Light from the lamp his father held illuminated the scene inside but all Chris could make out was a

dark figure with a bright light beside him. He knew there was someone already in there, despite the fact he could not see them. He could hear her. She didn't scream but instead there was a pitiful, desperate sound like a low wail. His father placed the lamp on the ground by the door of the big metal box.

Somehow Chris dared to move closer until he had a clearer view of his father, who still held the shotgun but now had something in his other hand. It looked like a little plastic bag, and he drew something from it and held it in his right hand while he kept the gun pointed forward with his left, then moved further into the box and disappeared. The sounds from the woman became shriller for a moment, then they were muffled until, finally, they ceased. The door was pushed to, from the inside, until it was almost fully closed. Only a thin line of light came from one side now, a tiny gap, because his father had been careful not to lock himself inside it by accident.

Chris would never know what pushed him on, but he began to move forward, abandoning all caution, along with his usual dread of retribution from his father. He wanted to know the secret of the big box. He had to know it, in fact.

He reached the door. Initially he had wanted to creep up to it and observe without being seen but that was impossible now. Instead he opened it, and his presence was immediately detected. His father whirled, wide-eyed, and pointed the gun straight at him. He was shocked, angry – frightened, too, by the look on his face. It was only later that Chris realized his father could have turned and fired at him in one movement, without even thinking. From that range, the twelve-bore would have ripped him to pieces.

But he didn't fire. Instead he lowered the gun and they both looked at the figure on the bed. A girl? A woman. A woman not so very much older than Chris. Curvy, with long brown hair, like the girl in one of his father's paintings that hung in the hallway, and she was asleep, her clothes half removed. The damp cloth on the floor smelt strongly of chemicals. That was what his father must have removed from the plastic bag as he entered the box.

'Chris,' said his father, lowering the gun, and he was suddenly terrified. He braced himself for the onslaught, the beating, the accusations of spying and betrayal, but none of that came.

'It's okay,' said his father. 'I was going to tell you anyway. It's time you knew about the work.' Both of them stared at the girl lying on the bed. 'God's work,' he added quickly, as if he was likely to undertake any other kind: 'Now you are old enough to understand.' Chris noticed there was what looked like a fresh tear in the arm of the young woman's blouse. The skirt she wore had been pulled up to her waist and her tights and underwear wrenched down.

Perhaps Chris looked scared then, because his father said, 'It's all right, it's okay.' Then he smiled at Chris. 'I'm saving her.'

Chapter Sixty-nine

That night Jenna insisted on buying Tom a meal. 'It's a lot cheaper than paying a blackmailer,' she told him when she had finally exhausted his protests. He relented then, partly because he enjoyed Jenna's company but also because he had no desire to go back to an empty house with Helen away.

'I can't believe it's over,' she said when they'd finished their meal and she had paid the bill. 'I haven't slept properly in ages. I want to thank you, Tom. You've been very kind.'

'Nobody should be allowed to get away with blackmail, especially a police officer. He had to be stopped.'

'It's not just that,' she said. 'You never judged me.'

'Why would I do that?'

'You know why.'

'Well, Jenna, I hadn't seen you for a long time and it wasn't as if you chose that life while I was seeing you. Things just happened to you.'

'Well, anyway, thanks for not judging.'

'You secret is safe with me,' he told her, but she still looked troubled.

'Is it, though?'

'Of course.'

She shook her head. 'I know *you* wouldn't tell anyone, but that detective isn't the only guy who knows about my past life.'

'Your clients, you mean?' He wasn't sure if that was the right word.

'Yes,' she said. 'I thought coming to a small village would mean I was less likely to bump into someone who' – it was her turn to search for the right phrase – 'knew me, but now I keep wondering.'

'Wondering what?'

'I went to the pub the other night,' she explained. 'They had an event on for charity. I usually enjoy things like that. Now when I look around the room I keep thinking someone might know me. It's silly, I know, but it doesn't feel quite the same.'

'You're a little unnerved at the moment, understandably so.' Tom knew her fear of exposure might be an irrational one, but he empathized with it. How many times had he parted the curtains in the upstairs bedroom so he could look down on to the street below to check there were no strangers loitering there? 'But that will pass, in time.'

'I hope you're right,' she said, 'because I'm not planning on going anywhere.'

'You decided to stay?'

'If that's all right with you, Mr Carney?'

'It's more than all right with me, Miss Ellison.'

'Good, because this is my home now.' She added: 'And it's nice to know I have at least one friend around the corner I can turn to if I need him.'

'You do,' he assured her. 'Always.'

'If your girlfriend doesn't mind, that is?'

'She'll be fine with it.'

'Really?' She smiled then. 'Did you tell her you were coming here tonight?'

Reluctantly, he admitted the truth, 'No,' he said. 'You got me. I probably should, though.'

'Yeah, you probably should.' She placed her hand on his for a moment. 'And I'll see you around, Tom.'

Tom thought about Jenna on his way home. He hoped and believed he'd been able to help her, but bad experiences lingered long in the mind. He understood that more than most, because he carried the scars from the cases he'd investigated that had ended badly, sometimes with a murder or suicide.

That stuff stayed with you and you couldn't really talk about it to anyone. There was only one person Tom could share the burden with, because she had been through it herself. Helen understood. Who else could he talk to when the costs of his decisions came back to haunt him, as they often did, and he wondered, for the umpteenth time, *What if I had done things differently?*

Bradshaw had his demons, too, but they never talked about them together. Men didn't do that generally, but Helen could on occasion coax it out of him just by asking, 'Are you all right, Tom?'

In the same way, Helen could talk to Tom when she was gripped by a panic attack or woke shouting from a nightmare about her former editor's murder. What would he do if she ever left? Was she really contemplating getting back with the odious Peter? He hoped she would see sense. He told himself he was only looking out for someone he cared about, but he had a selfish reason, too. If Helen ever left, something big would be missing from his life.

Jenna would need someone to talk to from time to

time, too, and Tom wanted to be that person. Despite everything that had happened to her since they broke up, she would always be special and he was pleased she had no plans to leave. He wasn't sure how he would manage to continue their friendship and keep Penny happy, but he resolved to make it work somehow, even at the cost of lying to his girlfriend, a prospect he did not take lightly.

By the time he returned home Tom was exhausted and the empty house cold, so he went straight up to bed. He read for a while until his eyes began to burn with tiredness then put down the book and turned off the light.

He was woken from a deep sleep after what felt like a few minutes but must have been hours because sunshine was streaming through the curtains. There was a sound coming from somewhere. It was a phone ringing. The landline. Tom stumbled from the bed to answer it. His alarm clock told him it was 6.30 a.m.

'Hello,' he said.

'Put Helen on the line,' the furious voice demanded, and Tom, still groggy from interrupted sleep, took a moment to work out what was going on.

'Who is this?'

'It's Peter.' When Tom didn't immediately respond, he added: 'Helen's Peter. Now put her on the phone.'

Tom resisted the temptation to say, *You are not Helen's Peter.* 'She's not here,' he said instead. 'She's with you,' and immediately realized how stupid that sounded, because Peter wouldn't be angrily calling him at such an early hour if she was. Had they had some sort of a row? Had Helen told him she was going to take the last train back to the North-East? 'Isn't she?'

'You bloody know she isn't!' raged Peter. 'She was supposed to meet me last night and she didn't show. I've been calling her and calling her.'

'I thought she was with you,' said Tom, trying to work out where she might be. 'Have you tried her folks?'

'Of course I've tried her parents! She's not there. You know where she is!'

'I don't, and you need to calm down.'

'You do know! She's with you. She's always with you! Now put her on the line!'

Tom didn't even bother to answer the idiot. He just hung up.

Immediately he dialled Helen's mobile number but was diverted straight to her voicemail. 'Hi Helen, it's me,' he said. 'Could you give me a ring as soon as you get this message? Peter called and said you never made it to him, so I just wondered where you are. Bit worried about you, to be honest, so, you know, give me a call, okay?'

As soon as he finished he called Bradshaw and silenced his protestations about the early hour.

'Ian,' he said, 'we have a problem.'

Chapter Seventy

1996

*Truly, truly, I say to you, if anyone keeps My word
he will never see death.*

– John 8:51

There was an eleventh commandment. Not one of the ones
on Moses' tablets, which had all been written by the finger of
God, but this one was just as important. Chris had to learn it
from a young age and repeated it whenever his father called
upon him to do so. There were to be no police and no doctors. His father made him recite this almost as often as the
Bible commandments he had been made to learn by rote.

You shall not murder.

You shall not commit adultery.

You shall not steal.

You shall not bear false witness.

No police and no doctors.

Police and doctors were bad things because, though
they claimed to protect and help people, they could take
Chris away. If they disagreed with the way he was being
brought up, for example, then they would steal him.

Father had drummed this in to him time and time
again, particularly when he detected concern or fear in

Chris's eyes. The more ill Father had become, the more scared Chris had been and the more he had wanted to do something to help, but the man would hear nothing about it. He would get well without the doctor.

Calling a doctor would mess everything up because non-believers would be jealous of them and try to end the special way they lived. And they had to live like this if they were to survive the coming Apocalypse that would purge the world with its fire, before the long-awaited Second Coming of Our Lord Jesus Christ. Chris certainly did not want to miss that. He yearned to be one of God's chosen few, like the Israelites or Noah and his family, and so he obeyed his father, even as the man's voice grew weaker and his body more frail, before he took to his bed and stayed there for days and days. Even as he failed to get any better, no matter how many of the Aunty Botics he swallowed from the old pill bottles in the bedside cabinet, still Chris did not break their eleventh commandment.

No police and no doctors.

Then one day his father gave him a special task. He had to fetch something from a locked store cupboard in the bunker.

'Did you find it?'

'Yes, Father.'

'Show me.'

Chris took the revolver from the bag and held it up.

'Is it loaded?'

'Yes, Father.'

'Then put it down on the bedside cabinet.'

He watched Chris do just that and nodded in satisfaction. 'Good,' said Father. 'Now it's time to die.'

Chapter Seventy-one

Helen woke with a sour taste in her mouth and no idea how long she had slept for. She struggled to remember the sequence of events that had led her to this bed in a locked room in the bunker, then it gradually came back to her.

She could recall the man with the balaclava and the gun, the deep, barked instructions to walk and the march across the fields, shielded from view by the ancient farm-house, until she reached the hatch in the ground that was concealed until they were almost on top of it. He made her wait while he turned the wheel that opened it and forced her to climb down, still at gunpoint, until she reached the bottom. Helen had to stifle her fear that she might never come back up as he prodded her with the gun and made her walk along the corridor until she came to a door, which he opened, gesturing for her to enter. He commanded her to lie face down on the bed with her hands behind her back and she wondered if he would simply shoot her right then. But why go to all that trouble to get her down here just to do that? The sound would be muffled by the bunker and maybe that was rea-son enough.

He must have put the gun down because next thing he was astride her, sitting heavily on her back and hands, lift-ing up her head painfully then forcing a soaked rag over her nose, against her lips and mouth. Helen tried to struggle, to fight him, but he was powerful and strong. That was all she remembered.

How long had she been down here before she awoke? She couldn't tell. He had taken her watch and her useless phone and had stripped her of her normal clothes and dressed her in these . . . what were they? Army fatigues? Prison garb of some kind? None of it made sense, least of all the relative comfort of this cell. She had a bed, a bedside cabinet, a shelf with books on it. She went over to scrutinize them.

They were children's books, old-fashioned titles from the fifties, and there were two copies of the Bible, one old and battered through use, and a newer one. There were also two wooden bookmarks, and Helen immediately wondered if they could be of use somehow, so she eased them out of the books they were in.

Holding them, Helen realized they would be useless as a weapon or a tool to scratch at the walls with. They were made of the lightest, flimsiest balsa wood. She started to feel nauseous then and the smell of whatever drug she had been given seemed to fill her nostrils anew. She gave up on the books, went back to the bed and lay heavily down on it again. All she could do now was wait – for her captor to return, for the nature of her fate to be revealed.

They were both rational men, so each offered up reasons why Helen might have innocently disappeared off the grid. She'd changed her mind about seeing Peter and wanted to avoid conflict; she was really at her parents' house or with her sister and had told them not to admit this to Peter; she had gone off on some spur-of-the-moment trip without telling anyone. None of these actions sounded remotely like the Helen they both knew.

Bradshaw made some calls inquiring about traffic accidents that might have resulted in serious injury or death and was relieved to find there had been nothing involving a young woman around Helen's age.

Tom contacted as many people as he could, including her sister and her parents. No one had seen her and he made light of the situation to avoid alarming them while becoming increasingly concerned himself.

'That's okay. She said something about maybe seeing you soon and I just needed to get hold of her about a story.'

They contacted all the organizations Helen had worked with on newsletters and even drove down to see Marie from the hearing-dog charity, but she hadn't seen Helen either. While the rest of the country concentrated on an historic polling day, with the likely election of a new government, Tom and Ian ignored it and instead focused all their energies on finding Helen.

'Where to next?' asked Bradshaw.

'That's everyone I can think of that she has regular contact with.' Tom wracked his brains for any ideas of where Helen might be. 'You don't think that Jimmy McCree . . . ?' he asked, fear in his voice.

'McCree is up for parole soon,' said Bradshaw firmly. 'Why would he risk it? Besides, I kept your name out of it for that exact reason. I didn't want anyone inside HQ knowing you were involved in case it leaked back to him. Only Kane knows about that and, if I can't trust him, then I can't trust anyone.'

'Then this must have something to do with the missing

women,' Tom decided. 'Helen thought of something or worked a bit of it out – but why the hell didn't she tell me?' He felt guilty then. 'We had a bit of a falling-out,' he admitted, and he told the detective about their argument over Peter. He wondered now if Helen hadn't felt like sharing a confidence with him because of it. Maybe he had been too preoccupied with Jenna and her blackmailer for Helen to involve him. Either way, he bitterly regretted it now and was determined to find her.

'Where the hell could she be?'

'I know she didn't buy that whole white-slave-trade theory.'

'I'm not sure we did either, if I'm honest. Do you think she tried to do something about it?'

'On her own? I doubt she'd start poking about in those other scrapyards or anywhere else, do you? Not without us.'

'In case she accidentally discovered the man behind this. No, not on her own.'

'Exactly. Helen is a brave lass, but she wouldn't do that unless she . . .' He thought for a moment: '. . . felt safe.'

'What are you thinking?'

'Just something we said before, about someone not looking like a killer.'

Helen's captor wouldn't talk to her. He had been in her cell twice since she had come round from her drugged sleep. She thought of it as a cell, because that's what a locked room was, no matter how many books it contained.

It didn't matter what she said to the masked man, he never once acknowledged her, and his brooding, silent presence oozed menace. She asked him why he was keeping her here and what he wanted from her. She explained that people would be looking for her, that they would know where she was, but it didn't seem to provoke any reaction, though it was hard to tell with him wearing the balaclava. When he came he brought her food on a tray and some water, but even that was in a plastic glass so she couldn't use it for anything else.

It was his second visit that gave her hope.

Helen had noticed something. It was the way her captor quickly locked the door behind her and immediately marched away. Helen heard the door lock, but there was no scraping sound as the key was withdrawn. Was he leaving the key in the lock? She went to the keyhole and checked. It was blocked. The key was still in there, she was sure of it. It wasn't that he was careless, exactly, just hasty and preoccupied, perhaps, or he didn't want to carry lots of keys around with him. He would naturally assume it was safe to leave them in the locked door if she was on the wrong side of it. Helen heard his footsteps retreating back down the corridor almost as soon as he had turned the key, and that made her think of a way out.

Not careless, she thought. *Just not careful enough.*

Chapter Seventy-two

'Helen thought this place was weird,' Tom explained as they got out of Bradshaw's car and walked towards the cottage. 'I've seen a lot of weird in my time, though, and my tolerance for it is higher than hers. Maybe it was just female intuition.'

'You really believe in that?'

'Not really, but I do believe in trusting your instincts, so perhaps I should have trusted hers. I don't know why she would come back here, but I can't think of anywhere else she could be.'

There was no one at the cottage and nobody in the scrapyard. They knocked and waited, then knocked and waited some more. They both walked around the cottage and peered in every window. There was no one there and nothing hidden from view, not even a drawn curtain to prevent them from checking the place out.

'No one home,' said Tom, then he realized Bradshaw had noticed something. 'What is it?'

Bradshaw stepped back and let Tom take his place. The journalist peered through the window into a small lounge with a sofa, a single armchair, a coffee table and an old fireplace with a chimney. 'What am I looking at?'

'Above the fireplace,' said Bradshaw. 'The painting.'

Tom looked again. The room was gloomy but he could make out a large print of a painting with a distinctive brushstroke; a Van Gogh, perhaps, or maybe a Renoir? The portrait was of a young girl wearing a simple dress and a bonnet. She was looking right back at the artist. The most striking aspect of it was her most dominant feature, the long red hair that fell down below her shoulders. She even held some in her hands to draw attention to it.

'The same hair colour as Eva Dunbar,' said Bradshaw. 'And Cora Harrison.'

Without taking his eyes from the painting, Tom said, 'Coincidence, right?' then he turned back to Bradshaw. 'Or maybe someone likes redheads because of this old painting?'

'Or has this painting because they like redheads.' Bradshaw shrugged. 'Either way, none of the other girls have red hair.'

'There are more in the hallway,' Tom told him, 'and framed sayings – proverbs, some stuff from the Bible – and paintings of women. I say we keep looking. Come on. It's not trespassing if I've got you with me.'

They carefully explored every inch of the yard, walking between lines of cars stacked on top of each other.

'What makes you think Helen came back here?' asked Bradshaw.

'Nothing. I don't know. It's more that I can't think of anywhere else she'd've gone. The young woman gave her the creeps, but why would a woman take women?' He shook his head. 'It doesn't make a lot of sense, but we're here now, so let's keep looking round, shall we, to rule the place out, if nothing else?'

They walked until they reached the end of the yard then stopped and surveyed the land beyond it. There was a wooden fence, but it was a low one with a gap in it wide enough for a person to walk between two fence posts. The field beyond this had a well-worn path trodden into it. Tom and Bradshaw exchanged looks and without a word they both made for the gap.

They walked across a large field which sloped up and then down again and when they reached its uppermost point they saw there were more fields beyond it. 'What's that?' asked Bradshaw, pointing ahead of them to some dark shapes in a hollow some way up ahead.

'Let's find out,' said Tom.

The next time he came in with the food, Helen stayed silent. She lay on the bed, curled up in the foetal position, one arm clasped to her chest, the other hand tucked up so that it lay under the pillow, seemingly seeking comfort. Her eyes looked dead.

The man stared down at her silently for a while, as if he didn't know what to do or say to her. Then he uttered a single word, 'Eat,' and put the tray down on the cabinet next to her bed. Was there actual concern in the word? Why did he give a damn whether she ate or not?

He backed away and opened the door, stepped through it and pulled the door closed behind him. Helen had been waiting for that moment. She knew she only had a second. She pulled her hand out from under the pillow and sprang to her feet. Her bare soles made no sound on the floor as she ran to the door and thrust out the hand that had been hidden under the pillow.

Just before he turned the key she slid the thin wooden bookmark into the crack between the door and its frame.

It was so flimsy it bent when the key turned in the lock and she thought it would give way, but it didn't break. Instead it buckled against the latch bolt. But it held.

Helen stepped back from the door, waiting for the moment when the man behind it would notice that the latch bolt had only gone in part way, blocked as it was by the balsa-wood bookmark. If he tried to remove the key at that point it would probably stay in the lock, and she was gambling he would leave it there, like before. Helen braced herself for the door flying open and the man in the bala-clava stepping inside to beat her in a fury, but there was no sound, apart from the steady, regular *slap-slap* of his retreating footsteps on the tiled floor. She didn't dare believe that this might actually work.

Helen let out her breath as silently as she could and found herself gasping, her heart beating hard. She waited till she could no longer hear the footsteps then pressed her ear against the door. Moments later she heard a faint clang of metal that could surely only be the hatch dropping back down in place again, then there was a less distinct metallic, scraping sound, which she took to be the locking wheel on top of the hatch being turned from the outside.

He had gone.

Please let that be true.

She waited a full minute, just to be sure, before turning her attention back to the door mechanism. This could work, couldn't it? She had managed to jam the latch bolt before it fully engaged in the door plate on the frame. If she could just lever the wooden bookmark without break-ing it, perhaps she could prise the bolt back a little, and then she might just be able to open the door.

Helen took a breath and clasped the flimsy wooden bookmark. She bent it slowly, fully expecting it to break into pieces any second, and it buckled alarmingly then splintered, but, as it did so, she could see the bolt begin to push back against it until it was forced free of the frame. Helen grabbed the door handle, turned it then pulled, and the door swung open.

Chapter Seventy-three

The shapes seemed to be too small for buildings, but as they drew nearer Tom worked out what they were. 'Shipping crates.'

Three of them were set to one side of the hollow. They weren't new but they didn't appear to have been there for a long time. Only one of them was old and rusted and it stood apart from the others on the opposite side of the hollow right by some trees. All four crates were locked and could not be prised open. The two men banged on each one, but there was no answer from within.

'Didn't the stoned girl say she was kept in a box?' said Tom.

'She did,' said Bradshaw, 'and she also said she was taken underground.' He looked around him for any sign of a subterranean prison, but saw only grass and fields.

'Could be an entirely innocent explanation,' said Tom facetiously.

'For having four shipping crates in the middle of an isolated field?' answered Bradshaw. 'I mean, who wouldn't do that?'

Bradshaw shared Tom's sense of unease. He took out his mobile phone. 'I think it's time we told someone where we are, don't you?' He looked at the screen. 'Shit, no signal. Maybe we need higher ground.'

'We're here now,' said Tom, 'there are two of us, and we can both handle ourselves. I say we carry on.'

Helen closed the door behind her and locked it then ran barefoot all the way down the corridor until she reached the ladder. She climbed up to the top; the hatch was closed and sealed from the outside. There was a wheel on the underside of it which she tried to turn, but it wouldn't budge. She tried again and again, using all her strength, but there was no indication that it was going to give from the inside. She had to stifle angry tears of frustration. For a moment she thought she had broken free, but now she realized she was just as trapped as before. What would happen if her captor came back and found she had broken out of her cell?

Surely, though, a bunker this size would not just have a single entrance? There had to be more than one way out, in case debris fell on the hatch from the outside. Helen climbed back down the ladder and retraced her steps cautiously along the corridor until she reached her cell then carried on beyond it, following the lengthy passageway, passing doors she dared not open or knock on for fear of what might lay beyond them. She told herself she could not allow herself to be distracted by trying to find the others – if they were to be rescued from the bunker at all, Helen had to get out of here and alert the world to its presence. Her priority now was her own survival, for her sake and theirs.

She rounded a corner and her heart sank because the ground was sloping downwards, which meant she had to go deeper and deeper underground. She could hardly go back, and so she followed the passageway, telling herself she had no choice but to go down.

It didn't take them long to find the hatch. They went across the fields and reached a point where the ground rose before meeting a border fence. The hatch was obscured from view until you were right on top of it, and they were some distance from the road by now. If you were going to build a secret bunker, then this would be the ideal place to sit out a nuclear war. No one would even know you were here.

They didn't even debate it. Tom bent to grab the wheel on the outside of the hatch and gripped it tightly, expecting it to resist, but immediately it began to turn. 'It's moving. It's not stiff at all.'

'Open it,' urged Bradshaw, and Tom finished turning the wheel then lifted the hatch.

'Bloody hell,' said the detective as he looked at the ladder that went down deep into the bunker. 'It looks like something out of a horror film.'

'And there's a light on.'

'What do you want to do?' asked Bradshaw, wondering if Tom was as nervous as he was.

'Obviously, I don't really want to go down there, but what choice do I have? Helen could be in there.'

'And whoever took her could be there, too, waiting with a chainsaw. Have you thought of that?'

'Of course,' said Tom.

'Maybe one of us should go down and the other stay here, in case he comes back and closes the hatch.'

'Do you want to go down there on your own?'

'Hell, no,' said Bradshaw

'Neither do I. If we're going to do this, I want you to cover my back.'

'Okay.'

'Can you get a signal from here?'

Bradshaw inspected his phone. 'Nothing. How about you?'

Tom looked at the signal-strength indicator on his mobile phone, 'I've got one bar.' He handed it to Bradshaw. 'Worth a try.'

Bradshaw keyed in the number and dialled. 'Come on,' he said, then a second later. 'It's ringing.'

'Let's hope someone picks up.'

'Malone?' called Bradshaw down the phone. 'Is that you?' He looked at Tom. 'Line's terrible.' He winced as he tried to hear. 'I'm going to give you an address, and I need you to get down here with some people . . . I said I need to give you . . . oh, this is hopeless. I can't hear her, and she can't hear me. It keeps crackling.'

'Keep trying,' said Tom. 'She might be our only hope.'

Bradshaw kept on relaying his message in bite-sized chunks and when he had finished, he called, 'Got that?' Then he swore because he couldn't make out her reply, and then she was gone.

'Did she hear you?'

'I don't know. I think so, yes, but I'm not sure if she got it all.'

'Great,' said Tom. 'She probably thinks you just placed an order for a takeaway.'

'What do we do now, then? I wouldn't normally risk it, but it's Helen, so I say we do this.'

'Well said. Come on.' And Tom banished the considerable fear he was feeling and began to climb down the stairs.

Helen had been walking along the snaking tunnel for what seemed like an age but was probably really only several minutes. She had no sense of depth or direction, just a faint hope that there had to be more than one way out of there.

Finally, she reached the end of the corridor and found what she was looking for, but this time there was no ladder with a hatch on top of it. Instead there was a series of steps that went up in a circular pattern like a corkscrew. This had to lead somewhere significant, but would Helen emerge in an isolated location she could run from or would she suddenly appear in a room where the man would be sitting, nursing his shotgun – and what would he do if Helen saw him without his mask?

She had to force that idea from her mind and convince herself she had no choice but to go on. She couldn't go back the way she had come. At least this way her fate was in her own hands. Helen started to quietly climb the staircase, listening for any sounds of life from above.

She climbed forty steps, counting each one, and held her breath when she reached the top, where two large, thick metal blast doors signalled that the outside world was beyond them. They even had the words DANGER OF CONTAMINATION written on them.

Helen tried the large handle on one of them, fully expecting it to be locked, like the hatch had been, and felt a combination of fear and relief when it turned and allowed her to push the door slowly open.

When she walked through the doors she found she was at ground level, in what appeared to be a normal house – the farmhouse? It was dark and dusty and smelt of mould and . . . something else she did not immediately recognize, but it was a strong smell, like meat that had gone bad. She was in a hallway of some kind with three closed doors to choose from; one to her left, one to her right and one straight ahead. Assuming it to be the way out, Helen chose the door in the middle.

When she opened it she came face to face with a sickly-looking man wearing pyjamas, with a deathly pale complexion, and she realized the smell of rotting flesh was coming from him. He was sitting propped up in bed and looked as if it was taking all his energy to accomplish that simple act. He was holding a gun in his hand and pointing it straight at Helen at point-blank range. From that distance it would be almost impossible to miss. Before she could say a word in protest, he fired.

Chapter Seventy-four

Tom and Bradshaw had been exploring the corridor in the bunker. They walked silently and on edge, fully expecting to be attacked at any moment, but they met no one. They didn't want to start banging on doors or calling out for Helen yet, not until they were certain there was no one down here waiting for them, but they tried each door in turn to see if it would open.

Bradshaw walked up to the next door and turned the handle. Predictably, it was locked. Then he noticed there was something sticking out below the handle: a key. Puzzled, he looked around. There was no one there apart from Tom, who was looking back the way they had just come.

'There's a key in this door,' said Bradshaw.

'Try it, then.'

'I suggest we don't both go through it at the same time.'

'Fair enough,' agreed Tom, who was just as unhappy at the thought of being trapped in any part of the bunker.

'Watch my back,' said Bradshaw, and Tom nodded. He walked a few paces away from the detective so he could see back down the corridor and warn him if anyone was coming.

Bradshaw turned the key, wrenched the door open and found a woman lying on a bed. He recognized her immediately, but it wasn't Helen.

'Eva?'

Eva Dunbar blinked up at him from her position on the bed in the corner of the room and let out an involuntary cry. She looked startled by his sudden presence, terrified in fact, and he walked into the room to reassure her. She flinched as he entered and pressed herself back against the wall.

'It's all right, Eva,' he said. 'You're safe now.'

Everything happened very fast then. First the door slammed behind him and Bradshaw called out, 'Tom!' in his alarm. Then the key turned in the lock and they were both trapped.

Trying not to panic himself now, Bradshaw turned back to Eva. 'It's all right,' he told her again. 'I'm from the police. Everything is going to be fine.' This seemed to both calm and confuse her, but Bradshaw had no time to explain further. He turned back to the locked door as the sound of a scuffle began right outside it.

Chris had seen the two men coming when he was walking back across the fields after feeding the women. He knew if they kept going they would eventually find the bunker, so he went back into it and waited for them to come. He'd been leaving the hatch tightly shut following Eva's near-escape but this time he had deliberately left it loose so they could open it easily and come down. He left the key in the locked door of Eva's cell, to bait the trap. He hoped it would lure both men inside, then he could lock the door and leave them all in there. He would keep them for as long as it took, until their strength went and they gave up hope. He could starve them out, whether it took days or even weeks, then he would come back and bury whatever was left.

It had seemed like a brilliant plan, and it was. There

was only one flaw in it. When Eva screamed Chris had burst from the room opposite hers and slammed the door with one hand. His other hand was holding the shotgun and he quickly placed the weapon against the doorframe to free it up so he could turn the key and lock the door. But then he realized only one of the men was inside. He caught a movement from his left, which betrayed the presence of the second man, who immediately bore down on him. He finished locking the door, grabbed the shotgun once more and span to face the second man so he could blast him with it.

Tom had two choices when he saw the masked man with the shotgun slam the door: run and hope he could get round the corner then climb the ladder out of the bunker, or avoid that suicidal dash by going towards the threat instead. He chose the latter course and ran straight at the man as he grabbed for his shotgun then tried to level it.

As the gun came up Tom crashed into the masked man and they both went sprawling as both barrels discharged in a deafening roar that echoed through the confined space and left Tom's ears ringing. The gun hit the floor and both men fell to the ground. Tom landed hard and for a second wondered if he had been shot or if the impact with the ground had caused the pain he was feeling. He couldn't afford to hesitate and instantly started to grapple with the man on the ground, knowing that, if he didn't subdue him, he was unlikely to live to see the end of this day.

First there was a loud gunshot which reverberated in the corridor outside and shocked Bradshaw with its suddenness.

Then he heard the sounds of an immense struggle on the other side of the door. Scuffling noises, the sound of blows being landed and the cries of the men absorbing those blows were all audible, but he couldn't tell if anyone had been hit by the pellets from the shotgun or who was getting the upper hand in the fight. Tom was tough enough in the normal world, but this place was a long way from normal and their jailor far from ordinary.

Once again he pulled on the heavy, locked door, knowing it was useless and impossible to budge. He heard Tom cry out in pain, the sound of scuffed footsteps and then silence.

'Tom!'

But there was no answer.

Tom took punches to his face, and a knee was directed into his stomach, forcing the wind out of him. The blow was a sickening one that took some of his strength, but it made him angry and that was probably what he needed most to forget the consequences of losing this fight. He butted his head forwards and crashed it into the man's nose then pummelled him with both fists. The masked man cried out and struck back, landing body blows on Tom's torso which made him shout in pain, but Tom kept up the fight and they traded blows as they struggled viciously on the ground. Then the man bit Tom on the arm, drawing blood. Enraged, Tom grabbed the man by the ear and banged his head hard against the floor. The masked man did not pass out but it gave Tom a precious second to wriggle free and get to his feet.

He immediately went for the gun and the masked man grabbed him around the leg, trying to drag him away.

Tom lashed out with his foot. It connected with his opponent's jaw and he was knocked backwards. Tom was free, and he levelled the gun.

'Don't come any closer,' he snarled.

The man in the balaclava got slowly to his feet and stared at him for a long moment. Then he took a step forward, then another.

'Get back,' Tom warned him, but the man took a third step, until he was almost close enough to reach out and touch the barrel of the shotgun.

'The gun is empty,' the deep voice told him, as if to show Tom why he wasn't stopping.

'I know that,' hissed Tom, then he sprang towards the man and pivoted, swinging the gun round fiercely with his right hand so that the butt of the shotgun came across in an arc and smashed hard into the side of his assailant's face.

The other man fell sideways then backwards, his legs buckled and he dropped to the ground. He landed heavily on the tiled floor then lay still.

'Tom!' called Bradshaw again, but still he received no reply.

Then there was the sound of metal against metal as a key turned in the lock. Bradshaw took a step backwards and drew back his fist, ready to land a blow as soon as the door opened.

'Christ,' he hissed in relief when he saw Tom standing in the doorway. Tom was breathless and bent almost double. He seemed in considerable pain from the fight, but at least he was alive. Behind him on the concrete floor was the unconscious figure of the man in the balaclava.

'You got him,' said Bradshaw, and relief flooded through him. The two men moved closer and Bradshaw peered down at the motionless figure. 'Out cold.' He looked at Tom for an explanation.

'Hit him with the gun,' he explained. 'Bloke almost had me.'

'No such thing as rules in a fight,' Bradshaw reminded him. 'Particularly one you can't afford to lose.'

Eva shrieked then, and before either man could react she shot past them both and went straight for the prone figure on the floor, kicking him hard in the head then drawing her foot back to do it again. She landed a second sickening blow which made the unconscious head wobble alarmingly, before Bradshaw managed to grab her and pull her away. She was cursing and trying to kick out again. 'I'll kill the bastard!' she roared, and Bradshaw was relieved, because it was the first words he had heard from her. Perhaps she wasn't as damaged as he had first thought.

Tom bent low and carefully examined the unconscious man, alert to any sudden movement from the prone figure, but there was none. He glanced up at Bradshaw, who was still holding Eva back, then he grabbed hold of the bottom of the balaclava and drew it up over the face of the unconscious attacker.

'Oh my god,' he said, and Bradshaw leaned forward to understand the reason for his friend's shock.

They both stared at the man's face for a moment and, in his confusion, Bradshaw let go of Eva. He needn't have worried, though, for she too was having difficulty processing the sight before her.

'That man,' Bradshaw said needlessly when he was finally able to find his voice, 'is a woman.'

Some of the doors had keys in their locks and others didn't, so Bradshaw took the keys from Chris's belt and began opening all the doors in the bunker's corridor. The keys were numbered to coincide with the rooms, so it was a simple matter. Some of them were empty, but not all. To Bradshaw's intense relief, he opened one door to find one of the missing women cowering behind it, then he opened the door to another, and another, until all five of the Disappeared were assembled together, standing in a disbelieving huddle, their terror only diminishing when they saw their rescuers and the unconscious figure of their captor lying on the floor.

Bradshaw recognized each woman from the photographs in the case files that he had studied so closely. There was something of a miracle in the appearance of each one. Though they were shaken and in shock, they appeared, at first glance, to be physically unharmed. It turned out that Alice Smith's mother was right and she wasn't dead after all, and Jessica Davies' fiancé would not have to live for ever with the knowledge that his inability to give her a lift home that night because of his drinking had cost her life. Whatever marital issues Stephanie Evans might have to explain because of her missing wedding ring probably paled into insignificance right now, and the reappearance of Sandra Lane might even snap her largely mute parents out of their shock. Then there was Eva Dunbar, the only one of the five who still had the presence of mind and composure left to thank him.

'My pleasure,' he said, and they both looked down at the figure lying inert on the floor. 'The nightmare is over.'

She shook her head. 'I need to get home,' Eva told him. 'My mother's not well, she won't be able to manage without . . .'

Bradshaw placed a hand firmly on Eva's shoulder to calm her. 'I've met your mother, Eva. She's coping. She was beside herself with worry about you, of course, but as soon as she knows your safe she'll be okay.'

'Thank god,' she said. 'Then the nightmare really is over.'

'It is,' he assured her. 'Now let's get you all out of here.'

Tom had taken off his belt and used it to bind their abductor's hands behind her back.

Tom regarded the women and waited till Bradshaw had checked every room. 'No Helen,' he said.

'She's probably fine,' said Bradshaw, unconvincingly. 'You know Helen.'

'If anything has happened to her, then I swear this piece of shit will . . .' Tom's anger prevented him from finishing, but Bradshaw got the message and resolved to intervene, to protect his friend from a murder charge.

Helen had watched as the old man squeezed the trigger. She had fully expected to die. Instead of a bang, however, there was only a click, and the man stared at his gun in disbelief. Helen didn't wait for him to fire again. She turned and ran, bursting from the room and running through the nearest door, which to her immense relief opened into a hallway with a front door directly ahead of her. Not daring to look back over her shoulder in case the old man had managed to climb from his sick bed and pursue her, she went straight to it.

She drew back the bolts on the inside of the door and turned the key. She pulled hard and the door opened. Helen ran out through the door and emerged in the courtyard of the farmhouse once more. The light hurt her eyes after so long underground and it took her a moment to realize she was back at the spot where she had been taken by the man in the balaclava. She sprinted through the courtyard and around the house, went to the gate, climbed over it and realized her car was gone, so she ran down the road as fast as she was able.

She was free.

Bradshaw took off his belt and threw it to Tom. 'I say we tie his . . . *her* . . . feet together and leave her here.'

'I'm good with that,' said Tom. 'Let's get everyone out of here.'

They went back down the corridor and guided the stunned women up the ladder one by one, then out through the hatch, still open from when they had entered the bunker.

They trudged back across the fields and when they were halfway there picked out the flashing lights of four police cars in the distance. 'Malone,' said Bradshaw. 'She must have heard me.'

By the time they reached the scrapyard the cars were pulling in, lights still flashing. DC Malone got out of the first one, then a familiar figure dressed in unfamiliar clothes slowly climbed out of the back seat.

'Helen!' cried Tom, and he ran to embrace her.

Chapter Seventy-five

I charge my daughters every one
To keep good house while I am gone,
You and you and especially you,
Or else I'll beat you black and blue.
  – From an early version of *Mother Goose*

'This one is a criminologist's wet dream,' announced Kane when they assembled in his office the following afternoon. 'Chris' – and he paused for effect – 'is actually Christina.'

'It's official,' Bradshaw told Tom. 'You were beaten up by a woman.'

'Correction,' said Tom, whose face was bruised from the fight. 'I was *almost* beaten up by a woman, and believe me when I say this: there is no shame in it. That is one powerful female.'

'All this time she was pretending to be a man?' asked Helen, recalling the meek and softly spoken woman at the cottage and trying to reconcile her with the balaclava-wearing figure wielding a shotgun at the farmhouse who had imprisoned her. 'But why?'

'I don't know,' admitted Kane, 'but when the professor finally gets here maybe he will enlighten us.'

'We got an expert in from the university to speak to Chris,' explained Bradshaw. 'A Professor Flannery.'

'An expert on what?' asked Tom, who was wondering how anyone could ever be qualified to comment on a case as bizarre as this one.

'Pretty much everything,' he said, and when he saw the look on Tom's face, Bradshaw added: 'Sociology, psychology, social anthropology . . . that kind of stuff. Anyway, he's been with her all morning.'

Kane waved a hand dismissively. 'Whatever he ends up telling us, the main thing is you got the women back alive. I think we can agree it's a job very well done, and I know you all went through a lot, particularly Helen.' He nodded at her. 'So, thank you.'

'It's not over, though, is it?' said Helen. 'Not until we find out what happened there and why. The women who disappeared recently have all been rescued, but the others . . .' She couldn't bring herself to say how horrific the fate of the earlier victims must have been. 'We owe it to their families to at least find out why this happened.'

'The father isn't talking, and his son' – Kane corrected himself – '*daughter* is a basket case. Maybe the professor will get something out of her.' He looked over Tom's shoulder towards the wider office outside Kane's. 'And this looks like him now.'

A self-important figure dressed in a tweed suit walked into Kane's office and greeted them. Professor Flannery was a man in late middle age with wild curly hair and reading glasses on a chain that hung around his neck. The DCI made the introductions, explaining that Helen, Tom and Ian had all personally experienced the bunker.

'What did you find out?' Kane asked him when the

formalities were complete. 'Apart from the obvious . . . that she's barking.'

Professor Flannery blinked at that description. 'It would seem that Chris has been living as a boy for most of her life,' he began. 'She becomes quite agitated when you point out the obvious, that she was born female.'

'Is she a whatsit?' asked Kane, searching for the word. 'A transvestite?'

'No.' Flannery shook his head dismissively. 'A transvestite is someone who derives pleasure from the act of wearing clothes normally associated with the opposite sex. Chris has no interest in wearing a man's clothes other than practicality.'

'Does she want a sex change, then?' asked Kane.

'Apparently not. Chris knows she is a woman but simply chooses to present herself as a man, and that is enough for her.'

'How could she?' snapped Kane. 'If a bull has tits, it's a cow.' Then he muttered, 'Sorry,' at Helen, who was looking at him in disgust.

'Chris isn't a transvestite or transgender and as far as I can see does not have any recognized condition such as gender dysphoria. She doesn't feel emotionally as if she *is* a different sex, she just wishes it so because her father would have preferred it that way.'

When this pronouncement was greeted with blank stares, the professor grew impatient, either with his audience or his own inability to explain himself to them. 'I'm saying she's a one-off. Chris has, in effect, for want of a better word, been brainwashed. She has had very little contact with the outside world. Her life has been spent almost entirely with her father and no one else. He taught her everything she knows, quite literally.' Then the professor quoted, 'Give me a child until he is seven and I will show you the man.'

'Who said that?' Bradshaw asked, meaning the professor's quote.

Before Flannery could explain its origins, Helen said, 'Aristotle.'

'You really are posh,' Tom told her.

'I am not posh,' she retorted firmly.

'Was she pretending to be a boy, then?' asked Kane.

'Pretending . . .' mused the professor. 'Is it pretending if you believe it to be true because you have willed it that way?' he asked hypothetically. 'Chris lived her life in almost total isolation, brought up by a father who raged when his wife left him. He told her women were abhorrent, the creator of most of the world's problems, the catalyst for the release of man's basest nature and the cause of his expulsion from the Garden of Eden, when Eve tempted Adam.'

'In other words, it's all a woman's fault,' said Helen. 'I might have known.'

'That was Samuel's view,' explained the professor, 'and when his daughter heard all this, she resolved to live her life with him as a man, or as close to it as she could. I think she reasoned she would then be more worthy of his love.'

'But when we met her it was obvious she was a woman.'

'She couldn't alter her physical appearance entirely in day-to-day life,' he said, 'but in the bunker she could pad out her clothes and wear a mask. Behind it, she could be whatever she wanted to be, and she chose to be a man.'

'Is she a lesbian?' Kane asked.

'Not according to her. I understand none of the women that were abducted experienced sexual attention of any kind from Chris. She claims she never touched the previous victims. That was left to her father, who raped them.' And he turned to Helen then and shocked her by saying, 'You and the other most recent victims were spared that ordeal, but only because of his ill health.'

'Are you saying she willingly went along with her father's plans to kidnap and rape women?' asked Helen.

'Yes,' he said, 'but she did not view those acts as either abduction or rape.'

'Then what did she view them as?' asked Tom.

'She told me her father was saving the women.'

'Saving them?' asked Bradshaw. 'From what?'

The professor frowned then. 'Some form of Biblical Apocalypse. It would be caused by man but decreed by God. Chris is convinced war is imminent and the world will soon be devastated by nuclear Armageddon. She keeps asking to be returned to the bunker. Right now, she is genuinely in fear for her life, because she is no longer able to retreat back underground.'

'Her father told her war was coming?' asked Tom.

'She knows no other reality, doesn't believe the newspapers, has no TV and no perception that the Cold War is over. Chris thinks the world will soon be destroyed. Only she and her father will survive, along with the women they save.

'When her father became ill and could no longer do God's work, she had to do it for him. Posing as a cab-driver, she could choose suitable candidates for salvation.

376

This whole thing has been about following in Daddy's footsteps. She even took five women to exactly replace the five he kept underground, until the day when the world as we know it would end.' He looked at Helen. 'She planned for you to be a replacement, for one of the women who hadn't cooperated.'

It took them a few moments to let all this sink in and they sat in silence for a time while they processed the professor's appraisal of Chris, a woman who wanted to live like a man not because it felt more natural to her but to appease her father, a madman who had poisoned his daughter's mind against her own sex.

The professor must have found the silence oppressive because he cheerfully observed, 'I must say I have never come across a case like this one before. She's really quite unique. I'll probably write a book about it.'

'You'd better be quick, then,' quipped Kane, and he glanced at Tom: 'Before he beats you to it.'

The professor looked unnerved then, as if realizing that the journalist would indeed very likely finish his less academic study of the Keoghs before him.

Helen's head had started to throb, and Tom noticed her discomfort. 'You okay?'

'Headache,' she said. 'This whole case is making it spin.'

'I'll drive you home. You've been through a hell of a lot and it looks as if we're finally done.'

'Almost,' said Bradshaw, 'but not quite. I've got to go back out to the farm. There's one last thing I still have to do.'

Chapter Seventy-six

As Tom drove her home he told Helen, 'At least you didn't miss much while you were down there. Only a General Election with a Labour landslide.'

'Can't believe I didn't even vote.'

'Me neither,' he smiled. 'I was a bit busy.' Then he said, 'You also missed what's-his-name.' Tom always made a point of not using Peter's name.

'Yeah,' she said. 'Probably for the best, judging by the voicemails he left me when I didn't show.'

'Was he worried about you?'

'No, he just assumed I'd stood him up deliberately, and his messages got angrier and angrier. There was quite a lot about how humiliated he felt.' She smiled. 'Your message was much nicer.'

'I was genuinely worried. There was a lot of work to be done and I didn't fancy doing it all myself.'

'I'm touched,' she said, 'and I have to admit you were right about Peter. People don't change.'

The job had taken far longer than anyone expected and now they were forced to wait for DC Wallace, who had driven back to HQ for something he loosely described as 'a special tool'. The newer shipping crates were simpler to break into but nothing they had tried so far had worked on the doors of the dented, heavily corroded old shipping crate set aside from the others, and they stubbornly refused to yield.

In their impatience, while they waited for DC Wallace to return they were beginning to speculate that the whole exercise might just be a complete waste of time.

'Why would he need it anyhow?' asked one of the officers tasked with opening the crate. 'He's got the newer ones over there and a bunch of rooms underground. I'm betting, when we finally pop this bugger open, all we are going to find is a bunch of rusted tools lying in a pool of mucky water.'

Before Bradshaw could contradict him, one of the other men said, 'And maybe we'll discover the bodies of every person who's disappeared from this county in the last twenty years. That cross your mind at all?'

'It did,' the DC conceded. 'I'm not saying we should give up.'

They didn't give up. Instead they waited and stood around smoking and talking, about politics ('Nothing ever changes, not really'), football ('Newcastle United will never win 'owt, no matter who's playing for them. They're bloody cursed, man') and women, specifically DI Tennant and whether they would or they wouldn't ('I definitely would, as long as she didn't expect me to call her ma'am during it').

The other men laughed at this, but Bradshaw grew tired of their pathetic appraisals of Tennant. 'She'd eat you alive,' he said, and he walked away from them.

Bradshaw strode towards the highest point of the dip so he could wait for the return of DC Wallace. He was already trudging across the field towards them. Bradshaw was expecting him to be carrying an expensive power tool and was surprised to see him loosely holding something that looked more like an iron bar with a grip on one end.

'What's that, then?' he asked when Wallace finally reached him.

'It's a sort of skeleton key for shipping crates.' He was out of breath. 'I'm not joking. We picked this one up when we lifted a bloke who was using it to break into them after dark.'

'Can *you* use it, more to the point?' asked Bradshaw.

'We'll see, won't we?'

Cigarettes were extinguished and everyone gathered to watch DC Wallace. He placed the open end of the bar over the protruding seal in the middle of the shipping crate, took a step back and pushed outwards from the other end. It took him a few goes but soon the seal began to give and then quite suddenly it bent backwards so it was away from the doors and no longer preventing them from opening.

'Nice one, Bob,' said another officer, who had an enormous crowbar and a heavy-duty metal hammer. He placed the narrow end of the bar into the gap between the doors and struck the opposite end with the hammer twice until a small gap opened up between the doors and the crowbar slid in. He placed the hammer on the ground and put his weight on the crowbar then levered it until the left-hand door began to slowly open, scraping on the ground as it did so. Others started to help, and several pairs of hands pulled the door till it was dragged entirely back. Wallace used the hammer to bash the right-hand door then, striking it from the inside until it swung outwards. Both doors were now wide open and the light from the outside illuminated the shipping crate for the first time in years.

It smelt of mould and decay, of contents undisturbed for a very long time, and they could still make out the shapes of the larger items inside the crate. All eyes were instantly drawn to one thing. Like the other crates, this one contained a camp bed. The bed lay in the far corner, had a stained, discoloured mattress on it and a pile of . . . something.

The men exchanged looks and, without a word, Bradshaw and Wallace stepped into the crate to take a closer look. As Bradshaw drew nearer he could make out a body: a badly decomposed human figure dressed in rags that may once have been a dress. It was little more than a heap of bones that had rotted till they had turned black. The figure was curled up in a foetal position and, as Bradshaw drew nearer, he saw the hairless human skull, its sightless eyes and a mouth that was wide open, as if frozen in a final scream of anguish. Around its neck he could just make out a tarnished chain that clung to what remained of the corpse. As he moved closer he noticed it still held a simple faded cross.

Chapter Seventy-seven

The last enemy to be destroyed is death.

– 1 Corinthians 15:26

They hadn't been able to get much out of Samuel Keogh. He would claim he was too ill to talk to them or that his life had no meaning now and it would soon be over, so why should he bother to help them?

Bradshaw had to step aside while more senior men tried to persuade Samuel to talk, then they brought in Professor Flannery to see if he could understand the man and, when that didn't work, someone had the bright idea of sending for a priest. The latter was sent packing because he was 'no more than a godless Satanist in league with the Pope!'

'He must be a Protestant then,' observed Bradshaw wryly. 'What a pity nobody bothered to check.'

'It wasn't my idea to send him in,' said Kane.

'I'd like to have a go,' Bradshaw told him.

'What makes you think you'll get anything out of him when no one else has? He's just a religious nutter.'

'But I'd like to try,' Bradshaw told his DCI, 'and I think I've earned the right.'

Samuel Keogh was held in a secure hospital bed while he was treated for various ailments. They had managed to at least stabilize the open sores on his body and limbs and reduce the effect of the severe blood poisoning he was suffering from, which was most likely caused by a deep, infected cut from a rusty car he had worked on.

His voice was a weary rasp, the croaked words of a dying man. 'I'm done anyway, and everyone knows it, so what difference does it make whether I explain myself?'

'It doesn't really,' said Bradshaw calmly. 'I understand. I understand completely, in fact.'

The man looked at him warily but there was the merest trace of interest in his eye. 'Do you?'

'Yes,' affirmed Bradshaw. 'It doesn't really matter what we do in this life.'

The man regarded the detective closely. 'Are you mocking me, Copper?'

Bradshaw shook his head, '"Blessed are they which are persecuted for righteousness' sake: for theirs is the kingdom of heaven,"' he announced placidly.

Keogh was surprised. 'That's Matthew?'

'It is.'

'Are you a God-fearing man, Mr ... ?'

'You can call me Ian,' he answered. 'Most certainly. Isn't everyone?'

'Not everyone, no.'

'Well, they should be,' he said. '"The Lord will take vengeance on His adversaries, and He reserveth wrath for His enemies."'

'That's right,' agreed Keogh, 'so spaketh the Lord. You're a believer?'

'I have faith, yes,' said Bradshaw, 'so help me to understand

and let *Him* in turn understand. Only then will you be sure of everlasting life.'

'It's over. There'll be no trial. Look at me. I haven't got long. I don't think I even have the strength left to tell you what happened.'

'But you must, Samuel,' Bradshaw urged him. 'Only God can judge you, but how can He do that if He does not hear you? Remember Proverbs?' he asked the man. '"Whoever conceals their sins does not prosper, but the one who confesses and renounces them finds mercy."'

Samuel looked at Bradshaw with wonderment. 'All right,' he said. 'I'll do it.'

'Come in, Kane,' said the deputy chief constable, who had summoned the DCI to his enormous office on the top floor. 'It's about these expenses you've been incurring.' Edward Tyler held up the papers he'd been scrutinizing.

Kane knew he hadn't done anything dodgy but wondered if he had inadvertently done something that might *appear* to be dodgy. 'Which expenses, sir?'

'The additional manpower for the investigation into the missing women. The journalist.'

'Oh, that,' said Kane, relieved.

'Or should I say *journalists*?' Tyler let the last letter of the final word linger, making it sound particularly damning.

'I did get prior approval for that, sir.'

'To hire this Carney chap as an investigator,' Tyler nodded slowly, 'but not to pay two journalists.'

Kane noticed a slight gleam in the senior officer's eyes. It was almost a look of triumph. This wasn't about the budget. This was about slapping Kane down for allowing Bradshaw to embarrass him.

'They come as a team. Their fees have never been a problem before.'

'They should have been. This bill is far too high. You can pay one of them, but not both, and that's my final word on the matter.'

Kane wasn't prepared to accept that, 'You're telling me to go back to two people who have worked with us, helping to save lives and risking their own in the process, and now you won't pay them? What the hell am I supposed to say?'

The deputy chief constable's voice was icy. 'That you exceeded your authority, Detective Chief Inspector. I don't much care which name you put on the form when you resubmit it, as long as there is only one.'

'They'll never work with us again,' protested Kane.

'Oh, believe me,' snapped Tyler, 'you are entirely right about that.'

Listening to Samuel Keogh's long, self-serving account of his life was exhausting, but Bradshaw persevered. He wrote it all down, too: names, dates, every crime the man had committed in the name of his God.

'My father was an ungodly man who cared for nothing but Mammon. Bible studies made that obvious to me.' Samuel explained how he had studied chemistry at university but left college before graduating and joined the RAF, to escape the pull of the family business, much to his father's fury. It was while serving in the forces that he had his epiphany. Mankind was going to destroy itself and most of the planet with it. Being on the front line, he could see how easy it would be. One trigger-happy reaction to a single misunderstood blip on a radar screen would unleash a disaster of Biblical proportions.

Samuel owed it to God and his family to make arrangements for the coming of Armageddon and beyond, when the world would be reborn and repopulated.

'That's why you took the women?'

'To save them, yes.' He nodded at his own selfless act. 'Only five, though, because of the room we had and the supplies. I couldn't take more.' He said that with regret, as if he had let down others who could not be saved.

'But they didn't understand, did they?' probed Bradshaw.

'No.'

'They resisted, even though you tried to explain.' Bradshaw was offering up a possible version of events. 'That's why you had to subdue them. Methoxyflurane? From your studies, you knew what it could do.'

'It eases pain,' he explained, 'and they were sometimes in pain.' He said this as if he had been administering morphine to a wounded soldier, not rendering a woman unconscious so he could rape her.

'That wasn't the only reason, though, was it?'

'They were my wives in the eyes of God.' He was wild-eyed and angry again suddenly. 'They would not submit to me. I had a right, and they had to help me repopulate the world, but they couldn't do that if they refused me.' He looked bewildered then. 'but they were all barren. Not one of them was fertile.'

'The Methoxyflurane made them ill. You used it on them every time and it damages the internal organs. That's most likely why none of them ever got pregnant.'

'I never knew that,' he said.

'And one of them got out,' said Bradshaw, 'but she was already too far gone to survive, even before the car hit her.'

'I was sorry when she wasn't saved.'

'So you replaced her, but what happened to the others?'

'Dead,' he said. 'All dead in the end. They got ill and just gave up. I buried them by the magnolia trees.'

'Did you always replace them?'

'At first, in the early years, yes. I wanted five, always five, but when my health was taken from me I couldn't do it any more.'

'Chris took over then.'

'He thought God would make me well again and we'd go on like before, only with new wives.'

'You were trying to create an Eden?'

'Not an Eden,' Samuel corrected him. 'An Ark.'

'For you and your family and the women you saved. What about your wife? What happened to her?'

'Ingrid was a whore,' he said flatly.

'Was she?' Bradshaw forced sympathy into his words.

'I tried to save her, but she couldn't be saved. I wanted to teach her how to behave, but she couldn't find it within herself to be happy, even when it was just the three of us. That was why I bought the cottage, the land, the farm and the bunker.'

'How did you know about the bunker beneath the farmhouse? It was so secret the nearest villagers weren't aware of its existence.'

'I was posted there for a time. You had to sign the Official Secrets Act and couldn't tell anyone, but I saw it and knew it was about to be decommissioned. It was intended to be a place of last resort for the local government to retreat to in the event of war, but they built a new bunker right under the streets of Newcastle. A few years later I used the money from my father's estate to get hold of it.'

It seemed so simple when he explained it. Samuel Keogh had a ring-side seat to the Cold War and used that inside knowledge to snap up the bunker.

'You faked your own death,' Bradshaw said. 'Why?'

'So you wouldn't come looking for me, but if you did, I intended to go through with it anyway. It would have been better than this.' He gestured to his cell.

'If you intended to commit suicide, why were there no bullets in your gun?'

'Chris must have taken them out, to stop me from killing myself if the police came' – he laughed without humour – 'because that would be a sin.' Bradshaw realized Helen would have been dead now if Chris hadn't emptied the gun.

Bradshaw stopped writing for a moment. He had heard it all. Almost. There was just one bit of the story that Samuel hadn't told him.

'What happened to your wife, Samuel?'

He evaded the question. 'It was meant to be just be the three of us. We had the fields and the orchard. It was our Garden of Eden, but it wasn't enough. Like Eve, she wanted more. They always want more.'

Bradshaw knew exactly what she wanted: some freedom to come and go as she pleased and not be kept in a prison, whether it had an orchard or not.

'In the end I told Chris. I said, your mother is no good, *women* are no good. She's gone. She's run off and left us. Chris knew what she was like, she saw and she learned.'

388

'No, that's not right,' said Bradshaw, 'because your wife didn't leave, did she, Samuel?' The other man refused to look him in the eye. 'A man like you wouldn't allow it. Do you honestly expect us to believe she ran away and left her daughter with a monster like you?'

'She ran off,' he mumbled. 'Ran away with her fancy-man.'

'Bullshit. Who was that, then? If you never let her out of the house? Who was she ever going to meet?'

'That's what happened.'

'You're a liar, Samuel. Want to know how I know? We opened that big, old rusty shipping container that's set back away from the others.'

Samuel opened his mouth like he was about to say something then he clamped it shut again.

'Know what we found?'

'Shut up.'

'Human remains. A badly decomposed corpse. It's your wife, isn't it? She never left. You locked her in there. Know how we'll prove it? DNA. We just have to match it to a blood relative, so it's convenient that we have her daughter in custody. We'll prove it's her, if you aren't man enough to admit it.'

Samuel put his hands over his ears then. 'Shut up!'

'I won't shut up, not yet. I still have one last question. Did you at least have the decency to kill her before you sealed her in there?'

Samuel started to sob then and when the tears came it was like a dam bursting. 'Shut up . . . I can't bear it . . .'

'Thought not, you evil bastard. I can't imagine what that poor girl went through before she died, but one thing is certain, Samuel Keogh. If your God really does exist, you are going to burn in hell for ever for this.'

DCI Kane spent an uncomfortable quarter of an hour on the phone to Tom Carney explaining he wouldn't be paid the full amount that he and Helen were owed. The journalists didn't take it well, as Kane fully expected and, for once, the DCI felt no need to mask the truth or demonstrate any loyalty to the man who had refused to sign off the money they were legitimately owed.

'Half? You're kidding me, right?'

'I'm sorry, Tom.'

'The bastard,' said Tom, when he realized there was absolutely nothing he could do to rectify the situation.

'Yes,' admitted Kane. 'I'm afraid he is.'

There was a long pause before Tom concluded, 'Make sure you put Helen's name on the sheet when you resubmit it.' And before Kane could ask him why, the journalist was gone.

A moment later Ian Bradshaw reappeared. He stood framed by Kane's office door, as if he didn't know whether he should come in.

'Bloody hell, Bradshaw, you've been ages. Did he say anything?'

'He did,' said Bradshaw, and he held up his notebook.

'Well, come on then, out with it,' Kane said impatiently.

Bradshaw looked intensely weary. 'Have you got all day?'

'How do you mean? What did you get?'

'Everything,' said Bradshaw. 'I've got it all.' And he tapped the notebook with his free hand. 'Chapter and Biblical bloody verse.'

Chapter Seventy-eight

Two days later DCI Kane was summoned once again to see Deputy Chief Constable Tyler and instructed to bring DS Bradshaw with him. Once they were safely behind closed doors, Tyler, who looked apoplectic, produced a copy of the *Daily Mirror* and virtually threw it at Kane. 'What the hell is this?' he hissed.

Kane blinked, looked down at the front page of the newspaper then looked back up at Tyler, who was glaring at him malevolently. He fished the paper from his lap and began to read the article.

The headline was 'TOP COP'S BLUNDER FREES KILLER TO STRIKE AGAIN'. The strap line below it said, 'Durham's Next Chief Constable Let Murderer Slip through His Fingers'.

The byline underneath the article proclaimed it to be the work of Paul Hill, but that was fooling no one, least of all Tyler. Hill was Tom Carney's former colleague and was known to be a buyer of Tom's stories. Deputy Chief Constable Tyler might not be aware of that link, reasoned Kane, but that probably didn't matter because who else, apart from Tom, was in a position to write this piece without insider knowledge of the case?

Tyler's name appeared in the first paragraph, to ensure there could be no doubt which top cop was personally responsible for the killer's ability to strike again. Kane read every word of the damning report then he looked up and said, 'Oh dear.'

'This was you!' thundered Tyler. 'You know it and I know it.'

'This has nothing to do with me,' protested Kane truthfully.

'Nor me,' said Bradshaw.

'I'll sue you both for this. It's defamation.'

'We didn't write this.' Kane was trying to stay calm. 'It's the *Mirror* you want to be suing, but . . .' The words trailed away because he wasn't sure how far he wanted to go with this.

'But what?' snapped Tyler.

Kane took a deep breath and steeled himself. His career was over anyway. He could tell that by the look of deep, vindictive hatred in Tyler's eyes. 'It's true. You did interview the girl, and no one took her story seriously.'

'How dare you presume to know what happened in that interview, Kane? I've never come across such insolence and insubordination! You're just a DCI, for God's sake!' He made that sound like the lowest of the low. 'Oh, you think you're so bloody clever, don't you? I'm going to prove you are behind this story . . .'

'I repeat: I had nothing to do with it.'

'Are you seriously suggesting this article wasn't written by Tom Carney?'

'No, I'm not, sir,' replied Kane. 'I'd say, on the balance of probability, he almost certainly wrote this.'

'Because you put him up to it,' Tyler said.

'Because you refused to pay him.'

Tyler avoided this uncomfortable truth. 'I want him

arrested for leaking confidential information while on our pay roll.'

'But he isn't on our pay roll. I put the girl's name on the form.'

'Then arrest her!' Tyler was so angry he was starting to sound unhinged.

'But she didn't write the article and we can't prove Carney did. The *Mirror* will never reveal their source.'

Kane wanted to say, *That's what you get when you shaft a journalist*, but at that point Chief Constable Newman walked in. He, too, was holding a copy of the newspaper. Great, thought Kane, as if things couldn't get any worse.

'Ah, James, I'm glad you're here,' Tyler said, forcing himself to calm down. 'I feel like I might need a witness.'

'You know,' he continued, not bothering to mask his contempt, 'I've been giving a lot of thought to CID, and I reckon it needs a bit of a shake-up. We could do with some new keen, fresh officers who don't find it quite so hard to obey orders or feel the need to go off on witch hunts with tabloid hacks.'

Oh well, thought Kane, Siberia awaits. At least he was a proper cop, though, not like this empty uniform currently lecturing him. 'In short, I think a new broom is required around here.' He turned to the man he would soon replace and said, 'Don't you agree, sir?'

'Perhaps,' said the chief constable, and his deputy's smile was one of triumph, until his boss added: 'But I'm afraid it won't be you, Edward.'

'What?' Tyler's shock was palpable.

'I wanted you to hear it first, and I wanted you to hear it from me,' the chief constable explained. 'I'm withdrawing my support for your candidacy and will be recommending we go outside the force for the next chief constable.'

Kane stared at his boss in bewilderment.

'But why?' Tyler almost wailed. 'I haven't done anything. That whole business with the girl was years ago. I defy anyone to have done it differently.'

The chief constable waved his excuse away. 'I'm not talking about that. Frankly, the only person who really knows what happened back then is you.'

'Well, then!' His voice was a high-pitched plea and Kane could see how desperate he was to stay in the game.

'It's never really the act itself,' explained the chief constable, 'it's the cover-up. It's always the cover-up.'

'What do you mean?'

'Well, someone removed those notes from that file.'

'It wasn't me!' Tyler blustered.

'Who, then?' his boss asked simply, and no answer was forthcoming. 'And you applied pressure to a subordinate to omit you from an account of the initial investigation.'

'I did no such thing.'

'I've been to see him, Edward. I knew Hugh Rennie when I was a chief super. A good man, but liable to wilt under pressure, though he did at least put Bradshaw here on to you at his leaving do.'

All eyes turned to Bradshaw, who nodded his agreement.

'This is ridiculous,' blustered Tyler.

'You hindered an investigation into several missing women. They might have died.'

'You can't prove that. No one can.'

'I don't have to prove it. You won't end up in jail, though some might say you should. I'm merely withdrawing my support for your candidature, which I have a perfect right to do.'

'Without your backing they won't pick me!' protested Tyler.

'Probably not,' said the chief constable, and Kane knew there was no *probably* about it. Edward Tyler was finished.

'I'll resign then, if that's what you want.' His boss didn't seem too perturbed. 'You never liked me.' It was the accusation of a schoolchild.

To Kane's surprise, the chief constable said, 'No, Edward, I never did, much.' He let that sink in before concluding: 'But I didn't have to like you, just respect your judgement. Then I would know this force was in safe hands.' He shook his head. 'And you just said it yourself: you haven't *done* anything, except cover your own arse, which, frankly, is unforgivable.'

Tyler knew he was finished. 'So you thought you'd tell me this in front of an audience?'

'I did that for the same reason you were initially happy to see me. I wanted witnesses. If this incident has taught me one thing, it's that you cannot be trusted.' With that, Newman must have decided he had said enough, and he made to leave the room. When the chief constable reached the door, he turned back to face Tyler. 'Oh, and Edward, I accept your resignation.'

Chapter Seventy-nine

Tom thought Helen would want to hear the good news about Tyler's professional demise right away, even though Bradshaw tried to tempt him with the prospect of a celebratory pint. He thought about it, but for the second time recently he turned down the detective's offer. Later, he would wonder to himself what the consequences might have been if he had met Ian at the pub instead of heading straight home.

Tom parked up and went inside. He called her name, because the lights were on and he assumed she was in the kitchen, but there was no sign of her there, so he took a bottle of beer from the fridge and walked into the lounge. He found Helen there, unconscious, lying on the floor.

The ambulance reached him in minutes, but it still felt like an eternity.

'I found her like this when I got home,' he blurted as they started to put her on a stretcher. Tom thought he had lost Helen when she went missing, then they had got her back, and now it looked like he might lose her again. There didn't seem to be any sign of forced entry and he couldn't see any obvious injury to her, so what the hell had happened?

He rode with her in the back of the ambulance and, to his immense relief, she came round groggily before they reached the hospital. Helen blinked at Tom and he took her hand. Then she realized she was in an ambulance. 'What happened?' she asked, as if he knew the answer.

'I was going to ask you that,' he said.

It was several hours before Tom was allowed to go to her bedside, by which time Helen had been tested for a variety of ailments, from low blood sugar to epilepsy.

'You shouldn't have waited all this time,' she scolded him.

'I was glad of the skive,' he said. 'Hospital waiting rooms are brilliant. I get to read all the old magazines I normally never have time for. How are you?' he asked, then he smiled at her. 'The things you'll do for attention.'

'Don't,' she said. 'I feel enough of an idiot as it is.' But he noticed she was still too weak to fully sit up. 'At least I didn't miss another election.'

'But you did miss the Eurovision Song Contest,' he informed her, 'and Britain won.'

'Gutted I missed that.' She rolled her eyes.

'Are you okay?'

'Basically, yes. There's nothing actually wrong with me. Unless you count syncope, which I don't.'

'What's that?'

'It's the technical word for fainting. I passed out, possibly due to a temporary blockage of blood supply to the brain, or maybe just because of hyperventilation. Either way, I feel like a complete fraud sitting here, but they told me to stay in for a night, just in case.'

'Helen, you were held at gunpoint by a maniac who drugged you, then locked up in a cold bunker with little food and hardly any sleep. You escaped, then the maniac's father fired a gun at you.'

'Which didn't contain any bullets.'

'You weren't to know that,' Tom reminded her. 'You could have been killed. Anyone would have a reaction to that. I'm surprised it took so long.'

'I kept thinking about those poor women, and I think I panicked. I was only down there for a little while. They were there for years.' She shuddered. 'I could have been, too, if you and Ian hadn't worked it out.'

'You were doing a pretty good job of rescuing yourself when we arrived,' he reminded her. 'It was every man for himself down there for a while, but let's not go over it again now.'

'Agreed,' she said, 'and things could be a lot worse. Apparently, my kidneys and liver are in reasonable condition' – she smiled – 'and, considering I've been living with you for a while, I'd say that's pretty amazing.'

'I don't know what you mean.' He surreptitiously glanced at his watch then and she noticed.

'You don't have to stay, you know.'

'I don't mind.'

'I don't need looking after,' she assured him, 'and I can be my own company. They're just keeping me here for observation.'

'Okay,' he said doubtfully. 'Well, if you're sure.'

'I am,' she said firmly. 'Have you got somewhere to be?'

'It's Penny's birthday.' He sounded apologetic.

'Then you should go, obviously. Where are you taking her?'

'Nowhere flash,' he smiled. 'She's a student. She prefers pasta or pizza.'

'Then have fun.'

'You really don't like her, do you?'

Helen was tempted to say, *No, she's a pain in the arse*, but she had modified her view since getting to know Penny better. Instead, she opted for, 'I'm just not sure she's right for you, that's all. She's very young.'

'I'm not planning on marrying the girl,' he said, 'but I do like her, Helen, a lot.' For some reason, this stung. She was hoping it was just a physical thing between them – physical things usually burned out. 'She makes me laugh and I really enjoy her company. It's not just the . . . I know you think it is, but . . .' He left the sentence unfinished but he must have read her mind.

'I didn't say that was all it was,' she managed, 'and I'm happy for you both.'

'Anyway,' he said brightly, 'who else would have me, eh? An ageing journo with commitment phobia living a hand-to-mouth existence. Penny kept me from being a complete Billy-no-mates when I couldn't drag you away on that holiday with me, even on the rebound.' Tom got up out of his chair, lifted his jacket from the back of it then picked up his bag. 'Get some sleep, pet.'

'I did come.'

'What?'

Helen blurted it without thinking of the consequences, and now it was out there and she didn't even know why she had said it.

'To meet you,' she said, her voice cracking a little. 'At the pub before your flight, but you'd already left.'

'You're joking?'

399

'No,' she said. 'You'd been sitting outside, but there was just a pile of newspapers, an empty glass and those bloody sunglasses of yours.' He was always losing them.

Tom looked at her with a mixture of confusion and shock. It was almost comical how easy he was to read.

'I thought you wouldn't come,' he said. 'You kept saying you wouldn't, and I believed you.'

'A woman's prerogative,' she told him. 'I changed my mind, but our timing was a little off.'

'Our timing is always a little off,' he said quietly.

'It is,' she admitted, 'and you should go now, before you're late.'

'Why didn't you say anything?'

'It was my own fault and I figured it was probably for the best.'

'Because of the business?'

She managed a little nod that made her head ache.

'So why tell me now?' he asked. 'Other than to mess with my brain?'

'Don't know.' She was telling the truth about that. 'Perhaps I hit my head when I passed out?'

There was a silence between them then that was full of meaning, until Tom said, 'I'm seeing Penny and . . .'

She held up a hand. 'It's fine,' she told him. 'I know. I shouldn't have said anything. I'm sorry.'

'All right then,' he said, and there was a long pause before he added: 'I'd better go,' though he seemed far from certain about that now. Tom didn't leave, not at first. Instead he walked up to the side of her bed, leaned in and kissed her very tenderly on the cheek. 'Get well,' he said, and then he was gone.

'Oh god,' she said to herself after he left. She could see he was as conflicted about what she had said as she was.

She rolled over, eager to embrace sleep and willing to bet she would get more of it tonight than Tom.

Chapter Eighty

'Calzone!' she said triumphantly.

'What?'

Tom looked so startled that Penny laughed and clicked her fingers. '. . . And you're back in the room,' she said, as if she was a stage hypnotist waking him from a trance. 'I'm going to have the calzone.'

It had taken Penny an age to choose what she wanted for her birthday dinner and, normally, that would have irritated Tom but he had barely given it a thought.

'Sorry,' he said. 'Look, I can take you somewhere a bit better than here for your birthday.'

'You keep saying that, but it's my favourite.'

He wondered what she liked so much about the budget Italian restaurant with its PVC tablecloths and empty wine bottles with candles burning in them. 'What's the matter?' she asked him.

'Nothing,' he said, knowing he had been miles away.

'You seem preoccupied.' She leaned over and took his hand. 'Is it Helen?'

'No.' How the hell did she know that?

'You shouldn't worry about her. She's in the right place. They'll look after her.'

'You're right.' He realized she only meant that Helen was in hospital. Then he smiled. 'I'm sorry. No more fretting about Helen, I promise.'

He squeezed her hand then and they had a moment, but it didn't last. Tom's mobile phone started to ring shrilly, causing more than one head to turn in disapproval.

'Sorry,' he said to Penny. 'I'd better get this. It might be the hospital.' And he was up out of his seat and heading for the door to avoid disturbing other diners. 'If the waiter comes, you know what I want.'

Tom answered the phone before he was out of the door but as he passed through it and into a crisp, cool night he was surprised to hear Ian Bradshaw's voice on the line.

'Have you got a moment?'

'I suppose so.'

'How's Helen?'

'Resting. They think she's going to be fine.'

'Good,' said Bradshaw. 'And she isn't the only one.'

'What do you mean?'

'Samuel Keogh,' said Bradshaw. 'He isn't dying. Far from it, in fact. He's now in a stable condition and will undoubtedly be fit enough to face trial.'

'That's a cast-iron life sentence.'

'It is,' agreed Bradshaw. 'Now they just have to work out what to do with his daughter.'

'That's going to take a while.'

'I think it will,' said Bradshaw, then admitted, 'That's not the only reason I called.'

'I should have known. Okay, what's up?'

'Remember the evil stepdad?'

'The one you reckon killed his stepdaughter? Have you finally got him?'

'No.'

'What, then?'

'He's dead.'

'Really? Guilty conscience, eh?'

'Not exactly,' said Bradshaw. 'It wasn't suicide.'

Now Tom's interest was genuinely piqued. 'And I am guessing it wasn't an unfortunate accident either.'

'Not unless he fell on to a carving knife,' said Bradshaw. 'Fourteen times. I am led to believe it was a frenzied attack.'

'Any idea who did it?'

'Not yet,' admitted the detective. 'It could be someone who is as convinced about his guilt as we were. Then again, it might be the same person who is responsible for his step-daughter's mysterious disappearance. We just don't know.'

'Police baffled,' said Tom, quoting an imaginary headline.

'Aren't we always?' admitted Bradshaw dryly.

Tom thought for a moment. 'And they've given you the job of finding out what happened?'

'Who else do they call when they're bloody desperate? Actually, the whole team is on it. I'm back working for DI Tennant.'

'Well, good for you, mate.'

'We are still a bit undermanned, though, what with so many detectives suspended. There are just too many people out there killing each other these days. So we were wondering if you might like to lend a hand? If you're not too busy, that is?'

Tom smiled. 'We'll have to have a think about that.'

'Okay, but do me a favour.'

'What?'

'Don't think about it for too long.'

'Don't worry,' said Tom. 'I'll get my people to call your people.'

A Note from the Author

It is often said that life is stranger than fiction and I regularly read accounts of true crimes and think, if I wrote that, no one would believe it. I might have dismissed the idea of a secret bunker hidden under a large house as a bit far-fetched for fiction if I hadn't come across a real example. Two brothers were being shown around a farmhouse in St Andrews, with a view to buying it, when they asked what was behind a large door. The estate agent opened it and took them down a set of steps into an enormous decommissioned Cold War bunker that came with the property. When they recovered from the shock, the brothers bought the place and preserved the bunker as a museum, known as 'Scotland's Secret Bunker', and it is now open to the public.

Being a crime writer, I immediately began to imagine the worst and wondered what would happen if a person with more sinister intentions was able to purchase a bunker like this one and what purpose they might put it to. Imprisonment of any description would be awful enough for most of us, before you add in the underground element. The accompanying claustrophobia and dawning realization that no one could possibly know where you are makes this the stuff of nightmares. That was the genesis of the idea behind *The Chosen Ones*. I hope you didn't find it too disturbing. Sleep well and sweet dreams.

– Howard Linskey, June 2018

Acknowledgements

I would like to thank Penguin Random House for publishing *The Chosen Ones*. A special thank you goes to my brilliant editor, Joel Richardson, for all his hard work, great ideas and unflagging support while I finished this book. Thanks also to Maxine Hitchcock for her faith in me and to Jenny Platt, Beth Cockeram, Bea McIntyre and Sarah Day for their hard work on my behalf.

My superb literary agent, Phil Patterson at Marjacq, has helped me to write eight books now, and his support has been invaluable. Thanks also to Sandra Sawicka at Marjacq for overseeing the foreign-language versions of my books.

The following people have all given me their help and support throughout my writing career and I am extremely grateful to them all: Adam Pope, Andy Davis, Nikki Selden, Gareth Chennells, Andrew Local, Stuart Britton, David Shapiro, Peter Day, Tony Frobisher, Eva Dolan, Katie Charlton, Gemma Sealey, Emad Akhtar, Keshini Naidoo and Ion Mills.

My lovely, long-suffering wife, Alison, has to live with both me and these books. She witnesses the times when putting words down on the page feels like pulling teeth. Her reminder that 'you have done this before so you can do it again' always helps to get me over the bumpy bits and on to the finishing line. When I met Alison I told her I wanted to be an author one day and she didn't laugh at me, but that isn't the only reason I married her. Her love and faith keep me going.

My wonderful daughter, Erin, deserves huge thanks for making every one of my days brighter and better. The best part of being a writer is being able to stop when you come home, Erin, so we can spend time together. Love you always.

Alice Teale is missing.

**In a town full of secrets,
hers was the biggest.**

**Ian Bradshaw, Tom Carney and Helen Norton
return in the next gripping thriller from
Howard Linskey, coming in 2019.**

Enjoyed *The Chosen Ones?*
Discover the rest of the series:

No Name Lane

There's a serial killer on the loose in north-east England. Four bodies have already been discovered. A fifth girl, Michelle Summers, has just disappeared.

When a body is discovered, everyone fears the worst. But this isn't Michelle – this corpse has been dead for over fifty years.

Behind Dead Eyes

Tom Carney receives a letter from a convicted murderer who insists he is innocent. His argument is persuasive – but psychopaths are often said to be charming.

Across the city, Ian Bradshaw has a murder case on his hands. But he can't catch the killer if he can't ID the victim, and this woman's identity has been extinguished in the most shocking manner imaginable.

The Search

Susan Verity was only ten when she went missing. The police searched for years without finding her.

Convicted serial killer Adrian Wicklow was always the prime suspect. After decades behind bars, Adrian finally says he'll tell the truth . . .